Praise for
The Woman in Red

"*The Woman in Red* is an epic tale of one woman's fight to take control of her circumstances to create the life of her dreams. Anita Garibaldi is a modern woman in the nineteenth century who led with her heart despite circumstances so dire, most mortals would give up. Her passionate affair with Giuseppe Garibaldi freed her from a provincial life into one of passion, danger and purpose. Ms. Giovinazzo has crafted a spectacular story in this stunning debut."

—Adriana Trigiani,
New York Times bestselling author of *Tony's Wife*

"Anita Garibaldi, one of the greatest unsung heroines in history, comes to passionate life in Diana Giovinazzo's searing debut novel, *The Woman in Red*. Brazilian revolutionary, gaucho, and partner-in-arms to her husband, Giuseppe Garibaldi, Anita is a feminist icon to die for."

—Mary Sharratt, author of *Ecstasy* and *Illuminations*

"Diana Giovinazzo establishes herself as a worthy new voice in historical fiction with this irresistible tale of Anita Garibaldi: firebrand, lover, soldier, mother, revolutionary. Garibaldi isn't just fierce, she's ferocious. Her unstoppable energy propels this novel forward through tragedy and triumph, soaring all the way."

—Greer Macallister,
bestselling author of *The Magician's Lie* and *Woman 99*

"Anita Garibaldi is exactly the kind of courageous woman whose astonishing story of defiance and dedication—to freedom and to her passions—I've been craving. Told in her bold and unflinching voice,

The Woman in Red by Diana Giovinazzo brings this brazen, complex woman—and the man she fought beside—vividly to life."

—Erin Lindsay McCabe,
USA Today bestselling author of *I Shall Be Near to You*

"Captivating...Giovinazzo adds realistic details to the fast-paced narrative. The novel's focus on a strong woman who defied the odds to follow her heart will appeal to fans of historical fiction."

—*Publishers Weekly*

"A great swashbuckler...Epic in scope, adventurous in nature, dreamily romantic, and occasionally a nail biter, this is the story of a passionate love affair, a feminist before feminism's time, history as it happened in three countries, triumph, and tragedy."

—New York Journal of Books

"Giovinazzo gives the reader a fascinating look at nineteeth-century South America and its culture, where machismo prohibited women from any meaningful role or status in society. It's Anita Garibaldi's fight against those prohibitions that make her such an inspirational character...*The Woman in Red* is a finely crafted, exciting page-turner and is highly recommended for readers interested in learning about strong and empowered women."

—Historical Novel Society

"Giovinazzo deftly brings Anita and her story to life in this sweeping saga...Entertaining and educational, as well as a wonderful way for readers to meet a lesser-known historical figure whose own life story could very well help influence their own by encouraging others to dig deep within to find courage and bravery."

—Ovunque Siamo

THE WOMAN IN RED

DIANA GIOVINAZZO

GRAND CENTRAL PUBLISHING

NEW YORK BOSTON

This book is a work of historical fiction. In order to give a sense of the times, some names or real people or places have been included in the book. However, the events depicted in this book are imaginary, and the names of nonhistorical persons or events are the product of the author's imagination or are used fictitiously. Any resemblance of such nonhistorical persons or events to actual ones is purely coincidental.

Grand Central Publishing
Hachette Book Group
1290 Avenue of the Americas, New York, NY 10104
grandcentralpublishing.com
twitter.com/grandcentralpub

Originally published in hardcover and ebook by Grand Central Publishing in August 2020.

First Trade Paperback Edition: August 2021

Grand Central Publishing is a division of Hachette Book Group, Inc. The Grand Central Publishing name and logo is a trademark of Hachette Book Group, Inc.

Library of Congress Cataloging-in-Publication Data

Names: Giovinazzo, Diana, author.
Title: The woman in red / Diana Giovinazzo.
Description: First edition. | New York : Grand Central Publishing, 2020.
Identifiers: LCCN 2019049247 | ISBN 9781538717417 (hardcover) | ISBN 9781538717424 (ebook)
Subjects: LCSH: Garibaldi, Anita, 1821?–1849—Fiction. | Garibaldi, Giuseppe, 1807–1882—Fiction. | GSAFD: Biographical fiction.
Classification: LCC PS3607.I4686 W66 2020 | DDC 813/.6—dc23
LC record available at https://lccn.loc.gov/2019049247

ISBNs: 978-1-5387-1741-7 (hardcover), 978-1-5387-1742-4 (ebook), 978-1-5387-1743-1 (trade paperback)

Printed in the United States of America

LSC-C

Printing 1, 2021

Destiny toys with us with both hands. For my sins, I will pay, as all of us must. More, I think. But I still rejoice in the family she brought me.

—Anita Garibaldi

PROLOGUE

AUGUST 1840

Bad omens have followed me all my life. I was born in an unlucky month, under an unlucky moon. "August, the month of sorrow and grief." It is a saying I know all too well, and it haunts me now as I pick my way through the soulless bodies on a deserted battlefield in the middle of the Brazilian wilderness.

A low fog flows through the field, covering the ground with a thin mist. It's not enough to hide the carnage. These men, strewn about like broken china, were people I knew. They shared a campfire with my husband, hanging on his every word, just as I did once upon a time. So many men. I clasp my belly and say a silent prayer for my child as I wonder what will become of us. This battlefield that may have claimed my husband spreads out before me.

I look back at my captors, playing cards by the lantern light. Young men in tattered uniforms with unshaven faces. One of them slaps down a card and cheers as they continue to play. They want to leave, but I made a deal with the devil to be here. None of us can go until I am satisfied. These young soldiers underestimate me, just like so many others.

Slumping against a fallen tree, I rub my pregnant belly as I watch black vultures circle and swoop in a golden-red sky. My chest heaves with exertion as the stench sticks to the back of my throat, sweet and rancid. It threatens to overtake me, but I must continue. I have been here for hours, searching and wondering if these birds might be an omen. Is my husband dead?

I close my eyes at the childhood memory of a hunched old woman shaking her knobby fingers at me from the steps of the church as she proclaims, "This one, she will have a hard life. So very, very unlucky, this one," before spitting off to the side, to ward off the devil.

But her proclamations made no difference. My mother already knew I was unlucky. I wasn't born a boy. My life could have been infinitely different if I had been. Perhaps I would be one of the bodies scattered here among the mud and filth.

A branch cracks and I startle at the sight of a vulture walking in front of me. He dips his head down and pulls the flesh from a soldier, then turns to look at me as he gulps his meat. His black eyes shine in the dying light. We regard each other, this scavenger and I, and in him I recognize a creature not unlike myself. We do what we must to survive. The vulture flaps his massive wings and is gone.

My stomach churns and bile sets my throat on fire. Doubling over, I try to expel the acid, but nothing comes. I wish I had some water, anything to get the bitterness out of my mouth. Wiping my damp hair from my face, I look around me at the muddy field. My back seizes as I push myself up. Gasping against the pain, I catch an abandoned wagon before I fall face-first into another dead body. I close my eyes and try to control my breathing as I fight against the hopelessness that is setting in. This field is large and our losses enormous; there is no way that I can search through it in one evening.

My husband can't be here. Men like him don't die. He is too cunning. But in the back of my mind I can't help but wonder what it means for me if he is. There are so many men, it's not impossible to think that what they told me was true.

I turn back to the tree line as I realize, I could run. I could leave this place. I could sneak away from these incompetent *idiotas*. I could become something greater than my husband. They would whisper the name Anita Garibaldi in reverence.

Closing my eyes, I step forward, my boots sinking ever so slightly in the mud. Memories rush past me as I make my way across the field. Only time will tell if I am making the right decision.

PART ONE

Santa Catarina, Brazil

ONE

October 1829

I was eight years old when I was sent to school in the small trading settlement of Tubarão. But conforming was never my strong suit. I tried my best to be like my two older sisters, my hair in braids, my dress freshly pressed, but I couldn't sit still and pay attention. Our one-room schoolhouse was small and stale. I could feel the thick, hot air in my lungs making me struggle for breath.

This was once the justice of the peace's office, but the villagers' children needed a place to learn to read. He got a new building and we got the old one, yellowed with age and adorned with thick cracks that climbed the walls. Everyone was happy.

We sat at our desks, four rows across, every child dutifully listening to the basic lessons that would allow us to take over our parents' roles in the village one day. The teacher droned on, reading from a book.

Sighing, I looked out the window to where a cherry guava tree grew. One of the branches, thick with bright pink berries, bounced up and down in the morning sun. I leaned out of my chair to get a better look at what was making such a ruckus. The little black nose of a wild coati poked through the lush green leaves. I watched as the little creature carefully walked out to the edge of the branch, seeking out the ripe guava.

"Anna de Jesus! Get back in your seat!" the teacher yelled, snapping my attention back to him.

"But, senhor—"

He grabbed me by the arm to pull me in front of the class and made me hold out my hands. I tried to rip them away, but it only caused his grip to tighten. He slapped them firmly with his ruler. The sting resonated up my forearms into my elbows. "Do not speak back to your teacher. You are a girl. You should obey."

Hot tears stung my eyes. I wasn't going to reward him; I bit the inside of my lip to keep from crying out. Blinking back the tears, I could feel the other students' eyes on me. It wasn't until a giggle rippled up from the back of the room that my embarrassment led to anger. I grabbed the ruler from his hand and started to hit him with it. I could see nothing but my hand gripping the ruler as it made contact with my teacher's arms, raised in defense. It was the last time I ever went to school.

"What are we going to do with you, Anna?" my mother asked, red-faced, nostrils flaring like a bull's. We were in the safety of our small home with its thatched roof and mud-and-straw walls, away from the prying eyes of the village. My mother was always careful with what ammunition she gave the town gossips. I sat at the table, looking up at her, fear making my stomach clench.

"She will come to work with me." Neither my mother nor I had heard my father come in. He was standing in the doorway, wiping a damp rag under his chin and ears. Mamãe straightened her back as she eyed my father.

"You are too soft on her. This," she said, pointing to me, "this is all your fault."

"This is our daughter. We could use the extra hands with the horses." He looked down at me with his arms crossed, the hint of a smile on his face. I tried not to meet his smile.

My mother threw her arms up in the air as she walked in the opposite direction from my father. "I give up!"

I grinned broadly at her back as she stormed away. My father's face grew stern as he regarded me. "Wipe that smile off your face. This will be hard work." I nodded in agreement as he stalked off.

Working alongside my father with the horses and cattle was wonderful. Our area of southern Brazil, known as Santa Catarina, was a true Eden. No one loved the wild, rugged country like the gauchos, and Brazil couldn't function without us.

We spent our days taming the wild land of Santa Catarina. Every year more people settled here from Europe and northern Brazil, requiring more land, more cows, and more resources in general. When a rancher lost one of his cattle, it was my father and the other gauchos who went out to find it.

Santa Catarina would not be the country that it was without the gaucho, and the gaucho would not be the gaucho without Santa Catarina. We worked under a wealthy landowner, who was referred to as a patron. A patron would not think of muddying their boots to drive a herd of cattle from one clearing to the next. A patron would not rise with the sun to feed the horses and cattle that made them wealthy. A patron would not leave the warmth of their bed in the middle of the night to help a cow give birth to a calf, not caring about the blood and mucus that came with. But a gaucho would. We didn't need noble titles to know that we were the true owners of this land, with its lush green mountains that languidly stretched to the heavens. A wilderness that opened before us like the expanse of the ocean was better than any heaven promised to us by priests.

I was at my happiest when I rode out with these dirty, unkempt men who braved the wilds, through the downpour that attempted to cleanse all living things from the earth. No, I did not envy my sisters and former classmates. While they stayed in the airless classroom listening to a useless lecture, I was getting a real education.

Working as my father's apprentice at first, I lined up his tools, making sure they were all in working order for him. I quickly became experienced enough to work alongside him, a full gaucho in my own right. At the end of the day, we cleaned the tools together, talking. My father told me stories about his people, the Azoreans who resided on the lush, exotic islands off the coast of Portugal.

"When I was a child, my parents couldn't keep me on the ground." He smiled as he wiped the mud off his prized *facón*, the knife that he had kept by his side since he first moved here. "There was this one bluff in particular that my friends and I liked to climb. It was so high that you could see for miles over the ocean." He put the *facón* away and picked up another tool as I sat on the stool watching him. "When you stand on a bluff like that, you understand just how small you are."

"What did you do after you reached the top?"

"We jumped." His eyes got big as he tickled me. "But don't you go getting any ideas now, little lady. I will not have you jumping off cliffs until you are at least…twenty."

"Twenty? Why twenty?"

"Because by then you will be your husband's problem."

I wrinkled my nose at the thought, but then another question struck me. "Papai, why did you come here?"

He thought for a moment as he closed the toolboxes. After a while, he finally answered, "I understood there was more to the world than my little island."

TWO

JANUARY 1833

As ran the course of my life, the omens came, and with them came trouble.

One morning while my father and I were preparing for our day's labor we heard my mother call out from the house. We dropped the tools that we had been packing and ran to her side. She was standing in the kitchen, staring at a little black bird with a bright red belly, sitting on the back of a chair, his little head rhythmically bobbing up and down.

"This is bad. Very bad." My mother crossed herself as the color left her face. "There are spirits here." She crossed herself again. "Something terrible is going to happen."

I slowly walked up to the bird so that I didn't startle him, setting one foot cautiously in front of the other. The bird turned his little head toward me. His eyes, as black as his feathers, shone brightly under his white-streaked brows. Gingerly I reached out toward him, stroking his little chest. The bird didn't move or flinch. Our eyes met and for a moment I felt a kinship with this creature. Moving slowly, I scooped him up in my hands and carried him outside, where I released him back to the wild where he belonged.

It was a hot January day when my father volunteered to figure out where the leak was coming from in the community storeroom, where our small village's produce and dried meats were stored during the rainy season. Any amount of moisture in that hut and we would all be starving for the rest of the season.

I volunteered to go with him, but he wouldn't let me. "You're too small. You might get hurt."

"Just last month I helped catch a wild bull."

"And you nearly got yourself trampled." He gathered his rope and hammer. "You are eleven years old. You will have plenty of time to risk your life chasing cattle and climbing on top of rickety sheds." He kissed the top of my head and left. I sulked, wishing I could go with him. They may have let me help rope the bull, but it was only because I was quicker with the lasso than the rest of the gauchos we rode out with.

Later that morning I was out at the stables, grooming the horses, when the news swept in like a rushing storm destroying everything in its path. The whole village went running to see the damage to the storeroom. Bile rose in my throat as I began pushing forward.

"He was walking on the roof," one of my neighbors murmured. "They say he fell."

"Of course he fell; that roof was so brittle that I don't think it could even support the weight of a bird." Their words died on their lips as they looked down, noticing me for the first time.

Weaving through the crowd that gathered, I made my way to the center of the room. It was only when I gasped at the sight—my father, white and waxen as he lay impaled by a beam through the abdomen—that I think I screamed. I couldn't tell. Lurching forward, I tried to grasp his outstretched hand. That's when one of the gauchos grabbed me. He threw me over his shoulder and carried me out the door.

The next day family, friends, and other kin gathered for the processional to bury my father. They hollered and cried, thumping their chests and pulling at their hair. My mother led the group, the loudest mourner of all. When the horse-drawn carriage came to a stop, she threw herself over the coffin, beating the lid as she exclaimed, "How could you leave me?" Two women pulled her away, her wails a low fog rising above the crowd of mourners.

I stood in the back, watching the spectacle that played out before me. People crowded around me as the whole village pushed past me to follow the casket. Clinging to a tree, I did my best not to get swept away by the current of faces that moved toward the graveyard. Looking around, I could no longer see my mother or my sisters. Suddenly, I felt alone and scared in this sea of people.

Their noise was a cacophony that made me feel disoriented. Their sweat clung to my nostrils as I was jostled along the pathway. I had to leave. I was feeling myself go mad. Fighting through the procession, I made it to the river, my pulsing lungs on fire, and collapsed by a tree, gasping for breath. This world suddenly felt cold and dark without my father. He was the only one who understood me.

That was when I heard the footsteps behind me. I turned my head sharply, expecting it to be a wild animal, only to see Pedro, the village drunk. He smiled; half of his teeth were missing, and I could see his tongue in the gaps.

"Such a little thing. So sad that you are all alone now."

"Go away, Pedro," I said, looking back at the river but keeping watch on him from the corner of my eye.

He swaggered over to me and took one of my braids in his hand. "Such pretty long hair you have." He let the braid slip through his dirty fingers. "Such a shame that you don't have a father to protect you anymore."

"Leave me alone, Pedro." I went to move away but he grabbed me by the arm, throwing me against a tree.

"You do not speak to men that way." He was so close I could smell his cologne of alcohol and urine. "I should teach you a lesson." He pressed me up against the tree as he fumbled with his pants.

I began to struggle. He pinned me harder, licking my cheek. "Be a good girl." His words were thick and wet.

Instinct kicked in and I stopped struggling. I went limp, slipping through his clutches, and ran faster than I had ever run in my life back to our house.

Most of the guests were gone by that point, but my mother was just outside our front door, having said goodbye to someone. I ran to her and wrapped my arms around her, feeling safe in her strong embrace.

"Anna, what has gotten into you?"

I buried my head in her neck, unable to bring myself to speak. When I finally did, I told her everything. Her face went from pale white to crimson. "That louse. You are lucky you were able to get away." She held my head in her hands in order to look into my eyes. "You have to be careful. We no longer have your father here to protect us."

That night I lay in my bed with my older sister Maria snoring beside me. It felt like there was a chasm between us. Even though we were only three years apart, she acted as if she were one of the adults. We had never been close, but the ways we expressed our shared grief for our father felt like night and day. Where I felt stripped bare, she turned inward. Maria wanted to be left alone to the point that she would sneer whenever I came around. Now, as I lay beside her, I couldn't sleep, the events of the day racing through my mind. I stared at our thatched ceiling. Maria snorted and rolled over. I couldn't help but think, *Why do we need a man to protect us?* I worked alongside the men, doing the same work that they did. I could ride a horse better than most of the men of our village. I was given the most stubborn horses to break. My father was the one who taught me. The day that he had discovered that I had a natural affinity for horses was one of the best days of my childhood. And perhaps the most stressful for him.

I could taste the hay and horse sweat that the hot November air had carried through our encampment. The horse shook her black mane every few minutes. Her eyes were wild, darting from person to person, her breath loud and heavy with her anxiety. Whenever one of the men tried to approach her, she would rear up, kicking out in an attempt to defend herself against their whips. I stood next to my father, who sighed heavily. "That is not how you break a horse." My father had his methods, and this wasn't one of them.

When the men were preoccupied with their siesta, and taking a break from the horse, I approached the pen slowly, holding out my shirt like a basket in order to carry all the figs that I had collected. She stood there regarding me; with every step I took she stomped her hoof and let out an angry whine. I stood by the fence and watched her as I put one of the soft fruits to my mouth.

The horse stomped in protest again. So I turned my back to her and continued to eat. It took only a few moments for her to come to me. She nudged my shoulder with her muzzle. When I didn't respond, she nudged me harder, pushing me forward. I turned to look at her. We stared at each other until she quickly dipped her head. I smiled, holding one of the figs out in the palm of my hand. It was gone in an instant. Then another. Before I gave her a third she had to let me pet her. She shied away at first but by her seventh and last fig, her head was in my hands, letting me rub her as she sniffed for more food. At the sound of a cracking twig, she ran away, making laps around the pen. I turned to find all of the men, including my father, watching me. An old man leaned in toward my father, whispering something. My father grimly nodded and strode over to me. "It's time for you to get in there with her."

I had watched him break a horse a hundred times, horrified at the prospect of doing it myself. He nodded toward the horse as she nervously trotted around the pen.

"She's going to try to break you more than you are going to try to break her," my father explained. "Do not let her know she has scared you." The horse's ears were back as her large nostrils flared, releasing angry huffs. My father paused, staring down at the horse. "And for the love of God, don't turn your back to her."

Hesitantly I climbed over the faded wooden fence and stood there watching her. She shook her head, letting out angry huffs and snorts. Then she charged me. I stood my ground as she came barreling toward me, just like I had seen the men do. And at the last minute, she broke off, running the perimeter of the fence. I breathed a sigh of relief as I readied myself for her next attack. This dance between gaucho and horse was one I had seen many times. We continued like this for most of the afternoon, until she stopped, panting and huffing. She stomped her hoof into the dirt like an angry child. I made shushing noises as I approached her. Slowly I reached out a hand and stroked her sides. I was patient as I worked the rope around her. She trusted me and I wasn't going to violate that trust. I was my father's daughter.

Now as I lay beside Maria, I wondered if I would ever be trusted to work like that again. I could rope a calf in ten seconds, the fastest in the village. Was I not as good as the gauchos because I was a woman? I certainly did not feel that way. Why should I be treated any differently now that I no longer had a father to watch over me? I punched my pillow and rolled over. I needed to do something. That's when I decided that the next day, I would be the one to teach Pedro a lesson.

I spied the louse the next morning from a distance as he was doing his job, if you could call it that. He was a lazy farmhand who worked only if his boss was watching. He sat in the shade of a decrepit old pine tree, too focused on his drink to care about the oxen that were tied to the trunk with a thick rope. Years of termite damage made the pine slouch to the side like an old man in need of a cane. This was going to be too easy.

I kicked my horse in the hindquarters and she took off at a run straight for the oxen, who at this point noticed us. Their beady eyes grew large as they stopped chewing. The oxen pulled, trying to run away, bringing the tree with them, roots and all. Pedro, seeing this and seeing me, came right into my path with his arms raised in an attempt to stop me. He was just where I wanted him. I reached back and struck him with my whip, as hard as I could across his face. He cried out as if I had chopped off a limb. Blood seeped through his fingers and down his arm.

"Father or no father, you do not get to touch me." I turned my horse and galloped away.

A few hours later the constable showed up at my door. He brought my mother and me to the justice of the peace, Senhor Dominguez, to discuss my incident with Pedro. Senhor Dominguez was known as a fair man, but I didn't know if I could trust him. He was short and bald with a little black mustache that made him look official. My mother and I sat stiff-backed in our chairs on the other side of the desk. The air was thick and hot even though his windows were open.

"I understand that you attacked Pedro this afternoon and damaged a very old tree." He looked down his nose at me. "Do you want to tell me what happened?"

I stared at the dark spot on the wall above his head. He looked over at my mother, who shrugged. "I wasn't there but I am sure that *totó* got what he deserved."

He shook his head. "Luckily for you Pedro's reputation precedes him. I suppose you have to protect yourself somehow." He shuffled the papers on his desk. "Your father was a good man. I always enjoyed our talks. Just do me a favor and next time you try to teach someone a lesson, please don't make such a mess. We're still cleaning up after the oxen."

When we arrived home, my mother made the decision: We were moving eighteen miles away, to Laguna at the coast, to be closer to my godfather. We would be safer there.

THREE

June 1835

I hated Laguna. The city was a crowded jungle of houses that ran along the horseshoe bay. I could feel the heat that radiated off the homes painted in bright hues of blue, green, and yellow. The only things the houses had in common were the clay roofs that were baked into a deep red from the Brazilian sun. The people always yelled, one voice over the other trying to make itself heard.

Though every village had its gossips, Laguna's were malicious. I was a favorite subject for them. *How can a fourteen-year-old girl with no father walk the streets with such pride?* Women whispered as I walked past them, their hands discreetly over their mouths, pretending they didn't want me to hear. *She doesn't talk to anyone; maybe there is something wrong with her?*

Wandering through the streets, I tilted my head to the heavens, praying to God to deliver me from such a wretched place. I missed my horse and our early morning rides. The smell of the woods after a rain. My freedom.

In a city so full of people, I was amazed to feel so…alone. My sisters, Maria and Felicidad, had been married off shortly before our move. I was left alone with our mother and our godfather, a shipping clerk. My mother took work cleaning the homes of the wealthy.

I ran my hands along my waist, feeling my hips, which had spread due to my newfound womanhood. My angular lines had softened out, giving me what many called a pleasantly plump profile.

One day as I was filling up the water jugs, I noticed a group of the village women talking in hushed tones, looking over at me in turn. When they saw that I was watching them they sauntered over to me, their baskets resting on their hips.

"It won't take you very long to find a husband." The lead woman wiggled her eyebrows as an amused smirk slowly spread across her face. "At least not with birthing hips like those."

A petite black woman placed her hands on my hips, sizing me up. "*Menina*, if my hips were as wide as yours, I probably could have gotten a better husband. I certainly wouldn't have had a twelve-hour labor for my last child."

I tried to pick up my water jugs, but my arm hit my left breast, making me spill water everywhere. I could not get used to these things. They were suddenly always in my way. The women doubled over in laughter. "See, Gloria, I told you some women have all the luck."

My new body was the talk of the gossips. Unfortunately, all of this led to men following me around asking to help with the most ridiculous things. As if I were unable to do anything for myself. They really were such a bother.

One morning, as the light from the rising sun crawled across the city, a sniveling, sorry excuse for a man by the name of Manoel Duarte approached me. Short and squat, at full height he barely stood above my shoulder. He looked as if he had just finished crying; his eyes were red, and he sniffled uncontrollably.

If I didn't know any better, I would think that he washed his hair with grease.

"May I carry your water for you?" he asked, out of breath from having to take large strides to keep up with me. I picked up my pace as he trailed behind me.

The next day he showed up at the well again. He asked if he could carry my water, and again I walked past him without saying a word. Surely if I continued to ignore him, he would go away like the stray dog that he was.

A few weeks later, while the sun set over Laguna, I sat down for our meager dinner of rice and beans with my godfather and mother. "I received a letter from your sister, Maria, today," my mother said with a grin. "She is very happy with her husband. Ship caulkers make a fine living. She doesn't need to work. Only tend to the house."

"Good for her," I said, reaching for more rice.

"I understand shoemakers make a good living as well," my mother said. "One, in particular, seems to have his eyes on you."

I looked up, stopping midchew. "Who?"

"A certain young man who likes to walk home with you from the well." My mother smiled coyly as my godfather stared intently into his beans.

"Mother, I don't know what you are talking about. There is only one person who likes…Oh no, Mother, you didn't. Please tell me you didn't."

"I was paid a visit today by Manoel. He is a nice young man. He says that you and he—"

"He and I nothing!" I roared. "I have no interest in that man at all. Whatever he told you is a lie."

"It can't be that much of a lie. He asked me for your hand in marriage today."

"Mother, no," I said, fighting the tears that were building in my eyes. "Please tell me you didn't."

"A woman without a father is nothing. You need to be protected and taken care of." My mother kept a controlled coolness that made me angrier.

"No," I said, feeling my world crashing in. I was only fourteen. I wasn't ready for this.

"The contract is already signed," my mother said, as if she were buying produce at the market.

"I can't believe you did this without my permission! I shouldn't have to marry anyone!" I yelled.

"Anna!" She dropped her food onto her plate. "I am your mother. I don't need your permission to do anything. I could have you dragged out into the streets and beaten for your disrespect. No one would even question me. Whatever notions you have in your head, you need to get rid of them right now. You have two purposes in life. One is to get married and the other is to make children with your husband. That's it."

"If that is to be my lot in life, then why not pick someone better? Why not let me marry someone of my own choosing?"

"Because you will be foolish and marry for love. You are a dreamer, Anna, always with your head in the clouds. I will not let you make my mistakes. Manoel will be a good husband." Her voice shook as she pressed her fists against the table.

"How do you know? Do you know anything about him at all?" I asked as my eyes betrayed me, letting tears trickle out. Manoel Duarte had a small, run-down shoe repair shop in the center of town. It was a well-known fact that the reason his shop was so badly kept was because all of his profit was spent at the tavern. The tavern owner's wife liked to joke that Manoel was a gracious benefactor. It was because of his patronage that she was able to acquire so many new dresses. And this was the man my mother expected me to marry?

"You haven't gotten any other offers, and he promised that he would take good care of you."

"Yes, because the promises of a drunk are always to be believed." I stormed out of the house, running as fast as I could. I made it down to the docks, where I grasped my sides, sucking in deep, jagged breaths. My mind raced. I couldn't believe this was happening. I paced, trying to control my breathing. I looked at the ships rising and falling with the gentle rocking of the ocean. Perhaps I could get on one and sail away to some other land. I took a step toward the harbor. For a moment, I closed my eyes, imagining. I could go somewhere exotic, like France or Africa. I could run away. Be a merchant, have adventures. Sail the seas. Get out of this horrible town. I could...

I shook my head, wiping away my silly thoughts. Even if I ran away, what would I do when I got there? I raised my chin as I regained control of my breathing. There was only one thing I could do. I turned on my heel and walked home. I was going to get married whether I liked it or not. Because as my mother said, I was nothing without a husband or a father.

FOUR

August 1835

August 21, 1835, was the day I married Manoel. Gray clouds blanketed the sky above the steeple. The gloomy afternoon mirrored my mood. The night before my wedding my mother slipped into my room and petted my hair. "Don't be sad," she said. "This marriage will be a good thing. You have the spirit of men's longing in your eyes. And that is so dangerous for a girl. It scares me. Soon you will come to see that a marriage will tame you. Keep you safe." She thought she was making me feel better, but my despair only grew.

I stood in front of a yellowed mirror while my mother fussed with my veil, waiting for the ceremony to begin. I wore a simple dress that had probably been fashionable when my mother was a girl. She'd purchased it from a newly widowed woman after being appalled by my plan to wear the same clothing I wore when cleaning houses. Just to be safe from any bad luck, my mother had the dress blessed by the priest.

"You look so much like your father," she said, smoothing out a stray wrinkle in my dress. "Such a shame his looks did not translate well to a girl."

She stopped and met my eyes in the mirror. "Try to be happy today, Anna. You will now be a woman. Your life is finally beginning." How could it be beginning when I felt like I was dying inside?

Standing at the altar, I looked over my new husband as he said his vows to our priest. Manoel's hair was slicked back with oil, and a thin trail of sweat rolled down his temple. He was even greasier than usual. *How can that happen?* I wondered. He was beaming, as if he had just won a hard-fought contest. I said the vows I had practiced like I was supposed to, not giving him the pleasure of a smile.

A middle-aged woman I vaguely recognized loudly whispered, "You would think she was at a funeral with that scowl."

As we hurried out of the church my shoe slipped off. When I turned back to retrieve it, an old woman gripped it in her hands. "I am so sorry, this is a very bad sign." She crossed herself. "You should get a blessing from the priest. Your marriage is doomed," she whispered.

"I know," I whispered back.

Dreading my wedding night, I kept passing goblets of wine to Manoel, hoping that he would become too drunk to perform his duties. However, when the time came, drink didn't slow him. I held my breath as he climbed on top of me, feeling slightly smothered by his weight. Manoel fumbled with his member and then tried to kiss me, but I turned away, squeezing my eyes shut. For a moment, he hesitated, but then he started pounding like I was a shoe that needed repair.

Thankfully, it was over as soon as it began. He rolled off me, lying with his back to me. Meanwhile, I lay on my back, staring at the ceiling. *Please, God, I will do anything. Don't let me be pregnant.*

* * *

September 1838

For three years I dealt with Manoel. He worked making or repairing shoes; when business was slow, which it often was, he went out fishing. However, most of what he earned he drank away at the tavern. Somehow, we managed to pay our rent every month and were able to put a little bit of food on the table. I picked up work cleaning houses when I could, but it wasn't enough. I had to regularly choose between food, new clothing, and other basic needs.

I daydreamed of being out with the gauchos, reveling in my memories of riding through the hills as I stirred a pot of fish stew. We had been eating a lot of fish lately, given that it was the only thing we could afford. The deep red sauce bubbled, releasing a pleasant aroma through our little home. My husband was late again, but I didn't mind. I liked it better when I was alone. In those solitary hours I got to pretend I was my own person. I daydreamed about my time as a gaucho. As I stirred the stew, I tried to conjure the feeling of the air rushing past my face while I rode my horse. Unfortunately, Manoel stumbled through the door, bringing with him my miserable reality.

"Anna! Anna! Your prince has arrived!" he exclaimed with arms outstretched. He stumbled over his feet but caught himself on our table. "Where is my supper?" He looked around the room, dazed. "I demand that you have my supper ready when I come home, woman."

I helped him to a chair. "And I demand a husband who isn't a drunk. If only wishes were gold." I dropped a bowl in front of him. "Did you drink all the money that you earned today?"

He reached into his pocket and slammed a dirty fist on the table. Coins spilled from his fingers, spinning and rolling all over the table before he focused on shoveling food into his mouth. Half of it tumbled down the front of his shirt. I turned away from him in disgust. I heard his chair scrape along the floor. "I fought for you and I won. You are my prize. My prized jewel," he said, trying to reach out for me.

I pulled away, evading his grasp. "Well, it would appear that you were duped."

"Why do you not love me like other wives? They dote upon their husbands."

I rolled my eyes, knowing how this argument went. We had it every time he was drunk. He came home, complained about his life, and complained about me, culminating in a childlike meltdown. I sighed. "Because I never wanted to marry you."

"You shouldn't say such things to me. I am a good husband."

"If you say so." I walked into the bedroom, letting him follow me like a sick dog.

"Without me, you would be nothing."

I nodded.

He sat on the bed. "Why don't you make love to me? A good wife would perform her duties."

I walked up to him as he slowly blinked his bleary eyes. Reaching out, I poked him in the middle of his forehead. With a heavy thud, he fell back onto his pillows, asleep. I finished putting him into bed and went back to the kitchen to finish eating my dinner alone.

Two days later my mother arrived at my door. She sat down at my kitchen table with a heavy sigh. "Your husband came to visit me yesterday."

"Did he now?" I said, pulling my shawl tighter. A surprise visit from my mother required a gourd of strong *mate*. I went straight to the stove to begin brewing it as she went on.

"He tells me you are being a cruel wife again."

"When have I ever been a kind wife?" I asked, looking out the window. The sky was darkening with the onset of the afternoon rains. Every day at precisely the same time, the sky would open up and a torrential downpour would wash over us. It also meant that my mother would be visiting for longer than I would prefer.

"Anna, you have to be good to your husband. You don't want him to leave you, do you? Then you will have nothing."

"Mother, I have nothing now." I spread my arms out to show the expanse of my small kitchen with its tiny woodstove, wobbly table, and dingy cabinet that held what little food we had. I didn't even have a parlor. Below us was a general store; above us, another apartment, even smaller than ours. "I did as you told me and married the man. What more do you want? I cannot love a man I do not respect."

"Who said anything about love?" my mother said with a wave of her hand as I poured the *mate*. "A woman who marries for love is a fool."

"Why did you marry Papai?" I asked, setting the *mate* in front of her.

"Because he was exciting. I was just a girl in São Paulo; I wanted adventure, a new life." She sipped her drink. "Look at where it got me. If I had listened to my mother, my life wouldn't have been so hard. Maybe my sons wouldn't have died. A woman is nothing without her sons." She stared into her tea, scrying for what I could only imagine were the ghosts of the brothers I had never met—the two boys born in between Maria and I, the one who came out with the umbilical cord wrapped firmly around his neck and the other, who gasped for air but was too weak to live through the night. "Listen to your mother. Be good to your husband. You don't want to be a ruined woman."

* * *

November 1838

It had been over a month filled with tense politeness since my mother came to visit. Heavy rains rhythmically pattered against the windows. Manoel slipped into the apartment after a long day in the shop. His clothes were soaked, and water slid from his hair onto our floor, creating little puddles around his feet. I wrinkled my nose at the smell of mildewed old sweat that followed him. Manoel kissed my cheek before quietly sitting at the table. "I received a large order today."

"From who?"

"The Silvas." He refused to meet my eyes.

"Aren't they friends of yours?"

He shrugged. "What does it matter? An order is an order."

"Are you giving them a lower price?"

"I can't charge any less than I do already." He pushed his food around his plate: stewed fish and rice again. "Do you think we could—"

"No." I didn't even let him finish the question.

"It's been three months." He looked up at me. His eyes searched my features for a hopeful sign.

"I have a headache."

His grip tightened on his fork. "You've had a headache for three months."

I shrugged. "It's a constant ailment."

He dropped his fork. "I'm going out."

I watched as he stomped out of the room.

Two weeks later I was walking home from the market when I heard someone mention my husband. I paused, unseen by Senhor and Senhora Silva. "You can't keep giving Manoel money."

"I know." Senhor Silva turned from his wife's scorn.

"It is not your responsibility to take care of him."

"I said I know." Senhor Silva let out a loud puff of air. "We have been friends since we were children. I can't stand by and watch him become destitute."

"If he goes destitute it is his choice."

"Manoel has a wife he needs to take care of. Wouldn't you want someone to step in and help us if we were in that situation?"

I watched from behind a pillar as Senhora Silva kissed the palm of his hand. "You will never let us be in that position." Such a simple act, that kiss, but it filled me with immense jealousy. I wanted someone whose palm I could kiss in the middle of a busy street. Someone I could give little affections to, not caring who saw. Someone I could trust. I wanted a partner. My basket handle creaked under my tightening grip.

A few days later Manoel sat at our table, stinking of stale ocean and the pungent sour smell of iron and mud that comes from gutting fish. He wiped a dirty hand over his tired face as he watched me finish making supper. I dropped the plate of pan-fried fish and rice in front of him.

"Why do we have to eat this slop again? I know we have no money, but we don't have to eat the same food every day." He knocked the plate off the table with a swipe of his arm. "Pick that up and make me something else."

"No."

Manoel quickly stood up, throwing his chair back. "You will obey me! I am your husband and it is your duty to do what I say. I am tired of you defying me. Because of you I am an embarrassment! Now pick that up and make me something else."

"You can eat it off the floor for all I care. I am not your slave!" He reached his hand back to hit me. I stared at him without flinching. "Go ahead."

He lowered his hand without taking his eyes off me. "Why do you hate me so much? Why can't you be a good wife?"

"Because you picked the wrong woman. You are weak and

pathetic." My eyes narrowed, taking in his hangdog expression. "Look at you…You make me sick." I spit.

He stormed out of our house without saying a word. He was going to find comfort at the bottom of a bottle. I looked around me at my meager home, which I hated, living with a man I hated even more. This wasn't the life I wanted to live. It was time I made a change, even if it ruined me. I packed a bag and left the apartment, never to look back.

FIVE

February 1839

The disputes of the rich are the burden of the poor. The magistrates of Rio Grande do Sul, the state south of Santa Catarina, decided to break away from Brazil, led by General Bento Gonçalves. A former friend of Dom Pedro I, the great Portuguese king who had liberated us from colonial rule, Gonçalves considered himself a proud monarchist. He had stood by Dom Pedro's side when he declared, "I am staying!" in the face of the colonialist nobility that wanted to keep Brazil from moving forward. Gonçalves had escorted the Queen Regent Leopoldina to the historic meeting on that sunny September day in 1822, where she signed the declaration of independence keeping us from becoming a colony again.

However, after the deaths of his friends, he had been pushed aside. The young prince, Dom Pedro II, fell under the influence of men who did not have the interests of southern Brazil at heart—one of those interests being the sale of jerky. The gauchos became angry because their jerky, which was sold only in Rio Grande do Sul, was being taxed out of the market. Meanwhile, imports from

Argentina and Uruguay were not only able to avoid the tax, but being sold at a discount to the population. The gauchos rose up in defiance and Gonçalves, a native of Rio Grande do Sul, felt it was his duty to lead the rebellion.

The anger of Rio Grande do Sul spread into Santa Catarina, infecting everyone with its hunger for rebellion. Laguna buzzed with news of the riot in São Joaquim. Gauchos there had stormed the village center and burned down the constable's building, with him inside. People argued in the streets. Those who were loyal to the king thought the rioters were rogue gauchos from Rio Grande do Sul. Others, who didn't like the Imperial government's influence, found the events inspiring. If São Joaquim could rebel against Brazil, so could Laguna.

I was living in the small home of my godfather with my mother and sister. Maria, the glorious wife of the ship caulker, had been sent home by her husband in disgrace. After four years of marriage she had not produced a child. By law, he was able to set her aside for another, younger bride who might be able to give him children.

Our godfather was often out. A house full of three bickering women was more than enough for a man who intended to be a bachelor his whole life. His small one-story house was three hundred yards from the harbor, but my mother liked to tell the other women, "We are on the right side of Laguna, west of the cathedral. We all know the east side is for the poor." But really, there was not that much difference, especially since we were across the street from the cathedral.

At eighteen years old, I found my time at the washing well a welcome respite from my crowded home. There I could listen to the gossip while I took my time laundering our clothes. One morning while it was still cool I made my way down to the well. The rainy season was fading away and the bright sun poured over the city, giving it a pleasant warmth. As I was washing, I heard a soft sniffle behind me. I turned to find Manoel standing there.

Dark red veins spiderwebbed the whites of his eyes. He sniffled, wrinkling his nose.

"Hello, wife."

"Manoel." I bundled the shirt that I was holding into a ball in front of me. "Why are you here?"

Manoel smiled. "I just came to see you. It's been a while; you look well."

"What do you want?" I asked.

He sighed deeply. "I've joined the Imperial cavalry. We are riding south."

I felt the air escape my lungs. He was going to fight in the Imperial Brazilian Army. Useless Manoel, who could barely cobble a shoe. I gulped. "When?"

"Today." He looked down, kicking a pebble. I stood watching him, my fear keeping me rooted to the spot. It was customary for the women, whether they be wives, lovers, or *putas*, to travel along with their men so that they could cook and tend to their husbands when they weren't fighting. Like cattle or, worse, slaves. I silently prayed Manoel wouldn't ask me to join him. I wanted to leave Laguna, but not like this. My stomach tightened as he opened his mouth to speak again. I spoke first. "If you are coming here to ask—"

"No. At least, I already know what your answer would be if I did ask. It's just, Anna, I came to say that I've always felt like I have had to be something for you. Something more than what I am."

"Manoel, I—"

"No. I need to say this." He puffed out his chest. "I have never been able to live up to your expectations. No matter what I do I am never good enough for you. I need to move on with my life and show you and everyone else that I am not a fool."

He left me there, clutching my laundry in my fists.

* * *

June 1839

My days were tedious, spent doing household chores, occasionally helping my mother and sister in their work as housemaids for the wealthy. I looked forward to spending my evenings with my best friend, Maria da Gloria. We had met by chance, both washing our family's laundry. She had forgotten the lye. I had a little extra.

We were brimming with ideas of what the world was supposed to be like. It wasn't long before Maria became my closest friend in Laguna. For a while she was my only friend. I both admired and envied her. Her curly hair made an unruly crown around her head—the only reminder that she was a descendant of freed slaves. When Maria smiled, everyone around her shared her joy.

Maria's father, Carlos, was a known sympathizer of the rebellion. His home was a safe haven for the most vocal of the rebels. Carlos encouraged Maria to speak her mind. She was his only child and he took pride in her independence. Maria's mother, Dylla, was an amazing cook. She could make a feast for an army with just a little flour and chicken.

"It isn't fair that our own government favors the products of foreign nations over those of its own people," Carlos said one evening, slapping the newspaper down on their table.

"The loyalists claim it's a matter of quality," Dylla said as she stirred the beans.

"Quality? How are Argentina's cows better than ours?" Maria asked. She stood at Dylla's elbow, helping to prepare our dinner. "The people can't determine which one they like better if they can't afford both to compare."

"You are absolutely right," Dylla said as she added more herbs to the beans. "What do you think, Anna?"

I looked up in surprise. "I, um... That is..."

Maria elbowed me in the ribs. "In this house, we value a woman's opinion."

"'Value'?" Carlos smiled mischievously. "I don't think I would be able to stop the opinions even if I tried."

Maria threw a dishrag at her father, which he blocked just in time by raising his newspaper.

Dylla smiled reassuringly at me. "Come now. You've got to have an opinion. Please share."

"We'll only judge you if it's the wrong one," Carlos joked.

"Well, I feel..." I began, looking at the friendly, expectant faces. "That it's our government's responsibility to take care of its people first." I took a breath, feeling my thoughts start to come out faster. "In taking care of its people it must make sure that the people can earn a decent living, not to make them rich, per se, but enough so that they can feed themselves. The imports from other countries, whether it is jerky or something else, should be the expensive products. Not what is made here."

"Well said!" Maria exclaimed.

"Why, Maria, I do believe you have been a horrible influence on this poor girl," Carlos teased. "I don't think I have ever been prouder to call you my daughter."

Laughing, Maria hugged her father. I laughed along with them. I felt proud that my opinion had been so well received, but at the same time, I felt a twinge of pain in my chest. Why couldn't my family be this open and friendly?

The door burst open and a group of men spilled through, led by Francisco, Maria's fiancé. Francisco saw himself as the leader of Laguna's rebels. The son of poor freed slaves, he was eager to make a name for himself, and battling against the Brazilian Imperial government was the most expedient way to make it happen.

"You'll never believe it!" He hugged Maria before standing in the middle of the room. "The great Giuseppe Garibaldi is coming to Laguna!" Maria squealed with joy before wrapping her arms around Francisco's neck.

"This is such wonderful news!" Carlos exclaimed. "He will liberate Laguna. Where did you hear about this?"

"My friend is a sailor on his ship. He sent a letter ahead of them. They just finished a campaign in the north and are moving south. He's bringing with him the North American John Griggs and his fellow Italian Luigi Rossetti."

"Carlos, go get the wine," Dylla requested, wiping her hands on a towel. "The one we have been saving for a special occasion. Tonight, we celebrate."

I made my way to Maria, who was beaming, and leaned toward her, whispering, "Who is Giuseppe Garibaldi?"

She turned to me, her face full of shock. "You don't know who the Great Garibaldi is?" Maria questioned me so loudly that everyone stopped talking and turned to look at me as the heat of embarrassment rose up my neck and into my cheeks.

"No, I don't," I mumbled.

"Garibaldi is a man of the people. He lived in Naples," Francisco began to explain.

"Naples?" Carlos questioned. "I thought he was from Marseille."

"Marseille? That's part of France!" Dylla responded, putting the large bowl of beans on the table. "No, he's a Genoan."

"How do you know?" Carlos asked.

"Because all the women like to gossip about handsome foreigners." She wiggled her eyebrows as she kissed a scowling Carlos on the top of his head.

"The point is," Francisco interrupted, "he was banished. His people are divided. The northern Italian peninsula is ruled by Austria, while the south is a stronghold to a Bourbon tyrant. While in Piedmont he and his mentor launched an insurrection. He was arrested and sentenced to death by exile."

"And now he is here?" I asked. "Why?"

"He travels the world fighting for the freedom that has been denied to his own people." Maria sighed.

The situation between the gauchos and Imperial Brazil continued to deteriorate. General Gonçalves, recently escaped from prison, was making gains in the west with his band of rebels. They and all eyes were turning to the prosperous port that was Laguna. War was coming.

Notices were posted all over. Recruits were needed for the rebel army at the northern front. All were welcome. I stood by the wagons, grasping Maria's hands in mine.

"Come with me, Anna," Maria pleaded. "How wonderful will it be to have my best friend and future husband fighting beside me?"

How I longed to say yes, to taste adventure. But who was I? I could never hold my own in battle. I was only Anna. I was not as brave as Maria. Nor as idealistic as the men she marched with. My fate was here in Laguna.

"No, Maria, I am no warrior." Battlefields were for the heroic. I wasn't heroic. "My place is here. Tending to our wounded." It was true. I volunteered my services at our little hospital caring for wounded rebel soldiers. "You go. You have enough bravery for the both of us."

Maria gave me one last hug. "Watch over my parents, please."

"Of course," I responded, letting her go. I watched as she rode away in a haze of dust kicked up by the overflowing wagon.

I found solace in my work, apprenticing with the nuns. It was rewarding to be needed and to know that what I did made a difference. I dressed wounds, cleaned up after the men, and helped to feed them when necessary. The blood didn't bother me as it did some, nor did the nutty, putrid, sweet scent that signaled an infection, which clung to the air. It felt good to be useful.

I was wrapping a bandage around the calf of an unconscious soldier when my friend Manuela came running up to me. "Anna! Anna! They're here."

When Manuela and I had met at the hospital, we became close friends right away. She reminded me of the tall grass that grew along the coast, swaying like a dancer in the breeze. No one was too far below her class to deserve her kindness, which was unusual for someone in her position. Her husband, Hector, held a position with the local government that afforded them a pleasant life and respect within Laguna.

I looked at her curiously and started to form the question *Who?* before she grabbed me by the arm. "The Farrapos, silly. The Farrapos are here!" she exclaimed as she pulled me out of the hospital. *Farrapos* meant "ragamuffins," a name given to the rebels by the aristocracy. It was easy for them to laugh; they could buy new clothing whenever they wanted without going hungry. Manuela and I ran down to the docks hand in hand. We stopped just before the wall of people who stood at the dock cheering. I let go of Manuela's hand and fought my way through the crowd, wiggling and pushing against people who were as unwilling to move as a tree. I ducked under the thick outstretched arms of a large cheering man. Looking up, I spied the most beautiful man I had ever seen.

The sun gleamed over the head of Giuseppe Garibaldi, making his light brown hair shine with specks of gold. His broad smile filled his bearded face. It was dazzling. *He* was dazzling. For a moment, I felt blinded by him. I watched as he shook the hands of the people who stood around him, kissing babies and the pretty young girls who held them.

My admiration turned to disappointment as I watched women flock to him. Amid so many beautiful women, how could he notice me? I slipped back into the crowd and quietly returned to my duties at the hospital.

SIX

July 1839

Days after Garibaldi arrived, Manuela and I walked through the market. A slave with a basket full of oranges bumped into Manuela. Slaves were meant to be seen and not heard. If they crossed these boundaries, they risked being shamed or beaten. The slave woman took in rapid short breaths. "*Sinto muito. Sinto muito.*" She bowed repeatedly, refusing to meet Manuela's eyes. Manuela put a hand on the woman's arm, causing her to flinch. "It's all right, there is no need to apologize." She handed the woman an orange. "Really, it was all my fault."

"*Obrigada*," the slave woman murmured as she hurried away.

Manuela and Hector lived in a spacious bright blue two-story home that sat on a hill surrounded by their own personal orchard. I spent so much time there that Hector liked to tease that I was their adopted daughter.

The week following the arrival of the Farrapos, I took to standing out on Manuela's balcony to watch the ships. They looked like bucking ponies tied to their posts, anxious to get out and run as they rolled with the waves. How I envied them.

I closed my eyes, lifting my face to soak in the warm sun as my hair danced in the wind around me. Breathing in, I filled my lungs with cool salt air. My thoughts went to Maria and the last time I saw her, rolling away from me. "I wish I had gone with you," I confessed to the wind. "Oh, Maria, I promise I will not be so foolish next time." *If there will be a next time.*

I lowered my eyes to look over the harbor. "As God is my witness, if I get to leave here again, I will grab the opportunity by the mane and never let go."

* * *

Early one morning, at the end of the week, I arrived at Manuela's house to help her tend to the grapes that ran along the edge of her property. The smell of the ocean thick on the brisk air. We moved about the grapevines, trimming back the unruly leaves and harvesting what fruit we could before heading back to the warmth of her home at midday. "Will we be eating these for lunch?"

"Yes, though I was thinking I would give some to the church to hand out to the poor," Manuela said, picking up her basket. "That's assuming you won't be eating them all before we get in the house."

"I only stole a few," I said midchew as I followed.

When we reached the back door, Manuela paused in front of a bush of vibrant yellow flowers. "Go ahead without me, I just love the smell of fresh flowers in the house. These will be perfect on the table."

I went into the house but stopped quickly. Hector was sitting in his parlor talking to someone. From where I stood, within the safety of the kitchen, I could see Hector but not the visitor.

"I can't guarantee the cooperation of the magistrate. There are too many loyalists in our ranks."

"What makes these men so loyal? The rest of Santa Catarina is preparing to join Rio Grande do Sul in war. Laguna will need to go with them or be left behind," the visitor responded. "Hector, my friend, they must realize that Laguna is going to be the central point for the war, whether they decide to join us or not."

I could have sworn I had heard that voice before. It was an odd accent, not one from South America, but I couldn't picture who was speaking. The deep purr made my breastbone vibrate. It dawned on me: I knew who was in the other room with Hector. My feet melted into the floor, and I couldn't move.

"Anna, you silly girl! What are you doing just standing here?" Manuela shoved me, stumbling, into the parlor. A steady arm reached out and grabbed me by the elbow, keeping me from falling face first into the brown tiled floor. Sheepishly, I looked up into the shining eyes of the mysterious man who had been speaking with Hector: Giuseppe Garibaldi.

Everyone else in the room fell away as I stared into his face. His eyes grew wide as his mouth hung open. Garibaldi stood frozen, bent over me, his grip firm on my elbow where he had caught me.

My heart thumped against my chest like a bird trying to escape a cage. I could feel heat rising up my neck and into my cheeks. My vision rocked like waves in the sea. I tried to swallow but my mouth and throat were dry. My eyes drifted to his throat as his Adam's apple slowly bobbed.

"*Devi esser mia.*" The words tumbled out of his lips like a prayer he couldn't stop. I pulled back sharply; not being familiar with Italian, I had no idea what he'd said. His face grew pink with embarrassment.

I was suddenly acutely aware of where I was and who I was with. I looked at Hector and Manuela in turn. Hector was standing up in front of his chair, looking down at us. Manuela stood in the kitchen, her hand over her mouth. I felt a rush of embarrassment as I looked back at Garibaldi's hopeful face. Feeling like I had made a fool of myself, I ran.

I raced up the stairs and flung myself onto Manuela and Hector's bed. I wanted to hide away. How could I have been so foolish? What was the matter with me? I closed my eyes, trying to slow my rapidly beating heart. Manuela slipped quietly into the room, placing a tender hand on my back.

"Anna?" she asked.

"I am such a fool," I said into her pillow. "I don't know what came over me."

Manuela laughed softly. "My friend, you have the sickness."

"The sickness?" I asked, sitting up.

"Yes, it's called love." Her eyes sparkled with her smile. She reached out to feel my forehead and cheeks before making a tsking noise. "And by the looks of it, you have it bad."

I grabbed her hand as she pulled it away. "Manuela, you speak Italian, don't you?"

"Just a little."

"Do you know what Garibaldi said?"

Manuela smiled mischievously. "'You must be mine.'" She patted my arm. "I'll leave you to collect yourself."

I sat in the bedroom, trying to work up the courage to go back down the stairs. I took my time, smoothing my skirt and tucking back my hair as the pounding in my heart subsided. I scurried down the stairs back to Manuela, hoping that I wasn't seen. She smiled at me as she piled a tray with *mate* and pastries. Before I could protest, she shoved the tray into my arms, turning me toward the parlor.

Senhor Garibaldi's eyes burned a hole into me as I set the silver tea tray on the simple wooden table that sat in the center of the parlor. I took my seat on the burgundy couch, my back rigid with my ankles firmly crossed. With Hector to my right, I was as far from Garibaldi as I could manage. He sat in one of the twin armchairs that matched the sofa. Together the three of us waited for Manuela to enter the parlor before we began the tea service.

Manuela entered with a tray full of small plates and *biscoitos de maizena*. She set the tray down before beginning the *mate* serving ritual. The silver-rimmed gourd she held in the palm of her hand had an intricate leaf pattern carved into it. After scooping the tea into the hollowed-out inside, she shook it, a process as important as the tea itself. Gently, Manuela poured the water into the gourd. She took a sip of the tea from the silver *bombilla* straw before spitting the first bitter dregs into the fireplace. When Manuela was satisfied with the taste and temperature, she passed the gourd to her husband.

"May I offer you a cookie, Senhora de Jesus?" Garibaldi held out one of the blue-trimmed plates to me. The sugar cookies looked innocent enough sitting there. However, as I looked into the hopeful face of the man before me, I felt that they were agents in an evil plot.

Manuela's head snapped up. A guest, and a man at that, serving during the tea service was a grave misstep. I could feel the blush creep up my neck all over again.

Taking the plate from him so as not to cause further embarrassment, I mumbled, "*Obrigada, senhor.*" He released the plate gently, brushing his fingers against mine. His touch sent a sharp jolt of energy up my arm. "And please, call me Anna."

"Anna." The sound of my name coming from his lips caused heat to rise.

Hector took a sip of the *mate* and passed it to Senhor Garibaldi as they resumed their discussion of Laguna's politics. I did my best to keep my nerves under control as I tried to hide the emotions that flowed through me like a rushing river. All the while, I chastised myself for my foolishness.

"How do you like Laguna, Senhor Garibaldi?" Manuela asked. "I'm sure it's much different from your home in Italy."

"Oh, I find Laguna to be quite lovely," he said. "Perhaps the most beautiful town in all of South America." He looked at me over the rim of the communal gourd as he said the words. "Senhora Oliveira, this *mate* is unlike anything I have tasted. What did you do differently?"

"I added dried oranges. They're a favorite of Anna's."

"Is that so?" He passed the gourd to me. "I believe it will be a favorite of mine now as well."

I tried to keep the blush from spreading anew as I took the gourd from him. It was next to impossible not to think about our lips being in the same place, on the same straw.

Throughout our conversation I attempted to resist every urge to look at him. Failing, I slyly spied him out of the corner of my eye. His gaze quickly moved away and back to our hosts.

"Tell me, Anna, are you at all interested in politics?" Garibaldi asked. I met his chocolate eyes for the first time that evening. His gaze held me, momentarily causing me to forget how to form words.

"Anna had the most interesting perspective on the rebellion. Go ahead and share it," Manuela said with a smile.

I tried to brush off my friend's compliment with a wave of my hand. "No, really, it's nothing, I'm not a politician like the men."

"Please, I would like to hear what you have to say." His face looked hopeful as he waited for me to speak.

"A handful of gentlemen became impetuous children because the king isn't giving them their way." I sipped my tea, trying to collect my thoughts before going on. "There are justifiable reasons to be angry, but is it truly enough to break away from the rest of Brazil?"

"But can't you say that this is an opportunity for the people of Santa Catarina to gain a better station in life?" Garibaldi responded.

"Is it? This is Rio Grande do Sul's war. Not ours. What will happen to Santa Catarina when the war is over? We can't risk taking on the burdens of Rio Grande do Sul."

He leaned back in his chair. A small smile played on his lips. "Tell me, Anna, what would you have Santa Catarina do? Your state is caught in the middle between Imperialist Brazil and her brothers of Rio Grande do Sul."

"If we are to enter into war, we need to guarantee that our people's interests will be seen to. If the people of Santa Catarina don't see that there is something in it for them, they will never support your cause."

"And therein lies our dilemma!" Garibaldi exclaimed. "We are trying to convince the people of Santa Catarina that what we propose is truly in their best interest. If only I had you by my side. As one of my advisors." A thrill went down my spine at the thought of being by his side. He smiled at me, soft and shy at first, but broader as I met his gaze. What was it about this man that drew me in? For someone who preferred to be alone, I couldn't explain why I suddenly wanted the attention of the strange foreigner.

Garibaldi stood up. "If you will excuse me. I have business matters to attend to." He bowed to Manuela and me in turn before striding to the front hallway. We followed him, the four of us crammed in the narrow hall, Garibaldi and Hector in front, Maria and I behind them. As he reached the door he turned to Manuela and me. "If either of you ladies would be interested, I could arrange for a tour of the ship."

"That is a very generous offer, senhor." Manuela smiled politely. A ship was no place for a lady. Women who spent time surrounded by a bunch of sailors were known as *putas*, whores.

He bowed his head quickly before exiting through the door.

* * *

"Manuela, it would be rude for us to ignore his invitation." I hurried after Manuela as she carried an armload of sheets down the hospital hallway.

"Anna, it would be inappropriate."

"Not if you come with me," I pleaded.

Manuela stopped short in the hall, causing me to nearly bump into her. "Anna, only *putas* go on ships, with or without a chaperone."

"No one needs to know," I responded.

"But they will, Anna. You know as well as I do that this town is full of gossips. If word gets out that I was somewhere inappropriate, Hector could lose his position."

"Fine." I sulked. "This was my one opportunity to see the tall ships up close. I'll never get to do this again."

Manuela sighed. "All right! I will go with you, but not one word to Hector. Do you understand? Not one word." She turned and stormed off down the hall. "The things I do."

Two days later we went to the harbor. Manuela kept looking over her shoulder. "The only reason anyone would notice us is because you are wearing a cloak on a warm spring day. You look odd," I grumbled.

"Do you think I should take it off so that no one will notice us?"

"No one is going to see us. Nor will they care."

"You never know," she hissed. "There are eyes everywhere."

"Manuela, we are the least interesting people in Laguna. No one will be watching us."

"Not unless you let this flirtation get out of control."

I chose to ignore Manuela's last comment. I didn't need her to remind me. A relationship with Giuseppe Garibaldi was the last thing I needed. We walked in silence for a few more feet before she added, "You do look nice today, though."

"Thank you," I responded. I wore one of Manuela's old dresses, green with yellow trim. My hair was pulled into a modest chignon.

Fidgeting with the sleeves of my dress, I wasn't paying attention to where we were walking until Manuela placed a hand on my shoulder.

My breath caught in my throat as I spied Senhor Garibaldi's ship up close, without a crowd of people, for the first time. "It looks like a horse, doesn't it?" The tall ship sat proudly before us, large and beautiful, the masts reaching to the sun. It gently creaked with the smooth lull of the water. Men moved about the ship, engrossed in their work.

I looked back at Manuela and was disappointed not to see my enthusiasm reflected in her face. "Are you sure you want to do this?" she asked, holding me back as I tried to move toward the ship.

"I have never been on a ship before. This is so exciting." I tried to pull her forward with me.

"Anna, are you excited about the ship or about Senhor Garibaldi?" I stared at Manuela as she ventured on. "A ship is no place for a woman. We shouldn't be doing this; we can still turn around."

I pulled on her arm. "Please, Manuela. I promise I won't tell your husband if you don't."

Reluctantly she followed me onto the ship. Garibaldi paced on the deck but stopped when he saw us. He looked up at us and smiled. "Welcome!" A large smile spread across his face. "Let me show you around the ship." We let him lead us around as he talked about the ship's features with pride.

"I have climbed this mast myself, many times. Right up to the crow's nest at the very top," he said, slapping the thick wooden pole. "When the ship is at full sail it feels like flying."

Stepping back, I took in the expanse of the large beam in front of me.

"On a clear day when there are no clouds and the sun glints on the crystal-blue water, you can see for miles and miles, all the way to the horizon." He spoke as if in a dream. "You really feel like the ocean is yours. It is the most humbling feeling in all the world."

"I can only imagine," I said, trying to picture what it felt like. I looked back at Garibaldi, who was watching me, making no attempt to look away.

He coughed slightly. "There is something over here I would like to show you." I followed him to the other side of the ship, cautiously looking behind me to see Manuela distracted by a sailor. I came up to stand next to Garibaldi at the railing of the ship. He was looking out toward the mouth of the lagoon. We watched as small fishing vessels lazily slipped in and out of the harbor. His hands gripped the railing in front of him, almost touching mine. They held on so tightly that I could see the small muscles criss-crossed with tiny veins.

"You are married," he said, refusing to look at me.

I felt a sinking weight in my gut, like a rock that had been dropped in a pond. For just a little while I wanted to pretend that I was not a marked woman, I wanted this flirtation to keep going. To think that perhaps somehow, some way, life with him could be possible, even if it was pretend. I struggled to suck in a lungful of air against the pressure that was building in my chest as I watched the fantasy of having Giuseppe Garibaldi dissolve into small waves that slapped against the boat.

"Who told you?" I finally asked, refusing to look at him too.

"Hector," he said, still looking out over the lagoon. "I inquired after you." He sounded like he had to force the words out of his mouth.

"Oh." I felt the stab of betrayal. I would never be able to look Hector in the eye again.

"Do you love him?"

"Who?" I asked.

"Your husband."

"Oh. Him," I said, annoyed that I still had not rid myself of the albatross that was Manoel. "No. Could you love someone you were forced to marry?"

"I suppose, if time allowed." He shook his head. "All the same. You are still married."

I took a deep breath, letting the air slowly escape from between my lips. "If you want to call it that. Manoel was never much of a husband. And now? He could be dead for all I know."

"He left you?"

"He joined the cavalry about six months ago."

"You didn't go with him?"

I looked at Garibaldi, tears threatening to spill out of my eyes. Manoel was gone, but he would continue to haunt me for the rest of my life. I realized this now as I looked into Garibaldi's handsome bearded face. I was never going to be happy. "And make his meals, wash his clothes, pretend to be happy when he walked off the battlefield? No. I am not his slave. I would rather live as a widow than follow around a man I have no respect for."

He looked down at me, shocked at the bitterness of my words. "I am truly sorry to hear you feel that way." He reached out for my hand, still clenching the railing, but I moved it away before he could grasp it. "It was a pleasure meeting you, Anna de Jesus." His voice wavered ever so slightly.

I smiled, though my heart broke into a million pieces. "The pleasure is all mine," I said as I pulled myself away. I went back to Manuela, who suddenly acted as if she were very interested in the structure of a fishing net.

Hooking our arms together, we strode back to shore. I looked over my shoulder and for a moment I thought I saw Garibaldi watching us. Had it been my imagination? What would Giuseppe Garibaldi want with a married woman like me?

I dreamed of him. Every night Garibaldi visited me, always at the edge of my sight, taunting me. I heard his whisper, *Anna*, soft and deep. I woke in my bed, the memory of his face fading from my eyes. My ears were precisely tuned to hear his name from even the faintest sound. It drove me mad.

Two terribly long weeks later, I was at the hospital tending to a patient when one of my fellow nurses rushed into my ward. "Hurry! Clean up this mess. Senhor Garibaldi is here, visiting the hospital."

When I looked at the nurse in stunned silence, she hurried over to me, shooing me from my patient. I tried to get out of her way as casually as I could in an attempt to slip out of the hospital without anyone noticing me. I stopped short when I heard voices. Garibaldi and an entourage of people walked into my ward, blocking my only route of escape.

"Dona Anna, what a pleasure to see you again." Garibaldi bowed.

"Senhor Garibaldi," I responded with a nod of my head.

"I was hoping I would see you again."

"I suppose it's good that one of us is getting their wish," I snapped.

"It is a beautiful day. Do you think you could give me a tour of the garden? I understand it is quite impressive."

I opened my mouth to respond, but one of the other nurses spoke up. "Senhor, if you want to see the gardens, I do believe Dona Francesca would be a better guide."

"No," Garibaldi said. "I would prefer for Dona Anna to be my escort." He turned to his entourage. "You will not be needed."

"Very well," I said, suddenly feeling every eye on me. "This way, please, senhor."

I led him out the doors to the garden. When we were out of hearing range of the others, I turned on him. "What do you think you are doing?"

"Asking for a tour of the garden," he responded coyly.

"Don't you act charming with me, Senhor Garibaldi," I said, pointing a finger at him. "I know very well that you have no interest in plants."

"And how do you know that? Botany could be my hobby." He had the audacity to look offended. Though the corner of his mouth tilted upward ever so slightly.

I huffed in frustration. "A sailor interested in botany makes about as much sense as a farmer designing cathedrals."

Garibaldi tried to stifle a laugh.

"Well?" I asked with my hands on my hips, squinting at him in the bright afternoon sun. "Will you give me an honest answer, or shall I go back to my work?"

He looked down and kicked at an unseen pebble. "I can't get you out of my head," he said, looking back up at me with large eyes. "Why do you haunt me?"

I took a few steps back, feeling the shock of the words he said. "Most likely for the same reason you haunt me, but it doesn't change anything."

"I don't want to ruin your reputation—"

"Yes, because asking to speak with me in the garden by myself is not going to ruin my reputation. People talk. You have done plenty of damage already."

"If you would let me finish, I was going to say that I don't want to ruin your reputation, but I want to work around this unfortunate matter."

"'Unfortunate matter'?" I shook my head. "Is that what we are calling it? I will not be your whore."

Garibaldi looked stunned by my words. "I would never…I have never…"

"I did not mean to be so harsh, but don't I get a say in these *unfortunate matters*, as you call them? I wasn't the one who wanted to get married in the first place. I wasn't the one who chose to leave my family. A man gets to go out and live the life that he wants, but me? I have to live by the whims of men who want to work around my *unfortunate matters*."

"Well then, tell me, Anna, what do you want?"

“Freedom.” I threw my hands up in the air and looked at him. I no longer felt the strength to fight. “You.”

He was by my side in just two steps. His arms were around my waist. The smell of fresh ocean and sandalwood engulfed me. “Then I believe it is time you make your own rules,” he whispered against my lips.

His eyes held me in a trance. I placed my hands on his broad chest. I could feel his heart pounding in time with mine. As Garibaldi leaned down, I slid my hands up his neck, tangling my fingers in his curls. He pressed his lips against mine, drinking me in.

Giuseppe pulled an eyelash’s length away, making me immediately feel the pain of his absence. “The families of the soldiers are camped out to the south of the docks. You should join us there, tonight.” Unable to speak, I nodded yes.

He stepped away, placing his hat back on his head. “I look forward to seeing you again.” He flashed me a boyish, lopsided smile that made my knees weak. I touched my fingers to my lips; they still throbbed from his kiss as I watched him stride away.

SEVEN

July 1839

I stared at my reflection in the mirror, running a comb through my hair for the third time that afternoon. As I brushed my long locks, I thought over my scheme to make sure I wasn't noticed. For all that my family knew, I was going to be spending the evening with my respected friends. I plaited my hair in a braid and repeated my practiced speech: *I am going to the Da Gatos' for dinner. I expect to spend the night.*

My mother didn't even look up from the black beans that she stirred as I walked into our cramped kitchen. I made my announcement, expecting to elicit a suspicious response from her, but I got none.

"Too bad the Da Gatos can't adopt you. Has your ability to manipulate people started to slip?" Maria sneered.

"Go to hell," I said to her as I made my way through the kitchen.

"You first, sister." Maria turned back to her mending.

"Oh, will you two stop?" Our mother whipped around, shaking her spoon at us. "I swear, I never have a moment's peace when both of you are here!" Bits of bean flew from the spoon. "Anna, if you are going to leave, then leave already! Stop causing so much trouble."

"Why am I the one getting yelled at?"

"Because whenever there is strife in this family, you're the one to blame!"

I tried to shake off my confrontation with my sister as I made my way to the Farrapos' campsite. Dirty sailors moved about as they settled in for their dinners with their wives, women who looked as worn out as the men they catered to. It was in the center of the camp that I found Garibaldi, surrounded by a group of friends. Their shared laughter carried over the business of the camp.

What if his friends didn't like me? What if they thought I wasn't good enough for Garibaldi? I paused and contemplated retreating. *This is foolish*, I thought, smoothing the pale blue skirt that I usually only wore to church. *Did I really expect anything to come of this?* Then Garibaldi saw me. A large, warm smile spread across his handsome face and every fear I had evaporated.

"Anna! You made it." He walked closer before bending down and gently kissing my hand. My heart fluttered at the tender touch of his lips.

"This is my fellow countryman, Luigi Rossetti." Garibaldi pointed to the tall dark-haired man standing next to him. I took in his clean, well-tailored clothing, trimmed in lace. He reminded me of a stern schoolteacher. How could he be a soldier and yet be so immaculately dressed? There wasn't a single stain or tear.

Rossetti's piercing black eyes stared back at me with an air of superiority from over his large nose. His smile was small and polite, barely making his neatly trimmed beard move. "A pleasure to meet you." He bowed with a flourish as he reached out and lightly kissed my hand, his lips barely brushing my knuckles.

Garibaldi pointed toward the man standing on the other side of Rossetti. "This is our resident *norte-americano*, John Griggs."

Griggs wasn't quite as tall as Rossetti. He had a pleasant air about him, with eyes that looked like he had just woken up from a deep sleep. His smile was charming as he tipped his hat, revealing a full head of curly dark-blond hair.

"So, this is the girl that you've had your eye on since we sailed into port?" Griggs's smile widened as Garibaldi's face flushed pink. I looked back and forth between the men. "Normally a man uses his telescope to look out over the ocean. Not up into the hills to spy on a certain lady who likes to spend her siestas on her balcony," Griggs teased.

Before Griggs could say another word, Garibaldi led me by the arm to a spot by the fire. The flames burned brightly, casting an orange-gold light over everyone. The smell of roasting meats and smoke intermingled with the sweet sea air. There were people moving about, tending to their own fires and needs, but Garibaldi paid them no mind as he doted on me. Every few moments he stood to grab something more for me to eat or drink.

When he shifted his weight to stand up again, I reached out, putting a hand on his arm to calm him. I swallowed a bite of bread with concerted effort. "Please, Senhor Garibaldi, I am fine. Just sit."

He smiled, settling back down. "My friends here call me José. You can do the same," he stammered. "That is, I do hope you would call me a friend." His face turned red before he dropped it into his hands. "I am making a fool of myself, aren't I?"

I laughed. "No more a fool than I am being."

He suddenly grew serious. His eyes bored into me. "I would never think of you as a fool." This time it was my turn to blush.

Soon a group gathered around the campfire, consisting of myself, José, Griggs, and Griggs's woman, Ruthie. Ruthie had joined the camp to be with Griggs. An Indian girl, she was so slight in stature she barely reached Griggs's shoulder. She had a sly smile and hawk eyes that seemed to take in everything. Rossetti eventually joined us too, sitting at a small table a short distance from our little circle. His face was buried in a notebook that he furiously wrote in.

As we sat by the campfire under the dying light of day, Griggs rubbed his large callused hands together and began to tell the story of how he and José fought off a group of Austrian mercenaries employed by the Imperial army. They had managed to capture the colonel leading the division who was not the most amiable of people.

"Now, we thought we had this colonel secured, but the sneaky bastard broke free, scaring the horses to distract us. Like fools, we all went after our animals," Griggs said, at the edge of his seat, his hand flailing about as he told the story. "Little did we know said distraction was a signal to his friends."

"Meanwhile, I was with my cook. We were away from the rest of the camp," José interjected, turning to me. "He got the finest *yerba mate* from Argentina. A rare variety that only grows in the north." He turned back to Griggs. "That cook couldn't do much, but damn could he make a great cup of tea."

"I swear, I still dream about his feijoada—sorry, Ruthie." Griggs gave Ruthie a kiss on her temple. "But he was godawful with a gun."

"'Godawful' isn't a strong enough word," José responded. "Anyway, my cook and I are sitting down enjoying this tea." He turned back to me. "He and I had been talking about it for weeks. We needed a nice calm moment to truly savor it. Cook pours the first bit of water and we are waiting on the edge of our seats for it to seep into the leaves when we hear the infantry call. I turn and there is this wall of Austrian cavalrymen racing toward us."

I gasped, lifting a hand to my mouth, which encouraged José to go on. "Now, one would think that with all those targets, Cook would be able to hit one, just one of those soldiers on horseback, but he couldn't do it!"

"No, surely he at least shot a horse?" I asked in amazement, looking from José to John Griggs. "I was five years old when I picked up my first gun and I could certainly hit the large targets."

Both men laughed and shook their heads. "What is the saying you have in Nord America?" José asked.

"He couldn't hit the broad side of a barn," Griggs said, still laughing. "We could have a target as big as a ship and still he would miss!"

"What happened then?" Ruthie asked Griggs.

"Well, yours truly came to the rescue. We wrangled up the horses, just after realizing they were a distraction," Griggs said with a grin as he wrapped an arm around Ruthie. "My men were able to scare away those Austrian bastards."

"Yes, you scared them, right into the surrounding buildings. Some of them even went into the outhouses!" José said, getting control of his laughter. "They thought they could hide in there and fire on us."

"Joke was on them, though," Griggs said. "Still, I always look twice before going into the outhouse."

"Bloody Austrians." Garibaldi sneered. "The outhouses were too good for them."

"Why do you hate the Austrians?" I asked.

"The Austrians have my homeland by the neck, like a chicken being readied for slaughter. They take everything from us, leaving my brethren with scraps not even fit for dogs. To the Austrians we are second-class citizens, at best. If they have their way, all that is good about my home will be destroyed."

"Hear! Hear! Death to Austria!" We turned to see Rossetti looking up briefly from his book. "May the devil have pity on their souls, because they will find none with the Italians," he said before going back to his writing. "*Gli stronzi*," he muttered. *Assholes*.

"What is he doing?" I asked, motioning toward his notebook.

"Recording his great memoirs. So that when we have a unified

Italy they will know of his sacrifice," José responded with a half smile. "It's a bit of an obsession."

"Why?"

José stood up, reaching a hand out to help me. "His one true love is Italy. She is his damsel in distress to be rescued from the dragon. Come, it's getting cold out here in the open."

José led me to his spacious canvas tent, set apart from the others to allow some privacy. To the left sat a neatly made bed. Clothing spilled out of the trunks that rested beside it. To the right was a table surrounded by four chairs, covered with maps and papers. In the center I admired a large oak desk that had thick books piled on it.

Shortly afterward an attendant arrived with a tea tray. He set it on the table and then slipped away. I watched as José picked a box wrapped in cloth off his desk. As if it were a fragile egg, he slowly unwrapped it. He opened the tin and scooped *mate* into his gourd, then shook it vigorously.

"You make *mate* like a real Brazilian." I fumbled with my hands, not sure what to do with them.

"Thank you." He smiled as he poured a small amount of cool water into the gourd. "I only drink tea and I quite like your *yerba mate*."

"No alcohol?" I asked, watching him pour hot water.

"No, I find it clouds my judgment too much," he said with a wave of his hand. "You have heard so much about me. I want to know about Anita."

"Anita?" I asked. "Have you forgotten my name already?"

José blushed. "No, only, in my country, when a girl becomes a woman we add '-ita' to her name. Flora becomes Florita; Anna, Anita; and so on."

"And you think my name should be changed?"

"Well, yes. I have no interest in girls."

I felt a blush creep up my cheeks. I could hear the dying

activity of the day outside, the jingle of equipment being cleaned up, the hiss of doused fires. José approached me, drawing my attention back to him as he slowly slid an arm around my waist. I could feel him shake ever so slightly as he pulled me closer. The tip of his nose grazed my cheekbone before his lips found mine. I savored everything about him, from the scratch of his beard to the sandalwood scent that engulfed me. Willingly, I let him lead me to his bed.

José was tender; I could barely feel his fingers as they caressed me, lulling me, making me want to pull him closer to me. I trembled as he expertly undid the buttons of my blouse, his lips never leaving my mouth.

Afterward, I lay on my back with José's arm draped over my waist. He slept on his side, softly snoring. Absentmindedly stroking his arm, I listened to the sounds that lingered in the air from the camp outside. The footsteps of the guards crunched through the dry grass. Birds began to sing in an attempt to lure the sun back from its slumber.

I looked at the man sleeping next to me, my eyes tracing the scars across his chest and neck. The Great Garibaldi, they called him. He was the savior of the people. I couldn't help but wonder, *What happens next?* Would I follow him, like the other women who followed their husbands? Would he leave me behind? Surely he knew there couldn't be much of a future with me. My stomach began to knot as reality set in.

José stirred, stretching his body alongside mine. He watched me for a few minutes before kissing my shoulder. "You look troubled," he said, his voice rough from sleep.

"No," I lied through my smile.

He sat up on his elbow, studying me. "You are lying."

"No." I tried to laugh.

"Oh, now you are lying even more. I can tell when you lie, you get these little wrinkles, right here." He ran a thumb over my forehead. Stroking my cheek, he watched me. "I'll let you escape with this little lie, just this once."

"And next time?"

"There won't be a next time." He kissed the top of my head. "We will never lie to each other. It will be our one rule."

I settled in closer to him. "I promise."

"What do you plan on doing today?"

"I have to work at the hospital. I'll be there most of the day."

"And after that?"

"I don't know." I hesitated. "What are your plans for the day?"

"Well, a captain's job is never done. I am sure I will have plenty to do, but I was hoping I'd have another evening with my Anita."

The excitement that bubbled in my stomach made my toes curl. "I think that could be arranged."

"Oh, you think so?" He playfully pinned me onto my back. "It is so gracious of you to think of me." He dove for my neck, making me laugh in surprise. His kisses explored my shoulders, breasts, and face. My laughter turned to pleasure as I enjoyed the feeling of the soft bristles of his beard.

"Tell me I am yours." He ran his finger around the edge of my jaw.

I turned his face so that he was forced to look into my eyes. "You are mine, José Garibaldi."

He kissed me passionately as he took me again. He whispered in my ear, "You are my treasure, *tesoro mio*."

From that day forward, I snuck away at every opportunity to be with José. We would spend the evenings among his friends as they told stories of their adventures. When José's sun shone on me, everything felt wonderful. I was warm and blissful. However, when he was gone, I could sorely feel the cold loss of his absence. I determined that I never wanted to be without him.

We didn't talk much about our romance or show much affection in public. I was still a married woman. If I was seen with José it would ruin everything that he worked for. Plus, we had a nearly fifteen-year age difference, which would make people talk all the more. When we weren't together, we went about our business as if nothing was amiss. Both of us were careful to avoid each other in town.

Occasionally José and I ventured out together, paying visits to my friends the Da Gatos. They were the only people outside of the camp who knew about our relationship. They fondly welcomed us to their home for evening meals.

However, secrets never remain secrets for very long, especially in a small town like Laguna. We became careless, as most foolish lovers do, paying attention only to each other and not to what the people around us were whispering. We thought we were safe within the camp; it was the one place where we felt we could be open with our relationship. But the whispers seeped from the camp into the town. People openly talked and still we didn't notice. I stopped going home for long stretches at a time. It wasn't until I snuck into my family's house when I thought no one would be home that I realized exactly how foolish we had been.

"I didn't expect you to show your face here again," Maria said from a corner in the parlor. I jumped, noticing her for the first time.

"I came to get my things," I said, making my way to my bedroom.

"Your things? You've been away so much we assumed you moved in with your pirate." She stood from her chair and walked closer, her black eyes boring into me, her icy hatred freezing me down to my bones.

"What do you mean by that?"

"Only that I gave your things away two days ago. There is nothing left for you here."

"You did what?" I asked.

"I said I gave away all of your things. Well, actually, that's a lie.

I sold them." She shrugged. "I figured your pirate preferred his *puta* in better clothing, and Lord knows we could use extra money since you don't bring home any of your whore earnings." She set down her sewing and glared at me, a small smile spreading across her face.

"Earnings?"

"Well, yes. Everyone says that you are a well-cared-for woman now that you are the whore of Senhor Garibaldi. Some even say he passes you around in order to raise money for the cause." She took a step closer to me. "Our mother is sick with embarrassment. Papai would be ashamed if he could see you now."

I clenched my fists. "How can you say such things?"

"How can I? How could you? You have made a fool of this family. You are a married woman, Anna, and you've taken up with a pirate! Mother can never show her face in town again!"

"Don't forget that it was my husband who left me." I pointed a finger at her. "He's gone! He's never coming back. I have a right to my own life."

"Are those the lies your Garibaldi told you to get you into his bed?"

I shook my head in disbelief. "José has not lied to me. I chose his bed. I chose to be with him. We don't lie to each other."

Maria laughed. "Give it time, sister. He'll be lying to you soon enough. If you were a good wife you would have followed your husband." I opened my mouth to protest, but Maria raised her hand, silencing me. "You made a vow before God. A sacred vow that you have broken. You are a disgrace."

"What about Fernando's vow?" I hissed. Maria looked stung when I brought up her ex-husband. "I'm sure he's not thinking about his vows now that he has taken up with a new woman. You know, the younger, prettier one. Tell me, how many children does he have?"

Maria's face turned scarlet. I opened my mouth to speak again but stopped when we heard the slamming of a door. In unison, we turned to our mother, whose red-rimmed eyes stood out against her ashen face. She walked up to me in silence. I raised my chin as she regarded me. In one smooth motion, she reached up and slapped me across the face.

The sting radiated from my cheek and into my jaw. "I wish I could trade you for one of my dead sons. You should have been the child that died, not your brothers."

EIGHT

I rushed from my mother's home to the Farrapos camp. At the sight of José the tears that I had been fighting since I left my family spilled out and onto his chest, creating a large wet spot. "Anita, *tesoro mio*, are you all right?"

He pulled me away by my shoulders. I shook my head no.

"Let's go somewhere private and you can tell me what happened."

I couldn't speak, it hurt too much. A lump had stopped up my throat. It wrapped its tendrils around my voice, making any attempt to speak painful. José led me to his tent, stopping only once to whisper to his servant. He pulled me in close, wrapping his large arms around me. "Tell me, who has made my beautiful Anita cry?"

The knot of hurt deep in my chest clenched at me. José kissed the top of my head. "You are safe," he whispered over and over. The stranglehold on my voice melted. Slowly the words came out. Broken at first, but as I began to feel better, they flowed. I told him everything that had happened between my family and me.

"I'm sorry," he said as he stroked my hair. "I suppose this was bound to happen. The truth always has a way of making itself known, and we were foolish." He sighed. "Anita, to many I am a pirate. I have no riches. I have no house. All I can offer you is a life of hardship and poverty. Every choice that I make has to be about how I can get back to my homeland. How I can serve my people. I chose this life and I can't force you to make the same decision."

I lifted my head from his lap to stare at him in a bit of disbelief. "A life of hardship with you is better than a thousand lives filled with wealth." I cupped his cheek in my hand, feeling the soft bristles of his beard. "I have already made my choice."

He rested his forehead against mine. "Is it even possible to love someone as much as I love you?"

I laughed through my tears. "I certainly hope so."

He wiped the tears from my cheek with a stroke of his thumb. Gently he pulled me to him. The smell of him, the sandalwood and sea, pushed away the remaining thoughts of my family. His soft lips were on mine, coaxing me away from my sorrow. His spell was broken when the servant appeared in the tent.

"*Perdoe-me, senhor*. I have the hot water that you requested."

"Thank you, Pablo. Also, Anita and I will be dining in my tent alone tonight. Please have some dinner brought to us."

"*Sim, senhor.*" He left with a bow.

José kissed my forehead. "Rest. This is your home now." I watched as he prepared the tea for us.

"I should be the one preparing our tea."

José shrugged. "It makes no difference to me. Plus, I am old and set in my ways, and I like my *mate* prepared a certain way." He winked as he handed me the gourd. "Now if you will excuse me, I have some work to attend to." José sat down at his desk, reading letters and signing documents. Sitting on what was now our bed, I sipped the tea as I played with a thread that stuck out from the blanket and I contemplated my new future.

To be tied to a soldier meant that I would have a life of perpetually waiting for death. José's mortality was as tangible as the gourd I held in my hand. I thought back to the day Manoel left. The prospect of following him around Brazil had sickened me. I would have been trading my small cage in Laguna for a smaller cage, but with wheels.

But I was willing to tie myself to this man. I'd follow him to places that I couldn't even imagine. Why did this feel like freedom? Or was it just that I couldn't see the bars?

José looked up at me, flashing a soft smile before bending back over his papers.

There were no bars, and if this man were to die, I vowed right then and there that I would die at his side with him. As his equal.

A meek voice took my attention from my thoughts. "Hello?" I looked up at the sound of Ruthie announcing herself at the entrance to our tent, in a plain green dress that made her dark skin and hair glow. "I heard what happened with your family. I am very sorry."

José crinkled his forehead in confusion, but I turned to him with a half smile. "Laguna is a small town. News travels fast."

Ruthie held out a pile of goods. "I brought you these. They're clothes that I was able to get from the other women around camp. Things that a number of us don't mind parting with. There is spare fabric so that you can make some things for yourself. If you'd like."

"Thank you," I said, rising to accept the bundle.

"Oh, I almost forgot! I also brought you some thread and a few needles." She reached into her pocket and pulled the items out. "It's not much."

"It's wonderful. Thank you." I carried everything over to the bed and surveyed my new treasures, looking up to see José smiling at me. I knew I was at peace with my decision.

* * *

As the days progressed, I chose to stay in camp rather than venture into town. The fact that I was openly with José was freely discussed in the streets and I had no desire to face the accusing stares. My position at the hospital had been terminated via a letter from the nuns. José's temper flared as he read it to me. "How can they disrespect you like this?"

I took the letter from him and threw it into the fire. "People will say what they want. But it makes no difference to me." I slipped my arms around his waist. "They aren't the ones who have to live with the consequences of my decisions."

On a particularly sunny day I found myself feeling restless. I wandered through the Farrapos' camp, absentmindedly picking at a piece of sweet bread.

The camp was a hive of activity. Not just the men, who were busy with the tasks associated with maintaining an army, but the women as well. Many followed their men from camp to camp to tend to them. A group of women clustered together, their heavily painted faces cracked as they laughed and flirted with the men who passed by them. I couldn't help but watch them as they jiggled and fell over themselves to gain attention.

"Anita." I turned to find Ruthie approaching me, holding a basket with wet laundry to her wide hip. "I hope the cloth I gave you was helpful." She wiped some stray black hairs from her face that had escaped her ponytail.

"Yes, it was. Thank you very much."

She smiled up at me. "Walk with me. I'll give you a small tour on our way back to the officers' quarters." Once we were away from the women, she turned to me. "Don't let yourself be seen around women like that."

"I wasn't very close to them. I didn't think."

"It doesn't matter. They are *putas*," she hissed. "They find their way into camps like maggots. All they want is a warm meal and a warm body. Stay by the other wives, it's safer." I looked at the women over my shoulder. We weren't all that different. I was reliant on someone else for my well-being too. Only, someone had deemed me respectable.

We were quiet as we walked through the busy camp. I watched as Ruthie greeted everyone she passed. No one seemed to care about her relationship like they did with José and me. They smiled and waved back at her, the respect Griggs commanded echoing in their movements. "Are you married to Griggs?" I slapped my hand over my mouth. "I'm sorry, that was too intrusive."

Ruthie smiled slightly. "It's all right. We are not married, in the traditional sense." She looked at me, blushing slightly. "Most of us aren't married. It's just easier to refer to ourselves as such."

"I feel as if everyone knows about me, but what about you? How did you find yourself here? If you don't mind me being so forward."

Ruthie shrugged. "There isn't much to tell. I was a servant for the Gonçalves family. Then John arrived and, well, that was that."

"The family you served just let you go?"

"I'm not a slave." She giggled. "I asked for my leave and they granted it. They knew I wanted to be with John, and Senhora Gonçalves wanted me to be happy." Ruthie smiled; it was pleasant, hinting at some future dream. "Well, here we are at your tent. I should go hang these," she said, motioning to her basket before walking away.

Life with the Farrapos was going to be an adjustment. Their sense of morality was different from everything I had been taught, yet so much remained the same. Once a woman was shamed, she was ostracized, but their idea of a shamed woman was far different from what I experienced in town. A woman's station was based on her partner's position within the navy. Griggs was second-in-command to José, therefore everyone respected Ruthie. I was

José's woman, which meant that I was afforded even more respect. These *putas*, though, they were outliers. They weren't associated with any one man. The officers called them maggots because they seemed to appear out of nowhere and scavenged for whatever they could.

A few evenings later I sulked in front of the campfire by myself while everyone else seemed too busy to notice me. The smell of roasted meats drifted on the light breeze, along with bits and pieces of their conversations. I looked over to José, a few feet away sipping his *mate*. He was surrounded by a group of mostly women who hopped around him like attention-starved puppies.

The tall one wore a bodice that was tied extra tight, making her bust look like a small table strapped to her chest, which she seemed to push out to José at every opportunity. Another painted lady was squat and round, reminding me of a frog, complete with a large wart that seemed to have a life separate from its host on her humped back, just above her dress collar. A few sailors circled the group as well, looking eager to get their master's scraps.

I felt the sting of jealousy spread in my stomach, only to be suppressed by the chest-crushing doubt that seeped down from my shoulders. José had yet to come to me for his dinner, which I had taken over making from his servants. I stabbed a small potato with my fork. Had I made the right decision? Did José mean everything that he said?

"I wouldn't worry about them." A man's voice interrupted my thoughts.

Surprised, I looked up to see Griggs smiling down at me. "May I?" He motioned toward the log next to me. When I nodded yes, he sat down. "José is a leader. He has to be that handsome friendly face. Who wants to follow an ugly man into battle?"

I couldn't help but smile despite myself. Griggs took it as a cue to continue. "You see, it's always the ugly ones who get labeled as crazy or as failures. If someone has to put their life on the line, they want it to be for someone who looks like victory personified. They want someone who looks like our José." Griggs playfully bumped me with his shoulder. "However, I have it on good authority that you are José's most treasured friend."

I could feel a smile forming, betraying my cool demeanor. José's second-in-command pointed at me. "There it is. I knew I could get your real smile."

I nodded in agreement. "Yes, yes you did."

"I, by the way, am an expert when it comes to reading people. Take José, for example: I know how to tell his false smile from his real smile. See, watch." He pointed his fork at the tall woman leaning her heaving breasts toward José as she tilted her head and spoke to him, batting her eyelashes the whole time. "You see she just told him that she has a very large... er... dowry. Oh, now look, see that smile, right there? The corners of his mouth go straight out toward his ears." Griggs popped some chicken into his mouth and quickly chewed, swallowing it with a gulp. "You see, when José smiles, truly smiles, the corners of his mouth go up toward his eyes."

"You must really know José."

Griggs shrugged. "I only know what I see, and what I see is that José only truly smiles when you are around." He slapped his leg. "Now you. What's that one saying?"

I looked to where Griggs's gaze led. Frog Girl was making her attempt to flatter José. She pushed the tall girl out of the way and giggled so loudly that the whole camp could hear her. "She's telling José that she makes the best *quindim* in all Santa Catarina. What she doesn't know is that José hates coconut." As soon as I said the words, a false smile broke across his face.

"What's *quindim*?" Griggs asked.

"It's a dessert made with egg yolk, sugar, and coconut. My friend's mother, Dylla, made it for us once. José's face turned the most awful shade of green as he tried to swallow it down."

The memory of José's face as he tried to eat the food without gagging made me start to laugh all over again. "When he finally managed to get it down, he complimented Dylla. She was so pleased that the Great Garibaldi liked it, she tried to give him more. He looked horrified, but she wouldn't take no for an answer." Griggs and I broke into uncontrollable laughter.

We were too busy laughing to notice that José had walked up to us. "And what has gotten you two into such a fit?"

I tried to stifle the laughter that bubbled out of my chest. It was working until Griggs said in a shaky voice, "The finer points of coconut."

I couldn't hold the laughter in anymore as I bent forward, giving in to it, fat tears rolling down my cheeks. José looked stone-faced as Griggs and I carried on laughing.

"I take it my food is by our tent?" José asked.

"Yes," I said, wiping tears from my eyes. "I will be there shortly." I regained my composure and looked at Griggs. "Thank you."

"Anytime, ma'am," he said with a smile. As I walked away, I heard him call, "Does anyone know where I can find some coconut?"

NINE

OCTOBER 1839

Word reached us that the Imperial navy was going to begin a campaign against the shores of Santa Catarina, moving toward Rio Grande do Sul. The legion received orders to sail out and patrol the waters off the coast of Laguna. It was to be an expedition that lasted weeks. The night before we left, I was rushing around the tent preparing for our departure when José walked in, his attention focused on a paper that he was reading. He stopped short, looking up at me.

"What are you doing?" he asked, looking both confused and horrified.

"Packing. Oh, and look, I made a pair of breeches just for the occasion." I turned around in a circle so that he could get a full view of me. I had taken an old pair of pants that José no longer wore and tailored them down so that they would fit me. They were still a little loose in the thighs, and I'd had to sew a red patch by the knee that stood out in stark contrast to the faded black of the pants.

"I see, but I want to know why."

"Because we are leaving tomorrow." I laughed as I continued my work.

"*We* aren't leaving tomorrow. *I* am leaving. You are staying here with the rest of the women."

"No, I am not." I rounded on him.

"Anita, a ship is no place for a woman."

"Tell me, do I look like a slave?" My eyes narrowed as I slowly walked toward him.

"No." He took a step back.

"No. Hm, do I look like a cow?"

"Now, Anita—"

"José, I am not your property. I will go where I want, and I want to go with you."

"It's too dangerous," José said, pleading with me.

"Oh, so I look fragile to you."

"That's not what I said."

"I'm a weak woman who can't manage on a ship. Is that it? Goodness, I am lucky I have you around. I don't know how I managed to live eighteen years on my own."

"Will you stop putting words in my mouth?" José threw the papers he had been carrying to the ground. "You are not a sailor. You don't know two things about the ship, let alone fighting."

"What is there to know about fighting? I have used a gun. There is no difference between shooting a man and shooting an animal."

"You have no place on a ship!"

"My place is wherever you are. If you are on that ship, then so am I." I crossed my arms. "I will not sit by and patiently wait for you while you go off and play war. I chose this life, danger and all, when I chose you. I am not some toy that you can put on a shelf and play with only when it suits you. I will not be one of those women."

"I can't have you on the ship with me. When I am there my priority has to be those men. I can't take care of them when all I am doing is thinking about your safety." He reached out for me. "*Tesoro mio, per favore.*"

I pulled away from him. "I am not your treasure."

"Anita, you can be killed. Even if we are just patrolling the waters. The ship is a dangerous place, especially for a woman."

"Do you honestly think I fear death? The one thing that has been my constant companion since I was a child?" I shook my head. "What I fear is being left here alone. Can't you see that? Without you I have nothing."

José opened his mouth to speak, but I stopped him. "Tell me, what happens to me if you die?"

"I won't die," he said.

"You said it yourself: The ship is dangerous. I have worked in the hospital long enough to know that even the most skilled soldier can become one of my patients. Now answer my question. What happens to me if you die?"

His shoulders sagged. "You go on living, I guess." His voice came out meek and small.

"Oh, I go on living all right, but what kind of life will that be? My family has disowned me. I am a disgraced woman, José." He looked away from me. "Look at me. This is what I am to these people. I am not ashamed. I have made my choices, but if I stay here and you die, I have no way to take care of myself."

"Anita, you are exaggerating—"

"Am I? I have no family, no one to take me in. What shall I do for work, since no one wants to be around me? Do you think my husband will take me back, if he ever returns?" José turned his head from me, his face suddenly pale. I reached out to him. "I would rather die a thousand deaths than live one life without you."

He put his hands on my shoulders and looked at me. "You mean everything to me. I can't bear the thought of losing you."

"If you don't let me go with you on your ship, I'll sneak onto Griggs's."

"Anita, you will do no such thing. John Griggs is an officer in my navy. You can't go running to him every time you don't like something." He fumed.

"I will find a way. I've heard of women who dress like men in order to fight. I can do that, you'll never know I was there." I poked his chest. Immediately he grabbed my hand and held it away.

"This isn't a game, Anita." Blotches of red appeared on his face. "You won't be chasing cows in the middle of a field."

I pulled my hand away. "Don't insult me. Mark my words, José Garibaldi, I will be on one of those ships, and your only choice is whether it's your ship or someone else's." I crossed my arms in defiance. "If you really wanted to keep me safe, you would have me on your ship with you."

José wiped a tired hand over his face. "Very well...you can come. But I need you to promise that every order I give you, you will obey. No questions asked."

I jumped with glee, wrapping my arms around his neck. I went to kiss him, but he stopped me, awaiting a response. "I promise." I smiled.

The next afternoon, we went out to the docks together to prepare for the expedition. As the only woman there, I received curious looks from the men as they rushed past us in the hot afternoon sun, loading crates onto the ships. Rossetti shoved the cargo list he was checking into the chest of a sailor next to him when he saw us approach. He rushed up to José with his fists clenched. "Please tell me that what they are saying isn't true."

José's body went rigid. "Anita will be my responsibility."

"Jesus Christ, José, what are you thinking?" Rossetti crossed himself. "This is no place for a woman."

"I am the captain and what I say goes. You don't have to worry about her."

"But I have to worry about you losing your head!"

"Why must you question everything I do?" José asked through clenched teeth.

"Gualeguay," Rossetti said, moving closer so that his nose was only inches away from José's.

"What happened in Gualeguay has nothing to do with this." José's fists clenched at his sides.

"I seem to remember you losing your head in a very similar manner," Rossetti responded. "If it weren't for me questioning you, we would both be in a prison right now."

José let out a flurry of words in Italian. I could see a muscle clench in Rossetti's jaw. "Get a hold of yourself, man, she is only a woman," Rossetti hissed.

"Stand down." José growled. The men glared at each other.

I wasn't sure what to do until I felt a tug at my elbow. "How about you come with me." I turned to find Griggs at my side, pulling me away.

He linked his arm with mine and led me to José's ship. "I wouldn't pay them any mind," Griggs said, patting my arm. "One minute they are closer than brothers, the next they are at each other's throats. I am surprised Rossetti hasn't run José through yet."

José's ship, the *Rio Pardo,* was a hive of activity as the sailors prepared her to set out for our mission. I watched in awe as men scurried up the ropes, disappearing behind the sails. "What are they doing?" I asked.

"Tying off the gaskets. Without doing that, the ship won't be able to move." He clapped his hands. "All right, first off, we are going to teach you how to tie the ropes up properly. When we begin to weigh anchor, we need to have ropes prepped so the men can direct the ship. Whenever we aren't using the ropes they need to be wrapped up, but not just in any old way. A tidy ship is a safe ship. In this case, we wrap these ropes like this. I don't want to come aboard your ship and see a single thing out of place."

He expertly wrapped the rope around the belay pin, then unwrapped it. "Your turn."

I grabbed the rope and copied the movements he'd made.

"Fantastic!" He clapped my shoulder. "We'll make a little renegade out of you yet!"

He continued giving me lessons until José boarded the ship. José nodded tersely to John and then kissed me roughly on the head before heading to the helm.

"And that is the first command to prepare to set sail. Take a spot over there." Griggs pointed off to the side of the helm. "For now, sit and watch and learn. Watch what these sailors do: If they spit, you spit. Do what they do, exactly how they do it. Everything you see around you has a purpose. Learn from them. I'll see you soon, little renegade." He tipped his hat to me and left the ship as our sailors prepared to weigh anchor.

TEN

The war for independence raged to the north of us. The Imperial government wanted to squash this rebellion as quickly and as efficiently as possible; with two states rebelling, they were worried that more would follow suit. Larger, more impressive ships than ours were moving down the coast in an attempt to intimidate the people. It was our job to make sure that they did not reach any Farrapo-controlled port.

We didn't want word to get out that we were leaving, so we worked quietly and quickly during the day, then stole out of the harbor under the cover of night. It was imperative that no one know about our mission to patrol the rebel-controlled waters off the coast of Santa Catarina and Rio Grande do Sul. If we could cut off the Imperial ships, our harbors stood a chance.

I closed my eyes and reveled in the smell of the brisk ocean air that stung my cheeks and nose. The cold didn't bother me; it felt electrifying, like I was on the cusp of some grand adventure.

I sat up through the night, watching the sailors work until large patches of pink and gold splashed across the sky as the sun rose above the horizon. Light reflected off the water, making it hard to tell where it ended and the sky began. I pulled my shawl in closer to me as I sat in awe of the new world that surrounded me. I had never been this far away from home. Never this far from land, for that matter. This world was so much bigger than my little port in Brazil. I needed to see all of it. If only my family understood…but they chose their way, and I wasn't going to let anyone hold me back from this. Never again.

José eased down next to me, silently slipping a hand around my waist. Together we watched as the sun finished making its ascension. Content we had seen all of the sunrise, José pulled me by the hand, leading me to our cabin.

When we were finally by ourselves, we gratefully sank into the comfort of our tiny bed. José let out a heavy sigh as he rolled over to face me. My fingers traced the long scar that ran along his neck, a reminder of the time he was shot protecting his crew in Uruguay.

"I'm sorry I made you and Rossetti fight," I whispered. We lay in silence, listening to the creaks of the ship and the men moving about their business. "Do you regret—"

José sat up on his elbow. "I regret nothing." He kissed my forehead. "If Rossetti and I didn't fight about something I would think that he was ill. Now get some sleep. The life of a sailor is all the more tiring if you haven't had any rest."

I spent the next few days learning whatever I could from anyone who was willing to teach me, whether it was to haul up the mainsail or to brace forward. Many of the men were still hesitant to have me on the ship, but they were respectful out of their loyalty to José. After his disastrous experience with the cook who didn't know how to fight, he'd refused to hire another cook for his ship. A number of the men took turns cooking for the crew. Knowing that this was something that I could easily help with, I worked myself into the rotation. I hadn't told José, who was pleasantly surprised one day to find me in his galley serving our men. I handed him his bowl of stewed meat and rice with pride.

"Anita, you don't need to work on the ship like this."

I thrust a chunk of bread at him. "We all have our jobs to do, Captain. Now eat. We can't have you starving to death."

When the bustling activity of the day was over, I found solace in José's cabin. One night, when we were stretched out together on the bed after making love, tired but happy, José talked to me about his destiny.

"I believe that I was born with a purpose." He stroked my cheek. "Even though I am here, in Brazil, I know that my destiny resides in the fatherland." He gently kissed me. "We all have a destiny to fulfill, *tesoro mio*."

"I don't understand; why does your destiny reside in your fatherland?"

"My home is nothing more than clusters of feuding territories. I dream of the peninsula being one country." He ran his fingers through my hair, letting the strands slip through his fingers. "So many men have died trying to achieve this dream, but I really feel that I will be the one to make it a reality."

Later that night, I lay staring at the ceiling, trying to contemplate what my destiny was. Perhaps it was Destiny that led me to José, and it was quite possible she wasn't done with me yet. Whatever it was, I wasn't going to find it in this cabin, whose walls suddenly felt confining. I slipped out of our room, with a shawl wrapped tightly around me. The wind had stilled in anticipation of some unseen force. I could feel it, just out of reach.

I waved to one of the sailors. "Hello there!" I called out.

"Ahoy!" he responded. "What brings you topside so late at night?"

"I needed some fresh air."

He nodded. "Be careful."

I continued walking to the stern of the ship but stopped short when I saw the moon. It sat high in the sky, tinged with red. I gasped. *Blood on the moon*. My breath caught in my throat. Blood on the moon meant that there would be trouble ahead.

"You are sounding like an old woman," I said out loud. Not caring who heard me. "Next thing you know you'll be dressed in black, scaring young girls in the village." I shook my head, attempting to banish the fear that threatened to seep into my thoughts. Still, I silently crept back into bed with José, moving in close, letting his warmth banish my ghosts.

Early the next morning I heard the call. The crew spotted another ship on the horizon. I ran topside to see the new visitors. Four massive Imperial vessels barreled toward us. One ship loomed as large as all four of our ships combined. The sails were pillars of clouds climbing toward the heavens. One thing was for certain: We would not survive a battle with them.

José moved about the ship with an authority I had never seen. He bellowed orders, making everyone around him jump to action as he made his way to the helm. I ran to the side of the ship to stand ready at the weather braces for the next maneuvers.

Where their ships had strength, ours had speed. We left at full sail, catching a good wind that helped us speed away. The fleet headed east—that is, all of us but Griggs's ship. "Where is he going?" I asked the sailor next to me as we watched it head in the opposite direction.

The sailor stopped what he was doing as Griggs's ship, the *Republican*, was pursued by two of the Imperial ships. "He's sacrificing himself." The sailor made the sign of the cross. "He knows we won't stand a chance with all four of those ships on our tail."

My heart sank as I watched him sail over the horizon with two Imperial ships following him. Our ship pressed on, speeding away from the danger.

Once it looked like we were safe, José stepped back from the helm, letting one of the officers take control. Sitting down on the crates with a heavy sigh, he extended his arms and turned his hands carefully in a semicircle. I walked over to him, taking his forearm in my hands. He didn't fight me as I began to gently massage his wrists with my thumbs. We didn't say anything for a long time as he watched me work.

"You are not supposed to see me weak," he said with a half smile.

I made a noise, dismissing him. "I have shared your bed for long enough. I think that allows us to share some secrets." I set his arm down and motioned for the other one.

"And what secret does this count as?"

"That you are human." I smiled, looking up at him. He returned my smile before resting his head on my shoulder. "Do they always hurt after a long stretch at the helm?" I asked.

"No." He squinted up at the sun, which had peeked out from behind a cloud like a shy child. "Usually only when it's damp out, or if I have been holding my sword for too long."

He took my hands in his large callused ones, accentuating how small mine were. "You are my calm in the midst of the storm."

"Can I ask what happened to your wrists?"

"Gualeguay."

"Ah, the infamous Gualeguay."

The corner of his mouth lifted in a half smile. "There was this general, Don Leonardo Milan. He made it his life's mission to see me behind bars." He focused on our hands, interweaving his fingers with mine. "I thought I was going to visit a friend. Turns out that friend wasn't as much of a friend as I thought she was."

"She?" I questioned. José was no priest, but no woman liked to hear about her predecessors.

"Yes, she." José had the good sense to blanch. "I would meet with her every time I was at port in Gualeguay. I thought she and I had an understanding...of sorts."

"But you lost your head? As Rossetti put it." I tried not to laugh at the blush that spread up from beneath his beard.

"Yes, well." He shifted in his seat. "Don Leonardo was there waiting for me when I returned to port instead. He had intentions of making me give up my co-conspirators' names. Like I would tell him my secrets." He winced at the memory. "When I wouldn't share like he wanted, he whipped me. Several lashes across my chest. When that didn't work, he held me above the ground by my wrists for two excruciating hours."

I caressed his cheek.

"I've mostly healed. All but my wrists." He shrugged. "Between them and Rossetti I will never forget." He kissed my hand. "*Grazie, tesoro mio.*"

Our reprieve from the Imperial ships didn't last long. Just after the noonday sun began to lower, a call rang out. Two of them had found their way to us. We had no choice but to face them.

José asked me to go below. "And miss out on all the adventure?" I asked as I grabbed ammunition to distribute to the men.

"Be careful," he said before giving me a hard kiss.

One of the Imperial ships fired its guns first. I ducked, narrowly avoiding flying debris. Grapeshot soared over the deck of our ship, landing just shy of our mast.

Black billowing hell clouds reared up from the opposing ship as the boom of cannons reverberated through the air. The tangy sulfur smell of gunpowder engulfed us like a heavy wet fog. I tried to breathe through my mouth but ended up choking on the taste of soot and ash that burned the back of my throat. Looking around me, I was immediately reminded of the sermons of my childhood that preached hellfire and brimstone.

From my vantage point I could see the Brazilian sailors on the next ship. Deftly, they reloaded their guns, leaving little time for us to take shelter. I lifted a discarded gun to fire at them. One, two, three rounds. I ducked down, reloaded, and came up for more. The men around me yelled. I couldn't make anything out, just inexplicable noise. I shot one of the Imperial sailors in the head. My bullet pierced his eyeball. I saw his fellow sailor's anger flash across his face before I ducked down to reload. That's when it happened.

Men and debris rose into the air around me, then I realized I was flung into the air with them. I landed with a thud against a semisoft mass of bodies. I tried to get up, but my vision tilted, causing me to lose my balance. The noise of the battle was drowned out by the buzzing that filled my head.

"Anita!" I tried to get up to find who was calling me, but I was pulled back down by some unseen force. I fought, trying to push it away.

"Anita, Anita, calm down. It's me." I turned my head to see José's face come into focus. "It's me. I've got you." He picked me up and carried me belowdecks into our room.

"Stay here," he said, laying me down on our bed. He kissed me briefly before running out the door and back up to the top to rejoin the fight.

I lay in bed listening to the noise from above as the nausea from my dizzy spell passed. Once I began to regain my senses, I heard panicked, unfamiliar voices.

"He almost saw us."

"Shhh! He didn't, now, did he? His woman is still here. She may hear us."

"So what if she does? She's only a woman and anyway, she probably fainted. Did you see her?"

"It's what she gets for thinking she could be a sailor."

"Just shut up. The both of you. All we have to do is stay down here until the coast is clear. No one will ever know any different. We'll get our pay and still keep our necks."

Testing to make sure I had regained my balance, I sat up. Once I was confident I could stand, I grabbed one of José's swords that he kept in the cabin. I crept from our room and found the men, sailors hiding from their duty in the storage room next door. "So, I am only a woman, am I?" I asked, pointing the sword at them. "This woman has shown more courage than all of you jellyfish combined."

The one who appeared to be their leader laughed. "You should put that down, senhora, before you hurt yourself." He had a pointed face with a long, thin nose that resembled a beak. His coal-black eyes narrowed on me.

I stuck him in the chest. A little pool of blood welled up around the point of my sword. "While you were down here scared and playing the coward, this woman killed, and I am not afraid to do it again." I pushed a little harder with my sword. "Do you want to be my next?"

I looked at the two other men standing there. One was shorter in stature, with straight golden hair and a small beard that held patches of red. The one next to him was much shorter than the other two, and younger. Beads of sweat broke out across his forehead.

"You should be ashamed of yourselves. Only in this for the money, are you? So are most of your comrades above, but the difference between them and you is that they actually have the courage to be men and earn their living." I let my sword slide down to his belly. "Do you know what we do to cowards where I am from?"

One of the other men stepped forward. "All right. We'll go." He motioned for the other two to follow. Pointy Face motioned for me to go first, but I directed him with my sword to walk ahead. As we made our way topside, I kept poking him in the back for fun.

José came running up to us. "Anita! What are you doing? I thought I told you to stay below!"

"I did! But only to bring you more sailors." I pointed the sword at him. "Now get back to work before I come after you!"

"*Sì, signora,*" he said with a grin before taking off again.

I fought alongside the ragged crew that I'd brought up from below. It seemed that the battle would never end until the unimaginable happened. The ships disengaged. The enemy stopped firing, turned, and left.

Cheering erupted on the ship. I turned to look at José, but he stood at the helm, solemnly watching the Imperial ships sail away.

"It's all right to celebrate once in a while," I said as I approached José.

"There is nothing to celebrate," he responded, not taking his eyes off our fleeing enemy.

"Nothing to celebrate? We chased away the Imperial ships. That has to count for something."

He tore his eyes away from the enemy to look at me. "We didn't chase them away. They were testing us."

"What do you mean?" I asked.

"Anita, they wanted to know how strong we were. They could have easily sunk us but they didn't. There was no reason for them to disengage. The Imperial navy wanted to know how many ships we had and what it was going to take to defeat us. I'm afraid they got their answer."

I watched the ships now disappearing over the horizon as I began to feel dread for what was surely to come.

ELEVEN

November 1839

Of the one hundred and fifty sailors on our ship, only twenty-seven were injured, while five left to meet our maker. To most commanders this would have been a victory, but José was somber. We sailed slowly back to Laguna in mourning. I checked in on him but kept my distance. Sometimes it was better to let a person grieve in private.

Clouds rippled across the sky as we sailed into Laguna, which was shrouded in light rain. Upon arrival the injured were collected, along with any reserve supplies we needed. All of my patients were taken to the hospital, and with no work to be immediately done, I sat down for the first time, among the crates and supplies that were left in the cargo hold. Wiping the sweat and grime from my face and neck, I looked over what remained of our medical supplies. The quiet of the ship didn't feel natural. All that could be heard were the footsteps of the men topside and the lapping of the water against the hull. A quick rap at the doorway startled me. I looked up to see Rossetti regarding me. His hands were clasped firmly behind his back, his chin elevated so that he was forced to look down on me. "I heard what you did. In the battle."

I stood up, straightening my spine, pulling my shoulders back in an attempt to measure up to his unspoken standards. "Is there anything I can do for you, senhor?"

"I came to say that you are apparently different from the other women I have come to know." He shifted his weight from one leg to the other. "Or at least the other women José has called friends." I stood watching him in awkward silence. I wasn't sure if this was an apology or just a statement. Either way, I wasn't sure how to respond.

"Well, if you have any problems replenishing the medical supplies"—he nodded to the table—"please let me know." He made a short bow then turned on his heel and left.

Later that night as José and I sat down to dinner alone, I told José about my exchange with Rossetti. He laughed, a deep laugh like a cork being let out of a bottle. "You, my love, have done the one thing that no one, myself included, has been able to do."

"What is that?" I asked in confusion.

He kissed my forehead. "You, *tesoro mio*, have made Rossetti apologize."

* * *

Six days later we received fresh reinforcements led by General David Canabarro. A squat man, he walked around the dock with a perpetual scowl, as if he had just tasted something foul. Nothing went unnoticed under his beady black eyes. Gray hairs peppered the thin beard that ran along his jawline. According to José, he was an unapologetic opportunist. He had spent the first few months watching the winds of war before he decided to jump into the fight. Once he did, he quickly rose in the ranks, becoming General Gonçalves's counterpart.

We were sitting in the new general's tent debriefing him on the mission when Griggs burst in, his eyes wild and his face flushed scarlet. José stood up so fast that he knocked his chair over. "You're not dead!"

Griggs stopped, looking confused. "Of course I'm not. I was distracting them. Where the hell were you? I *thought* we were supposed to rendezvous to the south. I've been waiting there worried out of my mind!"

"No, we were always supposed to come back here," Rossetti responded, looking up from the paper in front of him. "There is no logical reason for us to leave Laguna."

As the men began to argue about the actual meeting location, a sailor snuck into the tent. "Dona Anita, you have a visitor."

As I followed the sailor, I wondered who would want to see me. I was a social pariah. No one in town wanted to know me. For a brief moment I hoped it was my mother or sister. That they had come to check in on me. The sailor led me to the edge of the encampment, where a woman stood wringing her hands and looking around nervously. As we grew closer I recognized the small nose, the bowed lips turned down into a frown. "Manuela!" I exclaimed, running to my friend, embracing her. It was the first time I had seen her since I left home to be with José.

She hugged me as tears streamed down her cheeks. "Can we speak somewhere more private?"

"Certainly," I said, as she grasped my forearm. She was pale, her fingers cold to the touch.

"I heard you went with the Farrapos. I searched the hospital for you."

"Why would you do that?"

"Because you went out there with them." She shook her head. "I thought you died."

I laughed. "Well, clearly I haven't. I'm all right, Manuela." I took her hands in mine. "In fact, I am better than all right. I am happy. For the first time in my life I am happy."

"I don't understand. Why do you have to do this? Why can't you just come home?" Tears flowed down her face. "Your reputation is ruined. Go home to your family. Maybe everyone will forget."

I let go of her hands, suddenly feeling very cold and distant. "Manuela, I am home."

"You can stay with Hector and me," she said, wiping the moisture from her cheeks.

"Manuela, you don't understand. José is my family now. I don't care what the village says or does. My life is with him."

"Are you sure? Anna, how can you be happy?"

"Anita. My name is Anita now."

"Anita." She sighed. "I don't know you anymore."

"Manuela, I don't think you ever did."

Manuela looked down at her feet. "Hector says that I am not allowed to talk to you anymore. That your actions will poison the reputation of anyone associated with you." She let out a small hiccup as she tried to control herself.

"To be honest, I am not surprised. Hector is a magistrate; you both have an image to uphold, and I am a tainted woman."

"But you aren't, Anita, don't you see? It's not too late, it can't be."

I took her head in my hands. "It is too late. There is no going back for me."

"You are taking a path that I can't follow."

"I know, but please, do not mourn me," I pleaded. "I swear to you I am happy."

Manuela slowly walked away, her shoulders hunched, her head hanging low. I sucked in a quick breath. It felt like the door was finally closed on my past; there was no going back to my old life. I should have been feeling elated. Finally I was free, but a strange feeling of remorse filled me.

The sea breeze blew through the palm trees that lined the coast.

It sounded like hundreds of papers rustling. At the base of the trees men steadily worked repairing the ships. As the sun broke through the clouds, the remorse still clung to me as I set out along the harbor to clear my head.

I couldn't understand it. I hated living here. Everything about this place felt like a cage. Why was it that I felt this sadness?

When I was a child, my father and I discovered a tamandua near our house. The tamandua looked like a little bear but with a long nose and tail. It was only after a few moments of watching it scavenge for termites that we saw the bloodied, mangled paw. Immediately feeling pity, I implored my father to catch the animal so that we could nurse it back to health. He obliged, throwing a blanket over it and bringing it back to the toolshed, where we placed it in a pen typically reserved for small calves. For weeks my father and I nursed the tamandua back to health, feeding it mounds of dirt filled with termites. I delighted in seeing its long, skinny tongue jut out and lap up all the insects.

When the time came to release it, it didn't want to go and I was more than willing to keep it with us forever, but my father disagreed. "You can't keep a wild thing. They'll always crave their freedom."

My father took down two large pieces of metal and clanged them together, causing such a ruckus that I put my hands over my ears. The tamandua ran as fast as it could, out of our shed and into the woods.

Was I like that tamandua?

"Hey there, little renegade. I heard you had quite an adventure." The sound of Griggs's voice brought me back to the present.

His sleeves were rolled up to his elbows and sweat dripped from his brow as he used a hooked blade to dig into the side of José's ship, the *Rio Pardo*. When he heard me approach he turned to me with a smile. "How are you holding up?"

I smiled despite myself. "I'll survive."

He nodded. "Come have a seat. Keep me company while I work."

I sat on a crate watching as he repaired the caulking on the ship. Meticulously, he pulled out the oakum with his blade, discarding it in a crate next to him. "Can you hand me that cotton next to you?"

I passed him the long cord of cotton, which he put in place of the oakum he had removed. Using his knife, he forced it into the gap between the planks, working until no more would fit. He cut off the excess and picked up two brushes. "All right, you are going to learn how to finish caulking a ship."

"I'm going to do what?" I took one of the brushes awkwardly in my hands.

"Basically, make sure the ship doesn't leak, because Lord knows your José is quite hard on his toys." He opened his mouth to say something more but stopped. "I have also found that when life has gotten you down, the best therapy is a little ship caulking." He adjusted the brush in his hand so he could brush the tar on parallel with the boards of the ship. "Do it just like this. Slow and steady."

I mimicked his actions as we worked together in silence, Griggs digging out the old oakum, me replacing it. Then together we painted the tar onto the ship. With each move, the pain ebbed away until all that was left was the ship, the tar, and my friend. My old life was gone, I didn't know what was going to happen tomorrow, and frankly, it didn't matter. I had left my cage behind.

Later that evening I sat on our bed brushing out my hair when José stormed into our tent. "I can't believe this!" He rattled off what I recognized as a string of Italian obscenities. "I can't believe the idiocy of that man!" He threw his hat to the ground.

"Who?" I asked.

José turned to me, a dark vein protruding from his temple, accentuated by his red face. "General Canabarro!" he yelled in frustration as if I should already know what he was talking about. "That *allocco*!" he grumbled as he slumped onto the bed.

I jerked involuntarily at the profanity of his words. I had heard the sailors speak this way but never José. He dropped his face into his hands, leaving behind a tired mass of a man. He slowly looked up. "I am sorry, *tesoro mio*, I didn't mean to be angry with you."

Cautiously reaching out to him, I took his forearm in my hands. "Tell me what happened," I said as I began to massage his wrist.

"Canabarro has it on good authority that Imaruí has turned on us. They have gone back to supporting the Imperialist regime." Imaruí was a small village twenty miles north of us. There wasn't much in the tiny town beyond sun-dried fishermen and broken nets.

"He ordered me to raid the town. Like a pirate." He shook his head. "I…I just…If we make an example of these people like he wants, the Imperial army will fall on us hard and fast."

"Then tell him no."

"I did. It was either follow his orders or leave." He turned to face me. "God help me, Anita, I can't give up. Not now."

In that moment I saw the boy that he must have once been. He was heartbroken over what he must do. I pulled him to me, holding on to him as strongly as I could. He surrendered to me, letting his weight press against me. In that moment I knew I had to be strong enough for the both of us.

José sat back up and looked at me. "Anita, I need you to stay here."

I opened my mouth to protest, but he silenced me by lifting a finger to my lips. "I need you to stay here because I need you to work with Griggs. I've tasked him with collecting every dinghy, boat, and raft available. You know this town better than any of my sailors. If I am right, we are going to need all of them. Can you do that? Can you help me prepare?"

Taking his hands in mine, I pressed them to my chest so that he could feel my heart beat. "Yes."

TWELVE

December 1839

I watched from the cart as the *Rio Pardo* sailed from Laguna under a rippling gray sky. My heart sank at the knowledge that José was on that ship without me. Wrenching my eyes from the ship, I turned forward. I had a job to do.

"Hee-ya!" Griggs called, snapping the reins, causing the cart to lurch forward. "So, little renegade, which way first?" he asked.

I pointed to the north. "The outskirts of the town should have plenty of poor men willing to sell off their boats."

Griggs nodded in agreement. "I want to move fast; we're going to get rain soon." He was right, the air was thick with moisture.

In the cart behind us I could hear the three sailors who accompanied us bantering. We worked steadily all morning through the mist. When we got back to town I led the men to a shop I knew to be loyal to the revolution.

"*Puta.*" The voice was gruff and cold as it reached my ears. The word stung, causing me to pause, but I knew it was better not to add fuel to the flame.

I continued to walk; however, as I turned to speak to Griggs, he was no longer behind me. He was standing nose to nose with a dirty-faced gaucho with six men around him. Griggs had only our three sailors for support. I rushed over to them.

"Where I come from, we don't speak to ladies that way," Griggs hissed through clenched teeth.

The man's eyes narrowed. "Well then, maybe you should go back to where you came from, *norte-americano*. Here we call a whore a whore."

"Enough!" I yelled, stepping into the middle. "We don't need this." I pulled Griggs's arm. "Come on." He let me pull but stayed put.

"Go on, *norte-americano*, let the *puta* give you orders." The men around him laughed. "I guess that's how they do things where you come from."

Without warning Griggs head-butted the man, instantly dropping him to his knees. The sailors pulled out their pistols, ready for a fight. I pushed Griggs in the chest with all my weight. He relented, backing up slowly.

One of our sailors laughed. "Take care of your comrade."

"She's still a *puta*!" one of the dirty gauchos called out as he lifted his friend off the ground.

One of our sailors, a large freed slave, grabbed his genitals. "I'll show you a whore!" He threw his head back in a fierce laugh, revealing a set of large, rotten teeth as the gauchos looked disgusted. "All your wives already know me," he taunted. They dragged their friend away, clearly not wanting any more trouble.

"What did you think you were doing?" I yelled, rounding on the men like a schoolmistress.

"Defending your honor." Griggs looked stricken.

"Oh, is that what that was?" I poked a finger in his chest. "When I need help defending my honor, I will be sure to call you. Fighting with a bunch of worthless drunks is not defending my honor." I turned, storming away down the street.

"North or South America, they're all alike," I heard Griggs mumble from somewhere behind me.

* * *

José returned to Laguna two weeks later. Griggs and I proudly lined up the twenty extra boats and the dozens of crates of goods and ammunition that we had scavenged. José clapped my shoulder like I was one of his sailors. "You have done an admirable job."

José's smile was different; the corners of his mouth weren't lifted. Something was wrong. He drifted away toward the ship. I looked to Griggs, who reflected my concern. I followed José onto the ship and into our cabin. "Talk to me."

"There is nothing to say." He got up to move past me to the door, but I stopped him.

"José, we don't lie to each other, remember? Tell me what happened."

He stood there for a moment. Twice he opened his mouth to speak but couldn't find the words to say. He turned from me, bending his head down, taking in two deep breaths. When he finally was able to speak, his voice came out hoarse and tense. "Canabarro had us pick up fifty extra recruits. Fresh..." He trailed off, looking beyond me, looking at the ghosts that passed across his vision. "My God, the destruction." He sighed. "We got to the town and they were like animals."

He sat down on the bed with a heavy thud. "When you plunder, there is an amount of devilry that as a captain you have to turn the other way on. Harassing the women, looting and burning, but these men...they didn't care." He dropped his head into his hands. After a moment's reflection he slowly looked up, wiping his hands over his face as he did. "They set buildings on fire, with no regard for who was in them. They openly raped women right in the streets.

"I killed one." He looked up at me with large, sad eyes. "I was riding through the carnage and I saw him having his way with a young girl." His voice cracked. "She was just a child. I was so disgusted, I...I ran him through as I rode by. I didn't even yell, didn't give him any warning. I killed him while he was on the girl. I killed my own man."

I sat next to him on the bed in silence. "You did what you had to under the circumstances." I reached out and took his wrist, beginning to tenderly massage it. "You can't control all of your men's actions all of the time."

"Can't I?" José pulled his arm away. "When I go into battle, I know my men. I know each and every name. They are disciplined. If I give an order, they do not think twice about taking it. They have to be that way. I can't bring them home unless we operate like a finely tuned machine. Those men, the ones that I picked up on my way to Imaruí, were demons, pure evil incarnate." José looked away, focusing on his boots. "Imaruí is gone," he whispered. "I had to scream like the devil himself to get them under control. If I didn't, I don't think they would have even gotten back on the ship. They would have followed the townspeople who escaped into the woods."

After a moment I reached up to touch his arm. He jumped. "We burned everything." He sighed. "There's nothing left."

"The Imperial army is going to retaliate, aren't they?"

"I'd lose respect for them if they didn't," he responded, looking back up at me.

THIRTEEN

January 1840

José was right. The raid on Imaruí was seen as a blatant insult to the government. The fourteen-year-old king, Dom Pedro II, wanted to put an end to this insurrection that his regents, a succession of three, each one weaker than the last, had allowed to continue. Dom Pedro II determined this was his opportunity to start his reign with a show of strength. He would not be a fragile ruler like the regents that preceded him. The king was prepared to bring the full wrath of the Imperial army down on the Farrapos and anyone who harbored them.

He called our attack on Imaruí a massacre. The articles in the papers decried the loss of life due to the horrendous actions of the mercenary known as Giuseppe Garibaldi. They went on to further provoke the monarchy, saying he was being made a cuckold. The young king decided he would put an end to our rebellion once and for all and that end would come at Laguna, the port town that dared to shelter the man responsible for making him a fool.

One morning, a month after the attack on Imaruí, while the ship was still, I lingered in José's embrace, listening to the sound of the water slapping against the hull. An alarm sounded, startling us from our slumber, alerting us to another ship in the harbor. When we reached the deck there wasn't just one, there were several large frigates sailing into view, their cannons drawn. Our little fleet didn't stand a chance.

José sprang into action, giving us all orders. As I was unloading crates, preparing for battle, one of the men fired his carbine, causing me to look up. My heart raced as these massive vessels blocked out the sun, slowly moving toward us.

These frigates wouldn't be able to cross into the shallow waters of the lagoon, but they would make an escape by sea impossible. They were commonly used by the Imperial Brazilian Navy when facing a large foreign navy, but rarely were they used on rebels. For a moment I felt some hope that we would survive this, but then in the gaps between the large ships came dozens of smaller vessels loaded with cannons and men. I watched in horror as these ships crossed the sand bar, their cannons firing as they approached. My heart raced. We weren't prepared for a battle of such scale.

Thick gray smoke filled the air in large billowing clouds, seeping into my very being. I tried to cough and spit it out as I worked, doing my best not to let it slow me down. I was engrossed in my task when José grabbed my arm, spinning me around to face him.

"I need you to pass a message to General Canabarro for me."

"No!" General Canabarro was on the other side of Laguna, and there was no way that I was going to leave José. "I am staying here."

"You are my sailor and you will do exactly what I say when I say it! You made a promise to me, Anita! So help me God, I will flog you."

We stared at each other as bullets flew past our heads. "Fine!" I relented. "What am I to tell him?"

"Tell Canabarro to send more men. Whatever he has. I want you to stay there and have a messenger bring back a response."

"Aye, Captain!" I yelled, giving José a mock salute. He grabbed my arm, spinning me back to him as I began to walk away. He pulled me close, giving me a rough, passionate kiss before releasing me to the rowboat.

Small violent waves rocked the boat, threatening our stability. Cannon smoke oozed over the water around us as we made our way to shore. I had a job to do, whether I liked it or not. When we landed, I took a horse and rode as fast as I could through Laguna to Canabarro.

The Imperial navy was not only targeting José and his ships, they were punishing Laguna for harboring the rebels. Cannon fire bombarded the city, causing panic and mayhem among the citizens. It was only a matter of time before the Imperial forces made their way into town to avenge Imaruí. I wove my horse through the streets between people running for safety and debris from falling buildings. The town was in utter chaos; for a moment I wondered if there were any familiar faces in the crowd. However, I regained my focus as a cart rolled in front of me, making my horse swerve at the last minute.

Time folded in on itself as I galloped through town. Had it been minutes or an hour? I couldn't tell. I was only concerned with delivering José's message. When I made it to Canabarro's camp I jumped from my horse just as he came to a stop. I dodged and bobbed through groups of people rushing about loading provisions to be taken away. I stopped and looked at this quizzically. *Why are they leaving?* I found my way to Canabarro's tent, where I was stopped by a large soldier.

"No women in the general's tent."

"I come bearing a message from José Garibaldi."

"I don't care if you come with a message from the president of the republic himself." The man grinned down at me.

I pulled my sword. "I will run you through. I have a mission and I aim to complete it."

Canabarro stuck his head out of the tent. "What is all this commotion?" He looked to the soldier first, then let his gaze travel along the sword and up to my face. "Ah, Anita, I should have known. Well, stop wasting time and get in here."

I sheathed my sword and looked smugly back at the soldier. "You should really find better help."

"Wartime." Canabarro shrugged. His desk was littered with papers and miniature wooden soldiers. Standing around it were several other men in officers' uniforms. Their faces were creased with worry, beads of sweat forming on their foreheads. "What news do you have of Garibaldi and his legion?"

"We can barely hold off the attack from the navy. Garibaldi asks for more men."

"I can't send them."

"What do you mean you can't send them? We are sorely outnumbered and are at a severe disadvantage."

"I can't send them because I don't have them," Canabarro responded. "The whole Imperial army has descended on Laguna." He waved a hand over the map covered with small wooden ships and toy soldiers.

"What are we to do?"

Canabarro sighed as he continued to study the map in front of him. Beads of sweat formed on his forehead. Not taking his eyes from the map, he swiped a handkerchief over his face. "Burn the ships."

I looked back at him in horror.

"Burn the ships and fall back. We'll rendezvous in Rio Grande do Sul, with whatever we are able to get away with. Laguna is lost."

* * *

I pulled my horse to a halt as the harbor came back into view. I allowed the horse to step back in trepidation as my breath caught. José's ship looked like it had taken more than its fair share of cannon fire since I left. I got down and slapped the horse on his haunch to let him run to safety.

Griggs's ship looked even worse than José's. Its mast lay broken at the top and the ship listed to one side. I ran to a small supply boat that was loading fresh ammunition. After helping the sailors fill the hull, I jumped in and we rowed back to the *Rio Pardo*. The men rowed hunched down, but I stood at the front of the ship directing the sailors. Cannonballs and bullets hurtled past me, but I didn't care. My eyes were focused on the *Rio Pardo*.

"What are you doing back here?" José called down to me as I climbed up the ship's ladder.

"I am delivering Canabarro's message."

"I told you to stay there!"

"There was no one else to send."

"Anita, I told you—"

"José, there was no one else!" I interrupted him before he could continue. "Canabarro has no men to spare even for a simple message. He says to burn the ships and fall back!"

"*Va fangul*," José cursed, throwing his hat down. "We need cover as we work on our retreat. Go back to shore."

"José—"

"That's an order, Anita!" He composed himself. "Go back to shore and operate the rear cannons. Let me clear this ship and I will join you."

I loaded the few things we needed along with as many of the men as we could fit inside the rowboat. I made several runs, loading up provisions before settling in on shore to lay cover fire. I ran up and down the line passing gunpowder and fresh supplies, pausing only briefly as the large cannon's boom shook the world around me. I wiped the hair from my sweaty face, gazing at the *Rio Pardo*. Flames licked their way up the mast toward the heavens.

José wasn't on the first boats to arrive on shore. I dropped what I had in my hand and ran toward them, hoping to see his face among the sailors. As the last boat slid onto the sand, I launched myself at José, using all my strength to embrace him.

"*Tesoro mio*," he whispered into my hair. "Come, we have work to do."

I joined José, Rossetti, and the other men as we rowed to each ship, ordering the retreat. We pulled what supplies we could and splashed rum all over the decks. The pungent alcohol smell mixed with smoke made me feel dizzy. I ran with the others off the ship once José dropped the match. When we made it back to the shore, we stood for a moment laughing at the ridiculousness of what we had done.

José and his men moved on to our final ship, the *Republican*, Griggs's ship. I stayed behind to collect the remaining bottles of rum. José came off the rowboat with a small group of his men. His face was pale and there were tears in his eyes. He took the crate that I held in my arms from me and handed it to one of his men.

"Anita, you are to stay here."

"What do you mean? I can help."

"Stay here!" he yelled.

"Wait, where's Griggs?" I asked, looking around at the soldiers who had evacuated the *Republican*. Why were there so few, and why wasn't Griggs with them? "José, where is Griggs?"

José took me by the shoulders. "I said I need you to stay here."

Something was wrong. He shook me slightly. "Anita, are you listening to me? I need you to stay here. Promise me."

I nodded my head yes.

"Say it!"

"I promise," I whispered.

He looked to Rossetti. “Watch her.”

Rossetti put a delicate hand on my shoulder, but I pulled away, taking a step to the side. José took a few men with him and went about the business of setting fire to the *Republican*. When he jumped out of the small rowboat again, he stood next to me watching the funeral pyre put the sunrise to shame. I reached out and clasped his hand. He squeezed mine in return and we watched in silence as the ship burned.

PART TWO

Rio Grande do Sol, Brazil

FOURTEEN

January 1840

Our navy was decimated and over half of our men were dead. The battle of Laguna was a devastating loss to the Farrapos. As we rode away to safety José told me the fate of Griggs and the men on the *Republican*.

"They took the full force of the cannon fire." He steered his horse closer to mine so that only I could hear his words. "When I found Griggs, I didn't know he was dead; his back was to me. I called to him to evacuate. It looked like he was leaning against some crates. His arm was up, like he was in the middle of giving an order. When he didn't respond I walked up to him, grabbing him by the shoulder, but he was already gone." José shook his head. "He was frozen in the look he had in life, but a cannonball had cut him in two."

"Oh God," I said, breathing in sharply. "At least it was a quick death."

"It was a soldier's death. The only way he would want to go."

My mind drifted to Ruthie. There was no cross to mark Griggs's grave. No place for her to mourn the man she loved.

Would there be a cross to mark José's grave? Where would I go to mourn him when he died? My heart hurt for Ruthie and Griggs. Neither of them deserved this fate. I didn't get to see her to say goodbye, but I knew she would go back to General Gonçalves's estate. Once a favored servant in the household, she would be welcomed back with open arms.

My thoughts drifted. When you are awake for well over twenty-four hours, your mind can make you believe just about anything. I could see the faces of every sailor we lost in the foliage of the trees we passed. At the turn of the bend, Griggs was there, his roguish smile on his face. He winked, then put a finger to his lips before disappearing. I shook my head and looked back over the path.

My limbs felt heavy. Keeping my eyes open became my sole focus on the trail leading from Laguna to the untamed northern border of Rio Grande do Sul. If it weren't for the angry rumbling of my empty stomach, I'm not sure I could have stayed awake.

"We should be moving faster," Rossetti complained loudly from two horses away. His long face shone with sweat. The perfectly tailored black suit that he always wore was tattered. He pulled sharply at his horse's reins, making the animal swerve sharply to the right. "We don't know whether or not the Imperial army is following us. I swear I could walk faster than this beast!"

"That's because you are doing it wrong," I called. I pulled my horse back and navigated to the right, bringing myself between José and Rossetti. "Don't hold so tightly to the reins, and when you want to move don't pull so hard. Just a gentle nudge will do." I looked over to José, who was struggling with his horse as well. "Your knees are pressing in too tightly. The more relaxed you are, the more relaxed she'll be." José did as I said, and his horse immediately calmed down.

Rossetti scowled. "How do you know so much about horses?"

"Because while your nose was in a book, I was trained to ride a horse. I've been riding since before I could walk." Without warning

I grabbed José's hat and threw it as far as I could out into the air ahead of me. Kicking my heels into my horse's side, I peeled away after it. As we approached the hat lying on the ground, I swung low from my saddle and scooped it up in my hands. I held José's hat high to the air as I pulled back on my reins causing my horse to rear up on her hind legs. "Perhaps not everything is better in Italy!"

I kept my horse positioned in the spot while she stomped her legs up and down, marching in place like the four-legged soldier she was. She preened with pompousness. Smiling slightly I handed back José's hat.

Rossetti looked like he had a lime in his mouth, while José beamed with pride. "Also, Senhor Rossetti, we do not travel at a faster pace because we need to conserve the horse's energy. A strong horse will get us much farther than a tired one. Likewise, these beasts, as you call them, are quite sensitive. If we ride them to the point of exhaustion, they will die."

"Oh, well of course." Rossetti sputtered. "I was just expressing my frustration." He turned his horse away from me, this time with a gentler touch.

Our band of survivors consisted of about two hundred and forty, a third of what we'd had in Laguna. In addition to our fatalities, a large number of the soldiers who had once been our comrades had deserted us.

The terrible secret that the new Rio Grande Republic was keeping had escaped: It was poor. So poor that it could not fulfill its promises to pay the wages of its soldiers. The Republicans had been counting on a quick and profitable victory, making oaths they weren't able to keep. Once people learned the truth, they left. Those of us who stayed were truly ragamuffins.

We moved along in silence, feeling the weight of our collective losses. We stopped to rest the horses and our tired, aching bones. The scouts that José had ordered to stay in Laguna caught up to our camp, letting us know we were not being followed, the

Imperialists choosing to fortify their new stronghold. We were safe for now.

It was a warm afternoon in late January when our troop stopped to make camp. The wind swiftly blew, caressing the hillside as it moved through the open land. I sat in the shade of a tree as I watched the men skirmish with each other while they taught José their style of fighting. "Why don't you come here and learn to fight with us?" José called over to me.

The other men's eyes grew wide as they looked from him to me. "Teach me to fight like a gaucho?" I asked, getting up and bringing my poncho with me. I picked up a nearby *facón*, testing its weight in my hands. "The thing you need to understand is that this is the only way a gaucho resolves a fight."

A slim gaucho reluctantly stepped up to be my sparring partner. I swung my poncho around my forearm, using it as a shield as I countered the gaucho's weak attack. I lifted my arm, creating an opening toward his soft belly, stabbing my *facón* at his kidney. I stopped just short of drawing blood. He was surprised and attacked again with more ferocity. I swung the tail of my poncho, whipping him in the face. He turned his head, exposing his neck, which I slashed at. "When you step back with your back foot, make sure your front foot follows," I instructed the gaucho. "Your movements must always be synchronized. Like a dance."

He smiled and nodded, standing aside to catch his breath. I handed the *facón* to a waiting gaucho so that they could continue training.

"You're pretty good," José said.

"You seem surprised."

He paused, assessing me. "I shouldn't be, should I?"

"No." I smiled, looking back over the men training. "My father taught me. He said if I was going to be a gaucho, I needed to learn to defend myself like one."

"So is the *facón* your weapon?"

"I'm pretty good with a bola." I looked at him from the corner of my eye; he had a lopsided smile as he intently watched me. I pointed to the two gauchos in hand-to-hand combat in front of us with their spurs. "Every tool that a gaucho has can be used as a weapon. Spurs are short knives; ponchos, shields. For us, nothing is wasted."

The sound of hooves approaching made us stop. A small regiment came to a halt before us. The man at the front of the group jumped off his horse. Removing his hat, he revealed a neatly trimmed beard that made his chiseled face look dignified and charming.

"Senhor Garibaldi, it is a pleasure to make your acquaintance. I am General Terceira and I come with orders from General Canabarro." The general nodded in my direction. "It may be a good idea to dismiss your woman."

José patted the seat next to him. "My wife stays."

Rossetti and I snapped our heads toward José. *Wife?*

"Very well." General Terceira cleared his throat and explained that he hailed from the western edge of Rio Grande do Sul. Our regiment was to combine with his before reuniting with General Canabarro's forces in the south at Vacaria to relieve them from Imperial control."

Later that night José followed me into our tent. I sat on our bed, watching as he removed his boots. "Why did you call me your wife?"

José froze in the middle of removing his belt, then shrugged. "What difference does it make?"

"Well, I'm not really your wife."

"Tell me, Anita, what makes a wife? Hmm? She takes care of her husband both emotionally and physically. She is his rock. She supports him no matter what. She is his partner in building a future." He removed his shirt, wiping his soiled face as he did. "Marriage is only a piece of paper. It shouldn't matter, as long as we know what we are to each other."

"But the priests— "

"Those priests know nothing!" José paused, composing himself. "Tell me, what does a priest know of having someone other than yourself hold control over your very being? What do they know of loving someone so much it feels like your heart is walking around outside of yourself and if anything were to happen to her, you don't… " His voice caught. "You can't imagine continuing on without her."

"Priests love the whole world," I said.

José climbed onto the bed next to me. His eyes focused on my lips. "Sometimes a whole world is no bigger than one person." He kissed me so passionately I felt like I was going to melt into him.

FIFTEEN

As we moved to the south, the pine trees that I knew in Santa Catarina faded away. Large trees whose tops expanded outward like overgrown parasols shaded us from the beating sun. Humid tropical air filled my lungs.

We made our way up steep ravines, slipping on moss and rocks. As we continued to climb, breathing became a chore. It didn't matter how much air I sucked into my lungs, it never felt like enough. Moving took more energy than normal; every movement was an exertion of grand proportions. It felt as if Vacaria were a whole other continent. We reached the plains just at the top of the first set of mountains. Sweeping valleys below us took our breath away, but we had more climbing to do.

When the men could barely move a muscle, José pushed forward, encouraging them. He was jovial and made us all want to continue to follow him. "At the top of this mountain we will be victorious! Remember, men, this is training at its finest! We'll be the fittest regiment in all Rio Grande do Sul."

José thrived on adventure. He lived for the next battle. The potential for glory fed his soul.

On the eve of crossing into Vacaria, General Terceira approached me as I prepared a humble supper for José and myself while José was entertaining his soldiers.

"Dona Anita, I was wondering if I could have a few moments of your time."

"Of course, General, how may I be of assistance to you?" I wiped my hands on my skirt as I turned from our campfire to face him.

"I understand that you like to think of yourself as a soldier of sorts."

"I suppose you could say that."

"I am coming to you as one soldier to another, out of respect for what you did in Laguna. Please, when we encounter the Imperialists, do not fight in the battle."

"Why?"

"I know the commander. He is a vicious man. He will seek you out and use you as bait for your husband."

José approached us with a broad smile on his face. He stepped between the general and me, kissing me briefly as he moved toward the entrance of the tent. "*Tesoro mio*, you missed a wonderful story tonight. The men ate it up." He paused, sensing the tension. "Anita," he said slowly as he drove his sword into the ground. "Is there something I should be aware of?"

"General Terceira came here to ask me not to fight in the upcoming battle." I turned to José, taking my eyes off the general for the first time. "I was considering his request."

"Senhora Garibaldi, it was not a request." He swallowed hard.

I pretended to be flattered. "Oh, it wasn't? Well, how could a simple woman like myself refuse an order?" I batted my eyelashes and tried to look as sweet as possible. "You have my word, General, I will not fight in the battle." I stood with my arms crossed, watching Terceira walk away.

"Since when do you take directions so politely?"

I looked over to José as he picked chicken from the spit.

I swatted him away from the still-cooking dinner. "There are other ways to kill a panther."

José laughed as he let me shoo him into the tent. "I look forward to being a humble student under your tutelage." He took my hand, pulling me inside with him.

A week later we arrived at the Imperial camp. Their forces had taken position in the valley below us. I rode out with our regiment, feeling like the Empress Leopoldina, the Queen Regent who helped lead Brazil to its independence.

General Terceira rode up to us. "Dona Anita, you do remember your promise, don't you?"

"*Sim*, General Terceira, I shall not take part in the battle, but surely you cannot rob me of my traditions." I smiled prettily. "I always ride out with my husband. It's good for morale."

General Terceira looked from me to José, who looked back at him with a cold regard. "Very well then," the general said as he continued moving down the ranks.

"José, your wife's smile always seems to feel like a threat," Rossetti said with a sigh, studying me as if I were a message that he needed to decipher.

José smiled devilishly. "I know, it's one my favorite features."

* * *

I rode off to my own vantage point to watch as our men charged down the hill to the camp below us. The Imperialists were waking up, exiting their tents, stretching after their stiff night's sleep. I wanted to laugh as I watched them jump and scurry to sound the alarm.

José and Rossetti were the only ones who knew of my plan. They had arranged for a small cart to be stashed in the bushes for me. After a time, I moved quickly, hitching it to my horse. Once I was confident it was secured properly, I rode down to the battlefield to make my first patrol looking for injured men.

"Anita!" I turned. Rossetti limped through the smoke, bearing the weight of a brawny young soldier whose arm was wrapped around his shoulders. He moved slowly, though he tried to pull the man along faster. The man clutched his side as blood seeped through his fingers. I jumped from my horse, rushing to Rossetti's side to help bring our comrade to my cart. Rossetti pointed off in the distance. "There are more up that way. Hurry!"

I acknowledged his order and got back on my horse to ride where he told me to. When I got there, seven men huddled under a tree. One languished over his broken leg while two others tried to help him. The rest, with minor wounds, stood at the ready, their guns drawn. I collected them all in my cart and rode away as fast as I could. We set up a makeshift medical camp a safe distance away from the battle. I dressed the wounds of the men I had saved before making another run through the battlefield.

I was tending to a soldier when José rode up on his steed. He launched himself from the beast as it came to a stop. With just a few steps he was by my side, wrapping his arms around my waist. "*Tesoro mio*, you again make me the proudest man in the Americas." He began to pull me away while I was still entangled in his massive hug.

"Husband, you are acting like a drunk."

"I am!" He whirled me around in a circle. "I am drunk with victory!" He kissed me so passionately I felt a blush of embarrassment pass over me. José pulled away as more men rode up. "We will be moving your patients to our new campsite at the top of the hill."

"Anita Garibaldi! I gave you a direct order!" General Terceira came stomping over to us, pushing soldiers out of the way. I looked at José, whose face had suddenly turned deep red. I put a hand on his arm to calm him.

"I specifically stated—"

"You specifically told me not to fight in the battle. Those were your exact words were they not?"

"Yes, but—" He raised a finger to make a point.

"I followed your order, General. I did not fight in the battle. I simply rode through collecting the injured."

General Terceira opened and closed his mouth like a fish gasping for breath. He looked from José to me, trying to form words. Rossetti came up behind him, putting his hands on the general's shoulders. "When you deal with the devil, don't be surprised by the results."

Rossetti laughed as he walked past him for bandages to dress his own wounds. General Terceira stalked away. José turned to me. "Come, the men will take care of this. I have something I want to show you."

"But I am dirty," I whined as José pulled me to him.

"All the better," he growled into my ear.

José and I rode through a twisting ravine covered in moss with a thick wall of trees on either side of us. Unseen birds high above us sang with an indifference to our horses as their hooves splashed in the stream bubbling through this peaceful paradise. Though the sun was beginning to set, the air still held the warmth of the late afternoon.

"Where are you taking me?" I asked as I urged my horse closer to José.

"You'll see." He smiled, looking back at me. As we rode up over the ridge, the valley that spread out before us took my breath away. The ravine opened up into a small cove, with a crystal-clear pool fed by a large waterfall.

"Beautiful, is it not? One of my scouts found this place, and when he told me about it I had to bring you here," he said as he got off his horse. José began to take off his clothes. "*Tesoro mio*, won't you join me for a swim?"

I peeled off my yellow dress, stained with blood and dirt, before wading into the pool after José. Goose bumps spread across my shoulders and arms in the cold water. "It's freezing!" I laughed.

José waded back toward me, reaching out a hand. "Then let me help keep you warm." He wrapped his strong arms around me, carrying me deeper into the pool. He pressed into me, my bare chest firmly against his. He kissed me tenderly. Closing my eyes, I inhaled. José smelled of gunpowder and earth, war and victory.

"I love you," I whispered.

He kissed my neck, my jawline, my lips. "You are the queen of my soul," he murmured into my ear.

I wanted him more than I had ever wanted anything in my life. He stroked my hair and face, looking deeply into my eyes.

I took his face in my hands, kissing him harder. He carried me over to a large smooth rock, and we leaned against it to make love. When we finished we lounged on the banks of the pool, entwined. I watched the stars as José lay with his head on my chest, his thumb making lazy circles around my navel.

"Tell me about Italy," I whispered, afraid to break the spell of the night.

"What is there to tell? Italy is a fairy tale."

"I like fairy tales." I could feel him smile against my shoulder.

"All right then. Well, once upon a time there was a man named Dante."

"The author of that book you and Rossetti love. The *Inferno*, right?"

"That's correct, *tesoro mio*. Up until the fourteenth century our peninsula didn't speak the same language. Every municipality had its own variation. You see, here, Portuguese is predominantly spoken due to Portugal's influence. The various dialects branched off from that one root, and though the way you speak may be different from someone in the north, you can still understand each other. However, in Italy, our one language was Latin. Over the centuries since Rome's fall, we've all gone our separate ways to the point where people from some regions can't even understand someone from outside of their homeland."

"That would be an awful pain. How can people trade or do business?"

"Exactly. Dante wrote the *Inferno* in the Tuscan dialect and it was so popular everyone wanted to read it, but they had to read it in Tuscan Italian."

I thought about it for a moment. "So because everyone wanted to read a book, they all learned one language?"

"Yes, and now most people consider Dante to be the father of Italian. For the first time since the Roman Empire we were unified in the way that we speak. Some men believed if we could all agree on one language, we could agree to be a country of our own."

"That's a fairly big jump to make."

"When the regions bicker among themselves like a bunch of spoiled children, you take whatever compromise you can receive." José sat up on his elbow, resting his head in his hand. "But as you say, it's not enough. The people still fight among themselves." His hungry eyes looked me over.

"But there are still people who believe in unification?"

"*Sì, tesoro mio*. Another man came along to water the seeds that had been planted by Dante. His name was Napoleon Bonaparte."

"Ah, the little French man! I've heard of him."

"One's stature does not dictate the size of their dreams." José tapped my nose with his finger. "Napoleon ruled the peninsula as one country"—he traced his finger from my collarbone to my breast—"then drove his army from Paris all the way down to Siena." His finger circled my nipple, making goose bumps appear all over my body. "The army conquered Siena"—his hand slipped to my navel—"then Rome." His hand started to slide farther south, but I caught it.

"Finish your story."

José gave me an exaggerated pout. "As you wish, *tesoro mio*. Under Napoleon we were left alone to be our own country. We were unified under him. Suddenly, having a country all our own wasn't crazy talk. We were finally one. However, after Napoleon fell, the European powers broke us apart. They pitted us against each other yet again. But the dream is still alive." José broke his hand free from mine as it found its way south. My fingers tangled in his golden curls as I gave in to the passion.

SIXTEEN

May 1840

We slashed our way through the thick underbrush that lined the Caminas River toward Praia Grande. It had been just over five months since that night at the waterfall. In those twenty weeks we discovered that I was with child.

I grew tired of everyone treating me like I was going to break. It was infuriating. Suddenly my life wasn't my own; a future person was sucking away everything that I was. My temper flared over the slightest infraction, causing people at camp to avoid me.

I still thirsted for action. When my mother had been pregnant, she had sat in her bed with her feet raised, ordering everyone about, for the sake of her babies, she would say. She instructed every woman with child that this was the way to act during a pregnancy if you wanted a healthy baby.

Between the constant digestive discomfort and the awkwardness of carrying so much extra weight in front of me, I hated being pregnant. It was against everything I was told that a mother-to-be should feel, and that scared me.

Every night I dreamed that we picked up camp and left my baby. José would be yelling for me to hurry up, constantly asking if I had remembered certain things. I remembered them all, all but my baby.

Early one morning, during an especially traumatic nightmare, I awoke in my bed with a start. Looking around I noticed José was gone. I dressed and washed my face in the basin, trying to banish the dreams that still clung to me. As I dried my face, I heard my stomach gurgle. I placed my hand to my growing abdomen. "All right, little one, I'll get us fed."

I made my way out of the tent and set about cooking breakfast. José came stomping up to our camp. "I can't believe the stupidity!" he yelled, snapping my attention from the fire to him.

"Do I dare ask who has made you so angry?"

"Canabarro, of course!" He threw his arms up in frustration.

"What transgressions has he committed today?"

José scowled at me. "The *bastardo* wants to walk away from the war. He wants to let the Imperial forces win."

"If he can find an amicable peace, what is the harm?"

"What's the harm? Anita, we need to wipe the Brazilian army from here if Rio Grande do Sul ever expects to be a free and independent nation." He sat down with a huff.

Sitting next to him, I took his wrist into my hands, in order to massage it. "What do you think?" he asked.

What did I think? This was a question José never asked me. *What do I think?* I pondered on the question a little longer, carefully choosing my words. "I think Canabarro has a point."

José ripped his arm from me. "What do you mean by that?" His lip curled up in a sneer.

"You asked my opinion and I gave it."

"But that's not the opinion you are supposed to give."

"Pardon me, José Garibaldi?" I asked, raising my eyebrows. "When we are in public, I will stand by you no matter what. If you say we need to go left, I will tell everyone that going left is the best course of action, even if we should really be going right. However, when it's you and me, I will not hesitate to let you know my true feelings."

"And what, my dear wife, are your true feelings? That I am an idiot? That I don't know what's best for Rio Grande do Sul? Am I rash? Can I not think about what will happen tomorrow?" He was a caged jaguar pacing in front of me.

"José, I do not think you are an idiot." I stood, readying myself for conflict. "We are fighting a losing battle. We may be winning little skirmishes here and there, but we are losing this war. The Imperial forces keep coming after us; how long are we going to be able to continue fighting? We have to keep in mind that when this is over, our men will have to go back to the families of those Imperial soldiers and beg for forgiveness. They are not just nameless faces. These people come from the same villages. They are neighbors. They are family." José turned away from me. I took a step forward, continuing with my argument. "When we are done fighting they have to be able to go on living together. Let us only do the fighting that is absolutely necessary."

"Only do the fighting that is necessary? I came here because they needed me. When I left Genoa, I sailed all over the Mediterranean. I could have kept on sailing, but the republic asked me to be here, they asked me to win this war for them. And like an idiot I said yes. Now that they have me, they don't want to listen to me! They don't want to do what is necessary to win!"

"You don't understand what it's like for us. You are a foreigner." The words tumbled out of my mouth before I could stop them. I knew as soon as they reached José's ears that I had said the wrong thing. I shrank back as his face grew crimson.

"Did you dare call me a foreigner?"

"It's not what I meant. You are not from here, you don't understand our ways."

"I am good enough to shed my foreign blood for you on those fields but not good enough to respect. Is that it?" His voice grew low and menacing.

"José, please." I reached out to him, but he batted my hand away.

He came up very close to me. I tensed, unsure of what was to follow. "Don't forget that the child growing in that stomach of yours is half foreigner too." He turned on his heel and strode away, cursing in Italian.

I was still hungry and knew that José would be too, once he came to his senses, so I made our breakfast. I finished eating, just a simple meal of beans and rice. I left a plate for José as I began my camp-breaking chores. An hour into my work he approached our tent.

"I'm sorry for being so angry with you earlier." He lifted my hand to his lips, gently kissing my fingers. "Do you forgive me?"

I was surprised. It was not like a man, any man I knew, to apologize to his wife. I stammered, "Of course you may have my forgiveness."

He smiled tenderly, giving my hand a small squeeze. "*Grazie, tesoro mio*." Sheepishly, he took the plate I left for him.

With a mouth partially full of food, he began to talk. "I was thinking about what you and General Canabarro said, and you make a valid point." He swallowed the large mouthful. "If we go southwest, we can also really entrench ourselves with the people, bolster our numbers. I hear the people there are more sympathetic toward our independence."

I regarded him as he ate, continuing to talk about his new plans. In José's eyes I was no longer the shy little girl from Laguna. In his eyes I was equal to him and his advisors. My chest swelled with pride. How many other women in Brazil could say this about their husbands? We spent the day breaking camp before setting off on the long journey to General Terceira's region.

SEVENTEEN

August 1840

In the time it took to travel back to the Vacaria region my belly grew to the point where I felt as big as one of the horses. Nothing alleviated the discomfort.

The Imperial forces that we encountered when we arrived were well fed and well armed. Everything that we weren't. My heart raced as the men took their places, preparing for battle, head on.

I sat on my horse, surveying the battlefield with General Canabarro as we directed other soldiers on where to deliver the supplies. The general's black eyes examined the battlefield. From our vantage point we could see the full expanse of the battle laid out before us. His frown accentuated his features, making him look like a toad. He mumbled to himself as he oversaw his soldiers, the Black Lancers.

The Black Lancers were Canabarro's pride and joy. A contingent made up of slaves who were promised freedom in exchange for their service in the rebellion, they were expert horsemen and fierce fighters. Canabarro assured José I would be safe with them during the battle.

Holding one hand to my stomach, while the other hand gripped my horse's reins, I scanned the field below, directing supplies to various points in the battle. I was too distracted, too focused on the task at hand to notice that Imperial forces had set a trap and I was their prize.

I heard the heavy thumping of hooves in the distance. Turning, I watched in horror as the Black Lancers' horses, devoid of their riders, charged past us. *Weren't the horses supposed to be with the soldiers?* was all I could think until the shouting began: "It's an ambush! The Imperials are here!"

Our men scattered. A large regiment stampeded toward me, their rifles drawn. Turning my horse in a circle, I could see that we were surrounded. There was nowhere for me to go. Panic clawed at my throat as my mind raced. *There has to be a way out*. Swallowing it down, I moved my gaze toward the cavalry in front of me.

I charged forward. If I couldn't scare them out of my way, I could at the very least trample them. A single gunshot reverberated like a clap of thunder. My horse collapsed, taking me down with him.

I put my feet out, allowing me to tuck into a ball and roll away when I landed. I felt myself come to a stop at the roots of a tree. I realized it was no tree. I stared at a pair of muddied boots, the leather slightly worn along the soles. My eyes traveled up pristine green pants, past a chest covered in medals, finally resting on a skeletal face. The man smiled, making him look even more dangerous.

"*Olá*, Senhora Garibaldi. It is a pleasure to meet you."

* * *

To the Imperial soldier's credit, I was treated with more respect than a regular prisoner of war. I didn't know if it was because of my condition or who I was married to. Two young soldiers helped me into the cart, not bothering to tie my hands behind my back. They knew as well as I did that at eight months pregnant, I wasn't going anywhere.

We stared at each other, my captors and I, as we rode down the bumpy dirt path. Their hollow faces, streaked with dried mud, were aged beyond their years. Blank eyes watched me, not betraying any emotions.

My heart sank as we rolled into the village that the Imperial army now occupied. Vacaria, much like Tubarão, the village of my childhood, was made up of gauchos and their families. Gauchos who were loyal to the rebellion. A loyalty that had cost them dearly. Most of the homes were burned to the ground. Only husks of what they once were remained. Hazy dust rolled across the remains and the smell of charred meat filled my nose. A sick thought crossed my mind: *Where are all the people?* Carts sat abandoned. Stray dogs gnawed on mystery meat that lay by the homes. I tore my eyes away from the gruesome scene and looked up to the fluffy white clouds that lazily floated above us.

They brought me to the abandoned courthouse, now serving as the headquarters for the Imperial army. Inside what was once the constable's office, papers lay scattered about the desk, interspersed with miniature cannons and saint statues collecting dust. My thoughts turned to José. *Where is he?* I placed my hand on my belly, where my baby kicked. I closed my eyes and pictured a panicked José in my head. Standing in the middle of the battlefield, realizing that I was gone. He was going to rescue me. I was sure he would be breaking down the door at any moment.

Hearing the sound of voices on the cool August air, I ventured toward the window.

"How much damage can she cause? She's only a woman, and a pregnant one at that."

"Just let me do the talking. I have a plan."

So, they had a plan? *This should be interesting.* I settled into a chair and demurely waited for the officers to make their way to me. After a brief knock at the door, my captor entered the room. I inspected his suntanned face, from his dimpled square chin to the crinkled corners of his eyes. The gray hair peppered with light brown made him look almost fatherly. But I wasn't fooled. The smile he flashed sent a shiver down my rigid spine. Clicking his boots together, he gave a small bow as a plump middle-aged woman slipped in with a tray of food. I watched her as she hurried away, head bowed, doing her best not to be seen.

"It is an honor to make your acquaintance, Senhora Garibaldi."

"*Boa tarde*, Senhor...?"

"Senhor Moringue." He smiled warmly as he handed me the plate of bread and cold chicken. "I thought you might be hungry. Women in your condition need to keep up their strength."

I took the plate and thanked him. "Do you have children?" I picked at the food in front of me. The truth was that I was indeed hungry, but I didn't want to seem too eager. I didn't want to show any weakness.

"No, God has not blessed me with a family. Not many women can handle life with a soldier, as I am sure you can understand." He laughed to himself, not caring if I found his joke humorous. He pulled out a chair and sat across from me. "I have to admit that I am very excited to finally meet the one and only Anita Garibaldi."

"Senhor Moringue, you flatter me."

"No, really. I have heard all about you. The brave woman from Laguna who fought off thirty Imperial frigates," he said.

"Six." I smiled politely. "There were only six Imperial frigates that we fought off and about six smaller vessels."

"Brave and modest! Such rare qualities for a woman." He slapped his knee. "You'll have to forgive me, senhora, my soldiers have been following your story. The old men say you are Atiola incarnate."

I laughed. "Atiola? The Indian earth goddess?"

"Yes, the pagan mother who blessed us with cassava." He held my gaze as we scrutinized each other.

I shrugged. "I never cared for cassava."

"I do have one burning question. Did Garibaldi really throw you over his shoulder and sail away?"

"Where did you hear this story of yours?"

"It is the story the men tell of how you found yourself to be with a pirate. They say he spied you from his ship and declared, 'She must be mine!' Then in a fit of passion he dove straight into the water. He threw you over his shoulder and the two of you have been sailing the Brazilian waters since, living happily ever after." He looked at me as if I were a child. "For really, why else would a woman leave her husband?"

I openly laughed, accidentally spitting some bread out of my mouth. "Is that what they are saying? I will have to be sure to tell José when I see him."

Senhor Moringue smiled, reminding me how dangerous he was. "If we had met under different circumstances, I think I would be quite fond of you."

"I wish I could say the same for you."

His face grew stern. "I am sorry we cannot continue with this lovely conversation. I came to speak to you regarding a more serious matter."

I picked some more chicken. "Well, as you have said, I am only a woman. I would not know much about serious matters unless they involve mending clothes and cooking." I spit the chicken I had been chewing into my hand before dropping it unceremoniously onto the desk. "That, by the way, is horrible. You should put your cook in front of the firing squad."

He said nothing as he continued to watch me. He gave two sharp claps, summoning an officer into the room with us. The soldier carried a faded poncho that he thrust at me. "Tell me, senhora, does this look familiar to you?"

I felt the garment in my hands. It had once been bright red, so bright that it stood out in sharp contrast to the mossy green trees. Now, after so much use it had faded. My fingers traced the patch I had sewn on the sleeve.

I had laughed when I first gave José his mended poncho back, saying that with the patch, he would really be the captain in the Ragamuffin War. I turned it over and saw a deep wine color blossom across the back. Gasping in shock, I lurched up, letting the chair clatter to the floor behind me as the poncho fell.

"I hate to inform you, senhora, but your husband was killed in the battle." Moringue looked at me as if he had won.

Swaying a little, I reached out and steadied myself at the desk. There was no way that my husband could be dead. He was the Great Garibaldi. Men like him didn't die.

Senhor Moringue leaned forward. "I can help you. I can protect you."

"Protect me?" I cackled. "Protect me from what? From your men? From the Imperialist government? From you?"

"Anita, your husband is gone. You have nothing left. Tell me what you know and I will—"

I spit at him. The yellowish mucus landed on his cheek. It stuck there while he calmly removed a handkerchief from his pocket, wiping the saliva away. "You're right, I have nothing left," I said, trying to control my trembling outrage. "What do I care what you do? The only thing I care about is that José was able to meet his destiny before me!"

He slammed his fist on the desk. A tiny statue of the Virgin Mary toppled onto the floor. "You are being hysterical."

I stared at him, making him squirm in his chair. He shifted his weight, reminding me of a mouse that knows it's about to be eaten by a snake. I couldn't trust a mercenary who was responsible for so much damage, but then again, I needed to know the truth. "I will tell you everything you want to know, as long as I see my husband's body."

His eyes widened briefly in surprise. "The poncho is not enough?"

I turned my head to the side. "Would it be enough for you? I want to see my husband's body for myself. I want my right, as his wife, to bury him."

"I can't send my men to search for his remains."

"Then I will search for them myself."

"I can't let you do that."

"How badly do you want my information?"

He got up and walked toward the door. "You drive a hard bargain, senhora." The door closed with a snap. My knees gave out as I sank to the floor, clutching José's poncho. My breath came in fast, short bursts as I held the tattered rag to my chest. The baby inside me kicked wildly as I wiped the tears from my face.

EIGHTEEN

If José was alive, I would find him at the base camp the rebels had set up. He wouldn't leave without me. He would keep the army nearby long enough to regroup and attack. While it was there, the Imperial forces outnumbered the Farrapos, but this wouldn't matter to José. I knew he would sacrifice the whole world to get me back, and I couldn't let that happen.

Running my hand over the frayed material, another thought came to me. A thought that initially scared me much more than José being dead. The soldiers knew who I was.

My reputation preceded me. Usually it was only José that they all talked about; he was the rebel hero. At least, until now. They called me the Atiola. I started to entertain thoughts of living on my own. I could become a notorious renegade, even more notorious than my husband.

I could run off into the woods. They would never find me. I could still seek out the Farrapos. A widow who lost her husband tragically, I could fight for José's causes in his place. People would fawn over me much like they did for my deceased husband. Maybe even more. My heart fluttered at the thought.

This must have been what Eve felt like just before she took the apple. For the first time in my life I had the opportunity to be my own person, and the temptation to take it was great.

A young soldier in a baggy uniform stepped into the room. "Senhora Garibaldi, come with us."

"Where are you taking me?" I asked, still clutching José's poncho. He ignored me as he led me to a wagon, gently pulling me along by the elbow. Another soldier sat on the driver's bench, and two others sat in the back with me. They said nothing as we took off. It was late in the day and I could feel the cold weather setting in. I slipped on José's poncho. The faint smell of the man I loved was bittersweet.

The wagon came to an abrupt halt on the edge of the battlefield. "What are we doing here?" I asked.

The driver turned around to face me. "You wanted to find your husband?" He motioned toward the field. "Go find him."

The sun hung low in the sky as the cold night air moved in around me, bringing with it the scent of decay. I heaved myself out of the wagon and walked through the remains of what had been. Breathing into my hands, I rubbed them together in a vain attempt to keep warm.

I bent down to get a closer look at the faces frozen in their time of death. The first group contained no one that I recognized, just poor nameless souls who had gone on to meet our maker. I moved down the field to where a pair of boots stuck out from under a bush. I pulled the body by his boots, my breath coming out in fierce white clouds. It wasn't my José but another soldier in his regiment. Moving on, turning over stiff, bloody bodies, I continued my search.

Using my skirt, I wiped the muddy faces of soldiers to get a better look at them. I had to find my husband. I had to know for sure. I moved on to the next group of dead soldiers.

As I got down on my knees, the weight of my stomach threw me off balance. I stumbled a little, catching myself on another mass of dead bodies. There were five men piled like broken dishes; the one at the very top rested facedown. I grabbed him by his shoulder and heaved him onto his back with all my strength. My stomach lurched as he slid down the mound, his face infested with maggots.

My stomach wanted to empty its contents right there all over the poor men. I scrambled back, filling my lungs with cold air that stung my nostrils. I looked up at the orange sky, watching as the vultures made elegant circles over the field. Gracefully they dipped down and came back up with a prize. If I was to find out the fate of my husband, I had to keep moving. I refocused on the task at hand, reaching down and pulling another body out of the decomposing pile. My stomach wrenched, and I spit bile into the muddy earth.

I stood up and nearly fell over as a spasm seized my back. There were so many bodies. Leaning against an abandoned wagon, I surveyed the wreckage around me. The remains lay slumped like abandoned playthings. Clutching at my stomach, I wondered how I was going to find my husband. One of the vultures swooped down and walked across the field, huffing as he went. My feathered comrade watched me. Taking a few steps forward, he turned his head from side to side, his black eyes meeting mine. He dipped his head, pulling out a juicy red treasure from one of the soldiers. Dry heaves racked my body as I looked away from the gruesome scene playing out before me.

Turning to the tree line, I realized how close it was, just a few steps away. I could disappear into the woods before my captors would even notice I was gone. The young soldiers in their tattered, dirty uniforms sat at the cart playing cards by torchlight on the other end of the field. They would never find me. I knew how to live in the wilderness a lot better than those boys ever could.

"Hey, senhora!" one of my guards called to me. "Are you going to finish anytime soon?"

"Not until I find my husband!" I called back to him. "Do you want to help?"

The men wrinkled their noses and went back to their card game. They were under strict orders to let me search, but those orders weren't needed. They seemed to enjoy their time playing cards and drinking from a communal jug.

I picked up my skirts as I stepped over the dead bodies I'd already examined. Leaving now would be the easy way out, the coward's way. I wiped away some hair that clung to my cold, sweaty face. I was no coward.

Moving methodically along the battlefield, I continued my search, stopping only when I saw a soldier I knew. I recited a short prayer for his soul before moving on to the next poor bastard. Not a single one was José, nor did any of them resemble him, with his auburn beard and curly hair. None of them had his soft eyes. I breathed into my hands and lifted them to my nose and face to soak in a bit of warmth. The field was large, and I was only one woman with a poncho, searching through the bitterly cold night for my husband.

As the pink morning sunlight cast its first rays over the valley of death, I moved along the northernmost perimeter of the battlefield. I turned to survey the work that I had done. In the course of the night I traveled north, going back and forth along the field. I stood there, shivering against the cold. José was alive, and I needed to escape.

But that was going to have to wait. I made my way back to the wagon. One of the soldiers yawned, opening his mouth wide and showing his rotted teeth. "Are you satisfied, senhora?"

"Yes." I smiled. "My husband is not dead." I got into the wagon willingly as the men exchanged nervous glances.

NINETEEN

Back in the village, the Imperial officers brought me to a small shack where another man stood guard. "Only one?" I asked. He wasn't much of a soldier. He was fat and old with thinning hair that had thick white flakes stuck in it. One of my captors pushed me into the house. I turned to look at him. "Careful, I am with child." He looked back at me with disdain before turning on his heel and leaving.

After the men left, I paced the room. I hummed mindlessly to myself, an old wordless lullaby my mother used to like to sing. Looking out my window, I watched as my guard slept. Unfortunately, there were still too many soldiers wandering the village for me to make my escape now. I yawned, feeling utterly exhausted.

As I began to settle on the small cot pushed against the wall, Senhor Moringue came in. He slammed the door open and stood there with his fists digging into his hips.

"I hear you had some problems finding your husband's body." His eyes gleamed as he looked down on me.

"Yes, well, it's hard to find something that isn't there." I sat up and arranged my skirts as I watched the color on his face change from white to red and back to white.

Senhor Moringue stepped toward me, puffing out his chest, trying to take up as much space in the room as he could. "That poncho you wear begs to tell otherwise."

"My husband's not dead."

"I have fulfilled my side of the bargain. Now it's your turn. Tell me what you know of the rebels." Moringue's eyelid twitched.

"I know you haven't actually killed their captain."

"Don't play coy with me, Anita Garibaldi. I have my ways."

"As do I," I said, turning my head to the side. "There is nothing worse than a mouse who thinks he has bested a snake."

Moringue raised a hand to strike me but thought better of it. "I never thought of you as a woman who would go back on her word."

"I'm not. I said I would tell you everything I know, if I found my husband's body." I spread my arms out. "Clearly, I have not found him."

He pointed a finger at me. "You are an infuriating woman!"

"I know, my husband tells me every day."

"I'll find out everything that you know, senhora, mark my words." Moringue left the room with a huff. The sad little cot felt like the most comfortable bed in the world. I curled up, letting sleep overtake me, knowing I had a long journey ahead of me.

My usefulness was running out. At some point Moringue would tire of my games. If I continued to resist I would wind up like the poor souls that used to live in this village. I needed to escape.

* * *

The next day I paced around the meager room, with its drafty plain walls. As I moved, I took stock of what was around me. A small lumpy cot was shoved against the back corner. My fingers traced a bloodstain that splattered the wall, and I wondered what had happened to the previous occupant. The dresser, leaning to one side, shuddered as I ransacked it. Disappointed in its lack of treasures, I made my way to the lone window that looked out over the remains of the village.

I waited patiently, watching everything that I could. The men came and stood at their posts. Hours later the shift changed, and another man would show up. Each one cared even less than the last.

The same guard from the previous evening appeared the next night, a large balding man whose stomach pushed against the buttons of his shirt. Before long he was snoring with his chin resting on his chest. This time I tested my luck. I opened the door and stepped outside as quietly as I could. My guard didn't move at all. I looked around, taking stock of the other soldiers, where they were and what they did. Only a few yards from my cabin was a pathway into the forest. I could take it, heading south to where I hoped the rebel forces remained encamped.

A westerly wind swept through the still village. I raised my head and took a deep breath. Something was stirring, I could feel it as the hairs on my arms began to stand up on their own. I slowly walked away from the house.

Keeping to the shadows, I crept farther and farther away. My steps quickened once I reached the path. I briskly walked at least four miles. My feet swelled. The muscles in my back seized. A pinching sensation shot up from the right side of my pelvis to my shoulder blade. I jammed my thumb into one of the aching muscles in a vain attempt at relief. Just when I thought I couldn't carry on,

I spotted a cottage in the distance. I ran to the door, praying that someone would be home and they would take pity on me.

"The devil himself better be on the other side of that door." An old woman wrapped in a dressing gown clutched a shawl to her chest as she opened the door. Her sleeping cap was tilted on her wild, graying black hair.

"I may not be the devil, but I do need help," I begged.

"Estella, who is at the door? Is it the devil?" Another woman appeared behind her. She had similar features as Estella, only more delicate.

"No devil, just a woman." Estella looked me over, finally resting her eyes on my stomach. "And she's pregnant!"

"Well, bring her inside, don't be such a *totó*," the other woman said.

Estella pulled me inside as I continued to ramble. "I'm running from the Imperial army. Can you please let me rest for just a little bit? I promise I won't stay long."

Estella made a noise. "You'll stay the night."

"But the soldiers—"

"The soldiers will be looking for you no matter where you go. Might as well fill your belly and get a good night's sleep."

"Estella, is she staying the night?"

"Yes, Lydia, get the ham out," Estella responded.

"Get the handle to what?" Lydia asked.

"HAM! HA-AM, Lydia, she's famished!"

"Oh, ham, you should have said that." Lydia shuffled over to the cupboard as Estella shook her head.

"Please excuse my sister, her hearing is not what it used to be," Estella said to me.

"You'll have to excuse my hearing," Lydia said, coming to me with a plate of salted ham.

"I just told her that!" Estella shouted. Lydia looked at her with a blank expression, shaking her head. "I just— Oh, never mind."

Estella threw her hands up in frustration. "Would you like some fruit, dear?"

"No, I am fine. Thank you," I said, letting my eyes wander over the humble whitewashed walls of the kitchen, yellowed from age. A benevolent Virgin Mary stared down at me from the opposite wall. The lump of ham stuck in my throat. *I bet you never put your baby in danger*, I grumbled to myself as my eyes lingered on the saint. This child that grew inside me still felt like an abstract stranger, yet I felt the violent urge to protect him. If only I didn't keep putting him in danger in the first place.

"What did she say?" Lydia asked, bringing my focus back to the kind old women who tended to me.

Estella pointed to her lips. "Thank you!" she yelled, over-enunciating.

Lydia smiled and nodded. "Not every day is your birthday," she said as she brought me more food. I laughed a little, feeling relieved for the first time in days. Estella sat across from me as Lydia continued to bustle around the kitchen, setting more plates on the table despite my protests. I took Estella's cue and let Lydia be.

"I surmise from what you've told me that they won't know you're gone until the morning," Estella began.

I nodded in agreement. "They left me alone until the morning, when they brought me breakfast."

"Then you will need to be out of here just after dawn. I'll have the horse ready for you."

"Oh no, I can't take your horse."

"Nonsense, child. Where are we going to go?" Estella gestured toward the cluttered kitchen. "The village is desolated; we have no need for him now."

"Really, Estella, your hospitality is too much."

She waved her hand in dismissal. "The Imperial army has taken everything from my village. The only reason we haven't left is because Lydia wouldn't be able to handle it. My sister and I have lived here our whole lives. I would rather our Guapo go with you than with those *bastardos.*"

I ate until I was full and spent another ten minutes convincing Lydia that I couldn't take another bite. Feeling very content, I let Estella order me to her bed, where I drifted off into a very deep sleep.

TWENTY

The next morning, I woke to a rooster crowing with all his might outside my window. I wandered out to the kitchen, where Lydia shoved a thick slice of bread with guava jam in my face. I was not allowed to leave her presence until I took a bite. "Mmm, very good," I responded through a mouthful as Lydia looked on with the pride of a mother at a job well done.

Estella was behind the house in their small stable. Guapo turned out to be a massive black steed. The horse tossed his shimmering silky mane from side to side. I approached slowly, and he settled as I stroked his muzzle. His nostrils flared with angry huffs of air. "Are you sure it's all right that I take your horse?"

"What are a couple of old women going to do with a horse like this?" She shook her head as she stroked the horse's flank. "Guapo needs to run. His packs are full with everything you'll need for the next few days, or at least until the next town."

I wrapped my arms around Estella's neck, hugging her with all my strength. "Thank you," I murmured into her hair with tears in my eyes.

She patted my back. "Take care of yourself and that baby."

Knowing it was only a matter of time before the Imperial soldiers would come searching for me, I climbed onto the horse and kicked my heels into his sides. Guapo relished the opportunity to run. He leaped easily over fallen logs and rocks as we escaped into the forest.

He was a beast freshly released from hell and I his demon. We ran so fast that I didn't pay attention to the road ahead of me, trusting in Guapo's skill. Charging through the ambush, I laughed as the men launched themselves out of our way. They scattered like birds, screaming for God to save them from Atiola.

I smiled into Guapo's mane. They thought of me as Atiola. I didn't think I could be prouder.

Once I was a safe distance away I decided to take a rest in the heat of midday. I let Guapo seek out sweet grass while I sat in the shade and ate some of the food from the pack. I knew José's army was going to be south of me, I just didn't know how far south. My only concern was that I get to the rebel army before they moved.

I may have been out of immediate danger, but I would not feel at peace until I found the Farrapos. I couldn't help but look over my shoulder as I got on Guapo's back. I didn't trust my surroundings; even the shadows had a threatening edge.

The sun was setting when I came upon two Farrapos scouts.

"Anita? Is that really you?" João, one of the scouts, asked in disbelief.

"You have no idea how happy I am to see you both." My heart pounded with relief. "Am I close to the camp?"

They both nodded. "It's just a few miles south. When you get to the fork in the road, go left. We were headed back toward the Imperial encampment. We were going to find a way to rescue you, which clearly we no longer need."

"There is a cottage with two women, north of here. They helped me escape. Please, make sure they are all right."

"We will do what we can," they said in near unison.

Night had fallen by the time I reached the rebels' camp. As I rode through, the men crossed themselves, staring at me from their fires. Rossetti paused on his way to the main tent, a bundle of papers in his arms. He did a double take before throwing them to the ground. "Anita!" He ran up to me as I dismounted from my horse.

"May God be praised!" He wrapped me in a large hug. I was momentarily shocked. Physical affection of any kind was uncommon with Rossetti. "José has been inconsolable," he whispered in my ear.

I followed Rossetti into the tent. The men were standing around a large table with maps. Rossetti coughed softly and they looked up. They froze when they realized I was there.

"Anita?" José whispered. His brow wrinkled as if he didn't trust his eyesight.

"Hello," I said.

He pushed everyone out of his way as he came to me. Grabbing the sides of my head, he kissed me. Pulling away, he began to examine me, his hands searching everywhere. "You're all right?" he asked as he continued to inspect me.

"Yes," I said, taking his hands in mine and kissing his knuckles.

"And the baby? I heard you fell."

I put his hand to my stomach, where the child kicked. "We are fine. We just had a little adventure."

He wrapped me in a massive hug. "Don't you ever scare me like that again."

"I make no promises." I laughed into his shoulder. His grip tightened as he buried his face in my hair, the muffled sound of his breath sucking in in sharp bursts.

* * *

That night we lay face-to-face, holding on to each other. José gripped my waist as if I would disappear if he let go. Later, I awoke by myself. My momentary confusion passed when I heard the voices of José, Rossetti, and Canabarro talking outside our tent.

"We can't continue this campaign," Rossetti stated. "I know she thinks she is indestructible, but a woman in her condition has no business hiking around south Brazil, let alone fighting in a war."

"I know, but I won't be separated from her." This time it was José talking. "I thought I lost her once. I won't risk it again."

"We understand. We really do." Canabarro's harsh voice. "That's why I am suggesting you and Rossetti take a regiment. You can scout the western region for us."

"I'll not let others do my work for me," José demanded.

"They won't. You can lead a reconnaissance mission while you wait for the baby to come," Canabarro insisted.

"José, we need to go somewhere safe so that she can have the baby," Rossetti said. "Who knows what damage the infant took when Anita fell? I know a family from the old country living in São Simão; the wife is a midwife. Think about your wife and child, brother."

I got up from the bed and walked outside the tent, where the men argued so intensely that I stood there unnoticed.

"When all is well you can meet the rest of the army back at the front," Canabarro tried to reason with José.

José ran a tired hand over his face. "I just don't know if Anita will agree to it."

Standing in the shadows, I thought about Rossetti's words. I didn't know what was in store for us in São Simão. Other wives and children followed their husbands, but they never followed them into battle. My hand caressed my stomach as I remembered the fall.

I was lucky. The baby still kicked, but who knew if he would be born with any permanent damage. Could José and I risk the well-being of this child again?

"I'll go." The men looked up at me in surprise.

"Anita, *tesoro mio*, what are you doing up?" José rushed to me as if I were an invalid.

"I figured that if my fate was to be the subject of discussion, I should have a say," I said, taking a step back. I refused to be treated like a fragile piece of china. Gauchos such as myself were made of stronger stuff than this, but I had to protect this child. "We have more to think about now than you and me. We will go to these friends of Rossetti's."

TWENTY-ONE

September 1840

As we rode in along the banks of the Rio Corrente, I marveled at the rugged beauty. The river was flanked by brown flatlands spotted with low green foliage. The winds whipped past us with a vengeance. The trees that were scattered along the grasslands bowed in reverence to the wind's power. We had a very small garrison along with a herd of cattle given to us as a form of payment. The Farrapos were running out of money and had resorted to paying the soldiers any way they could.

The Costa home was nestled within the small river community of São Simão. The settlement consisted of a smattering of cabins with a wide-open prairie where cows lazily chewed the long yellow grass.

When José, Rossetti, and I arrived at the Costas' door, Antonia was already out front waiting for us. She stood in the doorway with her hands on her wide hips. Her black hair was pulled into a knot at the nape of her neck, though a frizzy halo of black curls framed her face. As soon as I dismounted Guapo, Antonia had her hands all over my stomach, pressing at various places.

"Good. The baby seems to be in the right position, but we should prepare for your confinement. Come inside, I have your room ready."

"We still have unloading to do."

"Nonsense, let the men take care of that." Antonia waved me off. "You need your rest, Dona Anita. When this child comes you will never be able to rest again." Suddenly she was distracted by something behind me. "Patrizio! Get down from that wagon this instant! Paulo, get your son down from there before he drives the whole army into the river."

A portly bald man with wire-rim spectacles, who I assumed was Paulo, walked calmly over to the giggling child who wiggled like a cat as his father threw him over his shoulder. Antonia turned back to me. "And that is why you need to take your rest now, while you can. It's been nine years since I've had a moment to myself. Your boy will be a handful, as most boys are."

"You're certain it's a boy?"

"Yes, dear. Don't you know when a mother glows that means she will have a boy? When she fades, she will have a girl, because a girl takes her beauty from her mother. It's something my mother taught me, hasn't failed me yet." She cupped a hand to my cheek. "And you, my dear, are gleaming."

In total the Costas had five children. Giorgia, nine, and Beatrice, seven, had both begun assisting their mother in the midwife trade. Then there were the three boys that were an oncoming storm. The five-year-old, Dante, was the ringleader. He kept an eye on both his younger brothers, Patrizio and little Paulo, but also led them into trouble at every opportunity. I watched the boys with trepidation and joy as they ran around in front of the house like a pack of puppies, trying to picture my own black-haired child among them.

We settled into life in São Simão quickly. While I turned myself over fully to Antonia and her care, allowing myself to be her humble student, José spent his days tending to our new herd of cattle. One morning I stepped outside to find him petting the nose of one of our cows while she took hay directly from his hand.

"You would have made a good gaucho," I said, coming up to stand next to him at the fence.

"You think so?"

I reached out and petted the soft nose. The faint smell of milk drifted in the air as the cow's large eyes watched me. "The country life suits you." The cow nudged José's arm, looking for more food. "And you have a way with animals."

He laughed lightly, feeding the cow the last of what he had. He was quiet for a moment as he looked out into the field. The grass danced in the wind that pushed puffy white clouds through the sky. "Yes," he finally said. "I could have made a fine gaucho." He wrapped an arm around my shoulders. "If only Destiny didn't have other plans in mind." José buried his face in my hair, breathing in deeply.

Destiny. She was an old crone weaving a tapestry out of my life. I wondered as we looked out over the field if we could be happy with a life like this, or if we were too used to Destiny's influence over us.

Supper was a grand affair in the Costa household. Antonia and her daughters brought in platefuls of roasted vegetables and pastas, which were a new delicacy to me. I wasn't allowed to help but was given the first share of every dish, whether I liked it or not. It was another rule of Antonia's: An expectant mother had to have the first bite of every dish. "It's good for the baby," she said.

José nudged me as we sat at the table one night. "You should learn how to cook from Dona Antonia." I eyed my husband suspiciously. Suddenly, I envisioned being trapped in a life like my mother's.

"Has there been a problem with my cooking up until now, husband?" I asked, passing him a plate of pasta.

"I'd walk gently if I were you, brother," Rossetti warned from the other side of the table.

"All I am saying is that the Costas are the first Italian family you have been around, and it is an excellent opportunity to learn before we go to Italy."

I choked on my water. *Go to Italy?* José never brought up leaving Brazil to me, much less the Americas.

"Do you remember *stoccafisso in agrodolce*?" Rossetti asked after washing down his food with a large gulp of wine.

"Oh, I dream of it," José said wistfully with a hand to his heart. "There is nothing like it in all the Americas, but what I miss is mussels *alla marinara*. My mother used to stuff the mussels with anchovies. It was a thing of beauty." José turned to me. "Just wait until you get to Italy, Anita, you will grow deliciously plump."

"If that is what you wish, husband," I mumbled.

"We will eat like kings!" Rossetti proclaimed, raising his glass.

After dinner, while Antonia put the children to bed, we sat around the table discussing the men's plans for Italy, in the event they got to go back. "Once we have restrengthened the monarchy all of the northern regions will gladly join the cause," Rossetti said.

"Cause?" I asked, looking from José to Rossetti. I knew that Austria controlled Italy in the north, but I didn't know of any active resistance. If there was a struggle, José would want to be there. The question was, would he want me there too?

"The cause of freedom. Austrian rule is keeping us from uniting. They are corrupt. To question the government is to put your life at risk, like yours truly. Only the rich prosper. Our people are starving while the Austrians pillage our resources. And what the

Austrians are doing is the least of our problems; don't get me started on the hold the pope has over Rome," Rossetti said.

"The peninsula wants freedom, that is a given. However, it's our job to see to it that the freedom that they crave is in a unified Italy under the Piedmont monarchy." José moved the *bombilla* in his gourd around, refusing to meet my eyes.

"What of Ferdinand II in the Two Sicilies?" Paulo asked. "He is a progressive. Surely he would support a unified country?"

"Oh, Ferdinand started off well enough, cutting taxes, building railroads and steamships," José responded, "but when the people asked for a constitution, he suppressed them. We can't count on him. King Ferdinand wants only power and is the antithesis of all that we fight for." José took a long sip of his tea. "However, the Kingdom of the Two Sicilies is not my primary concern, at least not now. We first must contend with Austria."

"Austria will not let go of the north very easily. We need to expect a bloody war," Rossetti agreed. His cravat was askew and his lips were stained purple with wine. He filled his glass once again. "I've been hearing whispers."

"Whispers?" José brightened up. "What whispers?"

"There are two brothers, Attilio and Emilio, they are resurrecting the Carbonari guild. They are proclaiming that Italy must be unified. The fire has not died with the people."

José leaned forward in his chair. "Really?"

Rossetti shook his head. "They are gaining support in very high places. The brothers are recruiting others, from students to nobility. They even say the young composer Giuseppe Verdi is among these recruits. We may be going home sooner rather than later, brother."

The biscuit I was nibbling suddenly tasted like dirt in my mouth.

José sat back with an audible harrumph. "Home. Can we really go back? I had started to think it would never happen."

"All we need is a pardon from the king of Piedmont. He can

offer us his protection. If these whispers are true, then he is on our side."

"Can we really do what the Medici family failed to do? Can we create a united Italy?"

Rossetti smiled. "The Garibaldis will be the new Medicis."

José smiled and feigned bashfulness. "Some people would consider that blasphemy."

"You know what Machiavelli says: 'A prudent man should always follow in the path trodden by great men and imitate those who are most excellent.'" José joined in with Rossetti in reciting from Machiavelli, "'So that if he does not attain to their greatness, at any rate he will get some tinge of it.'"

Rossetti leaned forward in his chair. "We can pick up where these great men left off. Brother, there can be an Italy within our lifetime."

This talk of Italy made me sick. I got up from the table, stretching. "I'll see you in bed, my love." I kissed José on the head and left the room. Lying in bed, I waited for sleep to overtake me.

I was standing on a cliff, the wild wind blowing my hair into my face. I was alone. Truly alone. José was gone. Rossetti had taken him to Italy, and he was never coming back. My child and I had nothing left to live for. I stared down into the abyss. Suddenly the canyon looked even deeper than it had originally. Pebbles echoed as they tumbled down the rocky slope. I lifted my foot, taking a step forward…

I woke with a start. The dream felt so real that my hand shook as I poured water from the porcelain pitcher into the basin. I splashed the cold water on my face. Looking out the window I marveled at the brightly shining stars that stood out in contrast to the ink-black sky. My eyes scanned the heavens when José came into the room.

"I'm sorry. I didn't realize you were awake."

"It's no matter," I said, setting my towel down and returning to bed.

"Are you mad at me?"

"No." I got into bed, making a point not to look at him.

"All right then," he said, lying down on the other side. "I don't know what I did, but whatever it was I am sorry."

I didn't want to be angry. I didn't want to argue, but I couldn't sleep. My blood pumped so fast that I could feel it coursing through my veins. I sighed.

"It wasn't what you did. It was what you said."

"What did I say?" he asked, sounding honestly bewildered.

"Your talk of Italy." I tried to make myself comfortable, punching my pillow.

"Anita, I don't understand. We were only talking about going home."

I rolled over to look at him, giving in to the inevitable fight. "You talked about running off to start another war. You haven't even finished with this one and now you want to leave us? Finish what you started," I spat.

My words landed heavily between us. "I am not leaving anytime soon," José began, "but how can I not be excited about going home? My people need me."

"And what about my people? They still need you."

"I am committed to freeing southern Brazil. You know that. Anita, what is this really about?"

I looked at him, unable to answer. He reached for me, but I pulled away.

"Do you think I am going to leave you here?" When I was silent, he took my hand. "*Tesoro mio*, I could never leave you behind."

I let him stroke my face, blinking back tears that stung my eyes. "When you go home, what will become of me?"

"You will raise our son and the other children we will have. We'll grow old and sit under the olive trees, watching our grandchildren play."

"But José, I know nothing of your home. I don't even speak the language."

"Then Rossetti, the Costas, and I will teach you. The language really is not all that different from Portuguese." He wiped a tear from my cheek. "Don't worry. You'll learn."

He pulled me to him. "In fact, you already know two words."

"*Tesoro mio*," I said into his chest.

"My treasure." He stroked my hair. "How could I possibly contemplate leaving behind my greatest treasure?"

TWENTY-TWO

The next morning, I woke to find myself alone in bed. As I dressed, I could hear quite a bit of commotion; I picked up a small orange and made my way outside to investigate.

Walking to the shore, I squinted in the glaring sunlight, peeling my fruit as I went. The regiment was cobbling together a small number of boats.

"What's going on here?"

Rossetti continued to hammer, not looking up at me. "There is an Imperial garrison north of us."

"And you're going to fight them? Now?"

Rossetti set his tools down before squinting up at me, frustration shadowing his face. "Some of us have work to do. You're about to give birth. Shouldn't you be in your confinement?"

I took a breath, trying to control my temper. "Antonia says that walking is good for me."

Rossetti grunted as he turned back to his work. I continued to walk along the shore.

"*Tesoro mio*, what are you doing out here?" José was dragging a small rowboat to the shore. "Why aren't you resting?"

"I wanted to see what was going on. Rossetti says that you are leaving?"

José was slightly out of breath as he dropped the boat on the ground. "Yes, there is an Imperial garrison in the north. We're going to raid them for supplies."

"But now?"

"I know." He put a hand to my belly. "The timing is not ideal, but we may be able to keep them from joining the rest of the legion in the south, giving Canabarro's men a fighting chance." He kissed my cheek, then went back to work.

Already feeling tired, I went back to the house to rest. I settled into a chair by the window as my eyelids grew heavy. The rhythmic hammering outside served as an impromptu lullaby.

I watched as a woman with hair as black as the midnight sky on a starless night walked through the ranks in a white dress that flowed like the river as she moved. I leaned closer to the window, trying to get a better view.

She let her hand trace along the men's shoulders. Why didn't they look up? Why didn't they notice her? Something was wrong. She stopped at Rossetti and José, who were fitting a piece of wood to the bottom of a boat. My heart raced. I stood up, I tried to yell, but my throat seized. The woman ran a loving hand along the side of Rossetti's face as he continued to work. I pounded on the window. Not José. Please, not José. The woman turned her head to watch me. The air escaped my lungs in a rush. The face that looked at me was the same face that watched in the mirror.

"Dona Anita! Dona Anita!" I woke with a start, feeling disoriented. Immediately I looked to the window. There was no woman among the men.

"Dona Anita!" I looked down at the little hands that were shoving my arm. Little Patrizio looked up at me hopefully. "Fix.

Fix." He plopped a miniature wooden rocking horse into my lap. The legs were pinned at its sides so that when the horse rocked the legs would sway as if it were running. Evidently one had fallen off. I lifted it up and examined it.

"Patrizio!" Antonia rushed over, shooing her child away. "Bambino, let Dona Anita sleep."

"It's no bother," I said, giving the toy back to Patrizio. "He woke me from a bad dream."

Antonia shook her head. "I do not miss those pregnancy dreams."

* * *

Two days later I watched from the shore as our men sailed up the river to meet the Imperial army. My dream still gnawed at me, leaving a sense of dread in the pit of my stomach. The next two weeks were endless. Every minute felt slower than the last. I looked forward to when sleep would overtake me. At least in my sleep I got to see José.

In my sleep we were happy. We had a little ranch here in São Simão. We owned cows and horses and had a little boy who smiled like his father, but whose eyes sparkled like mine. Who knew, maybe José and I would have more children than the Costas. They would play and tumble over each other like a band of wild puppies, never knowing pain or the sense of struggle as they wandered through the Brazilian wilderness in search of grand adventures.

I reveled in the idea that I could watch the sun set from the same place every day. We could live unbothered by Destiny and her schemes. All I needed was my family and a small house here in São Simão. But as all dreams do, this one faded with the rising sun.

The day was dying when the boats floated down the river. I ran out to shore, eager to see José. My smile fell as the boats sailed closer. There were so many men missing from the ranks.

José's boat hadn't even reached the shore when he jumped out, waist deep into the muddy current. He splashed loudly as he awkwardly moved out of the water to me. He wrapped his arms around me, holding on as if he were afraid he would be pulled back into the river. I didn't ask what had happened. I didn't need to.

José pulled away as Rossetti finally reached the shore with the boat that José had been in. He held his silence, trudging out on the wet sand and organizing the men. "Did we accomplish anything?" I asked, watching the beaten soldiers and trying to find some hope to latch on to.

"Besides nearly getting killed? We may have weakened their forces just a bit, but I doubt it. Moringue has a grudge to settle."

I caught myself, freezing midbreath. José noticed my reaction. "Anita, this is not your doing. Moringue and I were enemies long before I knew you." He shrugged. "He'll never forgive me for making a fool of him in São Paulo."

"I know, but I'm sure I damaged his pride." I rubbed my arms against the gooseflesh that appeared. "A man whose pride has been damaged is a dangerous thing."

José kissed my forehead. "Moringue is not your concern, *tesoro mio*."

* * *

It was just before dawn when I woke with the pain. The damp linens clung to me, causing an initial sense of panic. I thought for sure this child was going to claw his way out of me. I called out for Antonia, who ran to my side within moments.

"What a fine morning to have a baby, don't you think?" She spoke pleasantly, as if this sort of thing were as common as milking a cow. Julia and Beatrice staggered into the room, wiping the sleep out of their eyes. Beatrice grew wide-eyed as she stared at me. This was apparently her first childbirth. I could sympathize with her, I was a bit scared as well. Antonia rushed over to them, giving them a number of commands in Italian before turning back to examine me.

"The baby is not quite ready to make his way out. So how about we have a little walk, shall we?"

Antonia firmly grasped my arm, letting me lean into her. She patted my hand and told me stories about the births of her children. "Now, Patrizio, he couldn't wait to come out of me. I swear that child entered this world running." She shook her head. "That boy will run around the world and never look back."

A pain shot from my abdomen around to my back, causing me to double over. Antonia stood by my side as the cramp passed through. Once I could stand back up she began walking with me again. "Now, Beatrice was just the opposite of Patrizio. I think she would have stayed in my womb her whole life if I let her. By the time she was supposed to come, I was performing every piece of advice I was ever told to encourage her to make her entry into this world. Including eating all of the peppers in the village!"

I tried to smile at the thought but was too scared and weary from the pain. The girls came back into the room with arms full of rags and fresh water. "All right, Mamãe, let's get to work," Antonia said, setting me down on a stool. "When I say push, you push like your life depends on it. Understand?"

I nodded, eyes wide with fear. Both her daughters stood on either side of me, letting me clasp their small arms. In that moment, I wondered how fragile they were. Minutes stretched into ages. It felt like every moment ticked by slower than the next as I worked to expel this child from within me. Half an hour later my son was born. All pink and wrinkly, screaming in victory.

Antonia handed the baby over to Julia for her to tend to as she helped me pass the afterbirth. I was grateful to be able to lie back in the warm bed with fresh linens when we were finished. Every muscle in my body ached, but I didn't mind. My child had finally made it into the world. This thing that had been so abstract for so long now yawned deeply as I held him.

José rushed into the room. "They finally let me come in!" He stood over my child and me in utter awe.

"Would you like to hold him?"

"Can I? Do you think that's wise?" His eyes opened wide with fear.

"Of course." I couldn't help but laugh a little. "After all that he's been through I doubt he will break."

He took the child gently in his arms. He stared at him for a long time before looking up at me. "We have a son," he said in amazement, "and he's perfect."

"Well, almost," I said. José looked at me with a mix of surprise and confusion.

I nodded toward our baby. "Look at his head."

José looked to where I was pointing and saw what we had all seen shortly after his birth. A two-inch ridge traveled from his crown to his ear. "It's from when I fell from the horse."

José smiled brightly. "Then he really is our victory child, isn't he? What's his name?"

I shrugged. "I did the hard part. Why don't you do the naming?"

"Did I ever tell you about my tutor?"

"Not that I can recall."

"Menotti was his name. He was one of the first people to not just talk about a unified Italy but to encourage the people to make it happen. He started the Carbonari, a band of men who began the call for unification." Our son yawned while stretching out his little fist, making José smile. "Menotti was revolutionary for his time. The people were just beginning to wake up to the idea of freedom. I for one soaked up all that I could from him. He was a kind man; if anyone needed anything, he was the first to give it to them. Even if he had just one loaf of bread, he would break off a small piece for himself and give away the rest. But he was too much of a revolutionary for his own good. The Austrians didn't like his talk about unification. Which, of course, would mean an end to Austrian rule. The governor had him hanged." He looked up into my horrified face. "Being one of his disciples, I should have died too, but I managed to escape. Death by exile." He turned his attention back to our son, who had grasped his finger. "We'll call our son Menotti. Menotti Garibaldi, our victory child."

For two more glorious weeks we lived in São Simão. I thought that maybe, just maybe, we would be able to settle here. That the life I had dreamed about might actually happen. However, on a rainy morning in October I realized that my dreams could never be.

I was nursing Menotti when José burst into our room. "Moringue is on his way here. We need to leave."

TWENTY-THREE

October 1840

Antonia was distraught over our leaving in the early morning hours, but we didn't have a choice. If we were there when Moringue came through, the whole village would be wiped out. We needed to lead the Imperial army away, find safer territory.

Santa Catarina had already given up on the rebellion. Rio Grande do Sul still fought with every last resource it had. The Farrapos needed to regroup. I knew this, José knew this; the only question was, did the commanders of our army know? The plan was to meet with the rest of the Farrapos in Rio Capivari. Once there we would reorganize and make a push to expel the Imperial forces from Rio Grande do Sul once and for all.

I could smell the rain in the air. All night I could hear the thumping of fat water drops, and by the look of the clouds that ominously clung to the mountains, it would rain again.

"But I don't understand. Why must you leave?" Antonia said, fussing with my gear.

I smiled. "Because I am just as much of a danger to you as the army is."

"That's ridiculous. You're only one woman."

"You'd be surprised how much trouble one woman can seem to stir up. Antonia, I have met Moringue before. He will not be kind if he finds me, nor will he show sympathy to anyone who harbors me."

She shook her head as tears filled her eyes. "Then we will hide you. Yes, hide both you and the baby. No one will ever know."

I took her hands in mine. "I appreciate everything you have done for me. You've been a true friend to us, but my destiny and my child's destiny are tied to José and the freedom of Rio Grande do Sul. We have to go where he goes."

She waved her hand in the air as if my words were an annoying fly. "Destiny is what we make of it."

"And I made mine a long time ago." I hugged her. "Thank you, Antonia. You will never know how much you mean to us."

I climbed on my horse with Menotti tucked in close to me. As we came to the ridge overlooking the valley I dared to look back, just one more time. Golden rays broke through the dark gray clouds, accentuating the emerald-green trees. I knew I would never again see São Simão, my almost home. I kicked my horse and followed José to Rio Capivari.

The road was lined with spring flowers bursting with vibrant hues of blue and gold. I smiled as I kissed my son's bald head, though my joy faded as we entered Rio Capivari. Mud splashed up the sides of tents and gathered in puddles along our pathway. The men, stained with filth, watched us pass, their eyes dull and blank as they sat on empty crates. Despair hung in the air like a thick fog. Our once glorious army was now reduced to empty, frightened men. The women paused outside their tents, balancing baskets or children on their hips long enough to assess how much of a threat we were. The sunken cheeks of the children who played at their mothers' feet made me shiver.

We settled into our shack, a small building hastily constructed of loose boards. I was fearful that one wrong move would send it crashing down around us. My arms filled with excess dry goods to exchange for fresh clothing for the baby, I traipsed through the thick mud to the women of the camp.

"You're Senhora Garibaldi, aren't you?" A woman eyed me, her black skin glowing under the bright Brazilian sun that broke through the rain clouds. The small child that she held on her hip grabbed her curly black hair with his tiny fist.

"I am. May I ask who you are?"

"My former masters called me 'girl,' but I choose to call myself Pedrina." Her almond-shaped eyes narrowed as she scanned me from head to foot, disdain evident in her sneer. "We aren't interested in charity."

"I was hoping to exchange these."

Pedrina leaned over and pulled at the sling that held Menotti to my chest. "You need fresh swaddling. Without it your baby is bound to get a rash. Especially out here." She sucked at her teeth while she watched me. "What do you have to give me for my swaddling?"

"Tea, dry beans, and a little bit of soap."

Pedrina sat back on her heels. "I'll trade you some swaddling for the beans." She turned her head and called out to one of the other women. "Imelda! Have any extra blankets for a baby?"

A stout woman with a mess of children, Imelda pried off the child who was clinging to her skirts before slinking over to us. She examined me, then looked to her friend. "Maybe. What can I get for it?"

"Tea or soap. I already took her beans."

Imelda spit to the side. "No need for soap out here." She eyed her friend. "I could have used those beans."

"Then you should have gotten here sooner."

Imelda turned back to me. "It gets cold here at night. I'll give you one of my blankets for your tea."

I turned over my goods. While Imelda inspected her tea, Pedrina said, "I heard about you and your husband."

"You wouldn't be the first," I said, growing uneasy about where the conversation might lead.

Pedrina shielded her eyes from the sun. "Your husband's the reason why I am a free woman right now."

I tried to hide the surprise that threatened to spread across my face. "How so?"

"He told Benito Gonçalves that he wouldn't join his army unless he freed the slaves."

"Oh," I responded, feeling relief. "My husband and I share the same feelings on the matter. He says a country cannot call itself free if its people are bound in the barbarous act of slavery."

At this point Imelda found her way back to our conversation. "My cousin told me she witnessed Garibaldi pulling a drowning slave out of a river. Is it true?"

I'd never heard the story before, but I affirmed the tale all the same. The women smiled. "You and your family are welcome back here anytime."

When I walked through the door of our small shack, I found José shuffling some papers on our bed while Rossetti leaned against the wall, eating an orange. I asked the men about the story. Rossetti choked on his food. "Where did you hear about that?" he asked, trying to compose himself.

"The women," I responded.

"Right, the women. Always the women." Rossetti turned to José with a slight smile. "Back in Rio de Janeiro I was always pulling your husband out of trouble. Whether it be with a magistrate or someone's husband."

"Someone's husband?" I questioned, looking from José to Rossetti.

"There was only the one," my husband grumbled, not looking up at us.

"Only the one that was married, but I distinctly remember there being a number of fathers and brothers quite unhappy with you fraternizing with their daughters and sisters."

"Rossetti," José began, looking up from his papers, "I would appreciate it if you didn't tell my wife all about my wanton youth."

"I'm sorry," Rossetti said, slipping the last bit of orange into his mouth and slowly chewing. My husband, satisfied that the conversation was over, went back to his paperwork. The Adam's apple on Rossetti's long neck bobbed as he swallowed. "I also remember promising that I would get even with you for all the trouble you caused, and today is your day of reckoning, my friend."

José slapped down the paper in his hand. "I did not always cause the trouble."

"Well, you sure as hell didn't hide from it!" Rossetti turned to me. "Besides the women, your husband anointed himself the emancipator of every slave in Brazil."

"Slavery is barbaric. No civilized society has any business participating in it," José said, crossing his arms. "You couldn't expect me to let injustice stand."

"I can when we are outnumbered by Brazilian soldiers," Rossetti responded.

"Yes, but what about the drowning slave? I haven't heard that story." I set Menotti down in his basket. If I didn't intervene, this bickering would go on for hours.

"I think I'll tell the story, if you don't mind?" Rossetti said, wiping the orange juice from his hands. "José and I were walking along the riverfront, on our way to an important meeting with a pasta wholesaler," he began, reminding me of my husband's merchant past. "Well, we heard screams and loud splashing. Your husband ran to see what all the commotion was. Now, let me remind you how important this meeting was. We had our best clothes on as we were running toward the danger."

"Hey, you don't get to complain about the running. You followed me," José interjected.

"As if you ever gave me a choice." Rossetti continued his story. "It turned out there was a slave fighting for his life in the river. Without thinking, your husband dove in and rescued the man." Rossetti shook his head. "You ruined a perfectly good suit and wound up going to the most important meeting of our import business looking like a drowned cat."

"And if I had not intervened the man would have died." José scooped up his papers. "You would think that with all the people standing around, laughing, someone would have done something."

"Yes, well that *someone* is usually Giuseppe Garibaldi." Rossetti's smile betrayed his scolding tone. "I also seem to remember the slave owner arriving shortly thereafter to beat and scold you and his property."

José harrumphed. "As if a human can be someone's property." He lifted his papers under one arm. "Come, Canabarro is expecting us." José kissed my temple. "I'll be back in time for dinner."

"And please, be sure to see me if you want more stories about your husband." Rossetti gave me an exaggerated bow. "I have plenty."

The men left, the sounds of their playful bickering filling the air as I started to prepare our dinner.

Our life in Rio Capivari wasn't much, but as José said, "We have four walls and a roof, that's all we need," and truly it was. Just having stability again brought me peace. I sat with Menotti one night in our little hut while he gnawed on a wet rag. His little arms and legs punched the air with glee. A rustling by the doorway caught my attention. José stood there watching us.

"I didn't want to disturb you. You both looked like you were having so much fun." He smiled as he came over to tickle Menotti. He acted happy, but there was a shadow that had passed over him. His smile wasn't genuine.

"José, what's going on?"

"Nothing." He lifted our son up, then brought him close to nuzzle his chubby cheek.

"José, please." I put a hand on his arm.

He took a deep breath and slowly let the air escape from his lips, puffing out his cheeks. "The Imperial army has made an offer."

"Surely that should be good news."

"I suppose." He shrugged. "According to General Gonçalves, the new Imperial general is willing to pardon all Brazilian citizens."

"Only citizens?" I sat back. "People such as myself and the landowners would be spared, but what about the others? The slaves?"

"The Imperial general made the terms of the offer very clear. Brazil will never free the slaves."

My heart sank as I thought of Pedrina and her family. "But Rio Grande do Sul promised they would be free. What will happen to them?"

José sighed and looked away. "They'll be sent back to their owners, who will probably kill them for running away in the first place."

"What about you and Menotti?" I watched my husband gently rock our son in his arms.

He shrugged. "We aren't citizens. Menotti, I am sure, would be fine, but the Brazilian government is no friend of mine. The official edict is that those who want to go back, who want to go home, will be free to do so. Those who choose to stay will do so of their own free will."

"And what will happen to those who stay?"

"The Imperial army will not be merciful." José went back to playing with Menotti.

"What are we going to do?"

José looked up at me. "I don't know."

A knot grew in my stomach. José always had an answer, a plan. If we stayed, we would be forced to fight a losing battle, but if we left we would have nowhere to go. And what of the freed slaves we had made promises to? José had insisted on their freedom as a condition of his involvement. I know my husband; he felt responsible for them. As irrational as it might be, he felt he had created the situation that caused them to be in limbo. If they were to die, the weight of their souls would rest on his shoulders.

José smiled up at me, and I stopped wondering what was going to happen tomorrow. So long as we were together we would figure out a plan together.

* * *

The Imperial army offer had its intended effect on our forces. Almost all of those who could leave did. The small number who stayed were those who were too stubborn to give up or who truly had nowhere else to go.

Rio Capivari rested on the edge of a small lagoon. On the other side General Gonçalves owned some property where he was able to smuggle goods through to sustain us—goods he paid for out of his own pocket, as he did for most things in this war. However, Gonçalves wasn't among the plebes, struggling every day. He rode for Brasília, to kiss the ring of the new king and find an end to this war.

Standing in the cold night air, I watched my husband climb into a skiff that silently slipped into the ink-black water of the lagoon. The soldiers were so quiet that all I could hear was the lapping of the water against the boat and the shore. I wrapped my thin shawl tightly over my shoulders as my heart broke for my husband.

He had once been a man of such pride. Now he looked like a

flower that had begun to wilt. I thought of the Rio Grande and all the ships that he had commanded once upon a time in Laguna. We'd all had such pride then. We were certain that we were destined for glory. We would be revolutionaries for this new republic. Now most of our friends were gone and José rode a canoe that could barely float.

TWENTY-FOUR

NOVEMBER 1840

The Imperial army tracked us from São Simão. It was only a matter of time before they would make their way here. With that threat looming just over the horizon, the decision was made to go in waves to the safety of São Gabriel.

To get there we had to travel through the highest section of the southern Brazilian highlands. There we would find refuge with those who were sympathetic to our cause. José and I were to leave in the first wave, the vast majority of the soldiers and their families marching alongside us. Rossetti was to take the second wave with his printing press, and a third wave of soldiers would travel with General Canabarro.

Rippling gray clouds filled the skies as we loaded the wagons. I moved Menotti from one hip to the other as I watched José and Rossetti loading the printing press onto a wagon.

"I don't understand why you must take this ridiculous contraption," José complained as Rossetti helped him load goods into the cart.

"Because if I don't, no one else will."

José threw his arms into the air in exasperation. "We don't need the printing press."

"We need to be able to stay in contact with our brothers in Italy. They need to know our plight." He leaned against the wagon briefly, wiping sweat from his brow.

"For once will you think about yourself? Telling our story doesn't have to be your job." José was now following him as they picked up more goods to put in the cart. "Brother, let someone else carry that burden. Just for a little while."

Rossetti paused. He looked up at me and Menotti, making eye contact for the briefest of moments. I thought José had gotten through to him, but Rossetti shook his head. "I cannot shift my responsibilities onto someone else."

"I'll buy you a new printing press," José pleaded.

"With what gold, my friend? No, that printing press and I have been through too much together for me to ever let her go."

José sighed. "You are a stubborn, foolish man. That press will be the death of you."

Rossetti hoisted a box onto the cart before leaning against it, panting for air. "Then I will die with a legacy."

I pitied the women who were not suited to this life. Shortly after we set out for the trail they began to complain with every step. Their children were heavy weights in their arms. Their feet hurt. The weather was too cold.

I was lucky, Menotti was only a few months old and not very heavy. The first two miles felt lovely, the wind crisp against my flushed cheeks, but the trail grew steep as we traveled up the ridge.

The lush green foliage became sparse as more rocks lined the sides of the trail in piles bubbling up along our route. Soon there were only rocks as far as our eyes could see. The rain, relentless in its punishment, pelted us like tiny pebbles, turning the ground into a slippery mess. We had to get off our horses and walk alongside them, pulling them by their reins.

When I was young, the gauchos would sit around the campfire telling stories of giants who lived at the tops of the vast mountains of southern Brazil. One tale in particular always caught my attention: A prince volunteered to climb to the highest mountain in search of a fountain made of gold that would save his father from death. The prince was warned, "Do not look to the right or the left, for if you do the giants will snatch you up and make you their slave forever." When the prince began walking on the path, he couldn't help himself. He looked to his left and a giant snatched him up and made him his slave.

Now as I stared up the steep path before me, I couldn't help but think that these mountains were the giants that the gauchos warned me about. As we journeyed the air thinned, making every breath a struggle. It didn't matter how deeply I inhaled, it felt like I couldn't take enough air into my lungs. The rain never stopped. I was frigid and I didn't think I would ever be dry again.

I struggled to keep our son warm in the sling. At one point during our ascent José stopped me. He stripped off his poncho and took Menotti from me. "Here, let me carry him for a while." He strapped the child to him and then covered himself and our baby with the poncho. Periodically, as we continued to climb, he lifted the collar so that he could breathe warmth over our son.

At night José and I placed the baby in between us to shield him from the wind that flowed through our feeble tent. Sleep didn't come easily. I still shivered uncontrollably as fat water drops plunked randomly onto my forehead. Our attempts to keep Menotti warm didn't work very well, and he shivered and cried almost all night. I both dreaded and looked forward to morning.

At the break of dawn, we picked up our little camp and started our descent at an increased speed. The rains paused, and we wanted to move as fast as possible while the weather was good. The descent was muddy, causing many to slip and fall. Carrying my son the way José had, I felt better about keeping Menotti warm and safe as I used the trees to guide me.

Halfway down the mountain, the rains began again. I was relieved only briefly by a flat plateau until José made us stop. The whispers began, and I wove through our company to the front. There were remnants of an Imperial army ambush. An abandoned camp, fires long since drowned by the torrential rain. The officers talked among themselves as they raided the supplies that had been left behind. We were going to need to be more diligent. I looked at the carcass of the camp. Even the Brazilian army couldn't withstand the harsh mountain weather. I at least had more strength than they did.

We trudged along but stopped again as a river came into view. It swelled with the rains. The current was so strong that little waves rippled dangerously. As I cast my eyes over the water, I began to lose hope. José sent scouts north and south to find a bridge or even some shallows so that we could cross the swiftly moving current. I eyed the water suspiciously. I had encountered similar rivers when I rode with the gauchos. Knowing the danger to ourselves and our cattle, we would always find a different way to get to the other side, even if it meant an extra day in the wilderness. A river like this meant the loss of cattle and life.

Looking around at my traveling companions, I could see we weren't prepared. Our horses were loaded with goods. The women and children who accompanied the regiment didn't know how to swim. But what could we do? If we went back we would be at the mercy of the Imperial army; if we went forward we were in danger from Mother Nature herself. The only question was: Which fate could we stand?

The scouts returned an hour later. "Senhor Garibaldi!" they yelled as they came closer. "There is no bridge."

"Did you search everywhere? Are you sure?" José sighed. His shoulders fell as he looked around at the rest of us.

"We are sure." The scout shook his head. "We looked everywhere."

José faced the water. "What are we going to do? We can't cross here." He said it as much to himself as he did to the scouts.

"There's a section downriver where we could cross." José turned to the young scout who had spoken. "It wouldn't be easy, but it's safer than it is here."

"We can't swim across the river!" one of the men yelled.

"Well, we can't stay here!" the scout yelled back. He turned to José. "Senhor, we have no choice, it's either cross or die. At least if we try to cross we have a better chance at surviving."

"Show me," José said.

José left with the scouts and two of his officers. He returned some time later. "We're crossing the river."

When we reached the crossing, the horses were unburdened of most of their loads. We could easily let our supplies float across with us; the rest we abandoned. Children clung to the necks of their parents, hanging off their backs like meat shanks. I pulled Menotti out of his solitude under my poncho. At the deepest part of the river, the water would come up to my waist, dangerously close to my son. I held Menotti close to me, saying a prayer as I stepped closer to the ice-cold water. He was two months old and yet he already knew the hardships of a soldier.

I gasped involuntarily as freezing water stabbed at my ankles and calves. Clutching Menotti high at my shoulder, I made my way slowly through the river. The horses kicked and bucked, sending cold sprays of water through the air.

It was at the halfway mark that I heard the screams. A little boy lost his grip on his mother. He was too small to tread the water, too light to fight the current. He was swept away. Imelda, the heavy-set woman I had met in camp, began to panic. Her older children had already crossed, but it was her young son, no older than three, who floated down the river. She screamed and dove in the water after him. I turned and watched, unable to do anything as she was pulled under and her screams were drowned out.

"Imelda!" her husband called. He let go of his horse, who started to go wild. It thrashed and kicked, startling everyone around it. In the commotion of the horse bucking, three other men tried to get it under control. Imelda's husband let the current carry him downriver. "Imelda!" His voice grew shriller as he tried to reach his wife.

He went under and never came back up. People stumbled and lost their balance, falling into the water. They panicked, their screams choked by the water they thrashed in. Those who could reached down to pull them up to keep them from falling prey to the mighty current. I froze, holding Menotti so tight that I think I would have put him back into my body.

"Anita!" José was ahead of me by just a few feet. "Keep moving!" He reached a hand out to me. I looked behind me at the commotion. "Anita! Come now!" Slowly I turned back around to face him, moving one foot in front of the other as he impatiently willed me forward. We made it to shore together and helped what was left of the company do the same. In total we lost nearly half a dozen people. A number of goods were washed downstream, and our horses trembled from fright. Nervous horses were dangerous.

We walked along the level ground for another two miles until we came to the next mountain. José made us walk up the mountain until we found a nice ledge far enough up so that we would be safe from the river. "We camp here for the night!" José ordered.

Unfortunately, the weather was too harsh to allow us to get more than a few hours of sleep. Rain sliced the air at sharp angles in the bitter, cold wind. We collapsed against the rocks before pulling ourselves up and moving forward.

We continued on through the piercing rain and frigid wind for another nine days until we reached São Gabriel. I would have been happier had I not been so cold and wet, or if I didn't have a baby who finally grew fussy from a rash.

TWENTY-FIVE

NOVEMBER 1840

The river that we followed into São Gabriel bloated with brown water, turning the adjoining grasslands into an indistinguishable mush. The sleepy makeshift village, made up of freed slaves and Farrapos, sat on the edge of another of the many properties owned by General Gonçalves. People moved about in their daily chores, tending to cattle, cooking their meals. The ravages of war seemed not to reach us in this rebel haven.

José claimed a small windowless cabin for us that had one bedroom and a common room that was a combination of parlor and kitchen. I settled into a chair with the door propped open, nursing Menotti and listening to the sounds of birds singing in the morning sun. We'd been here for almost a week and the hut was starting to feel like home thanks to José's ability to scavenge for us. Later that morning José came in carrying a large box.

"I found some goods for us." He dropped the box on the table. "I had more, a heavier blanket and a loaf of bread, but I saw the

Rodrigues family. They needed it more than we do. I hope you don't mind."

I set the baby down in the small crate that served as a crib and peered into the box. "This will do just fine. It's certainly better than what we had on our way here." I pulled José to me, kissing him gently at first, then letting the passion grow. It had been a long time since we'd had the opportunity to be alone. We took our time as I let José lead me into our little bedroom.

Afterward, from the comfort of my warm bed, I watched as José got dressed. "Why must you leave?" He turned and smiled that lopsided boyish grin that I loved.

"I want to be with the other generals when Rossetti arrives. It's the first place he'll go."

"It's still fairly early, he may have been delayed by the weather."

"He should be arriving any day now, he wasn't that far behind us." He leaned over to kiss me. "I won't be gone long."

* * *

One week later I stood next to José at the doorway of our tiny shack watching the rain pour down. Breathing in, I took in the smell of damp grass and earth. Every day at precisely two in the afternoon the heavens opened and continued to saturate us until after sundown.

Anxiety ate at José. He moved from the bed to the table and back to the bed, unable to stand still.

"Something's wrong," he said. I turned to look at him as he began to make another circuit through our cabin. "They should have been here by now."

"You know how long it took us to get here. The roads are probably worse for them than they were for us. Don't worry. They will be here in a few days." I grabbed José by the shoulders and moved him off to the side so that I could get to the pot collecting the raindrops that leaked through our ceiling. "He probably stopped for his printing press."

"Possibly."

"And he probably picked up the people we left behind. I'm sure they slowed him down as well."

José took a deep breath. "You're right." He returned to the doorway, shutting me out as he kept vigil.

* * *

Another week went by with still no word from our other garrisons. One night as the rain poured outside José sat at our table waiting for his dinner. He shook one of his legs, jostling his knee up and down. The noise got louder and louder until I rested a hand on his shoulder. "Sorry," he mumbled.

As we settled in to eat we heard a knock at our door. José bounded to it in two steps. General Canabarro stood there, soaking wet. His clothes were covered in mud, with smears of blood on his chest and pants. His eyes were rimmed in red and he looked as if he hadn't slept in days. "May I come in?"

"Where's Rossetti?" José asked.

"That's why I'm here." Canabarro swallowed hard, his Adam's apple bobbing with exaggeration. "I am sure you came across many hardships in your journey."

"Canabarro, get to it. Where is Rossetti?" José growled.

Canabarro shifted his weight from one foot to the other. "He's dead."

José took an involuntary step back, knocking over the wooden chair. It hit the ground with a clatter, waking up Menotti in his crate. "No," José croaked.

"José, there were few survivors," Canabarro responded almost in a whisper. "The roads were bad. He had to stop and readjust his printing press. Moringue caught up with them."

José's knees buckled. I caught him by the elbow as he tried to grasp the table with his other hand. "How?"

"Bayonet, through the stomach," Canabarro answered in a small voice.

"General, you said there were few survivors. How many?" I asked.

"Two. Moringue wanted them to bear witness and to deliver a message."

"What was the message?" I dared to ask.

" 'The republic is dead.' "

"Damn that *bastardo* and his printing press!" José threw the dish off the table. It crashed against the wall, shattering into a million little pieces. "He was always thinking of his glory." José's voice choked. "I have to go. Excuse me."

José slipped out of the cabin, leaving Canabarro looking at me in shock. "Should we go after him?"

I sighed. "No, it's best to let him grieve in his own way." I picked up Menotti from his crate, holding him close as he settled down. I looked beyond Canabarro to the door that still stood wide open, letting the rain splatter inside. Emotion did not serve my husband. It led him to rash behavior. I kissed Menotti's head, letting my lips linger on his scalp.

"Is that your son? I haven't seen him yet. He's beautiful." Canabarro tickled Menotti, who decided to play shy and snuggle in closer to me. "I remember when mine were that young. They grow up too fast, senhora. Hold on to him for as long as you can."

"General, would you like to stay for supper? Sit and warm yourself for a while."

"No, I should go." Canabarro started to leave but paused. "Oh, I have something." He reached into his satchel. "We found this next to his body. I thought your husband would want it." He set a book on the table. Flipping it open, I could see the thin scratch of Rossetti's handwriting. It was his journal.

"Thank you," I said. "José will appreciate this."

"I'm sorry for your loss," Canabarro said, placing his hat back on his head before venturing out into the rain.

Rossetti deserved better than this. We didn't always see eye to eye, but we were able to find common ground in our love for José. He and José shared a dream. Now my husband would have to forge a unified Italy without him.

As the days dragged on, I watched José. Every smile that he showed to our soldiers was a farce to try to keep up morale. His opinions, which were usually strong, were verbalized with a shrug and "Whatever you think is best." He slunk about the camp with Rossetti's book in hand.

I discovered that the one way I could bring him back to life was to make him interact with Menotti. Our son excelled where others failed. At even the slightest giggle or coo from Menotti, José would light up. It's how I knew the fire in him wasn't gone. If our son could coax it out of him, there was hope. In my attempt to get my husband back I talked him into doing the washing with me.

"But washing is women's work." José whined as I gathered my supplies.

I looked up at him with a start. "I suggest you rephrase that, dear husband. Now where did I put that lye?" I turned around in a circle, checking to see where I might have set it down. "Aha!" I found it sitting on top of a cabinet. "If anyone asks, you can just tell them that your wife was forcing you to spend time with your son. Which is what you will be doing," I said, dropping the lye into the basket.

José sighed, knowing he had lost the argument, and picked up Menotti from his cradle, a drawer I'd lined with old clothing and blankets. "It's best you learn now, little one, that when you have a wife, she's the boss." Menotti gave him a toothless grin as he shoved a drool-covered fist into his mouth. "Ah, bambino, we men have to stick together, don't we?" He kissed the baby's bald head as we set out for the river.

It was late November, and the spring warmth promised that a pleasant summer was on its way. The golden sun shone down on us, making the water glisten. I worked in the river beating and wringing out our clothing. José laid the baby on a blanket in front of him. As I worked, José sang to Menotti in Italian.

"*A bi bo, goccia di limone, goccia d'arancia, o che mal di pancia!*" José reached out and tickled our son's belly. That's when we heard another voice call out.

"*Punto rosso, punto blu, esci fuori proprio tu!*"

José and I looked at each other in bewilderment. There was a rustling in the bushes next to us. José went rigid. I took a step onto the shore. I could grab the baby if José had to fight in our defense.

A tall man with wavy brown hair that fell over his hazel eyes fought his way out of the bushes like he was clumsily beating back a wild animal. "*Buon pomeriggio.*" He shook the leaves out of his hair and smiled at us. In that moment, he reminded me of an overgrown puppy. "I heard you singing and I had to stop by. I couldn't help myself. Another Italian! I love when I get to meet a compatriot on the other side of the world." José and I continued to stare at him in disbelief. "Oh, I'm sorry." He wiped his palm on his leg. "I am Francesco Anzani, but everyone calls me Anzani."

"Giuseppe Garibaldi," José said, clasping his hand. José still sat on the ground with Menotti, so he had to stretch a bit to reach our new comrade.

"*The* Giuseppe Garibaldi! As I live and breathe!" he exclaimed, pumping my husband's hand up and down. "It is a pleasure, no, I mean an honor! You are the reason why I am here." He still shook my husband's hand with a vigorous force. "Well, not here exactly, but you are the reason why I do what I do. You are my hero!"

José smiled as he was finally able to remove his hand from Anzani's grasp.

"I was just a boy when you were exiled. I heard all of your stories. How you stole your father's ship to take it for a ride along the Amalfi Coast. How you cornered a group of Austrian soldiers, disarmed them, and then left them chained to a post with no clothing on for the whole town to see. That has to be my favorite."

José blushed a little. "I was a mischievous youth."

"Mischievous youth? There are some things in this life that don't change," I said with a wry smile.

"And you must be his wife, Anita. It's a pleasure to meet the lovely Senhora Garibaldi."

"Come sit down and tell me about yourself," José said, adjusting himself so that he could better see Anzani.

Anzani launched into his story. "Well, where do I begin? Let's see." He thought for a moment as he sat down. "I was orphaned as a child. My mother died in childbirth and my father was taken from me by the Austrians. Thusly, I was raised by my uncle Filippo. He was a stern man, he required I do nothing but study."

"Where did you grow up?" José asked as he absentmindedly bounced Menotti in his arms.

"Pavia."

"Really? That's not that far from Genoa." José looked to me. "Pavia is a lovely little village, right on the Ticino River."

"My uncle's home had a beautiful view of the Ticino. I know because I sat at the window daydreaming about sailing away when I was supposed to be doing my lessons. My uncle was a permanent bachelor and he thought of me as his protégé." Anzani shrugged. "I suppose that's why the Carbonari were so fascinating to me. You and your friends represented freedom. I could be a scholar *and* a warrior for my country. Just like the Great Garibaldi and his men. You know, I hid your newspaper clippings in my textbooks. I especially like the ones written by Luigi Rossetti. Is he here with you?"

José immediately looked down, becoming overly distracted by

Menotti. "You had to have been awfully young when the Carbonari disbanded," I said. These were the men José had fought with for the unification of Italy before he was exiled.

"I was, but that didn't keep me out of trouble. First I went to Greece to fight for their independence, then I became a Spanish soldier." He smiled as he seemed to recall fond memories. "While there I stumbled upon a wonderful Italian family. Like me, they were in exile. I loved them so much I had to make myself a part of their family." He blushed slightly. "Luckily for me they had a beautiful daughter, Luisa. She has followed me all over and is my rock."

"A woman like that is hard to find. Cherish her. I know I cherish mine," José said with a sideways glance up to me.

"Oh, believe me, I do. It was quite a coup that I married her. She was supposed to marry someone else." He pulled a face. "After the wedding we stayed in Spain for her to have our firstborn, then I came to Brazil. I've been helping the Rio Grande do Sul army for the latter half of the war."

"You've been helping with the Ragamuffin War? How have I not met you?"

"I have trailed behind, keeping mainly to the south, but alas, my time here has come to an end."

"You are leaving?" José asked, looking sad.

"Yes. My wife and children are in Montevideo, Uruguay. We have three sons now, but my wife is insisting it's time I come home so that she can have a daughter." He shrugged. "What are your plans?"

José paused for a moment, focusing on our son. "We haven't thought that far out."

Anzani stood. "You should think about coming to Montevideo. It's the Florence of the Americas. Every Mediterranean has settled there. Well, if you decide to go, come and find me. I'll be the man driven mad by his wife." He placed his hat back on his head and made his way through the bushes from where he'd come.

PART THREE

Uruguay

TWENTY-SIX

February 1841

We weren't sure what to do, but then José burst into our cabin one bright morning while I was trying to appease our angry child. "You'll never believe it. People from every region of the fatherland are living in Montevideo, and guess what they are calling themselves, guess!"

I was pacing, gently bouncing Menotti, who was teething, in my arms. I turned to José, prepared to make a sarcastic response, but his exuberant smile stopped me. He looked happier than he had in ages. "Tell me, husband, what are they calling themselves?"

"They are calling themselves Italians. Do you understand? They are gathering together from all over the peninsula. It's not Tuscany versus Umbria or Calabria versus Basilicata. They are unifying of their own accord." He turned me to face him. "If they are unifying in Uruguay, this means they can unify at home. It's happening, Anita, there will be an Italy."

My husband didn't need to say the words for me to know what

he meant. Leave Brazil. As I looked into my husband's hopeful eyes, a million questions filled my head. Brazil was everything to me, but then I thought about my father and the words that he had said to me so long ago. *There was more to the world than my little island.*

Brazil was the fabric that shaped me, but that fabric was now tattered, worn from the war. There was no way that my little family could have a life of peace in my home country. The Imperial government made sure of that. *There was more to the world than my little island.* "There is more to this world than Brazil," I said to my husband. "It's time we go to Uruguay."

* * *

The great rolling hills of Brazil flowed into Uruguay, spreading out into vast green prairie. Never had I been in a country so flat. Immediately I missed the giants of Brazil; the absence of those majestic mountains left me feeling exposed, as if one strong gust of wind could lift me up into the heavens. We traveled through the vast expanse until we reached the outer limits of Montevideo in southern Uruguay.

Every building in Montevideo was created with great care. Offices rivaled cathedrals in their architecture. The houses were not the hastily built shacks I was used to; they were painted in bright teals and pinks, lined up tightly next to each other. I was amazed. Montevideo bustled unlike any city I had ever seen. The sounds of people speaking Spanish could be heard as we traversed the streets, making me thankful for the nomadic gauchos that had periodically traveled through my village from Argentina. My stomach gurgled violently as the scent of wood-fired meats floated through the air, mixed with the fresh saltiness of the sea.

José drove our little cart down toward the docks. Pulling to a halt in front of a pink house, he looked up. "This must be it." We went up to the door, but it opened before we knocked. A miniature Anzani stood in front of us. "You're the Garibaldis!" the boy exclaimed.

"Indeed, we are, and who might you be?" José asked.

"Tomaso Anzani." The little boy stared up at us. "You look dirty. Did you have a rough journey? Did you fight bandits?"

"Tomaso, stop asking so many questions and let our guests in!" Anzani came up to the doorway with another small child in his arms. He tousled his son's hair before sending him away.

"That would be my eldest. This little one is Antony, and around here somewhere is Cesare." He waved a hand in the air. "He likes to find a cubby to curl up in with a book. We'll find him again when he's hungry. Speaking of hunger, you must be famished. Come with me."

He led us through their parlor, filled with overstuffed furniture and children's toys, to the kitchen. We sat down at a large wooden table just before Anzani started pulling out every bit of food from their cupboards. "I am sorry it's not much, Luisa has yet to get back from the market." Soon the table was covered with various fruits, cheeses, and sweetmeats. It was more food than I had seen in months.

"I've taken the liberty of securing a new home for you. It's down the street. I know the owner. He just needs to meet you and have you sign some agreements. It won't be much, a bit smaller than this."

I gasped. "That would be lovely. Thank you. Thank you so much." Tears of gratitude stung my eyes. I was not used to such kindness. As I sat at the table listening to José and Anzani talk as if they were old friends, the realization that this was the right decision spread through me. Here, we had a future. We could dare to have the life we had only dreamed about in the rugged wilderness of Brazil.

"Tell me about the Italians," José said, not hiding the smile that grew on his face.

"Most of us are from the north, Genoa specifically, but more are coming in from the south. They'll soon outnumber us."

"Why so many?" I asked.

"The Kingdom of the Two Sicilies, which controls the lower half of the peninsula, is ruled by an absolute monarchy," Anzani explained.

"We had such high hopes for the king when he ascended to the throne," José interjected. "He cut taxes for the poor, gave amnesty to his father's political prisoners. The Carbonari thought this was a monarch who could unite our country. A true leader. Then it all went wrong."

"What happened?" I asked.

"King Ferdinand believes that he has divine right to rule the country. He even backed his sister's usurper in Spain all because she wanted her people to have a constitution," José explained.

"The king has gotten worse," Anzani said. "He's created a special peacekeeping force."

José went rigid. "A peacekeeping force? What for?"

"I've heard there was a protest in Sicily, almost everyone came out for it. The people wanted a constitution. He sent his soldiers in to break it up. You can imagine what violent ends the demonstrators met."

"So that's why there is an influx of Sicilian immigrants," José said, as much to himself as to us.

"Not just to Uruguay, all over the Americas. It's safer for them to take a chance emigrating than to stay in the fatherland. If the peace force doesn't kill them, the outbreak of cholera will."

I blanched at the thought of the disease, which had yet to reach its deadly fingers into South America, though I had heard of it. A disease where you were dying of thirst no matter how much you drank. Where your body tried to expel every last ounce of fluid.

It left people dead within hours. No wonder the Sicilians were seeking safety on foreign shores.

Luisa Anzani floated into the house on a jasmine breeze. She was a tall, stately woman with light brown hair that was twisted up in a simple knot. She set her basket down with a sigh. "The market didn't have any of the fish you like, my love, so I got something else. The fishmonger said it should taste the same." She stopped short. "And I see that we have company." She turned to her husband crossly. "And that you have put them to work. Where are your manners?"

Anzani jumped up from the table, rattling off a string of words in Italian that I had a hard time following. Luisa nodded, looking faintly amused. "Well, if it isn't too much trouble, husband, why don't you take Senhor Garibaldi to settle in while I get to know my new friend Senhora Garibaldi?"

José handed me Menotti as he happily followed Anzani. "Well, now that they are out of the way, let's set about getting to know each other," Luisa said. "You are going to love this city. It's the only place in all of South America that feels like Italy. Frankly, it's no Roma, but really, no place can ever have the feel of that city."

Luisa scooped *mate* into a red gourd as she continued. "People from all over Europe have settled here. When I was walking through the market today, I heard four different languages. Four! Can you believe that? You're just going to love it here. I can tell," she said, sipping her tea with a wink.

I smiled as she passed me the gourd. Montevideo was already feeling like home.

* * *

Later that evening José and I made our way down to our new house, with bellies full of food and a basket of additional goods to get us through the night. The downstairs boasted a parlor and a kitchen with a large worn-out table, while the upstairs held two bedrooms, one of which had a bed. My spirits rose as I let my fingers graze along the wall. I prayed this would be the place where we finally settled.

TWENTY-SEVEN

March 1841

The Italian community thrived in Montevideo. José found employment as a mathematics teacher at a boys' school and I found a new group of women to surround myself with. Every week we and the Anzanis took turns hosting supper at our homes. Our house became the unofficial meeting place for all of our expatriate comrades to gather and find camaraderie with their countrymen.

It was during these evenings that I learned to be an Italian. The women gathered together in the kitchen to cook, and using the local gossip they helped me improve my language skills. As my hands deftly rolled out the dough for spaghetti one evening, Luisa came up behind me, placing her chin on one of my shoulders and her hand on the other. "If I didn't know any better, I would have thought you were born Italian." She kissed my cheek. "You were meant to be one of us." The other women laughed in agreement.

José held court in the parlor, discussing the formation of the first Italian newspaper, *L'Italiano*, in Montevideo. Uruguay valued its free press and the men wanted to capitalize on that by using the newspaper to share their liberal ideals. I chose to stay in the kitchen with the women. In the parlor the men talked, but it was in the kitchen that the important decisions were made.

I watched as the women gossiped and told stories of the fatherland. Moving from the table, I stood in the doorway between my husband's world of soldiers and glory and the world of women. It was then that I realized that this was where I would make the most impact for my husband's cause. Yes, I thrived at his side, but at the end of the day, these women held more sway over their husbands than José ever could. I listened as they talked. These were not passive women who were content to be led around the world by their husbands. They were active heroines of their own stories.

"I wrote to my sister yesterday," one confessed to Luisa. "Her husband's crops are failing, and they raised the taxes yet again." She focused on the rolling pin, putting more pressure on the dough as she spoke. "I told her how different it was here. How we can live off the work that we do. God, I hope she listens."

I went to the woman and placed a hand on her shoulder. "She will." Looking over the faces of the women, I could see that they each looked at me with a sense of awe. José had his soldiers, I had mine. "When you write home to your sisters, your mothers, don't be afraid to tell them what you have here. Jealousy can be a powerful thing. Let them grow envious of your life in Montevideo. Perhaps they can join us or perhaps they can claim liberty for their families in Italy."

The women smiled and began discussing their families and the ways they encouraged them to come here or to rebel against Austria and France. I squeezed the woman's shoulder. "Let me know when your sister makes it to Uruguay."

She smiled. "I will. Thank you."

The next day, while José spent his morning teaching, I tended to our home. It was a relief to be able to put down roots in one location, at least for a little while. If only my mother could see me, happily cleaning a home. She wouldn't believe I was her daughter.

I was quietly laughing to myself, imagining my mother taking in my humble little home, when I heard a knock at our door. Upon opening it, I found a plump middle-aged woman with a kind face and a large smile. She stood in front of me holding a small basket of sweet bread. Her slightly messy black hair was streaked with gray. "Hello, I'm your neighbor Feliciana."

Graciously accepting her gift, I welcomed her into my home and offered to share the little bit of tea we had. Feliciana's eyes followed me as we moved through the house, taking in the threadbare sofa, the wobbly armchair, and the sparse walls. She cooed over Menotti, sleeping on a blanket in the parlor. "They are just cherubs, aren't they?" Following me into the kitchen, she asked, "What brings you to Montevideo?"

"My husband and I are looking to make a fresh start."

"Oh, that's lovely." Feliciana took the liberty of breaking off some of the sweet bread for herself. "Fresh starts are always a fun adventure. Where did you come from?"

"Brazil."

Feliciana choked on her bread. "That's quite a way with such a young child." She looked back to where Menotti slept. "Where in Brazil?"

I paused. "All over, really. But enough about me, I want to hear about you."

At my suggestion, Feliciana delved into her history with abandon. They were natives of Montevideo, she and her husband, Marco. He was a mountain of a man whose shyness made him gentle. They had no children of their own but fostered a boy who worked as an apprentice and slept at their shop. Soon she was telling me which markets were best, when the right time to visit the washing well was, and where to sit at church, "in order to get the perfect view of the altar, of course."

"Of course," I agreed, knowing that I had no plans to step inside the church.

Her kind eyes didn't judge as I told her who my husband really was and about what I had done in Rio Grande do Sul.

"You mean to tell me you fought alongside your husband?" she asked.

"Yes, I wasn't going to let him leave me behind."

"How remarkable," she said in an awed whisper. "How did you meet? What made you want to leave your home? Tell me everything."

I sat across the table from her and began my story as she leaned forward, anxiously waiting to hear everything that I had to tell her.

After that first morning, Dona Feliciana showed up daily with pastries, wanting to hear stories of my adventures. I made us tea as she doted on Menotti, trying fervently to get him to call her *abuela*. I grew to look forward to my mornings with her.

One day, after Dona Feliciana sat down, the steaming gourd of tea looking large in her hands, she asked the one question I wasn't prepared to answer.

"Tell me about your wedding. I haven't heard that story yet."

I slowly turned to her. "Well, that's because there isn't much to tell."

"There has to be something. Was it a beautiful ceremony under the stars? Were you able to get a priest or did one of the generals marry you?"

I sat down opposite her, watching the steam rise from the tea. My heart pounded in my chest as I debated what to say. I had told this woman so much, more than I ever shared with my husband. This secret, that we weren't actually married, was something that weighed on me. Others wouldn't understand, and there was a risk that Feliciana wouldn't either. That she would walk from this house and ruin the good name José had worked so hard to build.

Yet, after everything, she hadn't left. "You see," I began, "the thing is, José and I aren't really married."

Feliciana gasped as she crossed herself. "But you act as if you are."

"Because in our hearts we are."

"But what about in heaven? You are living in sin," she whispered before crossing herself, yet again.

"What could we do? We love each other and there was no one who would give us their approval." Feliciana gave me a look and I felt the need to press my case. I didn't owe her anything, and yet I wanted her to understand. "There was so much danger. We had other things to think about. How could we take time away for something so frivolous when people were dying?"

"But what about your immortal soul?"

"My soul means nothing to me." My finger traced a knot in the wood. Why should I care for my soul when I barely believed in the faith of my childhood? My sins were many and when the time came, I knew I would not be warmly greeted by Saint Peter. But my son...what was going to happen to Menotti?

I wiped my eyes with the side of my hand as I stared into my tea. I didn't want her to see the sudden fear that I felt. I knew she would reject me. I took a deep breath, steadying my trembling hands. "I know I will have to atone for all that I have done; of that I have no doubt. What I care about is my family."

"Anita, what have you done?"

I took a deep breath and finally told her about Manoel. I hadn't uttered his name since we left Laguna. Manoel. The husband I didn't want. The man who was forced on me. I thought I had escaped him in Laguna, but he still haunted me.

Feliciana placed a warm, callused hand over mine. "I am sorry, I didn't mean to upset you, but we have to think about the well-being of your son in both this life and the next."

"We?" I asked.

"Yes, we." Feliciana firmly grasped my hand. Looking at her, I saw her smile at me in a way that made me wish she were my mother. "Leave it to me. I'll sort this all out."

I let the tears flow down my cheeks as I reached out to embrace her.

TWENTY-EIGHT

A couple of days later Feliciana burst through my door, her black hair flying around her face. "I've got the best solution for you! It's the answer to all our problems!" She danced about the room. "We only need to tell the priest that Manoel is dead! It's as easy as that!" She smiled broadly. "Well? What do you think?"

I took a deep breath. "From what I understand, the priest has to see that the person is dead, or I have to have a family member swear that I am allowed to remarry. My family will never do that. After all this time, I doubt they would even speak to me."

Feliciana slowly grinned. "I'll sign as your mother."

"Dona Feliciana, I can't ask you to lie for me. It would be breaking the law."

"Not if I got permission from a priest to do it. He said in order to rectify this situation he will absolve me of my sin." She reached out to me. "I am so sorry, I hope you can forgive me, but I have been talking to Father Lorenzo about your situation."

I pulled away suddenly, feeling defensive. Feliciana pleaded her case all the more. "He is on our side. He thinks you and José need to be married. He said we can find a way around your first marriage."

This was too much. Everything was happening all at once. Feliciana rubbed her hands up and down my arms in an attempt to comfort me. "Father Lorenzo only asks that you meet him for a confession. Nothing has to be decided today, but talk to José. See what he says. Then go talk to the priest."

I gave a short laugh. She didn't know José as well as I did. Convincing him that this was a good idea would not be easy, especially with his views about the church.

That night for dinner I prepared one of the Italian dishes that I had recently learned. Walking through the front door, José set down his satchel. In addition to teaching, he had begun selling goods imported from Italy, primarily tomato paste, which he kept in crates in our parlor. "I sold two whole boxes of paste today. I would have to say that is an accomplishment. Don't you?"

He made his way to Menotti, who giggled, waving his pudgy little arms in front of him. José picked him up in a great swooping motion as the giggles intensified. José kissed my cheek before sitting down at the table with a large smile on his face. Not knowing how to begin, I just blurted out the first sentence that came to mind. "What do you think about getting married?"

He stopped midchew. "I thought we already were."

"Yes, well in our own eyes we are, but not in the eyes of the church."

He dropped his fork. "Anita, we have been over this. The church is a vile and corrupt organization. What they say and do holds no sway over us."

"What about when you die? What will happen to me and your children?"

"Anita, why must you think of such things?" He tried to brush me away. "You shouldn't worry about me dying."

"José, you are always going out to battle. You think nothing of risking your life. Of course I am going to worry about these things."

"I am not fighting a battle now, am I?" He pushed his plate away as Menotti reached a small hand toward it.

"It doesn't mean you won't fight one in the future, and it certainly doesn't mean you won't drop dead in the middle of the street tomorrow!" I put my head in my hands in frustration before looking back up at him. "I am asking you to seriously think about your son's future. What will happen to him in the eyes of the law, if you die?"

"Anita, please."

"In the eyes of the law he and any future children that we have are bastards!" I watched José as a shadow passed across his face.

"For the love of Christ, Anita!" He slammed his fist on the table, making the dishes rattle. "You and Menotti are all I think about! Before I go to sleep at night I think, 'My God, this has been a wonderful dream. I hope I don't wake up from this.' Every morning I think, 'This woman can't still be here by my side in my bed.' And in the hours when I am awake and supposed to be carrying on with my daily life, do you know what I am thinking? Answer me, do you know what I am thinking?"

"No." Menotti began to cry so I took him from José. The scent of José's sandalwood still lingered as I gently bounced my son in my arms, trying to soothe him.

"I am thinking, 'What is Anita doing right now?' and 'I hope Menotti is happy.' So, don't you dare guilt me when you know damn well that you and my son are everything to me."

"I don't doubt your love for us."

"Then why are you making this such an issue?"

"Because if you die leaving us behind, in the eyes of the law I will not be your widow, and Menotti will be entitled to nothing. Your mother, back in Italy, will she accept your bastards?" I raged.

"All I ask is that you think about us. I just want to make sure that if the day comes when we have to live without you, we can. That even if you are gone, you can give your son the best possible future," I said as I held our crying child.

José stared at the table for a long time. "We'll get married. In the church." He pointed a finger at me. "But it will not be a huge affair. I take it you've already figured out how to get this done."

I smiled. "I have."

"Of course you have." He grumbled as he ate. He grabbed a chunk of bread, tearing it off like it was the head of one of his enemies.

The next morning, I made my way to the church to see Father Lorenzo. It was the first time I'd been inside a church since I left Laguna. The sanctuary felt foreign to me with its orange and brown stained-glass windows casting odd shadows over the empty, aging pews. A bald man in black priest's robes stepped out to greet me with a smile that rose up to the rims of the large spectacles making his kind green eyes look like small moons.

"You must be Anita," he said in greeting. "Please follow me, I'll be hearing your confession in my study. Since I already know who you are, there is no need for the formal veil."

His study was stuffed with books. There were multiple rows on the shelves, some slipped in on their sides. Several piles dotted the floor and climbed up the walls, forcing me to navigate around them to get to a chair. He sat down in a weathered brown wingback chair and moved a pile of books from the center of his desk so that he could better see me. "Dona Feliciana told me of your predicament. Can you tell me, have you heard anything at all from your husband?"

"José? I saw him this morning before he left for work."

"No, I mean your first husband, what was his name?" He shuffled through some notes on his desk.

"Manoel. Manoel Duarte, and no, I have not heard from him since he left."

"He left you?"

"He joined the Imperial Brazilian Army. I stayed behind in Laguna."

"You received no letters, no documents from him indicating that he might still be alive?"

I sighed, trying not to grow frustrated. "Manoel didn't know how to read. He could understand his numbers because he was a cobbler, but that was it. There was no need for common people to read where I am from. He was probably happy to get rid of me. I was a terrible wife."

"But you aren't now?"

"I would like to think not."

"During your marriage to Manoel, did you have any children?"

"No, thank God."

Father Lorenzo turned his head to the side. "Was it consummated?"

"Conso-what?"

"Consummated—did you have relations...er...um, sex."

I squirmed. "Yes, we were married and lived as man and wife for three years."

Father Lorenzo nodded his head. "I see, I see." He put his fingers to the bridge of his nose. "Well, the purpose of a marriage is to produce children, children to serve God. You didn't have this with Manoel, however; it would appear that you have more of a Christian marriage with Giuseppe Garibaldi." He took his hand from his face and looked at me. "If you were a man, I would be able to dissolve your first marriage, but as you know I can't."

"If I were a man I would have been allowed to do a great many things, Father."

Father Lorenzo gave me a sad smile. "As you know, your situation is complicated."

"I did what was necessary for my and my child's well-being."

Father Lorenzo held up a hand. "Dona Anita, I am not testing you for sainthood. The Lord knows, none of us, myself included, are worthy of that. From everything that I have been told about you I feel only admiration. You have braved so much, but what I am worried about is making sure that you and your innocent child are taken care of. Tell me, Dona Feliciana has been like a mother to you, has she not?"

"Yes, better than my own mother."

"Good. Well, I have a document signed by Dona Feliciana saying that she is your mother and that you are free to marry. I have taken the liberty of preparing the paperwork necessary to marry you and Don José. However, given that it is Lent and I am too close to the situation, I have asked a friend, Father Pablo, to come. He doesn't know anything about you or your past. All he knows is that he is marrying two people in love."

He handed me a handkerchief to wipe the tears that began to escape. "You have friends, Dona Anita, and we'll make sure you and your family are taken care of."

TWENTY-NINE

April 1841

The entirety of the wedding preparations took us only three weeks. My dress was simple, pale yellow with a tasteful V neckline edged with small ruffles. The bodice came to a point at my waist, which, according to Luisa, made me look taller.

What made me fall in love with the dress was the intricate embroidery of ocean waves just above the hem of the skirt, which Luisa said looked Roman. It cost us a small fortune. It was extravagant, unnecessary, and everything I didn't know that I had always wanted in a piece of clothing.

I looked at Feliciana through the mirror behind me as she dabbed her eyes with a handkerchief. "You are so beautiful!" she exclaimed through her tears, clasping her hands together. "This is what I always envisioned having a daughter would be like. Thank you."

I turned to her, taking her hands in mine. "No. Thank you," I said, beginning to cry as well. Luisa rushed into the room with fresh tears on her cheeks. "Enough of that. No more tears!" She carried a basket filled with small pink flowers and ribbon.

Luisa pulled and twisted my hair up with the bows and flowers, making me feel like a princess. Never in my life had I felt so special. On our way out the door, Luisa gasped. "Oh, I almost forgot!" She grabbed a long box tied with a large white ribbon that sat on my table. "Here," she said, shoving it toward me.

Nestled inside, wrapped in thin paper, rested a delicate lace veil yellowed with age, trimmed with an embroidered leaf pattern that took my breath away. It was so fragile that I was afraid to touch it. Luisa gently placed it over my head, where it lay gracefully. The faint smell of lavender lingered in the lace. "Your 'something borrowed,'" she explained. "I wore it on my wedding day, as did my mother and grandmother."

Tears started to well in my eyes again, but before I could say anything, Luisa stopped me. "The coach is here. If we don't leave now, we'll never get to the church."

The great stone cathedral loomed over us as we exited the carriage. Squinting in the sun, I could barely make out the outline of the statue of San Felipe staring down at us, giving his blessing to those who passed by. Feliciana's husband stood outside waiting for us. When we approached, he looked bashful. "I...I thought since Feliciana was playing your mother that maybe I could walk you down the aisle." He looked up at me, slightly scared. "That's of course if you don't mind."

"I would be honored. Now, let's get me married."

My heart skipped a beat and my breath caught in my throat when I saw José standing at the altar. He fidgeted with his suit, moving from one foot to the other. But when he turned to look at me all nervousness stopped. A peace fell over him as he watched me walk slowly up the aisle. A smile spread across his face as his shoulders relaxed. José stilled as his eyes locked with mine. His spine straightened, making him look taller as I approached.

Had it only been two years since I met him? It felt like a lifetime ago that I stumbled into Hector and Manuela's parlor. So much had happened. So much lost. So much gained. Yet here we were, just as in love, tied together by Destiny and now by God. I chose José Garibaldi and I would continue to choose him until my dying day, no matter where he took me.

THIRTY

May 1841

Montevideo stood on the precipice of war. Sitting around the table at the Anzanis' house, we gleaned as much information as we could about this new threat.

"What do you know of Uruguayan history?" Anzani asked.

"I know Uruguay is the reluctant middle child forever pitted between Brazil and Argentina," José said as he reached for the gourd of tea. "For a long time, no one wanted to colonize the region. It was a patch of barren land used to keep Portugal and Spain from warring."

"Yes, but the gauchos began to settle here, didn't they?" I asked, taking the seat next to my husband. "I remember my father saying that he thought about moving here, but then he met my mother and stayed in Brazil."

"Women change everything." José planted a kiss on my temple. "And yes, the gauchos eventually settled the land."

Luisa set a plate of cold meats and fruit on the table. "This isn't the first time that Argentina has had its eyes on Uruguay."

"God help us, if it weren't for the Treinta y Tres, we would have been under Argentine rule a long time ago," Anzani remarked before taking a piece of meat for himself.

"Who were the Treinta y Tres?"

"The Treinta y Tres were thirty-three men who formed an army to expel Argentina from Uruguay," Anzani said. "Our last president, Fructuoso Rivera, was a member. Too bad he resigned after his presidential term was over. I would rather have him than Manuel Oribe. At least with Rivera we would not be bending for Rosas and Argentina."

"Oribe is an ignorant man who takes every offense as a personal strike. Men like him, who have a weakness of character, are drawn to stronger men regardless of their motives," José added, using the *bombilla* to stir his tea. "Now we are forced to play nice with Manuel Rosas and his corrupt Argentine bureaucracy."

The danger was further pressed upon me the following week as our Italian family gathered together. I sat at the table chopping herbs as the women gossiped, and before long Argentina became the subject of discussion.

"It doesn't bode well for Oribe to be making alliances with Rosas," one of the women said, shaking her head over the pot of rice that she was stirring.

"We're safer if we make an alliance with the *homem do saco*." A number of women gasped and crossed themselves at the name of the mythical sack man who stole children.

"I don't understand. What makes Rosas so evil?" Immediately, I was sorry that I had asked. All of the women turned and stared at me as I shrank with embarrassment until Luisa's laughter, tinkling like a bell, filled the kitchen. The rest of the room broke into laughter along with her.

"My dear Anita, let me tell you a story. Once upon a time," Luisa began, "there was a beautiful girl by the name of Camilla. She came from a prominent family and was destined for a fortuitous marriage."

"To one of Rosas's cousins, wasn't it?" someone asked.

"No, his nephew."

"Ahem, ladies. May I continue?" They all quieted as Luisa began to talk again. "However, Camilla was in love with another. A meek and handsome young priest, with eyes like the sea and a face so handsome that women wept over his devotion to Christ. However, the priest could not resist the beautiful Camilla. It was a secret love affair until our young Camilla found that she was with child. It was then that the priest and Camilla stole away."

Luisa moved through the kitchen with the grace of a dancer. All our eyes were locked on her as she wove her story. "Our ill-fated couple found their way to another village. They thought they had run far enough away. They thought the ruse they invented, a young married couple looking to make a fresh start, was convincing. But what they forgot was, once you cross Juan Manuel de Rosas, you can never get far enough away.

"Rosas and his army found them," Luisa continued, "and our couple was brought back to Buenos Aires. There was no trial because in Argentina there is only one sentence when you break the law…death." Luisa paused for effect as everyone in the room crossed themselves. "First, they put the young priest in front of the firing squad, so that Camilla was forced to watch her lover die. Then it was her turn, but as she was tied up and the guns were raised, poised to fire, the archbishop called out for the soldiers to stop. 'What about the baby?' he protested. 'Surely Senhor Rosas could have sympathy for the child.' Rosas considered this, for after all he was a good Catholic. 'Baptize the womb!' he ordered. Camilla's belly was quickly baptized before the firing squad killed her."

I gasped.

"This is why, my dear Anita, we are all so nervous about our new president's best friend," Luisa said.

That night I lay in bed, tossing and turning. Every time my eyes closed the vision of a pregnant Camilla haunted me.

"*Tesoro mio*, what troubles you?" José turned on his side, his head resting in the palm of his hand.

"Is Rosas as awful as they say he is?"

José's face darkened as he focused on a spot somewhere around my collarbone. "He is worse." He met my eyes. "What stories were the women discussing in the kitchen?"

"We were talking about the priest and his lover, Camilla."

"Oh, that is a good one but alas, not my favorite." He rolled over on his back and closed his eyes.

"Which story is your favorite?"

"You can't sleep, and you want me to tell you a story that will give you nightmares?" The eye that he opened sparkled with mischief.

"Yes. I want to know," I said, playfully hitting his shoulder.

"Right, well, the one that always stuck with me more than any other is the ritual he has when he kills his rivals. He cuts off their heads and plays *fútbol* with them." He pulled me toward him.

"No!"

"You told me you wanted a story," he said, touching his forehead to mine, a laugh escaping his lips.

"I know, but good God, he is an awful man."

José wrapped his arms around me, pulling me in closer to him. I nestled my head in the soft space between his shoulder and neck. "Why would Oribe align himself with such a monster?"

José took a deep breath. "I do not know, my love."

I looked up at my husband. "What's going to happen now?"

"You let me protect you from the demons." His arms tightened around me as I drifted off into sleep.

* * *

Two days later José rushed through the door, returning home earlier than normal while I washed up from my and Menotti's lunch. He quickly moved around the house, checking the windows. "José, what is it? What's wrong?"

"Lock the doors."

"What are you talking about?" I said, one of my eyebrows rising to question my peculiar husband.

"I said lock the doors. We are not leaving this house until I say so."

"José, now you are just being ridiculous."

"Rivera, the former president, is planning a coup. It's happening tomorrow." He walked over to Menotti, picking him up, holding him close.

I dropped the plate I was holding, large shards scattering across the floor. "Are you sure? Where did you hear this?"

"I have my sources. They've been planning it. Rivera and his men are preparing to move in on the government. They've had enough of Oribe's alliances with Argentina."

"Are you going to be involved when it happens?"

"No," José said, looking back at me. "I can't abandon my family."

As José had instructed us to, we stayed in the next day and the day after that. José cautiously ventured out to see what had become of the coup while I spent another day at home. Later that day José came home with fresh bread, a smile on his face, and a box of pastries under one arm.

"Well, we have avoided the war for now," he said, setting the box on the table and picking up Menotti, who was already obsessed with what his father was carrying. "Oribe was ousted, it was all fairly peaceful. Rivera showed up with his army and escorted Oribe out of the capital." He broke apart some pastry and fed it to Menotti, whose eyes shone with joy at the flavor.

"Mo! Mo!" he proceeded to call out to his father before holding his mouth open like a baby bird.

"They say that Oribe ran off to Argentina to take shelter with Rosas," José said as he placed more food in our son's mouth.

"You're going to spoil his supper," I scolded.

José passed the box to me. "Tonight, we celebrate the little victories. Supper can be spoiled this one time, can't it?"

Thoughts turned over in my mind as I slowly chewed. "Why would anyone want to take shelter with Rosas?"

"Because Rosas is powerful. He will back Oribe up when he is ready to attack. After Oribe licks his wounds, of course. It doesn't take a fool to know that any government set up by Oribe will just be a puppet government for Rosas."

"There's going to be a war, isn't there?"

"I'd bet money on it," José said.

I sighed as I watched my husband and son together. My heart constricted with worry. Once more we would go to war.

THIRTY-ONE

July 1841

As José had predicted, war came to Montevideo. Two months after being ousted from the Uruguayan government Oribe returned with an army sponsored by Rosas. "They say Oribe is advancing in the north," José said, pushing his stew around in his bowl. "It's foolish to leave now, with rainy season on the way."

"Who are they going to send to meet him?" I asked, wrapping my shawl tighter around my shoulders as I watched the brisk wind rustle the trees through the window.

José shrugged. "I wouldn't know. I'm not involved with the military anymore. They don't tell me these things." He abruptly turned his attention to Menotti, letting the subject of the war die.

Days later, José became increasingly involved with the household as he sought out distractions from Uruguay's politics. As we sat down for supper one evening a knock on the door echoed through the house. I looked at José curiously before going to open it. On a cold winter day such as this, no one was leaving their warm hearths to visit their neighbors.

At the door was a man who looked like his clothes hadn't been washed in days. A shadow of fine bristles spread across his face. He held a worn-out hat in his hands. "Pardon me, senhora, but I am looking for a rat bastard with garlic breath by the name of Giuseppe."

I stared at him, not knowing what to make of this supposed guest. "Miguel Contreras?" I heard José ask as he approached from the other room. "Why, you pockmarked bull calf!" José embraced the stranger in a bear hug. "What are you doing in South America?"

Miguel shrugged. "I've been floating around here and there."

José, realizing I was still there, turned to me. "Let me introduce you to my wife, Anita. Anita, this is an old friend of mine, Miguel Contreras."

"I gathered that," I said, looking him over, trying not to grimace. "Will you be staying for dinner?"

"I could never turn down a free meal, thank you," he said with a small bow.

The visitor looked around our house as he followed us to the kitchen. "I still can't believe that Giuseppe Garibaldi is a married man."

"And a father," José added.

"Well, I hope that your child has all your worst qualities, unless it's a girl. Then I hope for everyone's sake she looks like her mother." Contreras winked at me.

"We have a boy. His name is Menotti," José said, beaming with pride.

"I'm sure it won't be long before he's plundering the Mediterranean and instigating mutinies, just like his father."

"He's going to need to learn to walk first," I said, setting the plates on the table.

José threw his head back and let out a full laugh. "Miguel and I go way back. He was my shipmate when I sailed out of Marseille."

"And then I allowed your husband to rope me into helping him oust a very annoying French captain."

"I'm sure his reasons were most noble," I teased.

"Naturally," Miguel said, raising a flask that he produced from his coat. "To the man who corrupted me! May I never be considered an angel again."

"What brings you to my door?" José asked the question that I had been wondering as well.

"I've been heading up the resistance to Rosas. Up until recently he has had his eye on Brazil. However, Uruguay seems to be the easier pearl to retrieve. Someone needs to keep that monster in check." He stifled a burp. "When I heard about recent events, I couldn't help but get involved. Argentina has its eyes set on Uruguay. If we don't stop them, they'll take over the whole continent."

"I agree, but from what I've seen of the Uruguayan military, we should be able to hold off the Argentine army," José said as he clutched the metal straw in his teeth.

"Until the coffers run dry." Miguel's fork scraped the plate, making me wince in irritation.

"Well, thankfully that won't happen anytime soon," José remarked.

"I wouldn't count on that."

"What do you mean by that?" José asked.

"You didn't hear?" Miguel looked up, stunned.

"No. What's happened?"

"The treasury is empty. Oribe took it all."

José dropped his fork. "How? How can that be? I've sat in on government meetings, I've heard the reports. That's impossible!" José's voice trailed off. "Oribe had his son-in-law doing the finances." José and I shared a look of realization. This wasn't good. "They trusted him," he said to no one in particular. "I thought if they trusted him so much then maybe I should too."

"You ignored your intuition," I whispered.

"This is bigger than Uruguay." Miguel cleared his throat. "Argentina and France signed a treaty."

José leaned forward in his seat. "Why would France align themselves with a monster like Rosas?"

"Trade. Why else?" Miguel said. "A few years back a few French citizens got caught selling Argentinian cartography to Bolivia. The French ambassador demanded their release, which resulted in Rosas closing the French embassy." Miguel took a big swig from his flask. "The French, being the proud people they are, decided to raise the stakes and blocked the port of Buenos Aires until their people were released from prison. It's been two years and they are just now allowing ships through."

"Well, now we know why Argentina wants to meddle in Uruguay," I said. "They want our coastline."

"Rosas won't stop until he controls all of South America," José said.

"José, we need you, my friend. We need you to organize the Italians. We want to create a legion comprised solely of our Italian brethren. There are so many of us from the old country here, and we want to fight for our adopted home, but we can't do it without you."

José studied his friend for a while before speaking up. "The people will need to become their own champions. I am a mathematics teacher now."

"Please, you can't tell me that you are happy playing house." Miguel looked to me as I bounced Menotti on my hip. "I am sorry, I mean no offense." He looked back to José. "I know you. I know you thirst for adventure. You can't sit back and let history happen in front of you."

"I am sorry, Miguel; my days of marauding are behind me. I have a family to take care of." He poured more hot water into his *mate* gourd, trying his best not to look Miguel in the eye.

Miguel's sharp eyes narrowed on my husband. "Well, I see I was wrong. I will not waste any more of your time." Miguel bowed to me. "Senhora." He placed his hat on his head and left.

I set Menotti in the parlor to play before I began clearing the plates. José continued to sit at the table. "You don't have to use your family as an excuse, you know."

"It's not an excuse."

"Isn't it? All you're doing is shifting the blame from one thing to another while I get the reputation of being the wife who holds her husband back. If you don't want to join the military, say you don't want to join. You don't owe anyone an excuse."

"And what, dear wife, do you think is the reason why I don't want to join the military?"

"You lost a lot in Rio Grande do Sul; we both did. It's only natural to be hesitant to get involved in another conflict."

José sighed deeply. "I guess you know me better than I know myself." He kissed my cheek. "I'm going up to bed."

"José..."

He waved a hand at me in dismissal. "I have a headache. I'll see you in bed." And with that he disappeared up the stairs.

Later, I went into the darkened bedroom. José lay on his side, his back to me. I crawled into bed next to him, curling up against his back. I could feel his breath rise and sink in a rigid rhythm.

"You have sacrificed more than anyone dare ask," I whispered into his back. My fingers ran along the crisscross scars, the remnants of a long-ago punishment. "There is no shame in not wanting to give any more."

His breath paused for a moment before beginning again. When he didn't say anything I ventured further. "Know that your family will be all right no matter what you end up doing."

For a moment I thought he might actually be asleep, but then he grabbed my hand and held it to his heart. It was in this way we fell asleep.

* * *

A few days later, as the sun set, José was playing with Menotti. I watched as they built grand towers that rivaled our table. As we sat enjoying our time together, a number of our Italian comrades showed up at our door.

"We have a problem," Anzani said, supporting a man twice his size. The men who followed him through the door had bloodied faces with bluish-purple bruises seeping through. As they began to tell the story half in Spanish and half in Italian, I grabbed my medical kit and moved about the men, bandaging wounds.

Anzani paced, his arms tightly crossed. "Tell him," he growled.

"We were at the pub when a large group of drunken Frenchmen came in," one of the men ventured. His lower lip was swollen and split open.

"Well, that was your first problem," José said, surveying the room. "Spending your evenings in pubs leads to things like this."

"The Frenchmen bragged about how they were the best military and the Americas should feel blessed to have them here. If it weren't for them the continent would plunge into chaos," another comrade added.

I went rigid. José froze, looking to Anzani. France had caused enough damage to Italy. They claimed to be supporters of Italian unification when the public's eyes were on them. However, everyone knew that Louis-Philippe was the patron of the Papal Army. Anything the pope requested; France provided. They were no one's savior.

"Tell him what happened next," Anzani added.

"They insulted us. They said we were cowards."

"Just because a group of drunken Frenchmen call us cowards is not a reason to fight," José scolded.

"They insulted you, José," Anzani interjected. "Our people got into a pub brawl because they felt the need to defend your honor."

"They said you were the biggest coward of us all," a young comrade interjected. "They said the reason we lost the Ragamuffin War was because you couldn't even save toy ships."

José's eyes became very focused on the block that he held in his hand. A deep red blush creeped up his neck.

My patient flinched, and I realized I was tying his bandage too tightly. I apologized, my cheeks growing hot at my beginner's mistake. I couldn't help but be distracted. A loud, boisterous José was not afraid to let you know what he thought; you knew exactly where you stood. But a quiet, contemplative José? There was no telling what you were in for.

Anzani kneeled next to him. "We need you."

I stopped tending to the men and watched my husband. A hush fell over the room. José continued to train his eyes on the block, turning it over in his hands.

Then he glanced up at me. He gave me the same look that he gave when he was about to apologize. I returned a curt nod before he turned back to the men staring at him, letting his eyes scan each and every one of their faces. He pushed his shoulders back and straightened. His chin rose as he transformed from my José to Captain Giuseppe Garibaldi.

"We are here in South America because the European powers have made it unsafe to stay in our own country. They have taken almost everything. I say 'almost' because they have yet to take our pride. Our pride in ourselves and our pride as Italians." He looked around the room. "I don't know about you, but as for me, I would sail the world twice over to challenge anyone who attempted to steal my pride." He got up from his seat on the floor. "We shall see to it these Frenchmen never speak ill of an Italian again."

* * *

José stood by the door offering kind words to each man as he exited, keeping vigil as they disappeared into the night. "I'm going to have to play the politician again," he said to no one in particular.

"I know." I walked up behind him, slipping an arm around his waist, burying my face in his back. The smell of sandalwood engulfed me, bringing me to safety. Bringing me to him.

"It's unfortunate. I was getting used to the quiet life." He gripped my wrist, holding me closer.

"We're not quiet life people." I laughed into his back. "We were bound to tire of it."

José chuckled as he closed the door on the outside world.

THIRTY-TWO

I stood by my stove talking to Anzani about his new baby boy, named Giuseppe Antonio Cingolani Anzani. I was more interested than normal in the details of the baby, as talking about them gave me an excuse to ignore Miguel, who sat at my table sighing and tracing a knot in the wood with his finger.

"I have never had a baby sleep so little." Anzani yawned. "Just when I think we might get a few hours of sleep he wakes us up again. I swear the little *bastardo* does it on purpose."

"How are the other boys handling it?" I looked out of the corner of my eye to spy Miguel frowning, the crease between his eyebrows growing tighter.

"Tomaso has been a godsend. Anything Luisa needs, he takes care of. The boys really look up to him."

José rushed into the house. He was taking more meetings with government officials, and they kept him busy at all hours of the day and night. Large bags hung under his eyes.

After refilling Anzani's mug with tea, I took a cup for myself and sat down.

Immediately Miguel looked up at me. "This is a business matter." He turned to José and Anzani for support, but Anzani intently watched his feet as an awkward silence fell over the room.

José cleared his throat and looked Miguel directly in the eye. "Anita gets to sit in on any meeting of mine that she likes."

Miguel leaned toward him. "But she's your wife."

José shrugged and met Miguel's eyes. "That just means I am going to tell her everything anyway."

"Clearly you've never heard about her exploits in the Ragamuffin War," Anzani interjected with a roguish grin.

José frowned. "We have more serious matters to discuss. I've learned some unfortunate news about the navy. It's apparently become a burden of the local municipalities to purchase their own ships."

"That means if Montevideo wants a naval defense it would have to come up with its own money to have one? And the same goes for every other city?" Anzani asked.

"Are they mad?" Miguel asked.

"No money," José said with a sigh. "By diverting the burden to the local regions, they can also divert the blame should anything go wrong." When Anzani and Miguel opened their mouths to protest, José raised a hand. "I know, I know, something will surely go wrong."

"Why not take money from something else?" I said, getting up for more hot water to refill the tea. "I'm sure the politicians have their pockets lined with gold."

"Well, good luck convincing them to part with it," Miguel added as he poured something from a flask into his cup.

"Which politician had the bright idea of making the navy a burden of the municipality?" I asked.

"Enrique Vidal," José said. A longtime politician, he always seemed to surface when the timing was most opportune for him.

Miguel swallowed a large swig of tea before responding, "Of course he did. Vidal cries fiscal responsibility in the streets while he lives the life of luxury at home."

Anzani nodded. "All we need to do is show them that Garibaldi can put together a group of sailors and make a profitable navy. If it doesn't convince the federal government, we can at least have some protection for Montevideo."

* * *

Over the course of the next few weeks José came home tired and crankier than Menotti just before a nap. The government was fighting within itself. A number of the long-term politicians wanted to do things the way they had always done them.

José tried as best he could to walk a thin line of encouraging change without being too radical. He would have been successful in his endeavors had it not been for Vidal. Vidal was the keeper of the treasury and he didn't want the sins of his predecessor to be repeated. Or so he said.

José held his head in his hands while he sat at the table as I cooked. "Vidal won't fund anything. I barely got him to agree to one boat. One boat! Tell me how I'm supposed to sail a navy with one boat?"

"I don't know, my love," I said, setting his dinner down in front of him.

He pushed the food around on his plate. "Vidal says he's saving money for the good of Uruguay, but I think he's only saving money until he has enough to live like a king in Europe."

I had been doing everything that I could to make his time at home peaceful. I listened patiently as he frequently complained about the current state of affairs. I made sure Menotti was as happy as he could be, moving his naps to the later part of the afternoon so that he was fresh and pleasant for his father. The next evening José came up behind me while I was cooking, startling me as he wrapped his arms around my waist. He kissed my neck tenderly before letting his chin rest on my shoulder.

"What put you in such a good mood?"

"Nothing. I wanted to show my appreciation. I know I haven't been the most pleasant person to live with lately." I let myself be pulled along as José swayed.

"We put up with a lot from those we love." I laughed out loud as José blew into my neck playfully.

That evening I watched as José played on the floor with Menotti. He even put his son to bed. Later in the evening I found myself draped over José in our bed, breathless after our lovemaking. I felt cocooned in his embrace. José gently stroked my arm as we listened to the sounds of Montevideo outside our window.

"The government gave me my first assignment. They are sending me on a delivery run."

My fingers traced his ribs. "Where?"

"Corrientes."

I sat upright. "Corrientes! It's surrounded by Argentinian forces. The province is already lost."

"I have to prove how desperately Uruguay needs a functional navy."

"You have nothing to prove. This is suicide!" I moved to slap José's chest, but he grabbed my arm, pulling it to his lips.

"It's only suicide if I let them catch me."

"You are voluntarily putting yourself in harm's way."

He pulled me to him by my arm. "*Tesoro mio*, I have been in tighter situations than this," he said before kissing me.

It was still dark when I awoke. For a moment I felt disoriented. I stretched out, realizing José was no longer in bed next to me. Sitting up, I scanned the dark room, listening, but there was no one. I checked in on Menotti, who reminded me of a miniature man in the way that he slept with his blanket kicked off and wadded between his knees.

I cautiously padded downstairs and into the kitchen. The moon shone through the windows, casting odd shadows across the table. It was then that I spotted the note. The little intimidating piece of paper that lay on the table.

I have sailed for Corrientes. I will return to you, tesoro mio.

—José

THIRTY-THREE

SEPTEMBER 1841

The eerie quiet of the house without my husband was unsettling. I regularly took refuge with Luisa, who was left to manage the Anzani brood while Francesco sailed with José.

Taking advantage of the warm spring sun, we brought the children outside to tire themselves out. I watched Menotti play with the other boys, thinking about the duty I had to keep our son safe so that he could grow into a strong man worthy of his father.

"I don't know what I did to anger God so much," Luisa said over the sounds of her fussy baby. "Not only did I not get my daughter, I got a willful child who hates everything. How can he be so stubborn? He can't even talk yet!"

"At least you didn't have an ugly baby."

Luisa held her son out from her to admire him. "If there is one thing Francesco and I are good at, it's making handsome, strong-willed children." She made a tsking sound. "Cesare, put that thing down, Lord knows where it's been!" Cesare's smile fell as he flung away the large worm he had been tormenting the other boys with.

Luisa scolded Cesare in Italian, then turned back to me. "Go on, read the article."

Luisa had been teaching me to read by following the articles in the newspaper about our husbands. Each day we met I grew a little stronger as we gleaned the only information we could on their well-being.

After a two-day battle with the Argentinian flagship, the Rivera *has been sunk.*

My mouth went dry and Luisa froze in place, in the middle of patting little Giuseppe. I coughed, clearing my throat, and continued on.

Captained by Senhor Garibaldi, the Rivera *was attempting to bring much-needed supplies to the people of Corrientes.*

Luisa crossed herself.

The men are believed to be dead since the wreckage is so extensive. Argentina has yet to inform Uruguayan officials of any prisoners.

I let the newspaper fall into my lap.

Luisa stared ahead at her children. "Our husbands aren't dead."

"We would feel it." I'd been told José was dead before. I didn't believe it then and I certainly didn't believe it now. I thought back to that cold day in Brazil when Moringue tried to tell me my husband was dead. There wasn't any wailing, as my mother had done for my father. I simply marched on, knowing there was no way for me to stop. I had always imagined that if José was truly dead, I would feel it with every fiber of my being.

"When I was pregnant with Tomaso, Francesco was shot. The

bullet went through his back, lodging itself in one of his lungs." Luisa looked down at the baby, who had finally started to settle, stroking his little cheek. I could see tears welling up in her eyes. "The doctors told me then that my husband would die, but I didn't believe them. I made Francesco promise me he would live long enough to see Tomaso become a man." She watched Tomaso as he played with the other boys. "Our husbands will return."

* * *

It was early in the morning, before the sun rose, when I woke from a dream that felt like a memory. I was back on our ship in the battle for Laguna. I could feel the ship shudder from the cannon fire. The faint smell of gunpowder filled my nose.

I bolted awake when I heard the booming cannon and realized that it was not a dream. My heart pounded as I took in my surroundings. I felt the firmness of my bed. The moonlight cast odd shadows over my floor and armoire. The boom of the cannon rattled the house. I threw off the covers and ran for Menotti. We rushed out the door, meeting Feliciana on the front steps.

"What's happening?" Feliciana asked, her golden-brown eyes wild with terror. Cannon fire boomed again in the distance.

"The city is under siege. We have to get Luisa and the children."

Luisa was already pushing her sleepy children out the door as we approached. "Are you going to the church?" she asked, slightly out of breath.

"Yes!" The church was a large stone structure in the center of the city. It had withstood every storm and war that the people of Montevideo could remember.

The cannon fire echoed like thunder in the air around us. Guided by moonlight, we ran as fast as we could in the warm air, pulling our frightened children along behind us. Others were now waking, rushing from their homes to seek the sanctuary of the church.

Father Lorenzo and the nuns were handing out blankets and steaming cups of tea as we walked into the church. The smell of incense drifted through the air, mixed with the scent of unwashed bodies as more than a hundred women and children staked out miniature camps. Every able-bodied man was fighting with the central Uruguayan army in defense of our country, leaving the women of Montevideo to fend for themselves. The flashes of light from the distant ships lit up the night sky, casting an orange and red glow through the stained-glass windows of saints praying over us. My eyes scanned the high white marble arches above. Cathedrals like this were intended to last when everything else had turned to dust.

Father Lorenzo greeted us as we approached him. "We are doing all that we can to make everyone comfortable, but I'm afraid that we can't meet everyone's needs. Morning is going to come soon and with it, hungry bellies. I am not Christ; I cannot perform miracles." We steadied ourselves as another great boom rocked the ground on which we stood.

"Do you know if anything is being done to fortify the city? Surely we must have some defense?" I swept my hair into a loose knot. I needed to know what the plan was to keep everyone safe.

Father Lorenzo shook his head. "The vast majority of Uruguay's men are fighting to the west; they left a small garrison to defend the city. But if Argentina is here now, then it means they broke through our front line." He watched the people filing in. "Rosas has had his eyes on our port for a long time. It looks like he may finally get his hands on it." Though Rosas had a treaty with France regarding the Buenos Aires port, he still had to tolerate them meddling in his affairs. If he took Montevideo, he would have a brand-new port, free from the long arms of France.

I looked around; most of the people were huddled together, dirty, crying, and visibly scared. I didn't need Destiny to send me any omens to know that my place was here with these people. I stood up on a pew and called out, "Everyone, I need your attention. We need to work together to save our city."

"We aren't soldiers!" a woman called from the back of the room. She looked immaculate, like she had arrived on a social visit rather than running for her life from cannons. I stood taller and pressed on.

"No, we are not, and that's what makes us an asset. We don't need soldiers to protect us; by working together we can manage to accomplish the work of ten armies." I looked around the room at all of the dirty, tear-streaked faces that were staring up at me. "We will go out in teams of six, four groups at a time. We'll work together to fortify the city."

Father Lorenzo stepped up beside me. "Montevideo used to be surrounded by a wall. It was torn down when the English invaded in 1807, but we could build on those ruins."

I nodded. "You'll need to grab the debris; boards, timber, whatever you can to create walls that they can't get through. We are also going to need supplies. From our homes and from our neighbors you will need to gather food, blankets, anything we can use to make our time here more comfortable. Those that aren't outside will watch the children."

A small woman with light hair shot her fist in the air. "That's ridiculous! We can't do that much work!"

"Then you can take the first childcare watch!"

I got down. "Luisa, you take a team with you. Feliciana, can you take the first childcare watch, as well?"

"Of course," she said, gladly taking Giuseppe off Luisa's hands.

Amid the smoke we fanned out into the broken city. Two groups focused their search on blankets and food to bring back to the church, first from their homes and then from the homes of their friends. The other two groups focused on building up the battlements. We ventured as close to shore as we dared, pulling together debris, fitting it into a wall.

Meanwhile, the cannons exploded around us. The all-too-familiar smell of gunpowder filled my nose. Some of the women jumped at the sound of the cannon fire as the ground shook around us. But I kept moving, feeling more alive than I had in ages.

"Move forward!" I called out over the chaos. These women had an incredible amount of strength, they just needed to use it.

* * *

After working for another hour, we headed back to the church, our arms loaded with as many blankets and as much food as we could carry. When we reached the church, we handed out the supplies we had gathered. It had only been a few hours, but we were already functioning like one of José's regiments.

Without warning, I felt the room tilt as a wave of nausea washed over me. I grabbed the back of a pew to keep from falling as my knees buckled. Luisa grabbed hold of my other elbow, looking on with growing concern.

"How far along are you?"

I thought for a moment. "No, I can't, I . . . " But I hadn't had my courses since before José left . . . and that was well over two months ago. Realization dawned: It was indeed possible.

Luisa steadied me as she brought me over to a corner with a thick blue blanket. "Sit, I'm going to get you some food."

"No, Luisa, I'm not hungry."

"Don't be silly," she said. "You need it just as much as they do. I'll tend to Menotti and the children until your next shift."

I curled up in my corner, turning from side to side, trying to find a way to get comfortable as I contemplated the possibilities of having a new child. My mind raced; there was still no word from José. I looked around the church as the women held on to their children in an attempt to soothe them. Menotti toddled behind Luisa's brood while they hoarded whatever pillows and blankets they could get their hands on. Periodically I would hear giggles coming from their little tent, making me smile. My eyes rose to the crucifix that hung over the altar. We needed to make it through the attack, if not for our sake then for the sake of our children.

We continued to work in our shifts throughout the next day as rain poured down on us, and well into the humid night. Smoke and ash clung to the raindrops, soaking us with dirty water. The battlements weren't much, but they would at least slow down the Argentinian army. We were our own disciplined army.

A few days later reinforcements arrived to lift the siege, releasing us from our duty to save the city.

"Who knew our women could be so brave?" one of the soldiers mumbled as they surveyed the church.

"And resourceful," another responded.

I smiled to myself as I gathered Menotti and made my way home.

Three days later I rose early to go to the central military offices to collect our rations. A thick cloud of depression hung in the stale air. No one smiled; they kept to themselves as they shuffled through the once vibrant streets. I stopped short as I made it to the ration line.

Women and young children wrapped out the door and around the corner. I gripped Menotti's hand to keep him from running away as we waited. The only difference between the officers' wives and enlisted soldiers' wives in the line was the color of the ration cards. Red stood for enlisted, green was for officers. I hid mine in my pocket, feeling a stab of guilt, knowing that I would get more food than many of those around me.

My morning sickness grew far worse than anything I had experienced with Menotti. My stomach churned as we slowly made progress toward our end goal. Menotti pulled at my hand that gripped his arm as his restlessness grew. A commanding officer stood at the front of the line, inspecting the ration cards.

My turn came, and I stood in front of the tall officer, who looked down his nose at me. "Name."

"Garibaldi," I said, handing over my card.

He handed the card back.

"Bread, oil, and salt? What am I supposed to do with this?" I questioned the meager supplies slapped down in front of me.

"That's not my concern."

"This isn't enough to feed my family. My husband is an officer, I'm supposed to be getting officer's rations."

"Those are officer's rations."

I stared at him in disbelief. "If these are the officers' rations, then what are the soldiers' rations?"

He looked at me, for the first time showing empathy. "You don't want to know."

I hid my food in my basket and made my way back through the town center. Menotti escaped my grasp and ran to a shop nearby. I scooped him up just before his little hands clasped the persimmons at the bottom of a beautiful pile, moments before he had the chance to send them scattering across the ground. I held him close, looking at the food longingly. How was I supposed to feed my son on only bread and olive oil? How was I going to feed myself?

Passing the Anzanis' house, I suddenly felt the desire to see a friend, even if it was just for a quick visit. The children were playing outside while Luisa put together a salad of stale bread, olive oil, and scraps of wilted vegetables.

"I see you got your rations as well."

Luisa huffed. "At least I can put together a decent *panzanella*."

I laughed as we brought the food into the backyard. Picking at my plate, I took in the garden, lined by the backs of at least six houses. "How many of the families here have husbands fighting?"

Luisa thought for a moment. "Most of them, I believe. Everyone is struggling like we are."

I kicked at the grass. "What do you think about starting our own gardens? I am sure we can trade for seed or something. Maybe we could get the other families together. It probably wouldn't be enough to fully feed us, but at least we wouldn't starve."

Luisa smiled. "I like that. Whatever we put in we can get out of it."

The other wives happily took to the idea. Over the next several days we gathered every plant and seed we could find, filling two shared gardens with vegetables and fruits.

THIRTY-FOUR

November 1841

It had been months since I'd heard anything from José and his men. Luisa and I took turns visiting the military offices to see if they had anything sent to them by messenger about our husbands. But more often than not we were shooed away for being a nuisance. I tried to push away any worries I might have about the fate of my husband and his men as I weeded our little garden. My pregnant belly was beginning to take shape. It wouldn't be long before I couldn't get down on my knees to garden. Menotti kneeled beside me, marveling at every bug and leaf. A true Italian, he loved tomatoes. Picking the small ones, he held them in his cheeks before slowly eating them. If I let my child survive on tomatoes alone, he would. As we gardened, we sang his favorite nursery rhyme together:

Minhoca, minhoca
Me dá uma beijoca
Não dou, não dou

It wasn't a very pleasant rhyme, having to do with kissing worms, but Menotti loved it because he had a fascination with the earthworms of our garden. As we were singing, we heard bright and clear:

Minhoca, minhoca
Você é mesmo louco

Menotti and I turned to see José standing in the garden before us in his tattered clothes, covered in dirt.

He was alive.

Menotti ran giggling to his father, who picked him up into the air, then held him close. José set Menotti down as I approached him, a little more cautiously. I still couldn't believe it was my husband standing before me, smiling with pure joy.

Gray clouds shifted, revealing bright November sun, warming my face as I looked up at my husband. José kissed me with a passion I hadn't felt since we were young in Laguna. He held me close, breathing the scent of my hair deeply into his lungs. I could have stayed in his embrace for eternity.

* * *

After José had the opportunity to wash and put on fresh clothing, we sat in the parlor, José playing with Menotti. José helped him pass blocks from one pile to another while I was in the nearby armchair, watching them interact. José was always so warm with our son. Always tender and loving. Somehow along the way in my crazy life I got lucky to have such a wonderful husband.

"I have only been gone for just over four months. How could he have grown so much?" he asked with wonder as he gladly received a block handed to him by our son.

"That's what children do. They grow."

José grabbed Menotti around the waist, pulling him into a hug. "You aren't allowed to grow up."

"No!" Menotti called out with a giggle.

"What do you mean, no?" José tickled and kissed Menotti, who squealed with delight before breaking away. "I noticed Menotti isn't the only one who looks a bit different."

"Did you now?" I raised an eyebrow, amused by the direction of the conversation.

José turned to look at me. "You do look different."

I smiled, toying with him. "Really? How so?"

He thought for a moment, trying to form words. It was a struggle that played out in his features. "You, you look…softer."

"Softer?"

"Don't mock me." He laughed. "No, really, you look softer, like the edges of a cloud, but at the same time you look…tired." His face fell into a concerned frown. "*Tesoro mio*, have you not been feeling well since I have been gone?"

I sighed with extra drama. "Truth be told, I have been falling asleep as soon as I get into bed, but it's clearly not enough for the baby."

"The baby?" He returned to Menotti, who looked back at him with an angry little scowl.

"No," he said, taking a toy soldier from his father's hands.

"Oh no, Menotti sleeps through the night. That's not the baby I am talking about." I couldn't resist the smile that began to spread.

José at this point got up onto his knees. "Another baby, does that mean, that you, that we are—?"

"Almost nineteen weeks, by my calculations."

"*Tesoro mio!*" José grabbed me, wrapping me in a large hug that pulled me to the floor. "Another baby." He laughed. "Did you hear Mamãe? Menotti, you're going to have a baby brother." I hit

José playfully on the shoulder. "Or sister. What do you think of that, son?"

Menotti's full, pouty lips puckered in displeasure. "No!"

José smiled, turning back to me. "All right then, now we know his opinion on that." He kissed me. "Another baby. I truly am the richest man in all of the Americas."

That night, in bed, José told me the full story of what had happened to him. "We were outmanned. My ship didn't stand a chance." We lay on our sides, face-to-face in bed. José held my hand in his, keeping it close to his heart. "The Argentinian flagship was the one that made the point of attacking us. I thought for sure it was going to sink us."

"But it didn't." I touched the tips of his fingers, each one of them right where it was supposed to be.

"No, that's the strange thing! Instead of firing the kill shot, it broke off. We lost the ship, but they let us escape."

"That's odd."

"Absolutely. The Argentinians have employed a *norte-americano* by the name of Brown. He has a fierce reputation, but I just don't understand why he let us go." José sighed as he reached out and stroked my arm. "Anyway, we found what was left of the Uruguayan army in Corrientes and made our way home. Fighting the whole time."

"It sounds like it was quite the adventure."

José kissed my hand, his lips lingering on my knuckles. "As strange as this sounds, I wished you were there. It was the kind of action you would have lived for, but as I understand it, you had a few adventures of your own."

"Adventures?" I asked, stretching out. "It was just an average day in the life of Anita Garibaldi." José and I broke into childlike laughter.

* * *

In the few weeks that José had been home, I marveled at our ability to fall back into the comforting rhythm of our old life.

José's exploits were written about in every paper in Montevideo—the small navy that stood up to the might of Argentina. José was a hero. Important people started talking; how embarrassing to have such a pitiful navy compared to the might of Argentina. Uruguay's finest fleet was composed of roughly patched-together rafts that could barely float. What would the great kingdoms of Europe say if they saw such ridiculousness? A rumor grew that the Argentinian navy failed to sink José's ship because they were so impressed by José's sailing capabilities. Argentina had hired Brown, who was an admirer of my husband's. Supposedly this North American told anyone who would listen that to kill my husband would have been to kill a beautiful piece of art.

José used the gossip as leverage to get the government to reconvene to assess its war plans. In the end, Vidal and his supporters were overruled. José was given a small fleet of ships, two already built with four more commissioned.

On one of those blissfully normal evenings, José came home and wrapped his arms around my growing belly. "I have a job for you."

"You are putting me to work now too?"

"The war council put me in charge of forming a legion. An Italian legion."

I whirled around, wrapping my arms around his neck. "They are giving you your own legion? That's incredible!"

"It is, but I need your help. Our men need uniforms."

"I suppose I could do something." I pulled at his shirt.

"*Tesoro mio*, you are so gracious." José kissed me. "Tomorrow you and Anzani will go to the tailor."

Anzani and I arrived at the tailor's the next morning just after the shop opened. The tailor looked up from his books, stifled a yawn, and then looked back down over the rims of his spectacles, leaving us to survey the wares on our own.

"Excuse me, senhor, do you have any recommendations for a newly formed military regiment?" Anzani asked.

"Blue is such a fashionable color." He slowly walked out from behind his counter, huffing over being interrupted. "This one is quite light, it would be good for the men." He held out the fabric for me to feel.

I ran a hand over the material and shrugged. "It's all right, I suppose, if we want to look like every other soldier in every other army."

"Are you able to get any other colors?" Anzani asked, studying the fabric.

The tailor shook his head sadly. "Only what you see here. The war, it's not good for business; I can't sell my bolts. I have some green left over, but the French Legion is using that. I was able to get some white fabric a few weeks ago."

I scrunched my nose. "And look like bakers? No, thank you."

My eyes landed on one corner with an excessive amount of bright red fabric. I walked over and rubbed it between my fingers. It was a soft, breathable material. I turned to the tailor. "You seem to have quite a bit of inventory here, senhor."

The tailor sighed. "Yes, unfortunately that fabric was supposed to go to the butchers in Argentina. However, with the war, I can no longer fulfill their order."

"The butchers, you say?" I looked back down at the fabric. "Anzani, don't you think red would be an intimidating color for our legion?"

"Red?" Anzani studied the fabric with his hand on his chin. "But this is supposed to be for Argentinian butchers. They are not respectable men. They are dirty..."

"They are intimidating. When you see a butcher, you know he is in the business of one thing and one thing only: death. Don't you want our legion to be that intimidating? Don't you want our enemies to shiver in their boots the moment they lay eyes on us?"

"Red is not a sanctioned color, at least not for any legion in Uruguay." Anzani gripped the material in his hands, turning it over and twisting it to test its strength. He turned his gaze to me. "All right…all right, let's get it."

I was thrilled when we received the uniforms from the tailor a few weeks later. "What do you think?" I asked José as I turned from side to side.

"It certainly is as red as Anzani said it would be."

"This one is mine. After I have the baby I will take it in, of course, but I thought it would be nice to have one of my own. Even though I don't get to fight anymore."

"You would be quite a force to be reckoned with. The Argentinians would certainly retreat in fear," he said, taking me in his arms, "but you shouldn't discount the work that you do with the wives." He cupped my chin. "Without you we would have no one to come home to."

THIRTY-FIVE

April 1842

While the government assembled José's fleet, the Italian Legion defended Montevideo from the Argentinian force's constant bombardment. To the Montevideans, José was their savior. The Italian Legion, which people affectionately called the Redshirts, were cheered as heroes. The Italians walked around with pride, wearing their red shirts even when they didn't have to. It was a pride I had never seen in our people.

With José's rise in popularity came a number of people who wanted to be around him, which also meant that they wanted to be around me.

Our home became a hub of activity and meetings. The women were always in my kitchen. I had no peace and quiet. In actuality it wasn't the constant stream of people who came and left at all hours of the day that drove me mad. It was the gossip. *Who wore the better dress? Can you believe it, Maria was flirting with the butcher? When she knows very well he's married.* It was a buzz that fluttered around my kitchen, sowing seeds of chaos.

For days I thought about ways to keep the women busy and productive, but nothing worked. That is until, by chance, Father Lorenzo brought up an intriguing opportunity. It was a lovely afternoon as I let Menotti play in the central plaza with a group of children. The boys ran in circles, playing by rules logical only to those in the thick of the game. Around us, people meandered from one shop to the next, sitting at cafés across from the plaza. It was as if the people of Montevideo had collectively decided they weren't at war.

"Dona Anita, what a pleasure to see you," the priest said with a smile as he approached me. "My goodness, you are going to have that baby any day now, aren't you?"

I smiled in return. "It would certainly appear that way."

Menotti, accompanied by two little boys, sweaty and out of breath, ran up to Father Lorenzo. The good father had gained a reputation for carrying sweets with him that he freely gave out to the children. He reached into the folds of his robes and produced a candy for each child. He offered one to me, which I tried to decline.

"Save them for the children," I said, trying to wave him away.

"I am. This one isn't for you." He winked. "It's for your baby."

I thanked him as I took the honey-flavored sweet, and we sat on a park bench to watch the children play. Father Lorenzo had a genuine care for his parishioners. He didn't view his position as a place of power but as one of assistance. "It is most fortunate that I should find you," he said, looking out at the children playing. "I understand you have some expertise in hospitals at wartime."

I nodded, squinting into the afternoon sun. "I worked as an aide during the Ragamuffin War."

"Montevideo's hospital could use you."

"I'm going to be very busy soon. I'm sorry, but I have to decline," I said, placing a hand on my belly, but soon a thought occurred to me. "But I may have a solution for you."

With Luisa's help, I formed the Montevideo Ladies' Brigade. While I prepared for the birth of my child, the women went door to door collecting money for the hospital. They also volunteered two days a week to help the sick and injured. The women were happy; they got to gossip all they wanted. Father Lorenzo received the help he needed. As for me, I got my house to myself.

I was sweeping the floors when I felt my waters slide down the insides of my thighs. "José!" I called out. "The baby is coming!" It was shortly thereafter that the cramps came, violent and so strong that I doubled over on myself. The child wasn't going to wait for the midwife to arrive, whether I liked it or not.

I lay on my side on the sofa and tried to breathe through the pain and hope that the child would wait. José rushed for the midwife, and within moments of her arrival my tiny daughter lay in my arms, wide-eyed and curious about the world around her. When she let out a little yawn from her tiny pink lips, I thought my heart would explode. José quietly slipped into the room, his happiness evident on his face.

"They told me I have a daughter."

"It's true." I smiled. "Come say hello." I passed our daughter over to him. His large hands cupped her head as they stared at each other.

"She is such a pretty little thing, isn't she? As pretty as a rose," José said, entranced by our daughter. "Our little Rosita."

"I thought girls didn't get an '-ita' added to their name until they became women."

José stood up, bringing Rosita back to me. "Not my girls. They will always be considered women."

THIRTY-SIX

JANUARY 1845

In the two and a half years following Rosita's birth, our shining city deteriorated into crumbling ruins. As I made my way into town, I felt sorrow for what it had once been. Buildings collapsed in on themselves, windows were broken, and the sickly sweet smell of garbage filled the air and stuck to the back of my throat. I was long past the morning sickness stage of my latest pregnancy, but walking through the streets of Montevideo made me feel ill all over again. José continued to run missions for the government while I led and organized the women. We needed each other in order to survive.

Argentina continued to tighten its grip on Uruguay, attempting to invade from the east and north. They effectively cut off any supplies from Brazil, leaving us to fend for ourselves. Unfortunately, we were not prepared for this, having spent so many years relying on goods from other countries. Meanwhile, the French sat idly by, claiming to be seeking a diplomatic resolution with Argentina. Making my way down Avenida Rincón, I could see that most of the shops were deserted, their windows hastily covered by boards. I walked into the candlemaker's shop, the tinkling bell echoing off the empty walls. Ghosts of what had once been haunted the dusty shelves. "Hello?" I called out for the shopkeeper.

He walked out from the back room, wiping his hands on a cloth. His wire-rimmed glasses rested low on his nose. "How can I help you, senhora?"

"I need some candles."

"Don't we all, senhora." The shopkeeper sighed, then reached below in his cupboard and pulled out a pair of tall candles. "This is my last pair."

"Your last pair? How?"

"I can't get any more wicks for the foreseeable future, senhora."

"Very well. I shall take them." I handed over my money.

"Senhora, this is too much."

"No, I believe this is what is necessary for taking the last of your supply. Have a good day." I took my candles and left before he could argue with me. I did the math in my head of what was left in my purse. We would be skipping meat again tonight.

As always, my little family seemed to weather the storm. Menotti continued to grow, reminding me of a small pony in the way that his arms and legs grew faster than the rest of him. He was a miniature José, looking more and more like his father every day—except for his dark hair and scrutinizing black eyes. All the women remarked on how he had his mother's eyes. They sat around my kitchen table telling me that this was a good thing, he would see the world as I did. I smiled; my son would never be taken for a fool.

Rosita was the beloved child whom everyone fought over to get just a little of her attention. Luisa, resolved in the fact that she would never have a daughter of her own, fawned over her. In her mind, being the godmother was the equivalent of being a second mother.

Always exploring, Rosita toddled after every child. She was a happy little thing. Her giggles, reminiscent of the tinkling of bells, lit up the room whenever she entered. She was the brightness we all needed in this dimming city. Her little brow would wrinkle with worry for just a moment when she was upset, then it would pass, like a cloud on a windy day. When a true storm was brewing, all we needed to do was produce a flower, any flower, and she would quickly calm. Rosita was obsessed with flowers. I often wondered if Menotti would have been like this if he had not known such hardships so early in his life.

One breezy summer afternoon I walked into the kitchen to find the table covered with flowers of every shape and color. "What is this?"

"My flowers!" she declared, throwing a little fistful into the air.

"Darling, we need to eat here. We can't have your flowers all over the table."

"We can eat my flowers, Mamãe!" she exclaimed, offering me a fistful.

"That is a wonderful idea, my love, but I don't think they will fill your papa's belly."

Rosita giggled. "Daddy has a big belly."

I couldn't help but laugh. "Don't let him hear you say that." I looked down at Rosita, her pretty, round face glowing with happiness. I couldn't make her throw away her precious flowers. "Take those up to your room." She gathered the flowers in her chubby fists and ran upstairs. "But don't put them in your bed!" I called out, realizing I was going to have a mess to clean up. Holding my hand to my large belly, I hoped that this baby would know Rosita's happiness.

* * *

February 1845

Early morning was the best time of day to wash our clothing. On this morning as the sun shone through the hazy sky, Luisa and I talked freely with the other women while the children played.

We were in the middle of our washing when the pains hit me with a sudden force that caused me to double over. In agony, I crumpled to the ground. Luisa snapped into action immediately. "Carlita, run for the midwife. Lupita, come here and help me." Between her and Lupita, I was brought home.

"He's too early. He can't come yet, he can't," I pleaded in between labor pains, wiping the torrent of sweat that soaked through my dress.

Luisa was walking me back and forth in the parlor to help ease me as we waited for the midwife to finish preparing. "Children come when they are ready, not when you are," the old woman said, bringing hot water to us.

When walking hurt too much, I tried to sit but that made it worse. The midwife had me sit in a chair as she checked the position of the baby. "You aren't ready yet. Keep walking." It had already been an hour since my pains started.

"Keep walking? How can this continue?" I paused, wincing under the pain that shot across my groin "My other two children were never this intense."

"I'm sorry, senhora, but every birth is different."

Another hour went by before I was finally told to start pushing. I braced myself as I followed the midwife's directions. With every ounce of strength I had in me, I tried to expel this child. The birth took an agonizingly long time.

It wasn't until the afternoon sun began casting long golden rays into our windows that my second daughter was born. She wailed, waving angry little fists in the air. The midwife swaddled her in a clean blanket. I pressed her to my chest to feed, marveling at this fierce small human. José, who had been waiting on our front steps the whole time, was finally let into the house. He slipped inside and went straight for our sleeping child.

"She is beautiful." He had that same look in his eyes as when he first viewed Rosita.

"What are we naming this one?" I asked as I tried to stifle a yawn.

"Nicoletta?"

I wrinkled my nose. "No."

He thought for a moment. "Maria? After my mother?"

"No, don't forget, my mother and sister were also named Maria. I don't want to think about them every time I look upon my daughter."

We both watched the baby as we thought. Finally I ventured, "I have always been partial to the name Teresa."

"Teresa?" He looked at our daughter as he gently bounced her in his arms. "I like it. Teresita Garibaldi it is."

Our baby yawned and stretched her arms. José kissed Teresita on her little nose before handing her back to me. "You have given me the most amazing children a man could ever ask for." He stroked my hair as we watched our daughter sleep.

* * *

December 1845

In the still of the evening I sat with José at our table as he sipped his tea. He wrapped his worry around himself like a blanket as he studied maps and books. This was a side of him that he wouldn't let the children see but I had seen many times before when we fought our way through Brazil. Every move that he made was carefully choreographed, taking into account what his opponent might do. Whenever he planned like this, a little wrinkle formed between his brows. A wrinkle that, to this day, I longed to kiss. It didn't matter what country we were in, what battle we were fighting; he was still the man I loved. He was still my José. He mumbled, tracing a finger along a river.

"Where is the blockade?" I asked.

"There." He pointed, without looking up at me. "Argentina has a heavy military presence in the north. I don't think we can break them."

The drink had long since gone cold, but José played with the tarnished metal straw that resided in the battered gourd. "Argentina is occupying the west and the north. There is no way for us to get anything through the Brazilian border."

"What of the emissaries to Brazil?"

"Dead," José said. He moved from stirring the tea to stamping the *bombilla* up and down in the gourd, masticating the tea leaves that had sunk to the bottom. I blanched at the thought of what the Argentinians had done to our men. "But it wasn't likely that Brazil would help. They don't want to go up against Argentina." He continued to stare at the map as the kettle screeched.

"The Brazilian government is foolish. Once Rosas devours Uruguay he'll double his forces and head straight for them," I said, pouring hot water into his gourd.

"Oh, thank you," José said, barely looking up at me.

"And the blockade at sea?"

"Too much of a risk. Spain is the only country that can match their ships in strength." He trailed off, sipping the tea through his *bombilla*. It went without saying that we didn't want Spain, or the rest of Europe for that matter, involved in our affairs. "I can't fail the people. There has got to be a way," he said.

The fame of the Redshirts continued to grow in Uruguay. They were the hope of the people and José knew it. It was a responsibility he did not take lightly. His eyes, puffy and ringed, showed how tired he was. I reached out and took him by the hand. "You will find a way, but not if you die from exhaustion."

Obediently he followed me to our bedroom. It was in these brief moments that we were able to be man and wife. When we could forget about the Redshirts, about the problems of Uruguay, and solely be José and Anita. It wasn't long after that night that I found myself pregnant once again.

* * *

José was in the middle of a long absence when sickness arrived in Montevideo. I wasn't surprised, for sickness always seemed to follow war. It might have been due to the famine induced by the blockade or the number of wounded soldiers who were brought back to our hospitals. Either way, Montevideo suffered. People stopped going out into the streets, stopped socializing at the community washing wells. Our regular gatherings of Italians came to an abrupt end.

Every family kept to themselves, but it wasn't enough. In the poor districts, people were found dead in the streets. Funerals became all too common, the church sometimes holding two or three a day. No one was safe from this invisible enemy.

I thought I was doing well until I heard a wet, scraping cough coming from the children's room one night. I threw back the covers and rushed to Menotti's bedside. The cough rocked his body, making him violently lurch forward. I reached out, putting the back of my hand to his forehead. He felt like a burning coal. His bedding was damp from sweat.

I picked up Rosita, who was starting to rouse, bringing her into my bed. Then I rushed back to Menotti and put him in a fresh nightshirt. I brought him water and placed a cool, damp rag on his head. I sat by his side as he coughed violently, letting him lean his head on my arm. He was tired, his heavy eyelids closing over and over again, but each time he started to fall asleep another cough would tear through him.

Helplessness overtook me. All I could do was soothe one symptom at a time and hope for the best. Rosita stumbled in with her favorite doll. "Mamãe, I no feel good." She whimpered, approaching me.

I pulled her to me; her cheeks were flushed. "Yes, my love, it would appear you are sick too."

A cool compress rested on each of their heads. I set to vigorously rubbing the children's feet to pull down the fevers. My arms grew tired, but I didn't stop. This was when I felt the sting of José's absence. I tried not to think about him, but my heart clenched at how much I needed him. Not just for the extra pair of hands but for the stability. I blinked back tears as Teresita began to stir in the other room. I needed to keep her away from her siblings in hopes that she wouldn't get sick. When their fevers broke, I took my pillow and blanket from my bedroom and curled up on the floor next to their bed.

I woke from my spot on the floor to the sound of someone walking around downstairs, opening and closing my cupboards, clanking dishes. I cautiously ventured into my kitchen to find Feliciana toasting bread. My floor was clean, and a fresh pitcher of water rested on the table.

"Feliciana, you need to leave; the children are sick."

"I will leave when I know you've gotten some help." She waved me off. "I am going to go to the apothecary to see if he has any medicine for their coughs." She handed me some toast. "Eat something, Anita. Don't forget to keep your health up as well."

I brought some weak tea upstairs and woke the children, making them drink it. Rosita looked ghostly pale, her lips dry and cracked. I looked to Menotti, whose eyes were red and puffy. He kept rubbing a fist against his chest in a vain attempt to find comfort. Putting an ear to each of their chests, I could hear their lungs crackle like brittle paper.

As soon as a fever broke in one child, another would grow in the second. I had seen what a lung infection could do during my time in the hospitals, and I feared what it would do to my children. The first thing the nuns taught us when working in the hospital was that the more emotional we were, the more emotional our patients would be. It was something that I carried with me from that humble hospital in Laguna, through the wilds of Brazil to here, in my children's bedroom in Uruguay. Now as I looked over my suffering children, I mustered the strength to show them that I wasn't as terrified as they were.

The next day Feliciana dropped off a satchel of herbs. I was to brew it and make the children breathe in the steam. She didn't need to tell the doctor our symptoms; he already knew. We were just a few of many that had already developed pneumonia.

The next night the children cried in between their coughing as I tried to keep the fevers under control. Though Teresita was separated from her siblings, she too spiked a fever.

I had stared down cannon barrels, withstood torrential downpours, even escaped captivity, but this was unlike anything I'd ever had to endure. I wanted to step in and battle this for them, to take the unseen bullets, to fight for them like I had for José, but I couldn't. Feeling useless in their battle was a pain worse than death.

I leaned against the doorway as my vision swam in front of me. Lifting my hand to my forehead, I felt the familiar heat of the fever. Rosita stirred in her sleep, taking me away from my thoughts. She turned over, clutching her doll, the sheets damp from her perspiration. She coughed, her body violently shaking. Slipping in next to her, I tried not to succumb to my depression.

I awoke the next morning to the sound of Teresita crying. Checking Rosita, who still lay next to me, I could hear that her breathing sounded heavy and shallow.

I turned to Menotti. He had kicked off his covers, sweating through another fever spike. He opened his watery eyes to look at me and his sister, then moaned and turned over in his bed. Tentatively I reached out for him. He was hotter than my stove. We needed help. I made my way down the stairs as my world began to spin out of control. I reached out to steady myself. I could hear Teresita crying in the distance.

From the corners of my eyes a blackness crept into my vision. I blinked, trying to keep the darkness at bay, but it made everything look farther away, like I was staring down a tunnel. I leaned against the wall, rooted where I was by fear. I had to keep going down the stairs. I willed myself to move on, gingerly putting one foot down, then another. I was almost to the front hall when I couldn't hold back the darkness any longer. I tripped. The bottom of the stairs rushed toward me as my world went black.

The warm sun seeped through my skin, blinding me before I even opened my eyes. I roused, hearing the sounds of children giggling. I took in my surroundings: I was no longer in my home. I was in a field, which looked strange but somehow familiar. Just a short distance away stood a small house.

It had a thatched roof that hung over the stone walls, which leaned ever so slightly to the right. It took me a few minutes to realize why I recognized this house: It was my beloved childhood home. "This can't be real," I said as I wandered toward the front door.

"We're over here, little one!"

I stopped. I knew that voice. Why did I know that voice? The giggling children caused something to lurch deep within my being. Those were my children. I followed the sounds of the laughter just beyond the house to find my children playing with the stranger.

"Papai?"

"Anna! How nice of you to finally join us!"

My children, realizing I was there, ran to me, wrapping their arms around my legs. "What are you doing here?" I asked, looking around me. "Where are we?" My children ran off again through the field.

"Those are questions I cannot answer, little one." Together we watched them play. "You should know, you have brought more honor to our family than you realize. That's why I am proud to be the one to collect Rosita."

I shook my head, taking a few steps away from him. "No, I won't let you. Rosita! Menotti! Come here now." Menotti ran over to me, but Rosita went straight to my father.

He lifted Rosita up into his arms. "I am truly sorry, we have no control over these things."

I held Menotti by the shoulders, pressing him closer to me. Together, we watched as my father turned and walked toward the setting sun. Rosita looked over his shoulder, waving to us as they disappeared into the light.

THIRTY-SEVEN

I woke gasping for air, as if I had just emerged from being trapped underwater, the blankets pulling me back down into the abyss. Frantically, I took in my surroundings: a large open ward filled with rickety metal beds. The sound of coughs peppered the air. Finally, my eyes settled on Feliciana, who sat at the foot of my bed, watching over me. A frown, so unusual for her, accentuated the wrinkles around her mouth, making her look older.

"Where's Rosita?" Startled by my own raspy voice, I swallowed and tried again. "Where are my children?"

Feliciana took my hands in hers. "Menotti and Teresita are in the children's ward. Marco is with them."

"Where is Rosita?"

Feliciana looked down, focusing on a spot on the blanket. "She is at the church with Father Lorenzo. You've been unconscious for two days."

I pulled my hands from her grasp as she continued, "He has already performed the last rites, but we wanted to wait for you before she was buried. I am so sorry, Anita, sometimes God has a plan for these things."

I turned my head away from her. My veins turned icy with anger. Rosita was the sweetest, most honest soul on the planet, and she was taken from me. Our beautiful little flower. I turned back to Feliciana. "Tell me what happened."

Feliciana smoothed out her skirt as she searched for the right words. "I could hear Teresita's wails from outside. When you didn't answer your door, I knew...I knew." Her voice caught. She swallowed hard as she composed herself. "You would never let her carry on crying like that unless there was something wrong. I made Marco break into your house." Feliciana looked up at me with tears in her eyes. "You were just a heap on the floor. I thought you were dead." She shook her head. "Menotti still breathed, but Rosita...Rosita, the poor little lamb, she struggled. There was nothing the doctors could do."

I closed my eyes, failing to fight back the tears. If it hadn't been for Teresita, we all would have been dead. But my Rosita, my beautiful little girl, was gone. I looked around the ward as the nurses hurried past to tend to the groaning patients. I wanted so desperately for it all to be a horrible dream. I wanted to close my eyes and wake up in my bed with José. He would laugh as he petted my hair, whispering words as sweet as caramels into my ears. We would never be the same again. My Rosita, my bubbly, happy daughter, was gone, and no amount of wishing or dreaming was going to change that.

According to Feliciana, Luisa had made multiple trips to the central military offices to beg them to send word about his family to José. Each time she requested a messenger be sent to him she was informed that either it was too dangerous to send any or she had just missed their riders.

"She's there now," Feliciana said. "She's trying to get word to José about the family."

A few days later, when I regained my strength, I made my way to my children. My cough still lingered, but I needed to see them. Teresita lay curled up in a crib at the foot of her brother's bed, whimpering in her sleep. She calmed down as soon as I held her.

Kissing her sweet-smelling head, I whispered a thank-you. If it hadn't been for her cries, who knew what would have happened to us. Menotti stirred and stretched in his bed, then looked at me. He froze, then blinked as he watched me for a moment before crawling out from under the blankets toward me and Teresita.

I sat on the end of the bed and wrapped my free arm around him. "Where did they take Rosita?" he whispered.

"Rosita went to heaven, my darling."

He frowned, looking more serious than any five-year-old I'd ever seen. "Will they take me too?"

"No, my love, I won't let them take you."

"Or Teresita?"

"Or Teresita."

He thought for a moment more. "Are you still having the baby?"

"Yes, dear."

"He won't know Rosita, though."

"No, my darling boy, he won't."

"That's very sad." He rested his head against my arm. "Don't worry, Mamãe, I'll tell him all about her."

I kissed his forehead. "Thank you."

I needed to take care of Rosita, one last time. The next day, Marco helped me outside to a waiting carriage. We rode slowly through the semideserted streets. "Can you stop by my home?" I asked.

Marco nodded, pulling the carriage to the left. He came to a stop in front of our little house. I sat there staring at the front door. I wanted to get up and go in but couldn't. The house looked back at me, empty and cold. I had faced armies of more than a hundred men; I had stood on a ship, braved a hail of bullets, and never once felt the slightest bit of fear. But the house terrified me. Marco put a hand on my arm. "I can go in for you if you want."

"Thank you." I put my hand on his in return. "I need to get Rosita's doll."

Marco got up from the driver's seat and made his way into the house. After a while, he returned with the well-worn porcelain doll carefully held in his hands. He handed it to me before taking the reins. As we rode through the streets to the church I looked down at the doll. My fingers smoothed out her blue floral dress. Her porcelain head sprouted messy brown ringlets. With a shaking hand I petted the stray hairs in a vain attempt to tame them. I smiled to myself, thinking about how much Rosita loved her.

The day José bought the doll for her had been rife with chaos. Menotti and Rosita were bickering every chance they got. Then Teresita fell. She tripped, as all children do, but managed to tear open a large gash on her forehead; there was blood everywhere. And her wails! That child screamed loud enough for all the angels in heaven to hear. I went upstairs and found our savings box sitting empty on our bed. In addition to everything that was happening, I thought someone had robbed us.

I needed José's help, but he'd disappeared. I cursed. As soon as he walked through the door, midafternoon, I pounced on him like a cat. "How could you just leave me here?" I hissed, "The children are at each other's throats. Teresita hasn't stopped crying, and to make matters worse I think we've been robbed. Where have you been?"

He grew sheepish, looking down at his feet. "I'm sorry."

That's when my anger subsided, allowing me to notice the three brown paper packages that he clutched in his arms. "What are those?"

"Presents, for the children. I wanted to make them all happy. I thought I could help. I'm sorry, a messenger came by just as I was leaving, there was a meeting for the generals. I got delayed.

I intended to come home sooner." He shrugged as Menotti and Rosita wandered in.

"I was hoping to buy a roast," I grumbled.

José looked over at the children. "So I go without a roast. At least our children will be happy."

Rosita reached for her father, but he handed her the box instead. Kneeling down, José helped her open her new treasure. Inside was the doll. From the wide-eyed look on Rosita's face, you'd think that José had handed her the world. From that day on Rosita and her doll were inseparable. Now, looking at this doll as we made our way to the church, the only thing I could think was how upset Rosita must be without it.

Slowly, I walked into the church. The empty building felt cold and intimidating, making me feel conscious of the hollow clicking echo of my shoes against the polished terra-cotta-tiled floor. Dread filled me with every step that I took. Father Lorenzo sat in the front pew, staring at the altar.

As I drew closer, he turned in his seat to look at me. He stood, silently motioning for me to follow him. He led me down to the basement of the church. It was cool with an earthy mildewed scent. Rosita lay in a little coffin on the table in the center of the room. "I'll give you some time alone."

I turned back to Rosita as Father Lorenzo walked away. My beautiful little girl, gone. I reached out, brushing a light brown curl from her face. Silent tears streamed down my face. She was so peaceful that, for a moment, I thought she could have been sleeping. How I wished it were true.

I tucked her beloved doll in with her, smoothing out both their dresses. At least Rosita wouldn't be alone. "I am sorry, my love." Gently, I kissed her forehead. "I should have done more to protect you." I left the church, the silence crowding around me, making it hard to breathe.

THIRTY-EIGHT

I held Teresita closer to me against the gloomy December sky as Menotti and I stood side by side at the threshold of our home. "We should probably go inside," I said, transferring Teresita to my other hip.

My brave son nodded, but neither of us moved. Feliciana had offered to let us stay at her home until José got back, but I turned her down. I took a deep breath and steadied myself for the battle ahead as I twisted the tarnished brass knob.

The air in the house smelled stale. Dust motes swam in the slivers of daylight cutting through our windows. I set Teresita down as I moved about, bringing life back into the house.

Searching through the cupboard, I was disheartened by how little we had. I jumped slightly when I heard Menotti come into the room and sit down at the table.

"My darling, what are you doing here? You should be upstairs resting."

"I don't want to." His lower lip popped out as he bowed his handsome little head, refusing to look at me.

"Would you like to go to your friend's house?"

"No."

"Well, I won't have you sitting here. Go upstairs and open the windows. Get some fresh air flowing through here." Menotti grimaced. "What is it? Do you not want to go upstairs?"

"No." He traced a finger around a knot of wood, looking very much like his father. "If I open up the windows we'll lose all of Rosita's flowers."

I thought for a moment and then went into the parlor. I pulled out Rosita's favorite storybook. It contained fables from all around the world. "Here, Menotti, put your sister's flowers in this before you open the window."

He took the book from my hand before slowly climbing up the stairs.

I wondered if word of Rosita's death had reached José. Shuffling into the kitchen, I pulled out the plates for our dinner. I set three plates down and then froze. My brain slowly processed the fact that we no longer needed three plates. The loss hit me all over again. My daughter was dead. I fought the army of tears that welled in my eyes as I shoved the extra plate back in the cupboard.

* * *

January 1846

José burst through the door unexpectedly in the afternoon while I sat in my chair doing my mending. Eyes wild with panic, he quickly scanned the room before training his gaze on me. With two large steps he was in front of me, lifting me up from the chair, pressing me in close. Breathing in deeply, I took in the scents of sandalwood, hay, and dirt. José buried his face in my hair. I could feel his warm breath, ragged and uneven, that of a man who thinks no one can hear him crying.

When he finally pulled away, wiping his face, he spoke. "They didn't tell me you were sick. I didn't know."

"Don't blame yourself."

"No, Anita, I should have been here." He cupped my face in his massive hands. "I arrived in Montevideo this morning to find all of Luisa's letters written to both me and Anzani. The military didn't want me to know what was happening with my family."

I tried to smooth the tangled hair that flew out around his head. "If you had known, you would have left the front lines and returned to me."

He put his forehead to mine. "That's no excuse. I should have—" His voice caught. "I should have been with her. With you." He pulled a hair's breadth away and put his hands on my growing abdomen. "And how is this one?"

"He's well. Strong, like his father."

"Good. We leave for Salto at the end of the week."

"Salto? Why do you want us to go to Salto?" Salto was a three-day ride by horse.

"Argentina is invading from the northwest, cutting us off from Brazil. If we do nothing, we'll have no choice but to give in to Argentina's demands."

"'We'?" I questioned. "We can't bring two small children with us on such a long journey."

José shrugged. "It'll be an adventure."

I narrowed my eyes, preparing for a fight. "Giuseppe Garibaldi, I am not going to Salto."

"And I will not lose another member of this family!" José bellowed.

Heavy footfalls pounded on the stairs. We glimpsed Menotti,

who we hadn't seen come downstairs, as he ran up to hide. I moved to follow after him, but José stopped me. "I'll talk to him." José kissed my temple and went after his son as I slipped into the kitchen to make tea and ponder José's proposal.

As I waited for the water to boil, José's words clung to me. *I will not lose another member of this family.*

Just as I started pouring out the tea, José joined me in the kitchen, taking a seat at the table.

"How's Menotti?"

"He'll be all right," José said as I handed him his faded red gourd. "I had to convince him I wasn't taking you away."

"He is grieving for his sister in his own way," I said as I took a seat opposite him.

José thoughtfully took a long sip. "We all are."

I watched as he used the *bombilla* to slowly stir the leaves around in his gourd. "Tell me, why do you want your family to pick up and follow you to Salto?"

"My orders are to escort a general to Salto in order to lift the siege of the city. It's the first step in beating back the Argentinian army."

Refugees had been spilling into Montevideo as Argentina pressed in from the west, burning villages along the way. They had filled in along the edges of the city in makeshift camps, and the increased population meant tighter restrictions on our food rations. Filth filled our city, overflowing from the gutters and spilling into the streets. Pneumonia was no longer our only concern; cholera had finally made its way to Montevideo.

The political situation wasn't faring much better. The Uruguayan army was doing well in its defense of the capital, thanks in no small part to the Redshirts, but there was discord within the government. Rumors abounded; many weren't happy with Rivera, our current president. Would there be another war inside a war already raging?

"A pregnant woman and two small children are going to help?" I frowned.

"You'll be on the ship. It will be a grand adventure. Just like when we were in Laguna."

I sighed. "I don't need to be reminded of what happened in Laguna. The children and I don't need a grand adventure."

José regarded me. "When you were with me in every one of my battles, I was able to keep you safe."

"You kept me safe as much as I would let you. I seem to remember a number of occasions when I tested that. Hell, there were a few times I thought you were going to kill me yourself."

He smiled that lopsided, boyish grin I knew so well. "The point is, when we are together, we are stronger. We are safer. I don't want to be apart from you and the children anymore."

I crossed my arms. My husband had a point. All the negative things that had happened to us—the sickness, Rosita's death—it had all happened when we were apart. We were stronger when we were together. "Then we will go to Salto."

THIRTY-NINE

February 1846

The Río Uruguay served as a natural border between Argentina and Uruguay, its only outlet being the Río de la Plata, the bay that separated Montevideo from Buenos Aires. We sailed from Montevideo to the mouth of the river. Thanks to France's meddling, our ship, carrying two hundred and fifty cavalrymen, went unnoticed as we made our way toward Salto.

The Argentinians had already crossed the river and occupied the little towns that dotted its banks all the way down to Salto. The Uruguayan army had been keeping them at bay from the east, but needed the reinforcements we brought to attack the southern Argentinian lines. As we sailed north on the murky river, Menotti stood on a box in front of the ship's wheel, helping his father navigate. The men called him *piccolo marinaio*, "little sailor." I felt proud as I watched him learn how to sail the ship. José beamed with pride standing next to his son, his hand on the wheel, letting Menotti think he was doing all the work. Teresita was fast asleep in our little cabin, giving me the opportunity to soak in the morning sun in peace. I savored the feeling of the wind as it stung my face and pulled my hair.

I stood at the bow of the *Rivera* watching the dark, tranquil water of the Río Uruguay ripple ever so gently with the movement of the boat. The river beckoned me with its smoothness, but I knew different. My body trembled at the memory of being swept away by the current on our escape from São Gabriel. I tightened the shawl that hung around my shoulders, hugging it closer to me against the memory of the frigid river that nearly took me and my child.

Later that night, as our ship charged through the black stillness, José woke me from a deep sleep. He put a finger to my lips to keep me quiet so that we didn't wake the children. With a sparkle in his eye he led me to the bow of the ship. The stars glittered around a sliver of the moon in the tranquil night sky. José pulled me to him, gently kissing me.

"I am so happy to have you by my side again," he said, brushing his warm thumb against my cool cheek.

I smiled, placing my hand on his neck, caressing the soft bristle of his jawline with my finger. "It's where I belong."

The boat came to a slow stop just outside of Salto as all our men climbed up top, Anzani among them. He walked through the ranks, hands clasped behind his back, watching as they seamlessly moved to their positions near the little rowboats. Anzani, normally so jovial, reminded me of a stern schoolteacher. He slapped a slouching sailor on the back, commanding him to straighten his spine.

When Anzani was satisfied, he raised an arm straight into the air. The men took their places in the boats. José raised his arm with his fist tightly clenched, a mirror of Anzani. After a thirty-second count, José lowered his fist. Anzani followed suit, and as he did all the boats were slowly lowered into the water.

"*Tesoro mio*, watch." José pointed to the tree line, and that's when I saw them: one hundred gauchos dressed and ready for battle leaving the shelter of the trees. They looked magnificent. They sat on their horses with their colorful ponchos and formidable weapons, each one leading an extra horse for our men.

"How were you able to gather together so many men?" I asked, looking over the edge of the ship in wonder.

"They have a deeper resentment for Argentina than most of our own men. It also helps that up until the siege, Salto was a major trading post. Argentina put a stop to that."

"Naturally," I responded, watching our men quietly slip through the water.

Anzani went into a violent coughing fit just as José and I turned from the bow. When he regained his composure, he joined us. I watched as he put away his handkerchief. An unmistakable shock of crimson showed on the ornately embroidered white cloth. Our eyes met, and he quickly shoved it in his pocket. He turned to José. "Our ship is ready whenever you are."

"Go ahead. I'll be right behind you." José turned back, kissing me gently. He pulled away so that his lips were just a breath away from mine. "I have left a small detachment to guard you and the children. I would prefer for all of you to stay below during the fighting."

I nodded my agreement. He kissed me again before leaving to join his men.

The gentle lapping of the oars as they hit the water was the only sound to echo across the river as the soldiers rowed to shore. When I could no longer see José, I went belowdecks to be with the children. Menotti and Teresita huddled together on the bed, their eyes wild with fear.

"Mamãe, what's happening?" Menotti asked.

"The men are going to battle, and we are to stay here."

Menotti looked to the door, his brows furrowed in concentration.

"Don't worry, my love. We are perfectly safe." I got into the bed with the children. Pulling Teresita close to me, I relished the faint scent of cocoa and ocean that clung to her. With most of its inhabitants gone, we could hear every gentle creak and pull of the vessel. "I was thinking this would be a good time for a story. How would you like that?"

Menotti smiled and nodded. Teresita snuggled closer to me. "Once upon a time, there was a girl. A lonely girl who used to dream of sailing away on the ocean looking for adventure. Every day she would go out to the balcony and watch the ships that sailed in and out of the port, pretending that she was on them. What she didn't know was that there was a very handsome sailor who stood on one of those ships. Every day he watched her with his spyglass. He made a vow; he said, 'She must be mine.'"

Menotti giggled. "That's silly."

"It is not. That's how your father and I met. It's why you're here." I playfully poked him, making him laugh even more.

The ship drifted forward along the river as the sound of gunfire thundered in the night air. I cast spells with my words, weaving stories about Laguna, about renegades, about sleeping under the stars and facing monsters in the woods. Enraptured by my words, I was able to draw their attention away from the chaos outside.

FORTY

February 1846

I sat in bed stroking the children's silky black hair. The noises of battle had long since died, leaving behind an eerie quiet pierced by the sounds of stray guns firing. I had started to doze off when a soft tapping roused me. Cautiously, I opened the door to see José standing in the passageway covered in blood.

"*Céus!*" I gasped, stepping into the hallway, gently closing the door behind me.

"Don't panic," he said with his hands in the air. "Most of the blood doesn't belong to me. I wanted to let you know I was all right." He paused, looking at the door behind me. "I don't want the children to see me like this."

"Of course." I grabbed my medical bag and followed him below, where some of his men had already set up a bath. They took one look at me and slipped out of the room, cheeks slightly pink. In the hours since the battle, we had sailed to docks at Salto, newly liberated from Argentine control.

José turned to me. "*Tesoro mio*, could you help me remove my shirt?"

I walked over and gently peeled the shirt off his body. One side was stuck to his ribs. I tsked, grabbing a rag to soften the dried blood around the wound. "José, what happened?"

"Oh, that." He shrugged. "It only took a little flesh. Nothing catastrophic."

I looked up at him in frustration as he peeked at me under his lifted arm, laughing.

"Have I told you about the time I was stabbed in the thigh?"

"No, and right now I would rather not hear about it." I stepped back. "All right, my love, you should be able to take your shirt off." He wiggled out of his tunic, stripping off his clothes and settling into the hot water in the basin. Crusted blood covered his body; his hair was caked with mud. I picked up a large cup and began to rinse him. "Tell me what happened today."

He sighed, his eyes closed, letting his head loll in my hands as I worked the blood out of his curls. "There were more men than our scouts told us there would be."

"How many more?"

"About one hundred. Give or take. It wasn't going well."

"I can tell by all this blood."

He chuckled. "General Gonzalez wanted to retreat."

"Obviously you didn't."

"Of course not!" He sat up straight, sloshing water out of the basin. "I raised my sword and yelled, 'There is no time!' And really there wasn't. If we hadn't pushed through, we would never have won."

I moved so that I could face him and wiped a wet curl from his face. "You are a stubborn man, José Garibaldi."

He smiled, pulling me almost into the basin, kissing my stomach. "With any luck, this child will be just as stubborn as his father."

"Lord help me." I laughed.

* * *

The children woke at the sound of us slipping back into the cabin. They jolted to life and sprang on José. Teresita attempted to hang from his neck while Menotti aimed for his midsection. "Careful. Papai got a little hurt," he said, wincing as he pried Teresita off him.

"Ow?" Teresita asked with great concern in her little eyes.

"*Sì, principessa.*" He pushed the hair back from her face and gently kissed her forehead.

"Can I see it?" Menotti asked, bouncing up and down slightly with excitement. José grinned and lifted up the side of his shirt as the children drew closer to peer at the wound.

I watched my family in a dreamy haze. Feliciana once told me you can never lose family. At the time we had been speaking of my mother and sisters, remarking on how I was dead to them. Sentimentality for what once was had left me with a pang of guilt, but here, as I watched my children climb over José, I knew that Feliciana was right. This was my family and I would never lose it.

"I have a surprise for you," José said, ruffling our son's hair. Menotti's face grew ecstatic at the prospect of a gift from his father. "But it's waiting for you at the dock."

Menotti rushed from the room and darted up the ship's stairs like a cat chasing a mouse.

"Be careful!" I called after him just as I realized it was of no use. José kissed my cheek and followed his son. Teresita and I made it topside shortly after Menotti, who was already at the railing, standing next to his father.

"Where is it, Papai? Where is my present?" he asked, jumping up and down.

José had a silly grin on his face. He pointed to a trio of horses that waited by the dock. "Do you see that pony? The brown one with the large white spot on his nose?"

"Yes," Menotti answered, his voice rising with anticipation.

"He's yours."

Menotti squealed with glee as he ran down the plank and onto the dock, dodging sailors until he made it to his horse.

"What do you think?" José called out to our son with pride as we followed him.

"He's wonderful!" He wrapped his arms around José's legs. "Thank you!"

José looked at me, a sparkle of mischief in his eyes. "It's about time we taught him how to ride."

I huffed. "When I was his age, I was already training horses." I got on my horse, holding Teresita in front of me. "What will you have us do?"

"Put on a good show for the people of Salto," José said.

We rode through the streets, followed by the Redshirts, then the Uruguayan army behind them. The people cheered, throwing flowers in our path. I watched Menotti in front of me. His large, genuine smile made him look like a miniature José.

That night the town threw a large fiesta in our honor. The whole garrison came out and mingled with the townspeople. Lanterns crisscrossed over the town square, making a canopy of light. We sat at the head table, flanked by the new mayor and the Uruguayan general who would be making Salto his home. The mayor, a short bald man, was anxious; he kept wiping his forehead with a damp handkerchief. His eyes darted all over the party and his hands shook as he reached for his wine. "He's so nervous," I remarked, watching as he loosened his collar.

"Well, I would be too, given what happened to his predecessor." José leaned in toward me. "The Argentinian army hanged him. It's the first thing they do when they come into a new town. It's how they establish their dominance."

The women of the village began delivering dishes of roasted vegetables and mounds of Spanish scented rice and black beans.

"They were cut off from all their supplies. How do they have so much food?" I whispered to José.

"This feast that they are parading before us is the last of everything they have from every village from here to Brazil." He nodded toward the food. "When Argentina swept through Uruguay, they burned all the villages, instructing the people to move to the other side of the river in Argentina, because they were now a part of the great South American empire."

"Only the people didn't go to Argentina," I said, looking over the crowd that had gathered.

"No. They didn't," José said. "There is one thing about the Uruguayans that Rosas has yet to learn: They will never do what they are told."

After we ate, the villagers pulled out their guitars and accordions. José pulled me by the arm, twirling me around in the center of the impromptu dance floor. Lost in my laughter, José pulled me close to him, kissing me passionately in front of everyone, making me blush.

"I need water," I said, catching my breath.

José nodded. He followed me back to the table where Teresita stood dancing with some of the children of the village. After taking a swig of water José picked up Teresita in one big swooping motion. "If you don't mind, I will be dancing with my other lovely lady." He kissed Teresita's cheek as he brought her out onto the dance floor with him.

I leaned against the table, savoring the cool breeze. Looking over at the other children, I noticed Menotti wasn't there. I scanned the crowd and couldn't help but laugh when I discovered him. He twirled on the dance floor without a care in the world with two girls. Both visions of beauty. Both at least six years older than my son.

My eyes drifted around the crowd of celebrating villagers; the Redshirts joined in the festivities with fervor. However, I noticed that one person in particular was missing, Anzani. There was something different about him lately. Gone was the man we had met in São Gabriel. In his place was a cantankerous imposter.

The party showed no signs of slowing down when José and I decided to retire. Teresita whined and fussed in my arms as her battle to keep her eyelids open was lost. After about ten minutes of searching and asking everyone if they had seen Menotti, we found him asleep under a table. José pulled him out and carried him back to the little house that the village let us use.

After we put the children to bed, José and I climbed into bed, savoring our time alone. The sounds of the party and the scent of wildflowers drifted through the open window on the cool night air. I lay on my side with José's arms wrapped around me. His hand was flat against my stomach, feeling our baby flutter.

"He's going to be strong."

I ran a hand along José's arm. "We make strong children. Did you see Menotti? He's taking after you already."

José chuckled. "Let's hope we don't have angry fathers pounding on our door too soon."

"He has your looks, we should prepare ourselves."

"You flatterer." He purred into my ear.

"Isn't that why you brought me with you?"

José laughed with me, but after a few moments he grew quiet, tightening his embrace. "I am truly happy to have you here."

"I know, and I am happy to be here with you."

With the sounds of the fiesta drifting into our room, I worked up the courage to bring up something that had been weighing on my mind. "I saw the blood on Anzani's handkerchief."

He sucked in a deep breath. "He's extremely ill."

I stared into the darkness, my thoughts racing. "Luisa never told me."

José shook his head. "I didn't expect her to. Anzani is doing everything he can to keep it a secret. He doesn't want the legion to know. He's afraid it will undermine his authority. Do you know about his lung injury?"

"Yes, that I knew. He was shot in the chest before Tomaso was born."

"The injury, though not fatal, made his lungs weak. They have been ever since. Until recently he's been able to treat his lung issues like a challenge to overcome, but they got the best of him. He's developed the consumption."

I rolled over to face him. "And Luisa just had a baby."

With every visit, Luisa had looked more tired, but she swore everything was all right. The baby was very small and had a light yellow tint to him, but he was eating. She had never mentioned Anzani's illness. I was so focused on my children that I hadn't stopped to think about my friend's problems. I could feel the guilt harden in my stomach. "I can't believe I didn't notice Luisa was hiding something so terrible."

"The illness has changed him; it's likely changed her as well." José rolled over onto his back, rubbing his hand over his face. "He's not the man we met in São Gabriel. He doesn't talk about his family anymore. It is almost like he is trying to separate himself from them so that they can get used to him being gone. Just like what dogs do." He turned his face back to me, his eyes glistening. "They sent Tomaso to Spain to apprentice with one of Luisa's brothers." José stared at the ceiling. "Why does death follow every person we care about?"

I massaged his wrist as I contemplated his question. Though nobody was immune to the hand of death, those we loved felt its harsh sting more than others. I kissed the inside of his wrist. Destiny controlled every waking minute of our lives, but I didn't want to think about her tonight. Tonight was for José and me.

FORTY-ONE

March 1846

Salto reminded me of my time in São Simão. The people smiled and said hello as they passed us in the streets, ready to help us at a moment's notice. We easily blended in with the locals. The women gushed over my pregnant belly while the children found new friends to occupy their time. José engrossed himself in the business of the village, helping them to reestablish their trade routes and place the refugees in new homes. The north may have been devastated by the war, but if José had his way, Salto was going to thrive. It would be the ultimate insult to Argentina.

The little house José procured for us had two bedrooms, a large kitchen, and a small parlor all on one floor. Outside we shared a beautiful garden with neighbors who were also Redshirts. The people of Salto thought of the Italians as their saviors and wanted us to live as such. Some of our men even considered settling there, having grown fond of the local women.

One cloudy morning I walked into the kitchen with a basket of laundry on my hip. José looked up, his face creased with worry.

"What's the matter?" I asked, setting the basket on the table.

"It's a letter from Rivera, with an impressive offer. He wants to offer thirty-five acres of land to be divided among the Redshirts."

"Thirty-five acres is a lot of land. Has he made an offer like this to the other legions?"

"Not that I am aware of." He pointed to a paragraph toward the end of the page. "Those thirty-five acres are from his personal land. This can't be sanctioned by the government."

I let out a huff of air. "I don't trust this. Why would he give all of this to our legion yet not offer anything even close to this to his own men? The Uruguayan army's uniforms are little more than rags, their families left to starve."

"I don't know why he wants to do this, but I intend to find out." He briskly kissed my cheek. "Expect company this evening. Menotti!"

Menotti poked his head into the kitchen. "Come with me, son, we have work to do," José said as he grabbed his hat, walking out the door.

As the sun began to set over Salto, the whole Redshirt legion stuffed into our courtyard, spilling out of the surrounding houses. The men perched against trees, crowded in doorways, and hung out of windows. The threat of rain blew in on the crisp fall air. The rustle of dry leaves competed with the chattering of the soldiers. I leaned against our kitchen doorway with my arms resting on my pregnant belly, watching the meeting unfold before me. José stood under the lone tree in the center addressing the men, telling them of the letter and its offerings. Audible gasps spread through the crowd.

"I bring this to you today because it is not my decision to make. This gift is being offered to all of us."

"You mean Trojan gift!" a young soldier called from the back. I couldn't see his face in the crowd.

"Comrade!" José called. "Please enlighten your brothers."

"No one ever gives anyone a free gift," the same soldier called back.

"Your wife did!" one of the other men called out, to ripples of laughter. I lifted a hand to my mouth to stifle my own laugh as José raised a hand and a hush fell over the men. Every eye turned to him, waiting with still breath for his next command. He pointed to the original sailor from the back of the crowd, who spoke up again. "The question is, what does Rivera want from us in return?"

"That, my comrade, is a wonderful question," José said, pacing before them. "Does he want unconditional loyalty? To have the greatest legion in all of the Americas at his beck and call, like a dog?" The men cheered as José said this. My husband paused, waiting for the noise to calm down before he began again. "I had a talk with some of the officers from the Uruguayan army today. None of their legions have been offered a gift even remotely close to this. We are the lucky few to be given this offer." I fidgeted where I stood. Something wasn't right.

José waited while the men whispered among themselves. "I know the Uruguayan army owes us, but I ask you, are we owed more than our Uruguayan brothers? Have we fought for our adopted country more than they have?" He looked out over the crowd, which was enrapt at his words. "I tell you no. We are not special. We are soldiers with a job to do and only deserve our fair share." He looked down at the ground, contemplating some unseen fact before looking back up at the men. Everyone, myself included, leaned forward, waiting for his next words. "I can't make the decision for you. It's your choice as to whether or not we accept this gift. We will have a vote."

Anzani stood up. "Do I have anyone in favor of taking this gift?" The crowd was silent; even the birds stilled.

"Feel free to voice your opinion; we are all comrades here. We are all equal," José added, but still there was silence.

"Any nays?" Anzani asked the crowd. It was with a unified

defining voice they all called out nay. I couldn't help it. I joined in with them.

"Very well. I will give General Rivera our answer. You are dismissed," José said.

The next day, as I cleaned up our breakfast and prepared for my morning chores, José sat at the table watching me. He leaned back in his chair. "I have to say, I really like it here. I could see us making Salto home."

"I do as well. Even though it was under siege, it doesn't feel like it was tainted by the war."

"It's also cleaner than Montevideo."

"There is nothing like the smell of decaying fish in the morning." Slowly a giggle bubbled up from my belly and spread to José. Before I knew it I was sitting on his lap laughing.

A firm rap at the door brought us back to our senses. I followed José as he opened it to find a young messenger boy standing there holding a letter. José took the letter and opened it, his smile dissipating.

"José, what is it?" I asked, growing concerned. "José?"

"The war is over." He left the house without another word.

FORTY-TWO

May 1846

José had sent out inquiries to his allies in Montevideo. Soon the news came trickling back to us. Rivera had in fact been having disagreements with the Uruguayan government. Rivera wasn't satisfied with the peace treaty offered by Britain and France—an agreement that put Rivera in charge of Montevideo and Oribe in charge of everything else.

"Well, now we know why Rivera made such a generous offer to the Redshirts," José said, slapping down the letter from the messenger. "He thought he could buy us."

"And with your support he would have reignited the war," I said.

"We have to go back to Montevideo."

"Why? What for?"

"The government called the legion back. Even though we are Rivera's tool, we still have to take orders from the Uruguayan government."

"I don't want to go back. We can build a life here."

José's face fell. "They gave me orders."

"And it wouldn't be the first time you ignored them."

"Anita, we have to go." José crumpled the letter. "Oribe is taking over the region and he doesn't want us here."

"If we go to Montevideo now, we'll risk me giving birth to this child on the road."

"You wouldn't be the first."

"José—"

"*Tesoro mio*, I know it's not ideal and if we could stay, we would, but we have no choice."

"Montevideo is dangerous, it's filthy, and I'm sure it's still riddled with disease."

"We'll be fine."

"How do you know?"

José got up from the table and placed his callused hands on my shoulders. "Because we'll be together." He pulled me to him, kissing the top of my head.

I felt uneasy, but José had a point. As long as we were together, we were safe.

* * *

August 1846

Frigid rain pelted the ship, forcing me to stay below in the stuffy cabin with the children, fighting with the cushions I was perched on. At thirty-seven weeks I felt like an overripe fruit ready to burst. All I wanted was to be on solid ground.

Even though I was relieved to make it to Montevideo, I was apprehensive over what we might find. The city hadn't recovered from the siege and it was crawling with French and British soldiers.

As we rolled through the empty streets, I could see the ghosts of what the city had once been. Gone were the peddlers selling their goods from little carts, the women who'd bustled from shop to shop in their brightly colored dresses, their laughter tinkling like clinking china over the sound of the buggies driving down the streets. Montevideo was no longer home. Rows of houses sat abandoned, the boarded-up windows a testament to the devastation we had endured. I looked down and rubbed my stomach. We could not afford to stay here for very long.

It was then, while in the carriage on our way home, that the pains came. I doubled over as they made me crumple in on myself. José whipped the horses, rushing them faster as I prayed that the midwife was still here.

We were able to get her to our home just in time for the birth. The piercing cries of my other babies when they had left me had been welcome relief. This time, though, my son was quiet. Panic washed over me. Children, when they enter this world, are supposed to cry out with victory, but my son did not. I sat up on my elbows. "Why isn't he crying?" Panic seized my throat. "He's not crying. Why isn't he crying?"

The midwife turned her back to me, ignoring my questions as she went to work. I could see her move her arms but still couldn't hear anything. *This isn't happening. Oh God, don't let this be happening. I can't lose another child.* One of the midwife's assistants tried to tend to me, but I swatted her away as I struggled to get up from the bed.

Finally, I heard the high-pitched wail of my son. Relief washed over me as the midwife turned back around, delivering him to my expectant arms. "Congratulations, Mamãe, your son is quite the fighter."

I rocked him ever so slightly. He had already settled, his wide eyes searching the new world he now lived in. "He's a fighter, just like his father," I finally responded.

"I wouldn't be surprised if some of that came from his mother."

The midwife shot me a knowing smile as she washed her hands in the basin.

José burst into the room a short while later. Pure joy spread over his features as he took his son into his arms.

"Another boy. What shall we name him?" he asked as he let our little son grasp his finger.

"Well, Menotti was named after a freedom fighter. Perhaps we could do the same with this one?"

José looked up at me and smiled. "That is a brilliant idea." He looked back down at our son, thinking. "There was a man back in Italy named Nicola Ricciotti. We became friends when I was living in Marseille. He had the kindest spirit, yet he was fierce when it came to his love for his country. He embodied the dream of a unified Italy."

"I'm sure the authorities didn't like that."

"Not in the slightest." José gave a short laugh. "When the Bourbons put him in front of the firing squad, he sang."

"He sang?"

José nodded. "He did indeed. That was just who he was, and let me tell you, he could not carry a tune."

"What did he sing?"

"It was the chorus from *Donna Caritea* that we all used to sing. He belted out, '*He who dies for his country has lived long enough.*'" José looked back down at our son in reflective silence. "I think Ricciotti is an appropriate name, don't you?"

"I do."

Over the next few weeks, we settled back into a routine of sorts. We didn't know how long we were going to stay in Montevideo, so we did our best to make it a home again, even though it didn't feel like home anymore. Feliciana and Marco took refuge with Feliciana's sister in the north, out of the reach of Rosas, leaving Montevideo a little darker. José stayed busy with the affairs of state while I did all I could to manage the household and the children.

There were very few resources available in Montevideo; I had to scrape together every little crust of bread and ounce of flour so that we could eat.

I had put Ricciotti down for his nap, allowing myself a few moments of peace, when José came storming through the front door. The baby woke, crying out for all the world to hear.

"You don't know what kind of day I've had." José frowned, accentuating the bags under his eyes.

"Now I have to go back and try to settle the baby. Your supper is going to be late and you have no one to blame but yourself." I saw his hat lying on the floor. "And pick that up! I'm tired of cleaning up everyone else's mess." I could hear José cursing under his breath as I went upstairs. An hour later I was finally able to get Ricciotti settled. Quietly I ventured back downstairs. It looked as if my pantry had exploded, and in the midst of the food debris were my husband and children.

Teresita sat on the floor playing with a wad of dough, flour coating her raven hair. José and Menotti stood at the table rolling out spaghetti noodles, the latter looking exactly like the former. "What is this?"

José turned to me. "I decided to teach the children how to make pasta."

"Pasa! Pasa!" Teresita giggled, waving her pudgy arms in the air before shoving the wad of pasta dough she gripped into her mouth.

"Don't worry. I will clean it up," José said, turning back to his work at the table.

I looked around our small kitchen. "José, this is all of our provisions. We don't have the money or rations to replace this."

"Don't worry about it, *tesoro mio*," he said, giving me a floury kiss.

"Don't worry? How am I supposed to feed us tomorrow? Or the day after that?" I crossed my arms, clenching my fists. I couldn't believe how foolish José was being.

"I have it taken care of."

"Menotti, take your sister outside. Mamãe and Papai need to have a conversation," I said as sweetly as possible.

"But Mamãe, we are making spaghetti." Menotti threw his pasta on the table.

"Right now, young man." I pointed to the door. "And dust some of that flour off your and your sister's clothes."

Menotti looked up at his father. "Go ahead, your mother and I have to talk. We'll finish after you have come back in," José said.

Reluctantly Menotti jumped off the chair he'd been standing on. I watched as he took his sister by the hand, then I turned back to José. He had his back to me, working on the pasta as if there weren't a problem. "Talk to me. Why are you behaving like a madman?"

He sighed, dropping excess dough into a bowl. "The French and English broke up the army."

"How? How can they do such a thing? They are foreign countries. They can't come here and do whatever they like."

"They can and they are," he said, not looking up at me as he kneaded the dough. "They aren't stopping with the army. They are breaking up the whole government. Tearing it down and starting from scratch."

I huffed. "I'm sure they will be putting together one that favors them."

José grunted in response. He still refused to face me. Instead, he played with the pasta on the table, rolling it into a long noodle.

"What does this mean for the Redshirts? What about us?"

"My men are in purgatory. They have yet to get any pay." He slammed a ball of dough onto the table. "As always, the English and French have no idea what they are doing." He took in a deep breath, regaining control of himself. "I'm getting my pardon. The king of Piedmont is calling all Italians living abroad home."

"Oh, José, that is wonderful news." I reached out and pulled him by the arm, forcing him to look at me.

"Don't forget, he's only the king of Piedmont. Not a unified Italy. If I go back, there is no guarantee that I will be safe anywhere outside of his realm."

"But it's a start, isn't it? And tell me, José, when have we actually been safe?"

José's shoulders sagged as he dropped the pasta he'd been working with on the table. "I know I should be ecstatic. After ten long years of exile I am finally able to go home. But how can I be happy when the men who stood by my side don't have a stable future? I can't leave until I know that any man who chooses to stay here is able to put a roof over his head and food on his table." He wiped the flour from his hands, looking at me with exasperation. "What am I to do?"

I wrapped my arms around his waist, holding him to me. "You will do what you always do."

"And what is that, *tesoro mio*?" he asked, kissing the top of my head.

"You will force these European officials who seem to think they know better to take your advice." I looked up at him, resting my chin on his chest. "You'll use your Garibaldi charm to make them see your way or run them through with a sword. Whichever comes first."

José let out an uncontrollable giggle before pulling me away. "You know me so well."

I shrugged. "It's a talent."

José kissed me just as Menotti came back into the kitchen, dragging his sister behind him. He grimaced when he saw us.

I pulled away and went over to Menotti. "Would you rather I kiss you?" I grabbed Menotti and began kissing his dimpled cheeks. He giggled as he tried to push me off him.

“Ew, Mamãe!” he exclaimed as he wiped his face.

“Come, my darlings. Let’s all learn to make pasta.” I picked up Teresita. “I have a feeling this is going to be a very valuable skill.” I gave José a coy smile.

PART FOUR

Italy

FORTY-THREE

December 1847

Our massive ships set off across the ocean, the hopes of over a hundred Italians propelling us forward, filling the sails and pushing away the clouds. I wished I could be as hopeful as they were, but the truth was that anxiety gripped my chest. I was moving to a land I had heard about in stories.

The only time I felt at ease was when I stood at the bow of the ship with the cold spray of the ocean on my face. Memories of a time when I thirsted for adventure and the lure of the unknown floated back to me on the sea breeze. Breathing in the salty air, I could feel something brewing just beyond the horizon. Rubbing my arms against the gooseflesh, I hoped the lonely crescent moon poking through the clouds wasn't a bad omen.

A young sailor with several missing teeth ran up to me. "You have to come below right now!" We rushed below to find that Teresita had ravaged a number of trunks in search of Lord knew what. I pulled her out, my snarling little monster, from the tangle of clothing and goods. On top of continuously corralling my two-year-old daughter, I had a fussy sixteen-month-old who seemed to be happy only when we were topside with the crisp fresh air on his skin.

At seven years old Menotti clung to José, choosing to be his shadow in all things, admiring his father as if he were a god. If his father was at the helm, Menotti would be there as well. If José was trying to calculate our navigation, Menotti was by his side trying to learn how to operate the delicate instruments. I saw him only in the evenings, yawning deeply as he collapsed into bed.

When I could spare a moment, my thoughts drifted to Luisa and her family. Our last visit together had been one filled with false bravery. While Anzani was going to be joining José on the campaign, Luisa and her children were going to her family's home in Spain. We had sat in her parlor, letting the children play for the last time.

"I have not seen my brother in five years." She watched them, avoiding eye contact with me. "It will be good for the boys to be around their cousins."

"I wish you could come with us to Italy."

"I was only a child when my family sought the safety of Spain. The Austrians made sure we didn't have a home in Italy to go back to." Luisa sighed. "I have been gone from Italy for so long that Spain feels more like home." She looked at me for the first time, tears swimming in her eyes. "I want to be with my husband, but we agreed it would be best for me to go to my family while he fights. Anyway, Tomaso has started his apprenticeship with my brother."

We grabbed each other's hands, the unsaid words floating in the air between us. Anzani's illness, the children, the very real possibility that we would never see each other again. "I'll write. I'll tell you everything and then when we are settled, you'll come and stay with us," I told her.

"Yes. I'd like that," she said.

* * *

March 1848

When we finally approached the port in Genoa, the children and I climbed above deck and made our way to the bow of the ship dressed in matching red shirts. Our anticipation grew, the children bounced in place, their little fingers gripping the railing. I clasped Ricciotti tighter as my heart fluttered. The question that had been plaguing me rose up like bile in my throat: *Will I be accepted?*

The docks of Genoa appeared on the horizon. A great throng of people crowded the harbor and they were yelling.

"*Viva Garibaldi! Viva Garibaldi!*" Their chants drifted out over the ocean.

"Mamãe!" Menotti exclaimed. "They're calling our name!"

"They are, aren't they?" I said in equal amazement. Menotti turned his attention back to the docks with their crowds of people.

When we disembarked the ship, Menotti pulled me to the left. Teresita grasped my skirt and pulled to my right, rambling about something unintelligible. José stood to the side playing the politician; shaking hands, kissing children, making everyone love him. Old women shoved bread and flowers at me. All of those people surrounding me, clamoring for our attention. I turned my head for a moment to look at my husband, and then my children were gone.

Panic flooded me as I clung to Ricciotti. "Menotti! Teresita!" I called as the throng of people continued to close in around me, like a rushing river. The choking smells of heavy perfume, sweat, and roasting meats nauseated me. All of the faces that I tried to shove past made my head swim. I just needed to find my children.

Tears began to well. I turned around in circles looking for the familiar faces of my son and daughter. Just when all hope seemed lost, I felt a firm hand on my shoulder.

"I believe these two belong to you." Menotti and Teresita wrapped their arms around my legs. Relief washed over me as I savored the feeling of having them close.

"Here, let me help you," said a tall man with a deep olive complexion, his dark hair slicked back. Dressed in the fine clothing of a gentleman, he spoke like an official as he cleared a path for us. I followed behind, continuing to examine him. He wore a silver-trimmed sword, and his shiny boots clinked as he walked along the pavement. He led us back to José, grabbing my husband's shoulder. José turned around, looking at the man with pure delight. They embraced as old friends before José and the rest of us followed the man toward a large gilded carriage, away from the throng of people.

"I am terribly sorry. I have not had the opportunity to introduce myself. I am Paolo Antonini," the man said to me with a flourished bow.

"Paolo is a comrade in the struggle for a unified Italy. His family will be our sponsors while we stay in Genoa," José said as we entered the carriage. Paolo was a fellow member of the Carbonari, the Austrian resistance, José continued to explain. While my boisterous husband had managed to find himself exiled, Paolo had gone underground. He felt the best way to undermine the Austrians was to do so without being seen. With the help of his brother who resided in Rio de Janeiro, he smuggled goods in and out of Genoa, bypassing the high taxes. He also had a knack for procuring whatever the resistance needed.

"Yes, what an honor to be living in such an exciting time. Senhora, I hope you will feel comfortable in my home. It is not much, but it will have all of your basics."

"Thank you, senhor. I am sure we will be quite at home." I smiled.

José and Paolo made small talk as our carriage rolled through the bumpy streets of Genoa. Past the bustling marketplaces and grand buildings in the center of town. Through the winding streets that climbed the steep hills surrounding the crystal-blue bay, which reflected the sky. It seemed every Genoan waved to us as we went by. The children hung their heads out the window, oohing and ahhing as we rode along. Our carriage stopped at the gates of a large red brick house trimmed in white. The long drive was bordered with triangular trees in deep green hues that stood out in sharp contrast to the grand house.

"It is such a shame that I only have this house to host you. Due to the Austrians' meddling we have to consolidate in order to survive with comfort. Alas, this is the only estate in Italy my family has left."

"Oh, Senhor Antonini, this will be more than enough for us." I looked back at our host and smiled. The grandness of the home was overwhelming.

"Please, if we are to live under the same roof, I would request that you call me Paolo."

There were two footmen waiting for us; one opened the carriage door, and the other held open the front door. We walked past the stoic young man into a black-and-white marbled front entry. Small tables held large vases with long-stemmed blood-red roses. Teresita made a dash for one of the tables, but I grabbed her by the shoulder just in time.

"Perhaps the children would be more comfortable in the nursery. Please follow me." Paolo led us up the winding marble staircase and to the left wing of the house. "The nursery used to belong to my brothers and me. I hope it will meet your standards," he said, addressing Menotti and Teresita as he opened the double doors to an expansive room filled with every leisure item our children could ever dream of. The walls were painted teal with a white trim along the ceiling and floor. One whole wall was lined with a large bookcase. Rocking horses and toys of every shape and size were scattered through the room. In the center of it all stood a dollhouse painted in various shades of pink. A small bundle of dolls draped over each other next to the little house waiting to be played with. The children let out a burst of laughter as they ran into the room.

"We didn't have much in the way of toys for little girls, so I had some made for Teresita."

"Senhor, your kindness is too much. You will spoil my children," I said as I marveled over the toys in the room.

Paolo waved a hand in dismissal. "Children deserve to be spoiled. Life as an adult will come too soon and with it many troubles. Let them be happy now while they can."

A young lady in a black uniform approached us. "May I take Ricciotti?"

Instinctively I pulled back, hugging my baby to me. Paolo put a kind hand on my arm. "This is Giulia. She will be the children's nurse."

"Nurse?" I asked, looking from José to Paolo.

"Yes." The woman smiled. "I am here to help you take care of the children. I am the eldest of twelve; rest assured your precious little ones are in good hands. May I?"

Reluctantly I gave him to her. Giulia smiled as she gently bounced him in her arms. He giggled and shoved a fist into his mouth. "When was the last time he ate?"

"This morning, before we docked."

She patted his bottom. "He could probably do with a change." Drool oozed out over Ricciotti's fist. "And maybe a bit of rabbit. I'll have the cook send up some treats for the children as well."

She walked past us into the nursery, where she proceeded to introduce herself to Teresita and Menotti.

"Come with me, I will show you to your room." Paolo led us to the end of the hall, where a set of double doors opened into an expansive suite. Our bedroom, if you could call it that, was the size of my first home in Laguna. A large canopy bed stood in the center. To the right I saw a small table with two chairs. On top of the table was an overflowing plate of fruit.

"There is fresh water in the basin if you would like to wash. Dinner will be served at eight. Feel free to rest until then." Paolo left the room, closing the doors behind him. I continued walking around our new dwelling in awe.

José sat down on the bed with a huff and watched me with a hunger in his eyes. "You know, you are allowed to enjoy yourself."

I stroked the gilded brushes that perched atop the vanity. "The smuggling business seems to be treating the Antonini family well."

"The Antonini brothers have sacrificed for the Italian cause time and time again. They pride themselves on being able to get almost anything under the long nose of Austria. They use this wealth to the benefit of the rebels. The Antonini family is devoted to making Italy a unified country. Life in Italy is going to be very different from the life we knew in the Americas. I suggest you start getting used to it."

"Different is an understatement. I could fit the whole village I was born in inside this house."

José laughed, pulling me toward him. "I can bet this bed is softer than any bed in Laguna too."

"I am sure it is," I said, letting him pull me down onto the bed. As José began to nuzzle my neck there was a knock at the door. With a sigh he let me go. Three months on a ship didn't allow for much alone time, and this disruption was not welcome. "Come in," José called, the sting of disappointment in his voice.

One of the footmen held a message out for him. "I am sorry to disturb you, sir, but it is urgent."

"Thank you," José said as he took the letter. After a moment of reading he looked up at me. "I have to go back into town. It's Anzani. They don't expect him to make it through the night."

"Well, wait. I'll go with you," I said, gathering my things.

"No. Stay here."

I stopped and stared at him. "You said that we were stronger together. We just got here and now you want to leave me?"

"Anita, it's not like that." He took my hands in his. "Italy is not like South America. The men, they wouldn't accept you as a soldier."

"I don't care what others think," I said, pulling my arms out of his grip. "And since when have you?"

He let out a puff of air. "The culture here is different. We need to tread lightly. Let the people get to know you. I am sure they will fall in love with you just like I have."

"I still don't like this." I was uneasy about being left alone, about not being useful.

"Think of the children," José said, trying to console me. "They need their mother."

"I *am* thinking of the children," I responded through gritted teeth. "It's not just our children's lives at stake, it's all the children of this country."

"You will have a role to play in this conflict. I promise."

José grabbed his things and left me with a kiss on the forehead. I pulled aside the blue curtains and stood by the expansive window that stretched from the ceiling to the floor. Watching the people move between the sprawling tangle of ruins and majestic steeples, I wondered if I was foolish to think that this place was just like South America. Instead of a land that resisted taming, I had found a place that had long since shed the wildness of its youth. I couldn't help but wonder if I would fit in.

I left the window and curled up in the large bed. Would I never see South America again? Staring up at the light blue canopy, I felt a momentary burst of nostalgia for the rolling hills that reached to the heavens. For hues of green that you could smell. For the community in Montevideo. But this was my home now. It had to be. I determined that I would love this place and make its people love me in return.

FORTY-FOUR

I awoke to polite knocks that steadily grew louder. "Come in," I groaned. Three maids entered the room, one tall, matronly looking woman leading two younger ones in matching uniforms. The young maids struggled slightly as they dragged my trunk. The older woman wore a simple black dress adorned with a gold pocket watch. Her black hair was pinned back in a neat knot. "*Buon pomeriggio*," she said with her hands firmly clasped behind her back. "I am Mrs. Mancini, the housekeeper." She consulted the watch in her right breast pocket, then pinched it shut. "Madam, it's nearly time for dinner. I thought we could help get you ready." She snapped her fingers. The two younger maids opened my trunk and began pulling out my clothes.

"I don't need assistance," I protested, getting out of bed.

"Nonsense. We are here to help," Mrs. Mancini said, overseeing her charges. Holding my clothing up to inspect, they divided it into two piles. I bristled at the sight of my things being pawed at by strange women.

Mrs. Mancini picked up one of my skirts between her index finger and her thumb. She crinkled her nose before handing it to one of her underlings, who took the skirt and put it in a separate pile of its own. I was about to protest but she held up a dress. "I think this should work for tonight. We will finish unpacking and laundering your clothing while you wash for supper. Cook gets irritable when people are late."

I felt uneasy about leaving my things with these women, but I did as I was told. This was a new country with new customs that I was going to have to quickly adjust to. When I was ready, one of the footmen led me down to the dining room, which was lined with ornate wooden paneling. Paolo sat at the end of a long wooden table, my children on either side of him. He looked up at me with a smile as I entered the room. "I take it you had a lovely siesta. The children were just telling me the most magnificent stories of their adventures."

Menotti and Teresita looked utterly pleased with their new friend. "Senhor Antonini said that we can have ja— ja—...What was it called again?" Menotti asked Paolo with all the charm of a seven-year-old.

"Ge-la-to," Paolo enunciated slowly so that Menotti could learn to say it properly.

"Gelato. Senhor Paolo says it's the best dessert I will have. But we only get some if we are good children," Menotti said with glee.

"I a good girl." Teresita beamed.

"I see you have found your way into my children's hearts," I said to Paolo. "Where is Ricciotti?"

"The nurse has already bathed him and put him to sleep."

"I like Senhora Giulia," Menotti said wistfully. "She smells nice."

"An' she has sweets!" Teresita said in agreement with her brother.

A plate of roasted vegetables on top of pasta was placed in front of me. "Any word from José?"

"No. None as of yet. Tomorrow morning the seamstress will arrive to measure you and the children for new clothing."

"That is very kind of you, but we can't afford such luxuries. We will wear the clothing that we have."

"Nonsense. Your stay and all of your needs are sponsored by my family. You and the children needn't want for anything."

"Truly, Senhor Antonini, José and I are used to being able to get by on our own."

Antonini straightened in his seat. "Senhora, your husband is the figurehead of our revolution. The Garibaldi family is the first family of Italy. It is my job to make sure you look the part. Tomorrow the seamstress will come and the whole family will receive new clothing. I will hear no more protest."

The awkward silence that followed was interrupted when Teresita leaned in to Menotti. "Uh-oh, no 'lato for Mamãe."

Paolo could not hide his smile. "I think we can make an exception for Mamãe, just this once?"

Teresita regarded me for a moment, her little black eyes narrowed as she contemplated her judgment. A cunning smile slowly spread across her face. "Yes, just this once."

* * *

The next morning as I sat down for breakfast one of the footmen handed me a letter from José.

Tesoro mio,

As you read this I will be journeying to Turin with the hopes of receiving an audience with Charles Albert, the king of Piedmont-Sardinia.

I am grieved to report that our dear friend Anzani died in the middle of the night, surrounded by dear friends. Anzani, always ready for duty, wore his red shirt, even in death. I've sent word to Luisa in Spain. Thankfully she has the support of her family to assist her in this difficult time.

In honor of our dear friend I have named the Lombardy garrison the Anzani garrison. Lombardy was Anzani's home. Do you remember when he told us that? It feels like so long ago that we met him on the banks of the river. I think I will always remember him that way, overly friendly and looking for an adventure. He dreamed of returning to the fatherland, and though I don't believe this was the way that he had wanted, he is more advantageous than some of us who were banished.

How I long to be with you and the children. I wish I could explore Genoa with you, sharing with you the places of my youth. Have Paolo take you to Il Rifugio Café. That was where I spent most of my time planning the future of this country with my mentor and comrades. I am sure that Paolo can share a number of stories of that time, though I will admit they will not be the most flattering of tales. Stroll through the piazza at sunset. It is a romantic place, which will be made all the more beautiful by the setting sun casting its elegant rays over the cathedrals. I know I will be picturing you there. I dream of the day when you and I sip our morning tea under the great olive trees as our children play. A peaceful life in my home country. Tesoro mio, is this too much to ask for?

Alas, what is the point of dreaming when there is so much work to be done? While I am in Turin and pulling our great country together I need you to be my eyes and ears. Tell me all that you know. I leave you with Paolo Antonini as your guide. Trust in his wisdom.

Until I return to you,
José

Later that morning, after being poked and violated by the seamstress, I met Paolo in his study. The dark wood furniture trimmed in leather and walls encased in books gave the room a dark, warm feeling. One window let in the bright golden light that tumbled over the high-backed red armchairs. Paolo sat with his legs crossed, reading a newspaper, ignoring the fact that I had entered the room. He delicately sipped from a tiny mug as he read. I gently cleared my throat and he looked up at me and smiled.

"Ciao, senhora!" He set his little mug down on the table next to him. "How do you find your stay here?" He folded his newspaper in his lap.

"Lovely, thank you, senhor." I sat in the matching high-backed chair across from my host as a servant poured coffee into an equally tiny mug intended for me.

"Good, very good." He tilted his head and studied me. "Though the regiment has left us behind, you and I have work of our own to do."

"And what work is that?" I asked, taking a sip of coffee. The bitterness caught me off guard. "No wonder you drink your coffee in such tiny mugs!"

"Too strong?" he asked, looking at me as if I were a child.

"Yes. In my country we prefer *yerba mate*. Though bitter in nature, it is not so bold. Yerba coaxes the drinker toward life; this, it kicks you on the backside like a mule."

"That would be because it is espresso, senhora." Paolo laughed.

I set my cup down on the table. "You said that we have work to do. Tell me, does this have anything to do with José being the figurehead of the unification movement?"

"Yes, this has everything to do with your husband being the face of unification. We need you to recruit for the legion."

"And how will I be helping the cause, specifically?"

"You will talk. There will be a rally tonight in town. You will tell the people stories of your time in the Americas. Let them know why they need to follow our Giuseppe."

"I'm not sure they will want to listen to me."

"Anita, you are the closest person to our Giuseppe. You know him like no one else does." He sat forward in his chair. "Tell them why you love him, and they will see it too."

I was an outsider. Why would they listen to me? I looked to Paolo, with his hopeful face and slicked-back hair. We each had a role in the war, and apparently mine was to talk, whether or not the people would listen. "All right. I'll do it."

"I will have Mrs. Mancini put together a suitable dress for you."

"No. I will wear my red tunic."

"But senhora, it's so old."

Within every fiber of that old red shirt clung my memories of everything José and I had sacrificed to get here. Yes, it was a simple shirt, but the hope of a nation resided in every stitch. "I will wear no other shirt but the red one."

Paolo watched me from his chair. "I have a feeling that red will be in fashion this season."

FORTY-FIVE

That evening Paolo, Mrs. Mancini, and I rode to Il Rifugio Café in our finest clothing. When we arrived, people were spilling out into the street. It appeared that men and women from all over Genoa had come here to listen to me speak. "José wrote to me about this place," I said.

My eyes traveled up the old stone building along the crack that rose from the bright green sign to the faded shutters of the apartments above the café.

Paolo smiled as he helped me from the carriage. "Yes, this was the backdrop to much of the trouble that José got me into when we were young men." He laughed. "Have him tell you about the time we ran from the Austrian guard, through this café and out the back. Only your José stopped short of the trash that had been piled up by the back door. I was not so lucky."

As we approached the people crowded outside, they parted, staring openmouthed as we walked by. I sat in a chair at the front of the café next to Mrs. Mancini, watching as Paolo walked to the front.

"Esteemed comrades, it warms my heart that so many of you have joined us tonight. As you have heard or seen, we have the Garibaldi family among us." He smiled at some of the finely dressed women in the front. "Alas, Giuseppe could not be with us today. He has left for Turin already. I cannot share his plans, but I can share with you his incredible wife, Anita. The beautiful young woman who ran away from her family to join our Giuseppe in his adventures." Paolo encouraged me to accompany him in front of the audience. Standing next to him, I scanned the anxious faces waiting for me to say something.

The little café was filled beyond capacity. Every face looked at me with hopeful eyes. This had never been my place. José was the voice; I was just the woman who stood in the back of the room watching him conjure his magic with his words. What was I supposed to say to these people? Why should they listen to me? I was just a girl from a little town in Brazil. I wasn't José. Realization dawned on me... I wasn't José.

"Senhor Paolo flatters me. I know you all came here out of curiosity so that you could hear about Giuseppe, or Peppino, as you call him. Or perhaps you are curious about the untamed Brazilian woman who left her family to be with your hero. Well, here I am, we can see that I am nothing special." I smiled mischievously. "Though my sponsor will be the best witness as to my wild ways.

"But to know my José is to know the people he surrounds himself with. These people shaped him as he in turn inspired them to be better men. Let me tell you a story. When I met José, all those many years ago, there was a man in his service, his name was Luigi Rossetti. Perhaps you have heard of him? Like José, Luigi found his foster home of Brazil because he was expelled from here, from the fatherland. Like José, Luigi wanted a unified Italy. Like José, Rossetti wanted a just and fair government for Italy. With each breath, he made sure we all knew this was every man and woman's right."

The audience collectively leaned forward, waiting for more of my story. "There were many nights when José and Rossetti would stay up until the sun rose talking about these ideas. Talking about how they could apply the lessons they were learning in Rio Grande do Sul's struggle for independence toward the unification of Italy."

I smiled to myself, looking down at the scuffed floor. My worn black shoes stood out in contrast to the tan tile. I wiggled my toes, noticing that my big toe was about to break through the old leather as I tried to map out my next thoughts. "Even though José was an ocean away from his home, he still talked about Italy every day. Sometimes, when he and Rossetti were so focused on their plans for Italy, I felt like I was José's mistress. Italy always has and always will be his first love.

"Rossetti had a mistress too—his printing press. You see, he felt his press was a lifeline to the fatherland. José always teased him about the printing press, telling him it was more demanding than a wife. Rossetti, every time, smiled and said if he didn't have the printing press, how would people in Italy know what he and Giuseppe were sacrificing while they were away? He wanted the Italian people to know that they were not alone in their struggle. Halfway around the world, people not all that different from them were struggling for a fair and just system of government." I took a breath, remembering. "Rossetti didn't smile very often, but when he did it was magical, like the sun suddenly appearing after numerous days of rain. The only one who could get him to smile was Giuseppe when he talked about coming home.

"Rossetti couldn't be with us today. He died in his struggle for a just government, not only for the Italians but for all of those who wish to be free. While trying to secure his printing press he and his men were overtaken by Brazilian Imperial forces."

I paused, looking around the room. The people were soaking in every word that I said. Their chests stilled as I told the story. "We couldn't even bury him here; his body was buried somewhere in the Brazilian wilderness. He is forever separated from the country that he sacrificed for. Rossetti could not live to see his dream fulfilled, but you can. José carries Rossetti's dream on his shoulders. Will you let him carry that weight alone?"

All around me cheers and clapping erupted. Paolo stood up next to me, calling out to the audience, "If you want to sign up to join the legion, see Vincenzo by the door. Join us! See the dream of these great men come to fruition."

As the men slowly made their way to Vincenzo to sign up, three women approached me. All wore dresses of the highest quality in matching shades of green. Their hair was perfectly coiffed. "Hello, madam, my name is Elisa. This is Sofia and Claudia." Elisa pointed to each woman in turn. "We would like to invite you to a luncheon at my home. We want your insight into how we can better help our husbands as they prepare for war."

"Mrs. Garibaldi accepts." Paolo spoke up before I could say anything.

"I do?"

Paolo leaned in to me and whispered with a forced smile, "When the wife of the most powerful man in Genoa invites you to lunch, you accept."

I turned back to the women, genuinely smiling. "I accept. Please discuss the details with my maid, Mrs. Mancini," I said as I felt Paolo begin to pull me around the room to greet the people who had come to see me.

It was late in the evening when we finally started rolling through the streets of Genoa toward home. I slumped against the seat in the carriage. The chilly air felt refreshing against my flushed skin.

"You were remarkable!" Paolo gushed. "We got more recruits after this meeting than we have gotten in months!"

"That is wonderful news." I turned to Mrs. Mancini. "When is my luncheon?"

"Thursday next. I wanted to give the seamstress time to finish at least one of the dresses for you."

"Excellent thinking, Mrs. Mancini," Paolo interjected. "We have another rally in just two weeks. Make sure the seamstress has another dress ready by then." He looked back at me. "And make sure she has plenty of red."

Elisa Profumo, besides being the wife of the mayor of Genoa, boasted a noble heritage. Her mother was the niece of a pope. Her father, the third son of the duke of Genoa, made his fortune exporting silk to London. At every opportunity, she bragged that her family's line could be traced all the way back to 1098, when one of her ancestors brought the ashes of John the Baptist, the city's patron saint, back from the Crusades.

On the given Thursday I arrived promptly for the luncheon. The tight blond ringlets on either side of Elisa's head bobbed as she escorted me around her large, elegant parlor, introducing me to everyone. Her burgundy chiffon dress made soft swooshing sounds as she floated among every prominent lady in Genoa. Elisa sat me at the head of her expansive dining table. She took a seat to my right, while Claudia sat at my left, Sofia next to her. As Elisa began to address all the ladies at the ornate table, footmen set down plates of thinly sliced meats and cheese on delicate china.

"As you all know, the reason I invited you here was so that we could learn from Mrs. Garibaldi's experience. She has stood side by side with her husband on and off the battlefield. Mrs. Garibaldi, why don't you tell some of these ladies about what you did while Mr. Garibaldi was away?"

"Well, he wasn't always away. I was often with him. Our custom in Brazil, and even to an extent in Uruguay, was for the wives to travel with their husbands, doing the cooking and other wifely chores that one would do at home."

One of the older ladies down the table gasped. "How barbaric!"

"Well, I would not call it barbaric, it's just the way things were."

I smiled as the women nodded reassuringly. "In my youth, before our children, I even fought alongside him, though I can't say many other wives did that."

"Wasn't it dangerous?" another woman questioned. She fanned her blushing face as she looked around the table.

"Madam, I believe that is the point of war," Elisa responded dryly after sipping her wine. She motioned for me to continue.

"I did not value my life as much as I do now. Then, it was just José and me. If I died in battle what would it matter?" I leaned to the side as a servant picked up my antipasto and set down a small plate of penne with marinara sauce. "Who would care that I was gone? But now there are three little souls that need me. The support I lent to José and our soldiers was given out of necessity. We needed someone to collect and tend to the injured, someone to volunteer at the hospitals."

"That is a novel idea," Elisa said, setting down her fork and addressing the ladies. "I believe Mrs. Garibaldi has stumbled onto something that will benefit all of us. As so many of you know, my family was integral in making Genoa the greatest city in all of Italy. Now, I know you all can't trace your families to the Crusades, but it is our duty to make sure Genoa is properly supported during the unification. Volunteering at our hospital is an important part of that." The other ladies murmured their agreement.

"Was this something you found easy to establish?" Claudia asked.

"Well, once the war began there were others who established the hospital. In Laguna, I was a volunteer. On campaign with José, I kept my own medical kits so that I could help our soldiers as needed. In Montevideo, we already had a hospital, but I coordinated the wives of the legion."

Elisa put a hand on my arm. "Your experience then will be most valuable." She turned back to the women. "First we need to fund our endeavor. Who has any ideas on how to fundraise?"

From there the conversation broke down as women discussed their ideas to raise money for our hospital. Our main course was taken away and delicate whitefish was placed before us. I thoughtfully listened and then a thought struck me. "Perhaps we could do more than just organize a hospital? People need to see unification in a positive light. They need to see that it can bring them happiness and fulfill their needs." By this time our third course had been cleared and delicate crystal bowls filled with blood orange sorbet appeared. The women's talk changed to ways they could be a positive influence on the unification effort.

I was surprised to find that once the sorbets had been finished the footmen came around once more, delivering large plates of fruit to the table and coffees for each of us. Elisa sipped at her coffee and then leaned toward me. "My husband and I have our own box at the opera. We were wondering if you would like to join us?"

"I'd love to. Thank you," I said, a bit surprised.

Elisa gave a little clap of glee. "It has plenty of room. Sofia, Claudia, and their husbands will be joining us." I looked to the other two women, who nodded in unison, their curls bouncing. "Oh, and bring your lovely sponsor. What was his name again?"

"Paolo Antonini."

"Right, bring Mr. Antonini. I simply hate odd-numbered groups when going about town. Antonini can talk business with the men while we plot our adventures." Her eyes grew big as she displayed a coy grin.

When I arrived home from the luncheon, Paolo stood in the middle of the foyer. He rocked on the balls of his feet. "Tell me everything. Who was there? What did you talk about? Was your dress fashionable enough? Do they accept you?"

I raised a hand. "Please, give me a chance to breathe." I related every detail of the luncheon to him. "And then just before I left, Elisa invited us to join her and her husband in their box at the opera."

"Madam, you have saved this revolution!" Paolo kissed me on both cheeks. "We need to plan what we will say. What will we wear?"

"You can do all of that planning on your own. For now, I am going to visit my children." I left the room as Paolo muttered plans and scribbled in a notebook. I found my way to the nursery. Relieving the nurse, I spent the whole afternoon playing.

FORTY-SIX

April 1848

The hypnotic patter of the rain against the window made my head feel heavy with sleep. In the brick fireplace a pleasant little fire crackled and spit, spreading its warmth through the cozy room. Not having any practical sewing to do, I took up embroidery. It was the hobby of all the ladies in Genoa, and for better or for worse, I was now a lady of Genoa. I set down the pillowcase in my lap as I let my head lean on the back of the chair.

Watching the rain beat on the window, I remembered the days when José and I would huddle together in a rickety little cabin or tent, clinging to each other for warmth. When I would clutch Menotti to my chest, praying that he would not become sick. If anyone had told me then that I would one day be embroidering a pillowcase for fun, I would have laughed. There had been too much to do. I didn't have to go out searching for ways to support our cause. I had to regularly remind myself that what I did here was just as important as what I used to do on the battlefield. Wars were fought in more than one way, and while my husband won battles through force, I had to be more persuasive as I fought for the hearts and minds of the people.

However, I hated being left out of the planning. The news that I received was filtered as it passed from one person to the next. I decided it was time to hear from my husband directly. I got up from my chair, letting the pillowcase fall to the floor. The delicate ivy trim would have to wait another day to be finished. Pulling out the first piece of paper I could find, I scratched out a letter to my husband.

Dearest José,

I trust that you have arrived safely in Turin. Since you have left I have made myself a productive member of Genoa society. At Senhor Antonini's request I spoke at your café, Il Rifugio. Paolo told me the most entertaining story of how you let him fall into a pile of garbage. It sounds as if you and he had many grand adventures!

I have accepted an invitation to the opera. Senhora Elisa Profumo and her husband own a box. Paolo and I are invited to be their special guests, along with a number of what Paolo refers to as "elite citizens" who will provide much-needed support for the legion.

The society women have embraced me as one of their own, looking to me for leadership as they prepare for war. We have begun working with the hospital in Genoa, collecting items for its stockpile. One of the women had the most novel of ideas. We distribute bread to the hungry and tell them, "With compliments of Italy," so that they know they will be taken care of once we are a unified country.

The people hunger for Italy, a country they can call their own. They are ready to stand behind you. Here I await your orders to be of more assistance.

With love,
Anita

Tesoro mio,

I am proud that you have fit in so well with Genoa society. Paolo is correct. You have indeed aligned yourself with the elite. Is Elisa Profumo the wife of Antonio Profumo? If so, keep her close. As her husband goes, so goes Genoa. Be sure to tell me about the opera; I envy you.

I wish I had happier news to share with you, but alas, the leaders who have the king's ear do not feel that my services are necessary to the cause. The ignorance of these men astounds me! They see experience and wisdom standing before them, but they turn it away. They have the audacity to call me a corsair! Me! Giuseppe Garibaldi! The man who has led several armies to victory! To be considered a dupe is a huge insult. They are fools. If we are not careful they will lose this battle all because of their ignorance.

They order me to Venice in the hopes that I will be pacified away from the battlefields, but instead I shall go to Milan. The Milanese have done the impossible: As we sailed for Italy, the people of Milan had their own successful revolution, expelling the Austrians. I am going there in the hopes of being of use to the new Milanese government.

I wish you were by my side once more. I know that you would force these men into submission by the point of your sword. Your strength and clarity have always been a balm to my soul.

Until I return,
José

Dearest José,

We travel across the ocean yet are still plagued by fools. I have faith that in time you will make them see reason. In light of your last letter we no longer tell the people "with compliments of Italy" when we feed them. It is now "With compliments of Giuseppe Garibaldi." I know you may not be comfortable with this, but if the people love you, they will be more likely to listen to you over those imbeciles who call themselves royalty.

Yes, Elisa is married to Antonio Profumo. Antonio is a great supporter of the Italian unification efforts. While at the opera, he and Paolo had a lively discussion about what was needed for Italy. They were so loud that they and the other husbands left the box so that they could talk in the lobby! They completely disregarded Giuseppe Verdi's latest opera, Macbeth. Senhor Profumo has given Elisa the liberty of his checkbook in order to purchase whatever supplies we may need for the hospital and our other endeavors.

My love, do not give up hope. You will find a way. You always find a way. My advice to you is to be like Malcolm in Macbeth, take a step back in Milan, and wait for the right opportunity to seize the army and unify our country.

With love,
Anita

Tesoro mio,

How I long to watch your words fall from your beautiful lips before me. Until I can be reunited with you, I will have to settle for your uplifting words on paper. I have made some progress: We've been able to get the provincial Milanese government to agree to give us uniforms. But with every gift there is a catch. We were explicitly told no red. The nobility doesn't care about the reputation of the Redshirts. They say it's because the color is not sanctioned, but I feel as if they will choose the opposite of what I suggest just to spite me. My second-in-command, Medici, and I were handed a catalogue and told that we could choose whatever uniform we wanted from its pages. The problem is, all of the uniforms have already been chosen! We could look like the French. We could look like the Prussians. Or as Medici said, "Lord help the poor soul who chooses to look like the Austrians. If we dress like the enemy, we'll be firing on ourselves and not even know it."

We have reluctantly settled on white. So now instead of butchers we look like bakers. Well, I suppose if all else fails we could always bake the Austrians a cake! Perhaps they will be so disgruntled by our pastries that they will be repelled from Italy of their own accord? Speaking of that, have Paolo's cooks make you a torta pasqualina. I have dreamed of it for a fortnight.

Now that we have our uniforms, we need to find munitions. The war council has yet to approve any weapons for us. They are slow to approve anything that we ask for. The Milanese government acts as if we are pests as opposed to the aid that they need.

Tesoro mio, my chest is bursting with pride over the wonderful work that you have been doing in Genoa.

Until I am able to return to you,
José

FORTY-SEVEN

May 1848

I stared out the window of my carriage as we rattled along the cobblestone road toward Elisa's spacious townhome in the center of the city. Fresh ocean air drifted in on the cool wind. I would have much rather walked on such a nice day, but Paolo insisted I take the carriage. "It would be unseemly if Mrs. Garibaldi did a common thing such as walk."

During our stay in Genoa I came to trust Paolo and his advice. A bachelor by design, he found the invasion of the Garibaldi family a welcome novelty. At the dinner table he often regaled us with tales of his adventures with his brother both during their childhood and as adult merchants exploring South America. To my children he was the entertaining *Zio* Paolo but behind the laughter and the exaggerated hand gestures, I could see that he missed his brother, who had yet to return to Italy with his family.

I jolted back to attention when the carriage came to an abrupt stop in front of an expansive town house covered with ancient ivy.

Striding to the large oak door, I knocked with all my strength. This visit had to go the way I planned; there could be no mistakes. I was ushered into Elisa's private parlor. Large purple irises bloomed from a crystal vase near the open window. The lace curtains rippled against the burgundy walls.

Elisa entered, her little feet tapping against the terra-cotta tiles. "Mrs. Garibaldi. I am so glad that you called upon me."

"The pleasure is all mine." I smiled, doing my best to charm her. "It is so important to hold on to friendship when you are in a new land."

"You are quite right, madam. Why, I was just remarking to Mrs. Polizzi the other day how pleased I am that you have been welcomed into our little social circle." She smiled warmly as a servant brought in a tray of espresso and small chocolate cookies. "The Garibaldi family is one of the oldest in all of Genoa. Though they are younger than mine, of course. We Genoan families have a duty to Italy."

"I couldn't agree more." I paused for effect. "Elisa, I was wondering if I could ask you something rather personal."

"Oh, by all means, Donna Anita, I am an open book, as the saying goes."

"Does your husband still allow you the freedom to purchase what you please?"

Elisa sipped her espresso from the milk-white teacup trimmed with delicate pink flowers. "Yes, but our recent escapades have caught the attention of the Austrian magistrates. I have been advised to use discretion. I hope you understand, we can't have the Austrians looking too closely at us."

"It is completely understandable. No one wants the Austrians at their front door." I sipped my espresso. Having the attention of the Austrians on us was going to be a problem. I looked over to Elisa. She admired me; it wasn't a secret. She wanted to hear every story I had. She wanted…"I was only hoping that we could have an adventure, you know, like the kind that I used to have back in South America. I am so homesick."

She reached a hand out to me. "Of course you are homesick, darling. You are in a strange land. I do hope that my fellow Italians have been kind to you."

I grasped her extended hand. "Oh yes, you have all been so kind to me. Especially you, Elisa. It's just that sometimes a woman like myself, well, you see, she needs to stir up a bit of trouble. To feel complete. Do you understand?"

"Oh yes, Mrs. Garibaldi. You have no idea how much I understand. You don't know how often I imagined that I was the crusader who brought John the Baptist's ashes here to Genoa. I heard the story so many times that I hoped I could be like him. Live up to my family's name." Blond ringlets dangled like earrings as her head tilted to the side. "Did you have an idea in mind?"

I smiled. This was playing out exactly as I wanted. "José's legion needs weapons. Paolo can obtain them, but we need a generous sponsor to help us. This is where you come in."

"This sounds like a mischievous bit of fun." She moved forward in her seat as if I were offering her candy. "I assume you already have a plan?"

"Only the fuzzy outlines of one, really, but I hear the armory makes fabulous gowns," I said before I took another sip of espresso.

Elisa laughed. "This sounds delightful!"

I made my way home to Paolo's study. He sat in his high-backed chair, reading a book. I removed my gloves and draped them over the back of the chair opposite him. "What would you say if I told you I had a solution to José's inventory problem?"

Paolo closed his book with a crisp snap. "I would say that not even you, senhora, are capable of such miracles."

I picked at my nails. "Well then, perhaps it's time for me to apply for sainthood."

Paolo's book slipped from his hands, bouncing with a series of dull thuds across the floor. "Anita, what have you done?"

"Nothing really, only procured the funding necessary to supply the army with weapons and ammunition."

"How? I can't get what he needs without help or without being seen, and no aristocrat is willing to risk being openly aligned with Garibaldi."

"Not unless said aristocrat has a wife with an expensive dress habit that requires ample funds and the freedom to buy whatever she likes."

"You mean Elisa Profumo?"

"She'll pay for the weapons and write in her books that the expense was to a seamstress. Meanwhile we procure whatever my husband needs."

Paolo sat with his mouth agape. "This is truly a miracle. I'll place the order right away."

* * *

June 1848

Three weeks later I walked into the house after a meeting with the ladies of Genoa. As I removed my coat and gloves, I called out, "Paolo! I have new developments to tell you about. Of course, in between all the gossip." There was an unusual silence.

"Genoan gossip is the stuff of legend." José's voice boomed from the doorway in which he leaned. I dropped my gloves and ran to him, wrapping my arms around his waist.

"*Tesoro mio.*" His voice rumbled in a deep, husky vibration as he burrowed his face into my neck. The woodsy scent of him, the sound of his voice—no other words were needed as he led me upstairs.

Later, as we lay entwined with each other, savoring our reunion, I massaged his wrist. "Tell me, why are you here?"

José's brow wrinkled as he twisted to look at me. "What do you mean? You aren't happy to see me?"

"I thought you were doing important work in Milan. I wasn't expecting you to come here."

José lay back down. "Milan doesn't want me."

"What do you mean it doesn't want you? Why?" I sat up so I could look at him. "José, what happened?"

José looked away from me, pulling his hand through his hair. "The provincial government decided that they didn't want my help. They say my style of warfare is barbaric and unbecoming of how an Italian should conduct himself. They feel they can do a better job of keeping Austria at bay without me."

I gently took him by the chin, turning his face to look at me. "The provincial government of Milan and the aristocracy of Piedmont are ignorant to what a true Italian is. The people of Rio Grande do Sul are better off because of you. Uruguay is independent of Argentina because of you. You are the smartest, most accomplished man I know. The eyes of those men are clouded, and they will learn. Trust me on this, they will learn what happens when they lose faith in the one man who can unite them all under one banner."

José wrapped his hand around my wrist. "I can do what Machiavelli and the Medicis couldn't, but these men, they dismiss me like a child."

"Then husband, make so much noise that they can't dismiss you."

José chuckled. "I am already screaming. I can't yell any louder."

"What is it that you tell Menotti from that book, *The Prince*?"

"There is a lot I tell him from *The Prince*."

"José, I'm being serious, what's the quote? The one about how people see you?"

"Everyone sees what you seem to be, few know what you really are."

"Perhaps it's time for them to see what I see." I kissed his forehead. "Make them see the great unifier that I know you are."

FORTY-EIGHT

September 1848

José stayed with us in Genoa as he reorganized his supplies, new weapons included. He decided it was time for his family to move to his childhood home in Nizza. There we would stay with his mother while he and his troops gained some much-needed rest.

As we sailed from Genoa, I felt a longing in my heart for the place that was our first home in this new land. Now we were going to live with José's mother, the loving saint I had heard so much about. My longing gave way to trepidation as a rough image of the woman formed in my imagination.

The port city of Nizza was beautiful with its richly painted homes. The bright houses reminded me of Montevideo. José held Teresita as we sailed into port, lightly bouncing her in his arms. "You'll be able to see where your papai grew up. Every morning you'll be able to smell bread from the bakery downstairs and your nonna will give you all kinds of treats."

José had often spoken of his childhood in Nizza. His father, a successful merchant, had provided for his family of four sons.

They had lived in a large second-story flat in the center of town, above a bakery. Every morning the aroma of baking bread rising up from the first floor would wake José. He spoke of his father being a fair, hardworking man. His mother was a gentle, loving woman, attentive, the picture of Italian womanhood.

I took a deep breath, steadying myself as we set anchor. Beyond the palm tree–lined beach, brightly painted buildings with burnt-red tiled roofs stretched out toward the soft rolling hills in the distance. For a moment I felt like I was home in Brazil. José placed a hand on the small of my back and said, "Welcome to Nizza. The most important city in all of Italy, my home." He moved to the railing, entranced by the coast. "The ancient Greeks named it Nikaia, after the goddess of victory, Nike. Over the years, the French have tried to lure it from us. They even call it Nice. A terrible name in my opinion, but I never seem to agree with the French on anything. "

José's father had died in his sleep within the first years of his son's exile in South America. His mother, though, was still alive, her notorious stubbornness defying death. Two of his brothers lived in town, having taken over their father's merchant business. Mrs. Garibaldi stood at the docks, a stout woman dressed in black. Her blond hair stuck out like straw under her black cap. "Peppino!" she exclaimed, grabbing José by the face and kissing him. "*Peppino mio.*" She brushed away tears.

She turned to me. "She is so dark! I didn't expect her to be so dark."

"Mamma," José said in an attempt to get her to stop.

Mamma Garibaldi looked up at her son. "Our family has prided itself on not looking like southerners." She reached up, touching his golden-brown curls. "It is a shame none of your children will have your looks."

"I think Menotti looks like his father," I said in defense of my children, feeling an annoyance grow inside me. There was always an implication when someone remarked that a child didn't look like their father, and I didn't like the downcast looks Mamma Garibaldi gave my children.

She huffed. "Perhaps if he had been born in Africa." She looked down at Menotti. "But what can you do when their mother is from South America." She tsked as she turned from us and started walking.

I looked at José. "I thought you said she was a kind woman."

José shrugged. "She'll warm up to you."

I looked to Mamma Garibaldi, who walked ahead of us, navigating the narrow cobbled streets with the deftness of someone half her age, not caring if we could keep up. I doubted my husband's words. "I have dinner ready," she said. "It's been getting cold. You should have gotten here sooner."

We followed her up the stairs to the family apartment, which took up the whole floor. "We will have to live like sardines with so many people in our tiny home," she complained as we entered.

The Garibaldi flat boasted a modest entrance hall, the cream tile gleaming in the evening light. The walls were decorated with paintings of faraway hillsides dotted with wildflowers. Mamma Garibaldi pointed to the left. "That way to the bedrooms. The children will share one room. José, you can have your old room. Anita will have the spare room next to mine."

"Mother, don't you mean that Anita and I get our own room?"

"No, I do not. My son will not commit bigamy under my roof," she said, leading us through a set of double doors into the formal parlor.

I stiffened. After all these years, an ocean away, I still couldn't escape my past. My grip tightened on Ricciotti as Teresita clung to my skirts. How could I be so foolish? I would never be more than the disobedient girl who never learned her place.

Red blotches appeared on José's neck and chest. He took me by the elbow and whispered in my ear, "Stay here, let me talk to her."

José led his mother out into the hall while I sat on the light pink couch holding Ricciotti, with Teresita and Menotti on either side of me. Bits of the conversation flowed into the parlor.

"She is my wife!" José yelled. Menotti flinched.

"I have heard the stories. I know what she is. She is married to another man."

"No, she is not. That man is dead. He died nearly ten years ago!"

Teresita leaned into my arm. I put a hand on her leg as she began to tremble.

"Oh, that is very convenient. I am sure she told you that story once she saw you. The girls always chased you. I only hoped you would not find one so devious."

Teresita took the liberty of covering her ears and looking up at me.

"She is my wife and the mother of my children! You will show her respect!" Both Menotti and Teresita jumped.

"And I am your mother! Where is my respect?"

I now knew where my husband got his stubborn head from. I handed Ricciotti to Menotti and slipped into the hallway. They both turned to me, red-faced, the same vein on the side of their heads popping up. "José, she is right. This is her house. While we stay here we will be in our separate rooms."

"Well, at least the woman has some respect. I guess they are not all savages in the Americas." Mamma Garibaldi stomped away from us.

I grabbed José by the wrist before he went into the parlor. "Promise me that if we are to live in Nizza for an extended time, we will have a house of our own. I will appease your mother, but this cannot be forever."

He kissed my forehead. "*Sì, tesoro mio*."

Mamma Garibaldi showed no interest in discussing the current issues of the day as we sat down to dinner. She sulked at the head of the table, a figure dressed all in black, ignoring our conversation.

Silverware clinked against the china as we ate in silence. Before we had even finished with the food, she popped up and cleared the plates from the table. Menotti's fork was halfway to his mouth when she whisked away his plate. He tried to protest but she ignored him. As the sun began to set, Mamma Garibaldi announced that she was going to bed, leaving us in the parlor in peace.

The furniture in the parlor was nicer than anything we'd ever had in any of our homes. Three delicate vases adorned the coffee table, while a porcelain statue of a maiden desperately clutching her hat against a bitter unseen wind sat on the table next to us. My stomach clenched at the danger these most likely priceless treasures were in with my children in the home.

Menotti curled up in a chair with his latest read, *Eighteenth-Century Battles of Europe.* He gripped the book with both hands, his face completely covered, the binding crinkling with every page that he turned. José sat on the floor with Teresita and played with dolls while I rested on the couch, slowly swaying from side to side with Ricciotti.

Teresita fell onto her father's lap. "I hu'gry."

"Me too," Menotti said, looking up.

"I'll see if I can scavenge some food for us," José said, getting up from the floor and heading into the kitchen.

"Mamãe, do we really have to stay here?" Menotti asked.

"Nonna mean," Teresita said over the head of her doll.

Mamma Garibaldi was not the pleasant woman my husband had made her out to be. I hoped she would take to the children, but Menotti and Teresita were acutely aware of the anger that emanated from their grandmother.

"Shh, don't speak that way about your grandmother, Teresita." I turned to Menotti. "We don't have to stay here for very long. Just long enough so that we can get settled in Nizza. We will have a house of our own very soon."

José stepped back into the room with a plate of cookies. I could tell he'd heard everything we said. His fake smile, the one that he reserved for the public, was all too plain on his face. "Did you know that this is where I grew up? I was born in this very house."

"Was Nonna nicer then?" Menotti asked, reaching for a cookie.

"Your grandmother has been living alone for a long time. We are chaos to her. How do you think you would feel if you were her?"

Menotti looked over to Teresita. "I suppose I can kind of see how she feels."

Teresita shook her head. "Nonna still mean."

José pulled her onto his lap. "Perhaps, little one, your nonna will soften as she gets to know you." Teresita wrinkled her face as she reached for another cookie.

That evening after I put the children to bed, I settled into my new bedroom. As I was preparing for bed, José slipped into the room. He wrapped his arms around me as he began to nuzzle my neck. I pushed him away.

"No, my love, not here." I rested my hand against his face, letting my thumb trace his cheekbone. Life under his mother's roof would be difficult; she already loathed me and if she caught me with her son, regardless of our marital arrangements, life would be downright unbearable.

"My mother is asleep and what she doesn't know won't hurt her. I will be out by morning." He went in for a kiss, but I stopped him.

"I gave my word." I didn't like it here, and I wanted to make sure he didn't grow comfortable in our new home either.

José pulled away. "Well, we will have to find another way." He walked back toward the door. "Are you sure you want to let me sleep alone?"

"Go, my love, before I change my mind."

He sighed. "Well, dream of me."

Early the next morning, before the sun had even risen, I was awoken by a light coming in from the hallway. I opened my eyes and saw Mamma Garibaldi standing in the doorway, looking at me. When she saw me stir, she closed the door and left.

On our second day in Nizza we began unpacking our trunks. Cautiously, like a wild animal investigating something new, Mamma Garibaldi would come around us. When she thought I wasn't looking, she would reach out and play with Ricciotti, tickling his belly or letting him wrap a firm fist around her finger. She wasn't sure about Teresita, given her energetic outbursts, but I often caught her looking sideways at Menotti. Her brows knit as she silently scrutinized him.

In the morning of our fourth day, José pulled me aside. "I have a surprise for you."

I looked at him curiously as he slipped his arms around my waist and whispered in my ear, "I found a way around my mother." I put both hands on his chest and gently pushed him away, looking at him in surprise. "Be ready to leave just before dinner."

"But the children, we can't leave them alone with her."

"I hired a nurse. She'll help my mother. I want her to get to know her grandchildren. Spend time alone with them, see how wonderful they are."

We stole away that evening while the children played with the nurse. We made our way to the ship, where José had a delicious dinner laid out for us on the deck. We ate by the glow of the setting sun, enjoying our time alone together. When dinner was finished, we retired to his cabin to finally have the freedom of being man and wife.

FORTY-NINE

February 1849

In the months that followed we settled into our lives in Nizza. This included staying on José's ship a couple of times a week. I wasn't happy with our arrangement but believed José when he promised a house of our own when this war was over.

One morning I woke up in our cabin to the familiar pungent scent of salt, old fish, and ocean. The smells brought me back to Brazil. As I stirred in our bed, feeling disoriented, a pang of homesickness struck me. In Brazil I was a fierce soldier, in Uruguay and Genoa I could mobilize the women, but here, here I was trapped in a gilded cage with pink cushions. After years of purpose, spending day after day in my mother-in-law's parlor made me feel like a limb that had withered from lack of use.

I rolled over and watched my husband sleep, my eyes tracing the scars that fanned out over his chest as it rose and fell with each breath. My fingertips grazed the puckered ridge of skin on his biceps, a harsh reminder of a bullet that missed its mark.

In the quiet of the early dawn, when only the lapping of the waves against the hull could be heard, I realized I longed not for Brazil but for the people we had been while in Brazil. Before the children. Before the glory. When it had been Anita and Giuseppe chasing the wind.

My stomach pitched and churned like the sea during a storm. I ran out of our cabin and rushed to the railing, making it to the edge just in time to lose all of its contents. Wiping my mouth on my sleeve, I began counting as realization seeped through me. José walked up behind me, tenderly rubbing the space between my shoulder blades.

"*Tesoro mio*, are you ill?"

I shook my head. "It would appear that we're going to have another child."

A broad smile spread across his face. "Another baby?" He wrapped his arms around my shoulders, pulling me close to him. He put his nose to my head and breathed me in, savoring the moment. "Another *piccolo* Garibaldi." His voice was distant, his eyes were closed, and he looked at peace.

"We're going to have to tell your mother."

José sighed. "Can we just show up with the child?"

I laughed. "You mean just walk in with a baby in my arms? 'Oh, look what I found at the market today.' I have a feeling she will notice before then."

José rested his chin on the top of my head. "We could say that you are becoming more voluptuous due to all of this wonderful Italian food." I elbowed him. "All right, we will tell her soon, but for now I want to savor this moment." I leaned my head back against his broad chest as we watched the water gently ripple around us.

I dreaded telling Mamma Garibaldi. She already hated me for ruining her son. There was only one way that she would take this. José formed a plan. We took her out to dinner at a local restaurant with crisp white tablecloths. Crystal water goblets sparkled with the reflections of the large gold chandeliers that were scattered around the ceiling.

When the chef found out that the Great Garibaldi was a patron of his restaurant he personally came out to greet us. Dressed in a fine black suit, the portly man bowed deeply. "What a lucky man to have such beautiful women by his side. I want you to know that you can order whatever you want. It is my pleasure to serve you at no cost."

"Sir, that is too kind," José tried to protest.

"No, no, my pleasure. I shall be able to say that the wonderful Garibaldi has eaten at my restaurant. It's very good for business."

The food was heavenly. Pasta in a decadent pesto sauce as well as roasted beef so tender that it melted on my tongue. All the while José poured wine for his mother. The more she drank, the more he filled her cup. When her cheeks grew as rosy as the wine she consumed, José said. "Mamma, Anita and I have some important news to tell you."

Mamma looked up at José with bleary eyes and whispered rather loudly, "Are you sending her back to the Americas?" She hiccupped.

José cast a worried glance at me before continuing. "No," he said slowly. "Anita is pregnant. You are going to have another grandchild."

Mamma Garibaldi looked over at me as if I had the plague. "Why do you hate me?"

"I don't hate you." The words flowed easily from my lips, unburdening me of their power. Regardless of what she said and did, she was José's mother. Hating her would be like hating a piece of my husband.

Mamma Garibaldi's watery blue eyes shimmered as tears began to flow down her sagging cheeks. "I have failed. I have failed as a mother. I don't know how I can go on living."

"Mother, you are overreacting."

"Overreacting. Overreacting! I have done everything that I was biblically supposed to. I go to mass every Sunday. I made you go to mass. I have done my duty by God. Why does he punish me as if I were Job?" She moaned loudly. I looked around the restaurant, which had fallen silent as people began to watch us. "Your father is turning over in his grave. He would never have wanted this."

"You act like such a fool." José's tranquil face grew dark and stormy. "What my father would have wanted was for me to find fulfillment, which I have indeed found." Mamma Garibaldi opened her mouth to speak, but José lifted a hand, stopping her. "Whether you like it or not, this woman is my wife. I don't care what you say or think. She is my wife. You will learn to accept her, or you will lose your son."

Mamma Garibaldi sniffled, bringing her tears to a halt. She stared at her son in wide-eyed disbelief as he added, "I will not continue to indulge your hysterical delusions."

"Very well," she whispered, setting her napkin on the table.

The next morning as I placed the children's breakfast in front of them, Mamma Garibaldi wobbled as she made her way into the kitchen. Forgoing her usual fruit and toast, she chose to only drink coffee. She closed her eyes and breathed in the scent of the thick black liquid. Menotti and Teresita, usually very lively, cast furtive glances at each other, unsure of what was happening and how to proceed. José, no longer caring what his mother thought, had slept in the bed with me during the night but left shortly after the sun rose to work, and to avoid his mother. He came into the dining room with a newspaper under his arm and a box of cookies in his hands. He set the box down in the middle of the table and shoved the paper under my nose. "You were right."

"Well, it's kind of you to acknowledge the obvious, husband, but I need more specifics," I said, taking the paper from him.

"Austria attacks Milan!"

I snatched the paper from him. Austrian forces had gone back into Milan. They had jailed every member of the provincial government and declared martial law.

"The Austrians have undone everything that the rebel forces put together." He smiled as he pushed a cookie into his mouth.

"You sound all too happy about this," I said, bringing the pan back into the kitchen while the children, abandoning their breakfast, descended on the box of sweets in the middle of the table.

"I am!" José called to me. I walked back into the dining room, handing him his tea. "This means that all the dusty old tactics that those archaic politicians clung to didn't work. I can show them that they can't operate that way any longer, not if we are going to win this. They have to listen to me now," he said with his mouth full.

"Does this mean that you are going to Milan?"

"No, it's pointless, Austria has dug itself into the city." José guzzled the remaining tea. "Contrary to popular belief, *tesoro mio*, I have not been vacationing here in Nizza. I have a plan. We are going to the Alps!"

"The Alps? Are you mad? You'll be taking the fight directly to their door."

"Precisely." One corner of his mouth lifted in amusement. "I'll be cutting off their supply line while simultaneously drawing them away from Milan. It's going to be brilliant!"

I took his head in my hands. "If you go off and do this, promise me that you will do things your way. You won't let them influence you like they did before."

"Believe me, I will."

"No, José, I mean it. It's time to put your red shirts back on. Forget what the nobility says, you do what you think is right."

José kissed me in response. "I have work to do." And with that he left for the day, ignoring his mother.

* * *

As our time progressed in Nizza, more of our comrades appeared at our doorstep, including our dear Paolo, carrying with him Teresita's dollhouse and plenty of other toys for the children. Standing a short distance behind him was a man with a messy crop of black hair and a well-trimmed beard.

"Anita, may I present Giacomo Medici." The man bowed before entering the apartment. A descendant of the famed Medici family, he felt the burden of a legacy that was built long before he came into existence. Giacomo swore to do the one thing the Medicis had failed to do, unify Italy. His legion, named for his family, adopted José's red shirts as a sign of unity.

Every evening more and more officers gathered at the Garibaldi house as they made their preparations. Mamma Garibaldi's moodiness came in waves. Some days she enjoyed having José's friends over. It reminded her of Peppino's younger days. She fussed, making sure everyone had full bellies.

Other times she complained there were too many people in her house. She'd poke her head into the dining room, where they focused over maps and planned their strategy. She'd mumble something about wanting to be able to have her supper and then shuffle off to her bedroom.

The men gathered their provisions together, including making new red shirts. The night before they left, I slept with José on his ship. They were leaving the fleet here in Nizza for their march to the Alps. Using uncharted roads, they hoped to surprise their enemy.

"Remind me again why we can't have a home of our own?" I asked him.

"Because being a patriot sometimes means sacrificing a salary that would help me take care of a growing family." He kissed my forehead. "Anyway, it is good for the children to know their grandmother."

I grumbled as I nestled closer to him. I hated living with his mother, but I knew our welfare was at the whim of kind benefactors, at least for now. "Promise me that once this is all over, we will have our own home."

José stroked my hair. "Of course. We'll have the villa we always talked about. A little farm with horses and an olive grove."

"I want orange trees," I said with a smile. "The olives will be for you, but the oranges, they'll be for me. I love the scent of fresh orange blossoms in the morning."

"I will plant a whole grove of oranges just for you."

I lay there for a moment, dreaming of this piece of paradise that we would rest in once this battle was over, but there was one thing that it needed. "We need a tree."

He chuckled. "There'll be no shortage of those."

"No, there has to be one tree whose only purpose is climbing."

He turned his head, raising an eyebrow to question me.

"When I was a child, I climbed every tree I could, much to my mother's dismay." I laughed at the memory of my parents pulling me from a tree after mass. "Children, especially our children, need to have adventures of their own design. They need to be allowed to climb trees."

José kissed my head. "Whatever you want, *tesoro mio*."

* * *

Weeks passed, and I hadn't heard anything from José. Every waking moment left me wondering what was happening to my husband and his men. There was hardly any news in the papers. I was going to go mad from either the lack of information or the forced solitude brought on me by my mother-in-law. When a messenger arrived at our door one morning, I pushed Mamma Garibaldi out of the way as I grabbed the letter he clutched in his hands. Furiously, I tore open the letter to find a note from

Paolo. José was gravely ill with a fever and unable to leave his bed.

"I am going to José. I will be leaving the children here with you. The nurse will be here daily to assist you," I said to my mother-in-law as she sat in her chair embroidering.

"Battlefields are no place for a woman. Besides, you don't like me tending to your children."

"Your son is sick. He could be dying. I would move heaven and hell to get to him, battlefield or not."

Her shoulders sagged. "When do you leave?"

"Tomorrow morning before dawn."

The next morning, I crept into the children's bedroom. Teresita and Menotti were already awake and sitting up in their bed together. Menotti would soon be leaving for school in Turin, at nine years old, my little boy becoming a man. Ricciotti still slumbered in his crib. I kissed Menotti on the forehead. "Be brave, my love."

Teresita wrapped her arms around my neck, burrowing her little face into my hair. "Mamãe, no go."

"I have to, my darling. Papai is sick."

Tears spilled out of her eyes. "No" was all she could say.

I wiped her black hair from her face. My four-year-old daughter, never afraid to speak her mind or push the boundaries. She and I were a lot alike, and because of that I worried for her. Teresita's life would not be easy. "My darling, I promise you I will return. Until then, be a good girl."

I pried her hands from around my neck and left for the north to be with José.

As we rode through the rolling hills of the northern Italian countryside, the messenger grumbled, "The rebel camp is no place for a woman."

"I can assure you I have seen far worse."

The young man looked at me sideways. The gray early light obscured his features. "My commander is going to have my head."

"Don't worry about your commander. I'll personally see to it that you are properly rewarded for your efforts."

The scoff coming from his direction told me that he didn't believe me. I paid him no mind as I turned my attention to the fairy tale cottages that we passed. This land was truly as beautiful as José had promised. In my time here, I began to see why he loved it so much.

When night fell, my companion grew nervous. "Madam, it's not safe. We should find an inn for the night."

"Don't be silly. You said the camp is in the mountains? We'll easily make it there before dawn."

"There could be thieves. Most definitely wolves." The boy shuddered. "Madam, I must implore you."

I turned my horse to face him. "We all must grow up sometime, young man. Now, show me where the camp is and maybe you can be worthy of that stubble you call a beard."

He rode on without a word. The moon was high and clear, leading our way.

The men had taken shelter in an abandoned castle. Half of the building had crumbled, stone scattered everywhere as the earth attempted to reclaim it. Many of them were in tents dotted among the ruins. I rode through looking for José's tent, watching as men came out to see who this strange woman was.

"Anita? Anita, what are you doing here?" I looked down from my horse at Paolo. His shirt was partially unbuttoned, his suspenders hanging from his waist, his face only half-shaved.

I hoisted myself from my horse. "Paolo!" I was relieved to see him. "Where is my husband?"

"He has a room in the tower, but I didn't intend for you to come here."

"What did you expect when you told me he was sick?"

I started to walk past him, but he grabbed me by the elbow and hissed in my ear. "No one knows that I sent word to you."

I placed my hand on his. "And they won't." It went without saying. I was a woman and therefore not wanted on a military campaign regardless of who I was married to.

As I walked through the crumbling building, I removed my gloves and riding cloak, tossing them to the side. Medici stood up from a table. "Madam, what are you doing here?"

"My husband. Where is he?"

"Mrs. Garibaldi, this is no place for a lady."

"I can assure you, Mr. Medici, I have seen worse. I ask you again, where is my husband?"

His lip twitched. He closed his eyes for a moment, composing himself. "This way." He led me through the common area and up the stairs. I pushed past Medici as he opened the door to José's room. Instantly I was hit with a warm breeze that smelled of sweat and sick. "Who has been tending to him?"

"I have— " Medici began.

"It's a wonder he isn't dead," I grumbled as I threw open the shutters. "You." I pointed to a servant. "Douse that fire." The servant looked from me to Medici, who gave the subtlest nod of encouragement.

My attention turned to José, who lay tossing and turning in his bed. I pulled off the damp blankets that were twisted around his legs. "Paolo, rub his feet. We need to draw down the fever."

I sat by the head of the bed. José's breathing was raspy. I put my head to his sweat-drenched chest. It was clear, and his heartbeat steady. I breathed a sigh of relief. The servant, a thin boy whose coal-black hair was cut close to his head, cautiously moved forward. "Madam, is there anything else I can get you?"

"Fresh water... and rags."

"*Tesoro*." My husband groaned in his delirium. "*Tesoro*."

"He keeps saying that, but I am not sure what treasure he is referring to."

"He's referring to me, Mr. Medici," I said as I leaned down and tore the hem from my skirt. "I am his treasure." I used my freshly made rag to wipe the sweat from his brow.

Working through my exhaustion, I spent the evening waging battle with his fever, pressing cool rags to his face. My eyelids began to feel heavy as the night pressed on, but my husband was still delirious with fever.

"Anita!" Feeling disoriented, I sat upright. The room that had been dark had sunshine spilling through the windows. I looked at the bed: José was panicked as he tried to get out of the bed. "Anita, tell me, where are the children?"

I laid a hand on his arm. "They are with your mother and the nurse."

He eased himself back down onto the pillows. "Thank you, *tesoro mio*, you have brought me back to life. I will see to it that you are escorted back home."

"You will do no such thing!"

"But the children need you."

"*You* need me! José, I can't stay there with your mother. I feel like I am going to wither and die." I took a breath, composing myself. "You have said it yourself: We are safer when we are together."

"Anita, I know you are used to a certain amount of excitement, but the men here will not be comfortable with a woman present."

"They will learn to live with me." I took him by the hand. "Husband, believe me when I tell you this: If you send me away, I will only come back."

He wiped a hand over his pale face. "I should learn not to argue with you."

I grinned. "That would be wise."

He fell against his pillows. "Tell me. What news do you have of my children? Has Teresita succeeded in breaking all of my mother's valuables?"

"She has been too distracted by the dollhouse Paolo brought

for her." A servant slipped into the room with a tray of bread and meat. "She plays with it all day and sleeps with her dolls in her bed at night."

José smiled as he bit into a chunk of bread. "And my boys? How are they?"

I took a deep breath. "Menotti is on his way to your old school in Turin." José stopped chewing and looked at me. "I hope you don't mind; they extended a personal invitation and, well, it was either that or he goes to the Catholic school your mother tried to enroll him in."

José tore his cheese and meat into smaller pieces. "No, I don't mind. He does have to attend school, after all. I just hope they don't expel him like they did me."

"Well, he does take after you, dear husband, so it's only a matter of time," I said with a knowing grin. "But it would appear that the Garibaldi name has gone up in favor. Every school is honored to have the Great Giuseppe Garibaldi bless them with the responsibility of educating his offspring."

José laughed. "I never thought I would live to see the day."

José quickly regained his strength. I could tell he was on the mend because he grew anxious with being confined to his bed. Often, I would walk into his room to find various maps and documents strewn about his bed. On one such afternoon, I found José thoroughly engrossed in a large map that was spread over his lap.

Books had fallen to the floor, spread open, their pages bent, while a slew of papers were crumpled around his legs. I set the lunch tray I had been carrying on the nearby table and straightened up José's mess.

"Stop that. I need those," he demanded without looking up at me.

"But they are thrown on the floor."

"Only because I have no room on the bed."

I put my hands on my hips. "José, this is ridiculous."

He met my eyes. "My work won't wait. If you would let me get out of this damn bed, I wouldn't have a mess everywhere."

I sighed. "Do what you want, but if you fall because you overexerted yourself, don't come crying to me."

He smiled. "I wouldn't think of it."

That night I sat in on a meeting with the Redshirts. I took a spot in the back corner of the common room, hoping I wouldn't be noticed. Only officers were allowed in the room for the meeting; however, I was immune to most orders given the status of my husband. The tables were pushed together in order to make one large table for the men to spread their maps across. The campaign along the Alps had been successful. Reinforcements had arrived, strengthening our blockade along the northern border. Now José set his sights on the crown jewel of Italy. He spoke animatedly, his hands going everywhere, emphasizing his words. "We need to strike Rome now!"

"Why now? Shouldn't we wait until we have a stronger force behind us?" Medici was studying the map, his hand under his chin. "We can go in now, but it will be risky."

"This is war. There are always risks," José responded. "The Austrians aren't defending the city; the bulk of their force is up here in the north. They won't expect us to have the *grandi coglioni* to take the city."

"*Grandi coglioni, ma sei pazzo?* This is madness. I am not going to lead my men into a battle that they will surely lose." His eyes swept over the map. "Rome is impenetrable. It's been protected for centuries. The walls are too high."

"But it has its weaknesses." José pointed to the map. "Here and here. All we have to do is break in and it's ours."

"Peppino, this is madness!" Medici exclaimed. "Even if we are to find a way in, how are we going to convince the Vatican to unify?"

"We don't have to," José responded. "By holding Rome, we hold the power. We can show Austria and the rest of Europe that we are a force to be reckoned with. We will not be bullied any longer."

"It's foolish," Medici countered. "You only want to go to Rome because you want to expel the pope."

"And what's so wrong with that? The Papal States are undermining everything we are doing."

"We need more troops."

The men stared at the map. "Peppino does make a valid point." Paolo had kept so quiet during the exchange that everyone, me included, had forgotten that he was there. "We need Rome. That is for sure; without it, we can never become a unified country. Rome is the heart of Italy. We can't have one sovereign nation within another." He looked at the men. "And taking it now is a power play. If we can take Rome, we can take the rest of the peninsula."

Medici huffed. "Just because we *can* take it doesn't mean that we should. I doubt we'll be able to hold it; we don't have enough men."

"I can get you more men," Paolo said.

"How?" Medici eyed him under the messy dark curls that hung over his eyes.

Everyone followed Paolo's gaze, which landed on me. "Her."

I squirmed in my seat. "I don't think I can be of much assistance."

"No," Paolo responded. "When you spoke in Genoa you moved the people into signing up. You were our best propaganda."

"But you don't need me for that. You have José."

Paolo looked to his commander. "Think about it, Peppino. You can speak to the people, you can rouse them, but they expect that. Let them listen to your exotic wife talk of your adventures and they will be falling all over themselves to sign up."

"Exotic?" I looked to Paolo.

"Yes." Paolo turned to face me directly. "The people of Genoa are still talking about you. The gossip is spreading all over Italy. You are the American they all want to see."

I struggled to find words.

"She'll do it," José said from behind Paolo.

"José—" I began to protest.

"Everyone needs to do their part, and you, *tesoro mio*, will be responsible for recruitment."

FIFTY

March 1849

For the sake of efficiency, the plan was to recruit as we made our way south to Rome, staying west of Milan and the Austrian forces that still encircled the city. Little white puffs of dandelion seed floated on the lazy summer air that drifted between the people who congregated outside another abandoned castle, of which only the frame remained. Our location sat on a great hill that overlooked an expansive lush valley below. Brilliant hues of green shimmered in the warm sunlight.

A hundred people from the town had shown up to hear what we had to say. They packed in around us with picnic baskets and blankets. Families gathered to see us. I gulped and turned to José.

"Are you sure you want me to speak? These are your people. Won't they understand you better than me?"

"*Tesoro mio*, you will be fine," José said, putting his hands on my shoulders. "The people will love you just like I do." Tenderly, he kissed my forehead.

"Sir! Sir!" José and I turned to the messenger who was running up to us. "I come with news from Rome." He paused, trying to catch his breath. "The French have landed. They are in Ostia."

José cursed. "How many?"

"Seven thousand," the messenger responded.

"Why?" I asked, looking from José to Paolo. "Why would the French do this?"

"The pope put out a call to all the Catholic nations for assistance," Paolo answered.

"You know this is only the first wave," Medici whispered to José. "There are going to be more."

"This is preposterous!" José began pacing like a caged lion, ignoring everyone around him. "This cannot happen. It has to be the whole peninsula or nothing. We cannot be a country that stands on its own with one of our legs torn out from under us."

"Do we call it off?" Paolo asked, watching José with uncertainty. "We've missed our window. If we attack now, we won't have enough men. It's impossible."

"No. We can't let the French get a foothold. How many do we have now?" José asked.

"One thousand," Medici responded. "We're outnumbered. There is no way we can do this."

"Then we get more men," I said, walking to the podium.

A warm breeze rustled through the trees that surrounded us as the sun set in the distance. My eyes scanned the people gathered on the common. They were families in their cleanest clothes, reserved for mass and special occasions, spending their day waiting to hear us speak…to hear *me* speak.

I cleared my throat. "*Buona sera.*" I tried to smile. There were twice as many people here as there had been at the café in Genoa.

A small group of children had been playing in front of the stage. When I started to speak, they froze in place, their ball slipping from a boy's fingers. I leaned down and picked it up.

As the ball passed from my fingertips to the boy, I thought of my own little ones back in Nizza and the future we were building for them. The small child grinned up at me before running back to his family. I smiled. "He is a good, strong boy," I said to his parents. "Perhaps one day he will play with my children. Maybe they will call each other friends, yes? By the time they meet it won't matter that your son is from Lombardy and mine is from Piedmont, because by the time they meet we will all be one. We will be Italy.

"My son's namesake, Ciro Menotti, dared to dream that. He dared to stand up to the Austrians and tell them that they could not oppress us any longer. That there would be an Italy and it would be glorious. But Ciro Menotti paid dearly for that dream. The Austrians killed him, all because he wanted a free fatherland.

"We are on the brink of seeing that dream come true. We are the lucky few who can stand here today and bear witness to the creation of a country. If you are lucky enough to see the hairs on your head go white or for your bones to creak, you can sit with your grandchildren on your knee and you can tell them you were here. You can tell them that you did something that mattered, that because of you they have a future. A future that is full of hope. A future that is free."

The crowd erupted into loud cheers. "Will you stand by and watch while others bear the burden of history, or will you rise up so that your children can go forth with pride, so that they can say, 'This is who I am. This is where I come from.' So that they can say, 'I am an Italian.' "

"*Viva Italia!*" The crowd erupted. "*Viva Italia!*"

I walked back to José and the other men. "You're welcome." I kissed José on the cheek as he took my place at the podium.

I listened to José as he rode on the energy of the crowd. For a while, he chanted with them. "*Viva Italia! Viva Italia!*" He grinned like he had on the day Menotti was born. He held up his hand and immediately the crowd stilled. "My *compagni*, wasn't my wife something? You can see why I stole her from Brazil, yes? As she so eloquently stated, we need unification." He looked around the crowd. "But France has determined that Rome should be its own country. That they shall not take part in our dream of Italy. How can we be unified when we have a country within a country? If your son is missing, do you not search for him? Do you not bring him back into the fold of the family hearth?

"While in exile I prayed, nay, *implored* God that I would see Rome one more time. The cradle of our civilization. The birthplace of everything we are. Everything we hope to be is controlled by a man who dares elevate himself to the level of sainthood. Who calls himself pope." Gasps rippled through the crowd. "Yes, I said it. The pope is only a man. For how can he call himself the voice of God when he does not want equality for every Italian, regardless of the color of their skin, their gender, or their religion? Pope Pius seeks to stifle us. Every day he passes edicts that restrict the Romans' freedom. That creates inequality. Join me! Together we will march on Rome and say, 'No more!' We are one people united by our devotion to justice! To freedom! To Italy! Together we will tell the world that we will no longer stand for other countries interfering in the business of this peninsula!"

The crowd cheered. Every able-bodied man signed up for José's war effort. Together, new recruits blended in with our soldiers. As a great mass we marched south, stopping to speak in more cities. Bringing more people with us. Until we found ourselves at the doorstep of Rome, a great horde ready to take back the heart of our country.

FIFTY-ONE

April 1849

On the morning before we left on our campaign for Rome, José pulled me aside. "I should tell you that it would be a good idea for you to go back to Nizza to be with the children."

"And I should tell you, you are a fool to think that after all this time I would actually listen to an order like that."

José snorted. "I know, but I thought I would try anyway. I don't know how we are going to get you in the ranks."

"You're the general; they have to listen to you."

At this point my husband openly laughed. "Not in this matter they won't. You are a woman; they won't accept you." He kissed me on the forehead. "I have to inspect the munitions. I'll see you this afternoon."

I absentmindedly stroked my loose hair as I watched my husband leave. As my fingers slipped through the strands a thought occurred to me. I searched through the supplies for a pair of scissors. Finding one, I took a deep breath and cut.

That afternoon I slipped into the stables while the men loaded provisions for the battle. My hair was cut short and I wore men's clothing. None of the soldiers looked twice at me. "Boy, can you pick up…" José paused and looked at me, his eyebrows furrowed. "Anita?"

I saluted him. "Private Garibaldi at your service."

"Your hair!"

"I know." I beamed. "None of the soldiers even noticed me."

He led me outside by my elbow. "You didn't have to do this."

"I had to, if I wanted to come with you. I'm not going back to Nizza. I was thinking I could have a medical station."

He wiped a tired hand over his face. "All right."

As we progressed toward Rome we picked up every able-bodied person we could, but it still wasn't enough. Our numbers, all dressed in red, totaled only 6,300.

"It's not enough," Medici warned as we prepared to leave for the city. "The French still have seven thousand plus a full battalion of field guns. I know the French general, Oudinot, will take advantage of every opportunity he can."

"Oudinot is cocky," José said. "He believes the Italians can't fight, and that's where he's wrong. We'll surprise him with our strength."

Medici opened his mouth to argue, but a young man spoke up. "Perhaps I can be of assistance."

José and Medici turned to this boy, who stood before them in an old blue coat that was too long in the arms. He pushed back the sandy blond hair that fell over his face. "And who are you?" José asked with his hand on his sword.

"Angelo Puglisi. I'm the commander of the student brigade."

"Commander?" Medici let out a burst of a laugh. "You have barely left your mother's breast. How old are you?"

Puglisi stiffened. "Eighteen, sir."

"Eighteen," Medici repeated. "This is not a game, child. Go back to your toy soldiers."

"We weren't treated like children when we rebelled against King Ferdinand. Trust me, Lieutenant Colonel Medici, this is not the first war we've seen," Puglisi insisted. "I brought with me one thousand lancers. We are all students from Sicily."

José grinned as he clapped Medici on the back. "Rome is going to be ours."

* * *

My small garrison, made up of Redshirts who had followed us to Italy from Montevideo, made its way to Rome to set up our makeshift hospital. We crested the hill, and I saw Rome spread out before me.

Over the years I had heard a number of stories about this city from José. He called it the most beautiful place in all the world, and from our vantage point I could see why. New buildings pressed in on ancient ruins while giant domes rose above the clatter of the chaos.

For thousands of years people had built Rome, stone by stone. How many beads of sweat and blood had soaked into its foundations?

To look upon Rome was to know that this city belonged to no one. Not the French. Not the church. Not even us. She was from this land, as natural as the mountains that rose in the north. We were only usurpers destined to be here for a short time. Long after we were gone this city would remain.

I finally understood. If José had to choose—his life or the freedom of Rome—he would choose Rome. As I rode forward with my contingent of medical aides, I knew too that I would make the same choice.

We took up residence in a nearby monastery. Once the home

of a martyred saint, it was a simple structure that dated back to ancient Roman times. The monks begged and pleaded for us to go anywhere else. They were a church, not a hospital.

Stepping closer, I placed my hand on the hilt of my sword. "Do you mean to tell me that you would turn away dying people because they don't bow down to your pope?"

The head monk's beady eyes narrowed as he took in my baggy, worn-out red shirt tucked into my black pants. "I know who you are," he whispered. "You're the woman posing as Giuseppe Garibaldi's wife. You can't be here."

He pulled against the soldiers who gripped his arms. "Please, she can't be here. She is a blasphemer, a bigamist. The sanctity of this church is compromised by her presence."

My second-in-command, Orgini, was a broad man who had been with the legion since Montevideo. "Lock the monks in the basement," he ordered. "We'll trade them for prisoners of war when this is all over. Oh, and bring up the wine and whatever else you can find. We have a long night ahead of us."

The pleas of the monks echoed in the distance as they were hauled away. "To speak of the dust in another's eye while ignoring the plank in your own," Orgini said to no one in particular. "And they wonder why the new republic doesn't embrace the church."

"Come, we have work to do," I said, leaving our new prisoners to their fates.

As rain poured down around us, we opened every window we could in a vain attempt to dissipate the thick humid air that clung to us. Throughout the night the war raged in the distance, and the bodies kept coming. By the break of dawn, all of my men were walking around with glazed eyes, trying not to trip over their own feet. "By the look of things, I would think that we are losing," one of them grumbled.

"The battles are not over yet," I corrected him, even though I shared his sentiment.

The morning sun had fully risen when José entered the sick tent, greeting the injured men who had not yet departed from this plane. I watched as he passed from bed to bed. He was blood-splattered and covered in mud. My insides clenched with fear. I couldn't tell if he was putting on a brave front for the sake of morale.

I noticed the slight limp in his walk as he approached. "We won," he whispered.

"You did? We have so many injured, I didn't think—" José put a finger to my lips.

"They were vicious, but we proved to be the better force."

I grabbed a rag and began to wipe the blood off him. "Are you wounded?"

"Nothing to concern yourself with." His gaze passed over me to the injured that filled the sanctuary. "Take care of our men for now. I have business to attend to, but be ready to move. We are going to occupy a fortress." His hand cupped my cheek. "Once we have settled in, we'll have some time for ourselves." He turned back to the men and clapped his hands. "Tonight we celebrate, for Rome is ours!"

Soldiers soon arrived to help my company move the patients and their things. Initially, I stayed close, supervising the course of action, but soon I became more of a hindrance than a help. I found my horse and made my way to the fortress.

I found José wiping his neck with a damp towel as he gave orders to the men around him, who were busy moving boxes onto carts.

"*Tesoro mio*, you have escaped!" he exclaimed with a broad smile. The blood that had covered his face was gone. He wore an old white shirt that hung loosely on his large frame. The bloody edge of a bandage poked out from underneath.

"José," I scolded, pulling him to me and lifting up his shirt, "you are injured."

"It's merely a flesh wound." His hands went to my belly. "Has he moved much lately?"

"Not really," I said. "But I get a reassuring kick here and there. He lets me know he's still with us."

"Good." José smiled. "Good."

FIFTY-TWO

July 1849

In the months that we occupied Rome, José was in his prime. He gave orders as we all settled into our new roles. I was getting closer to my time and didn't argue when José asked me to rest. Unlike with my other pregnancies, I felt an unending exhaustion. If it weren't for the blasted maid waking me up at regular intervals to try to feed me, I would've slept for days. My sleep was troubled, littered with horrible dreams that kept getting worse.

I opened my eyes one unusually sunny afternoon to find someone standing there in the middle of the rays. As my eyes began to focus, I saw my father standing before me. "*Olá, filha.*"

"Papai?" He faded away as a cloud passed by. I suddenly felt cold and uneasy. I had to escape this room and get out for just a little while. It was a beautiful day, so I decided to take a walk around the garden. I made one turn before I found myself yawning uncontrollably. As I stepped into the doorway, I felt the room tilt. I grasped at the wall for support. *When was the last time I ate?* I couldn't remember. Was it before my last nap? Or was it this morning? My head felt cloudy. I tried to focus on the wall opposite me, but it moved like ocean waves. I took in deep breaths, steadying myself. Once my vision cleared, I decided to make my way to José's room. Perhaps we could enjoy a small meal together.

When I slipped inside, he looked up from his papers, a smile spreading across his face, making everything brighter. "*Tesoro mio*, you are my good luck charm." I laughed as he pulled me to him, nuzzling my neck.

"Husband, have you been drinking?"

"I needn't drink wine when I have you." He led me to the sofa. "How is my child today?" He chuckled as he leaned down and kissed my stomach.

"Tired. We both have been."

He looked up at me, concern plain on his face. "Is that normal?"

"Yes." I shrugged, trying to cover my lie. "Every pregnancy is different."

I stood firm under his scrutinizing stare. "You will tell me if something is wrong, won't you?" he asked.

"Of course," I lied. My husband had enough problems. We had taken Rome, but at a price, losing nearly half our men. Our new objective was to find a way to keep the city.

José continued to watch me for a moment but didn't challenge me. "It feels like a boy," I whispered, trying to change the subject.

"Really? How do you know?"

I kissed his nose. "A mother knows these things."

Just then Paolo burst into the room. "The French have returned! We have to evacuate. Now!"

José stood at attention. "If the French have returned, then we will defeat them like we did last time."

"Not this time, Peppino," Paolo replied. "They have sent twenty thousand troops, and they will retake Rome."

FIFTY-THREE

August 1849

Retreats are hardly ever organized. They are sloppy; they are chaos in its purest form. Before we made our way into Rome so many months ago, José had made a point of showing me the lone house on the northernmost point of Janiculum Hill.

"If we are separated, we will meet here," he'd said, motioning toward the abandoned villa. Birds made nests in the windows as ivy climbed up the side over the exposed brick. The house had clearly been neglected for decades.

"How would we be separated?"

He just shook his head. "Always prepare for the worst, *tesoro mio*. It may not happen, but we will survive even if it does."

Now as I stood on that crumbling embankment watching José lead a group of men toward us, I began to feel sick. Nothing was going as planned and I could feel a pain, sharp like a knife, cutting through my right temple. I winced, placing my hand to the side of my head. Closing my eyes, I could see a multitude of stars burst before my lids.

The men had abandoned the horses and swiftly marched toward us. When all fifteen hundred of us had gathered on the property José climbed upon the nearest ledge and called out to them. "Soldiers, I release you from your duty to follow me, and leave you free to return to your homes. But remember that although the Roman war for independence has ended, Italy remains in shameful slavery." He waited, but none of the men left. "Very well. We stay in the woods, north of the road. We make no noise unless you want to be a special guest of the French." Without further warning he moved forward, expecting the rest of us to follow. Silently we walked as the orange rays of the sun filtered through the leaves. Only after we had traveled for miles and the deep blackness of night had set in around us did we stop. I curled up next to a tree and slept. I didn't wait for José. I couldn't.

I awoke to José shaking me gently. When I turned to look at him, he put a finger to his lips and beckoned for me to follow him. We stood well within the tree line as we gazed down to the road below. It was infested by the French. Silently we gathered up our small group and crept away, finding our way to the river. I was relieved when our soldiers suggested they would take the boats from a nearby house so that we could sail instead of walk. My limbs ached with exhaustion and my headache had expanded. The pain had spread behind my eyes, stretching from temple to temple. My vision crackled around the edges.

As our boat sliced through the calm water, I could feel the blackness attempting to creep into my sight. "Sir, we are going to need to go ashore," one of the weathered soldiers said. "There are shallows ahead; we won't be able to make it through."

"Very well." José gave the signal and the men diverted the boats to the shore. Once we reached dry land I stepped out and felt my legs begin to shake. The world swam in front of me. Reaching for a large rock, I tried to steady myself. "Anita!" José rushed to my side. "Are you all right?"

"Yes. I just need the earth to sustain me." My knees buckled and I felt José's sturdy arms wrap around me before I hit the ground. I could only hear snippets of conversation as I faded in and out of consciousness.

"I'll carry her."

"The scouts caught up with us."

"We've got to keep moving. Peppino, there is a price on your head."

"They can't be getting that close."

"They are close enough to smell our cologne."

I couldn't make out who was talking. I was placed in a boat with no control over what was happening. I looked around at the legs surrounding me, unable to see any faces. None of them was my José. None were wearing his clothes. He was gone. He left me. I struggled to sit up. "José? José? Where is my husband? I can't leave him. I can't."

José pressed my hand to his face. "*Tesoro mio*. I am right here." He kissed my palm. I closed my eyes, and recalled wishing when I was a young girl that I could have a husband who would kiss me like that. And now I had him. "Rest now," José whispered.

"She's getting worse," I heard him say. "Her fever can't be quenched."

"We'll do what we can for her." Was that Paolo? I couldn't tell anymore as I felt the comfort in the cool rag that was placed against my forehead.

I watched the sky as our boat sailed forward. The full moon moved from cloud to cloud as it followed us, lighting our way. It was so large and bright; I was sure that I could skim the bottom edge with my fingertips. José grasped my outstretched hand.

"Don't leave me. Please," I begged.

"*Tesoro mio*, I will not leave behind my greatest treasure. Ever."

Paolo said, "There is an abandoned farm up ahead. Let's take shelter there. Talk this through."

"I won't leave. I won't leave," I murmured.

The next thing I knew I was being carried up a hill into a house. "Anita, stay with me, love. Don't go."

I turned my head, trying to see José. I smiled. "Leave you? I crossed a continent for you. You can't lose me, we still have work to do. I…" A fluttering caught my eye; a little black bird with a bright red belly and white brows sat on the windowsill, and she bobbed, watching me. I knew who she was. Who she had been all along. Destiny. She waited for me. All these years we had played our games, fought with each other, and now it was time for us to meet, woman to woman.

José pulled me in close to him. The smell of sandalwood enveloped me. "*Tesoro mio*."

I reached up, stroking his beard. I snuggled into his neck, grasping the collar of his shirt.

"I love you," he whispered.

I closed my eyes, listening to the thumping of his heart. The rhythm lulled my eyes closed. He was speaking to someone in the distance. I couldn't understand his words anymore, just the vibrations from his throat as my face pressed into him.

It amazed me in that moment how two people could fit together so well. We never stop to think that it is not just the heart or the soul that is a match to our other. It is the body as well. José and I fit together. We always had. We always will. The world around me fell away and all that was left was me, my husband, and the bird in the window.

There was only one request. One thing left that I needed from her, then she could have me. I gathered what was left of my strength, forming the words in my mouth. "Take care of the children."

EPILOGUE

October 26, 1860

José

The wood creaks under my grip as I brace myself for another wave of memories, my fingers digging into the aging dresser. Faces of the people who went before me swim through my mind's eye. The tang of gunpowder fills my nostrils. *Not again*, I pray as I feel myself being pulled back to the fierce battles long since past. I press down on the dresser, resting my forehead against the cool mirror, bringing myself back to this tiny room.

Opening my eyes, I stare at the man looking back at me. I hate what I see. The graying beard, the eyes that have dulled, the vitality of youth faded from battle. *When did I become so old?*

Today should be a happy day. Victor Emmanuel and his entourage are waiting for me. I will walk down those stairs and sign a treaty that will create the Kingdom of Italy. This is the culmination of everything I have ever worked for. Everything that I sacrificed. I look toward the ceiling, pockmarked with mold, trying to avoid the old man in the mirror. The man who outlived them all, who casts a judgment that I am not ready to face.

"Anita." Her name escapes my lips like a prayer to my patron saint. I lurch forward as another wave of images catches me in the gut. That night at the dairy farm. The impromptu burial during a hasty retreat. The— Oh God, I can't even let myself think of what the dogs did after we left. Our unborn child. Guilt making my knees buckle.

And all at once I feel her beside me, like a warm Brazilian breeze. She is stroking my arm, like she did before. "I can't do this," I say to the presence.

"Yes, you can." I turn to find Anita perched on the bed, her hands neatly folded in her lap. That smirk, the one that lights her eyes, tells me she is set for mischief. "You will walk out this door and sign the treaty that will create a unified Italy."

My shoulders sag as I relent. "I have sacrificed so much to get here, for this moment." I look into her dark eyes. "I should never have let you leave Brazil with me. If you had stayed..."

My wife scoffs. "You couldn't keep me in Brazil even if you tried. You know very well I would have followed you to the end of the earth and back."

"I was selfish in the pursuit of my dream. I cost so many lives." I stare down at my boots, too ashamed to meet her gaze.

"You are only selfish if you think that the dream of a free, unified Italy was yours and yours alone." She rises from the bed and moves toward me.

"I can't do this without you," I finally admit.

"Who says I've left?"

My wife fades as a soft knock interrupts us. "Father?" Menotti enters, his dark eyes, his mother's eyes, full of concern, looking me over. "Are you ready? They are waiting for you."

He's wearing his new uniform, his cap tucked under his arm. His wavy black hair is neatly combed away from his face, revealing the scar that runs along the side of his forehead. He's a young man now. The future is for him and his comrades.

"Almost." I pick up the old red shirt from the bed. It's more of a rag now, faded from the years of use. I pass it through my fingers, letting the warm memories of my wife move through me. I tie it around me. "Now I'm ready," I say as I follow my son out the door.

Anita's last words hang in the air as I leave. "Take care of the children."

AUTHOR'S NOTE

It would be nice if life moved in the arch of a perfect plot, wouldn't it? Our story begins, we have the central conflict, and all comes to a glorifying end with a perfectly wrapped bow. Only, life is not that simple, especially for Anita Garibaldi.

When I set out to tell this story I did all that I could to remain as close to her truth as possible, relying heavily on her memoirs as she told them to her friend, Feliciana—a woman that we should all be eternally grateful for. But certain things had to be changed: Battles were compressed in order to tell a coherent narrative. Birthdates of her children, particularly Ricciotti's, were adjusted, as were the births and deaths of her two brothers.

In the story I have José and Anita making only one trip to Italy together, when in reality, José made multiple trips between Uruguay and Italy as he closed out business and got his soldiers settled. Likewise, in Anita's final years she traveled back and forth from José's side to her children in Nizza before the fateful retreat from Rome.

Garibaldi was a staunch abolitionist and insistent on freedom for all, a sentiment shared by Anita as well. It was important to me that the struggles of the freed slaves and the bravery of the black lancers be brought up even though I was unable to explore their stories more thoroughly.

I would also like to note that though there may not be anything left of the earth goddess Atiola, she was a deity whom Anita brought up more than once to Feliciana, even acknowledging that this goddess was on the verge of being forgotten. In all of my research I couldn't find anything beyond Anita's references to her. It would seem that her story is lost to time.

One thing I did not need to exaggerate was José's love for Anita. His pet name for her, *tesoro mio,* came from his writings where he often referred to his wife as his treasure. He also wrote the following in his autobiography: "Fate reserved for me that other Brazilian flower which I still weep for, and for which I shall weep while I live."

In crafting this story, the one thing that I didn't expect was to find a feminist icon whom I could look up to, whose strength inspired and encouraged me in ways I never would have imagined. I am proud to be a steward of Anita's tale.

ACKNOWLEDGMENTS

Writing can be a very solitary activity. However, to get a story from a rough sketch in a notebook to an actual book takes a community. If it weren't for these people, *The Woman in Red* wouldn't be published.

First and foremost, a huge thank you to my agent, Johanna Castillo. Thank you for seeing the diamond in the rough, for giving me opportunities, and for always being there for my questions and anxieties.

Karen Kosztolnyik, thank you for being such a great editor and for loving my book as much as I do. It has been a true pleasure working with you. You made a lifelong dream come true, and I am eternally grateful. Likewise, thank you Grand Central for all your hard work in making this book happen. *The Woman in Red* found the perfect home with you.

Ryan Tierney, my husband, the peanut butter to my jelly, thank you for not only seeing my vision but for also putting up with the overflowing laundry and dirty dishes just so I could write one more chapter. You were always my first sounding board and listened patiently when I needed to vent.

Thank you to my father, William Giovinazzo, for *nagging* me to pick up a book about Anita. As always, you were right, I did love her story. For my mother, Helen Hall, thank you for encouraging me to have more books than shoes.

Holly Kammier, thank you for being an early editor and for helping me to take *The Woman in Red* to the next level.

Erin Lindsay McCabe and Greer Macallister, you were always available for my questions and never failed to cheer me on and console me when I was down. Likewise, to the rest of my historical fiction high-vibe tribe: Mary Volmer, Heather Webb, Alyssa Palombo, and Stephanie Storey, thank you for your support, advice, and mentorship.

It is a special thing to be able to count an Amanda as a friend; perhaps I am especially lucky to have two Amandas in my life. Amanda Vetter, thank you for being there for advice and insight even when you had no idea what was going on. We've come a long way since the Gag Factory. Amanda Sawyer, thank you for being a fantastic critique partner. I am truly grateful for the friendship that we built over long-distance coffee dates and writing.

Antonia Burns and Eddie Louise Clark, thank you for being early readers and cheerleaders.

Thank you to the Women's National Book Association—Los Angeles, for supporting and sharing your resources.

There was a time, believe it or not, when I set down my pen and gave up on writing. If it weren't for you, Michele Leivas, I probably wouldn't have picked it back up. You believed in me when I didn't believe in myself. If it weren't for your persistence, neither I nor my book would be here today. You are the best co-host/co-conspirator/sorority sister a girl could ask for.

YOUR BOOK CLUB RESOURCE

READING GROUP GUIDE

DISCUSSION QUESTIONS

1. In your opinion, what draws Anita to Giuseppe and vice versa? Is it love at first sight? Do you believe there needs to be a reason for people to fall in love, or do you believe some people can have an immediately strong connection?

2. From a young age, Anita made clear that she had ambitions beyond the role of wife and mother. After training horses with her father, she became a nurse and, eventually, a soldier. How did her upbringing prepare her to take on the role of a revolutionary?

3. Before Anita meets Giuseppe, she is characterized as a troublemaker, as crazy, as a manipulator. After she meets him, she is characterized as a brave revolutionary, as a radical thinker, as a brilliant strategist. Her intelligence and take-charge attitude are only praised *after* she is

partnered with a great man. How does this shift in attitude exemplify women's continued struggle to be taken seriously in the absence of a male counterpart?

4. In chapter 16, Anita, pregnant with her first child, says, "Suddenly my life wasn't my own; a future person was sucking away everything that I was." Many women today struggle with the notion of losing themselves after a child is born. How did motherhood alter Anita's sense of identity?

5. In chapter 24, Giuseppe begs Rossetti to abandon his printing press as they travel to São Gabriel: "Telling our story doesn't have to be your job...Brother, let someone else carry that burden. Just for a little while." Discuss the symbolism of the printing press in this scene: its weight, its importance, and its capacity to establish a personal and political legacy. Do you believe Rossetti was right to prioritize the preservation of history and personal glory over his own life?

6. In chapter 25, Anzani describes Montevideo as the "Florence of the Americas," where expats from different cities in Italy came together and called themselves Italians. How else did Montevideo foreshadow a future, united Italy?

7. In chapter 27, Anita says, "In the parlor the men talked, but it was in the kitchen that the important decisions were made." Do you agree or disagree with this statement? How is this idea illustrated in South America? In Italy?

8. What do you think of Giuseppe's decision to leave Anita a note explaining his departure to Corrientes in chapter 32? Why do you think he didn't tell her he was leaving in person?

9. Why do you think Anita dreams of her father before Rosita dies? Before her own death? Is his presence an omen of death, or a subconscious attempt at comfort?

10. Discuss the importance of the color red in the novel, from its association with professional butchers to Anita's adoption of the color for her personal wardrobe.

11. What do you think of Anita's decision to shear off her hair and join Giuseppe on his campaign to Rome, leaving her children in the care of their grandmother? What decision would you have made?

12. Birds play a heavily symbolic role in the novel. In the prologue, Anita worries black vultures are a sign of her husband's passing; in chapter 2, a bird on a branch foreshadows Anita's father's death; in chapter 53, a little black bird personifies Destiny. In Brazil, the Bororo people believe the human soul manifests in the shape of a bird upon a person's passing. In Uruguay, the tero bird is a "common literary symbol for the audacious, bold, attentive, and vivacious nature of the gaucho." Discuss the disparity between these two interpretations and how they relate to Anita at various points in the novel. When the little black bird appeared in the final chapter of the novel, did you realize Anita was about to die?

13. Anita was born on August 30, 1821. She died at the age of twenty-seven on August 4, 1849. Though she lived more than 170 years ago, her story resonates with contemporary readers, as women continue to campaign for equality today all around the world. How does Anita's life represent women's ongoing struggle to be recognized for their work and overall contributions to society?

ESSAY FROM DIANA GIOVINAZZO

When I was a teenager my aunt showed me a black-and-white photo of an Italian soldier taken during World War II. It was in a box mixed with photos of birthdays, Christmases, and scores of family Sunday suppers. The lone young man in the photo stood tall in his pristine foreign uniform, staring back at us from the small rectangular box. There was no doubt he was a relative: Not only did he have the tell-tale Giovinazzo eyebrows, he loosely resembled one of my cousins. The back of the photograph was blank. No hint of who this boy could be, or if he even survived the war. No clues as to who he was or what he meant to my grandparents. Nothing.

So many of my grandparents' stories were lost to us along with the immigration stories of my great grandparents. My Calabrian grandfather died a few years before I was born, and I have precious few memories of my Sicilian grandmother before her untimely death when I was a child. Perhaps that's why the picture of the soldier stayed with me well into my adulthood as I began to comb through the historical archives for the ghosts of my family. When I started to search the Italian archives those questions shifted from *how?* to *why?*

The question of why my family immigrated to the United States became my primary focus. Why did my great grandparents leave Italy in 1913? What drove them to gather their few belongings and start over in New York?

I was having the traditional Italian family dinner at my parents' house when my father and I began to theorize what happened in Italy when our family made the journey. The subject of Italian Unification, also known as the *Risorgimento*, came up. That was when my father said "You should read about the Garibaldi's and Anita Garibaldi in particular. I think you would like her." Following his advice, I picked up a biography of Anita, and he was right. I was immediately taken by her fierceness. This was a woman who stood, unfazed, on the bow of a ship as canon fire whizzed by her head. She insisted her life was not valuable, that the freedom she fought for was all that mattered. Throughout her life, she believed in equality for everyone, regardless of gender or race.

It was this pre-feminist thought that lured me in. I say pre-feminism because the feminism that we recognize today can be traced back to only 1848 in Seneca Falls. But while the suffragettes were debating how to accomplish their goals, Anita was already sacrificing for the benefit of the citizens of three countries.

During Anita's life, the women of Southern Brazil were severely repressed. Being forced into marriage at the age of fourteen, something Anita experienced herself, was not unheard of. Especially considering a daughter was one less mouth to feed for those in poverty, as was the case for Anita when her mother married her to Manoel. Just as the Italian anarchist women did during the early labor movement at the beginning of the twentieth century, Anita compared marriage to slavery. A woman's worth was not just tied in with that of her husband, her ability to survive was entangled with whom she married. As result divorce was unheard of regardless of the circumstances.

Women during this time were doing more, whether it be in riding horses or breaking barriers in the fields of science, and they yearned to be recognized for it. Yet, they were expected to adhere to the same society norms that keep them repressed in the first place. The notorious Italian Anarchist Maria Roda said, "It is exactly because we feel and suffer that we too want to become involved in the fight against this society because we also feel from birth the need to be free, to be equal."

Anita's feminism was very much like Maria's in she believed women's rights are human rights. It is in society's best interest that women have the same freedoms as men. That equality was inherent in Anita's nature. While Anita's attraction to Giuseppe Garibaldi may have started as physical, it was his devotion to freedom that made her want to stay. He respected her and allowed her to make the choices that she wanted. Soon she found herself fighting to give others that same dignity and respect, regardless of their station in life. Anita carried these beliefs with her from Brazil to Uruguay, and finally to Italy. In each country, she not only fought beside the men, but she also spoke with the women, inspiring them to take up freedom's cause.

Over the years I have gotten closer to finding the history behind my great grandparent's immigration story. We still don't know who the soldier is but in searching for my family I discovered something more, I discovered a woman who inspired me. Who made me want to be like her, even if I never stand on a ship's bow as cannons whiz by my head.

Anita Garibaldi became my hero.

ANTOINETTE'S SISTER

Maria Carolina Charlotte, beloved sister of Marie Antoinette, has unexpectedly found herself the wife of the king of Naples.

Bursting with intrigue, adventure, and romance, follow Charlotte as she upends societal conventions and tries to save her sister from death while courageously living—and loving—on her own terms.

Please turn the page for an excerpt.

Here we are at the end of all things. You who thought you could best me. You are the Icarus, and I am the sun. All these years, you have been my constant tormentor. You took away my sister and my kingdom, but you can never take away my identity, for I am a queen, a Habsburg daughter, and you will forever be known as a usurper.

As you read this, know that the courts of Vienna have ruled in my favor. My husband and I will be restored to our rightful place as king and queen of Naples while you will be left with nothing. Which is more than you deserve.

Yours Faithfully,
Maria Carolina Charlotte
Queen of Naples and Sicily

CHAPTER ONE

1765

There were few things as enjoyable as being able to see the unveiling of a suitor's portrait. The event, attended by four of my six sisters, was an opportunity for us to assess what our mother's intentions were. Our mother, Empress Maria Theresa, was not only the ruler of the Austria-Hungary Empire, but was also the absolute ruler of the Habsburg royal family—all eleven of us. No Habsburg child, male or female, was immune to her strict cultivation. We were all expected to be rulers in whichever court the empress mother deemed appropriate, and as such, were savagely pruned by her sharp tongue.

On this day, my younger sister Antoinette and I skipped down the hallways quickly, passing the ornate tapestries depicting the proud double eagles of the Habsburg crest. Large paintings, commissioned by the greatest artists in all the kingdom, celebrated the greatness of the Habsburg dynasty.

"Did you hear about Josepha's new fiancé?" Antoinette said with an evil grin, her blue eyes sparkling with the news she was burning to tell me. The older we got, the more differences I began to see in our looks. At one point, we were considered to be indistinguishable, even though I was three years older. While her hair had maintained its ash-blond coloring, mine had darkened to the color of chestnuts. In every other way, our features were the same, from our blue eyes to our rosebud lips. Day and night, people would tell us; that's what we were. One the counterpart of the other.

"They say that young Prince Ferdinand is just as mad as his older brothers," Antoinette interjected, breaking up my thoughts.

"Where did you hear that?"

"Why, the maids of course. They know all the palace scandal." Her eyes widened with joy. "Now that King Carlos rules Spain, he has to reposition what titles his sons are going to inherit. They say his older brother died of severe melancholy. That's how he got the Spanish throne."

"What makes you think Ferdinand and his brothers are mad?" It was always a great annoyance when my sister heard the best secrets before I did.

"Well, everyone knows the eldest son, Philip, is an imbecile; they can't even include him in court life. They only trot him out on important occasions, and then he is shuffled back to his rooms. The poor prince had to be excluded from the line. They couldn't even consider him as a ruler. Carlos's second son, Carlos the Fourth, is of course destined for the Spanish throne. But Naples, that belongs to Ferdinand." She shrugged. "It's the lesser kingdom anyway, so it's probably for the best. I can't picture Josepha ruling anything more prestigious."

Of all six of my living sisters, Josepha was the one Antoinette and I liked the least. Well, not quite the least: Elisabeth, because of her great beauty, was Mother's favorite and therefore could do no wrong. It was no secret that Mother intended on her getting the best marriage out of all of us. While I, on the other hand, was always being criticized for my behavior.

The title that Mother sought for Josepha was queen of Naples, not one of the more pristine titles. The Kingdom of the Two Sicilies took up the southern half of the Italian peninsula. Keeping to itself, the kingdom was seen more as a puppet of Spain than an independent country.

Once, the Holy Roman Empire had held almost all the territories of the Italian peninsula, but, as Mother liked to lament, our grandfather had squandered them away. The Two Sicilies had been ours, and Mother wanted them back into the Habsburg fold, regardless of the cost. This marriage alliance was so important that Mother had attempted to marry our sister Johanna to the young king, but she died before the negotiations got very far. Now, it was Josepha's turn to fulfill Mother's will.

"How terrible this is for her," I lamented. "She has to marry our sister's intended husband."

"Only you would think that." Antoinette laughed. "You refuse to even share a name with a sister who died well before you were born."

I shrugged. "I don't want to be confined to anyone else's fate."

We turned the corner and skidded to a stop on the royal red carpet, just in time to avoid running into the large gold-and-white porcelain vase perched on the pedestal. The butler that stood nearby raised an eyebrow as I grabbed the wobbling antique vase, steadying it on its roost. "Sorry," I mumbled as we scurried toward the small royal parlor. The hallway, white with gold trim, was lined with paintings of former rulers. Pompous men, who didn't come close to the empress mother's fortitude. They each stared down at us in judgment. All except one, Francis I, the Holy Roman emperor. Our father.

It'd been only a few months since his death, but his absence could be felt throughout the whole palace. He was the one who had tempered Mother and brought a smile to her face. When he was young, they had called him the "sweet little cavalier." But for all his charm, grandpapa wasn't convinced that the indebted Duke of Lorraine was the best match. Grandpapa had regularly threatened to cancel the whole thing, but Mother had refused to marry anyone unless it was to her dear prince. And our father proved his loyalty to the crown when Prussia betrayed us.

When Grandpapa realized he could find himself with a daughter as an heir to the kingdom, he created the Pragmatic Sanction, a document naming our mother, Maria Theresa, as the next in line for the throne. But the document wasn't official until he had the support of another country. He managed to get the support he needed from Prussia, but once he died, Prussia invaded, thinking Mother was weak. It was our father who stood by her side, who helped her defend the kingdom. Together, my parents had sought the glory of the Holy Roman Empire, but now that Father was gone, it was up to Mother to keep the legacy alive.

"Charlotte, come along." Antoinette tugged at my arm. "We're going to be late."

"Well, there you are!" Elisabeth said from her perch opposite the door. Like the spoiled child she was, she held out a goblet for the servant girl to refill, never once bothering to acknowledge the lesser creature. "We were beginning to think that you wouldn't make it."

"I was trying to replicate your toilette," I said, "but I found that I just didn't have the number of creams and powders required. How many is it that you use now? Twenty?"

Elisabeth sneered at me in response before taking a long sip and shifting her gaze, with her ice-blue eyes, to Antoinette. Instinctively, I took Antoinette's hand and pulled her into the golden-trimmed armchair with me. She sat partially on my lap as we shared the chair.

The room covered in gold brocade was one of the more familial rooms in the palace. Though too quaint to hold all eleven of the empress mother's children, it was large enough to hold four of her seven daughters. We were spread out on overstuffed blue sofas and matching chairs. Mother had ordered the drapes, in blue as well, to be opened, so that we could better see the portrait of Ferdinand that sat covered in front of the marble fireplace. Near the front of the room, directly in front of the painting, sat Mother with my sister Josepha at her side.

Josepha was only a year older than me, but the difference between us could have been a vast cavern. Josepha tried to model herself after Elisabeth in both attitude and looks. She had little patience, especially for the likes of me, but spent as much time as she could doting on our eldest brother, Joseph, Mother's coruler and heir apparent. Next to Josepha was her governess, the serious Countess Lerchenfeld.

Lerchenfeld was Mother's intermediary in the care and upbringing of all of the empress mother's daughters. It was Lerchenfeld's duty to see that we had the best tutors, from music and dance to philosophy, so that the archduchesses would be the envy of the Holy Roman Empire. She also managed the other governesses, like Antoinette's and my own vile warden, Countess von Brandis.

"Ladies, I believe that now that we are all here, we can begin the viewing," Mother proclaimed with a little wave directing a servant to remove the burgundy cloth draped over the painting. For a moment, we all stared in silence. Shock, really. And then—I couldn't help myself—a burst of laughter erupted from my gut and traveled to Antoinette. Mother snapped her head to us, her hawk eyes fixed on our uncouth behavior. I pressed my face into Antoinette's shoulder, doing all that I could to hide my laughter.

"Well, he's..." The words died on Elisabeth's lips. There was no way to rectify the situation. The young king's beady black eyes stared back at us. They were a little too close together, but they weren't even the worst feature on his face. His nose, that poor bulbous appendage jutted out from his face like a beak. Only unlike a bird's beak, it had a rounded bump at its tip that resided just above a pair of exceptionally large lips.

"He is by far the ugliest man I have ever seen!" I exclaimed as my sisters turned to me.

"Charlotte, that is enough. We do not need your commentary," Mother said, not bothering to look at me. "This will be a most fortuitous marriage."

"For him, maybe," Antoinette whispered in my ear. I snorted as everyone's eyes turned back to me.

"According to his tutors, he is of amazing health," Countess Lerchenfeld stated. "He is strong and well loved by his people."

"At least he has that," Antoinette murmured.

"Ladies, I believe we have seen enough. You may leave. I would like to speak with Countess Lerchenfeld alone." My sisters all got up and filed out of the room, but I slipped behind the ornate door. Pressing my ear to the gap between the hinges and the wall, I listened intently to the two women discuss my sister and her future husband.

"Tell me, countess, how are Josepha's studies progressing?" My mother's commanding voice drifted from the room.

"Quite well. I feel that she is going to make a fine ruler."

"Good. Very good. This gives me comfort. The situation in Naples is far worse than I was led to believe." I could hear my mother set down her goblet. "King Carlos is worried about the mental stability of his sons; it is understandable after the problems he has had with his eldest. But it would appear that he is afraid all three of his sons have the illness."

"Are they indeed ill? More importantly, what of Ferdinand?"

"I don't know." My mother's sigh fell heavy about the room. "According to my ambassador, the regents who have been controlling him have sought to control the country. Their method for doing this has been to keep the young man out of all affairs of state. I am told that the young king spends his days hunting, playing games, and carousing with the common people. He has no sense of duty. No patience for matters of state. And I don't believe he even knows how to read. He may not be ill, but he is certainly a fool. And fools make incompetent rulers."

"What do we do, Your Highness? Is it too late to back out of the agreement?"

"It has always been too late to go back on the agreement. Catherine the Great is waiting for any opportunity to pick at our borders. We can't afford a war with Russia. Spain is the greatest military power on the continent, followed by France. If I can marry my daughters into those Bourbon families, then we stand a chance to secure the stability of the Holy Roman Empire." There was a long silence. "I just wish this didn't feel like I had to sacrifice Josepha."

"What would you have me do?" Lerchenfeld asked.

"Prepare my daughter to rule the country like a proper Habsburg queen. I don't want to do this, but I am a queen before I am a mother."

"Yes, Your Majesty."

I scurried down the hall, burning to tell Antoinette what I heard.

MARCH 1765

Dear Charlotte,

Out of all my children, your behavior worries me the most. Don't you see that every punishment I put in front of you is an opportunity to learn from your mistakes?

But instead of learning, you subvert me. I take away your supper, but you employ a small army of maids to bring you cake. (Yes, I know of your secret cake supply.) You say your prayers with the devotion of a housefly. And, worse yet, you openly call your governess an ogre in public! You are ill-tempered with all your ladies, particularly while they are dressing you. Charlotte, you will never be esteemed, much less loved, by those that you govern if you behave in such a manner.

Furthermore, you have a penchant for idleness, which is dangerous, especially for you. You and your sister play childish tricks. You make improper observations and raise your voice too much.

I am doing my best to raise you properly to be an honorable ruler, but I fear you will be wholly lacking in the virtue necessary to lead a kingdom. If I had shown even an ounce of your irresponsibility, I would never have been able to hold together my realm. If I carried on as you do, I would never have been able to competently lead my empire, let alone protect it from the men who tried to rip it away from me.

I pray that you will see the error of your ways and change before it is too late.

Yours,
Empress Mother

CHAPTER TWO

May 1767

A silent assassin called smallpox was sweeping through Vienna and the rest of Austria. This was not the first time that the virus had paid a visit to the Habsburg family. When it initially reached the doorsteps of Schönbrunn Palace, the royal physicians had implored Mother to try the new form of medicine called inoculation. "The process involves taking the virus from a pustule from an already infected person and introducing it to an otherwise healthy person. The process is showing great promise in the city of Boston in the American colonies," they told her. Meanwhile, Mother's religious advisors disagreed. "To do this would thwart the will of God. Man was not meant to intercede in such an unholy manner," they said.

It wasn't until our brother Joseph insisted that he get inoculated that Mother relented, deciding to allow the older children to get the inoculation if they wanted it. Those three were my brothers Joseph and Leopold and my elder sister Johanna, soon to be married to the king of the Two Sicilies. And while Joseph and

Leopold lived, Johanna did not. She died from the inoculation. After that, Mother took her chances with the virus.

The family was regularly checked for fevers and rashes, but in the end, no one was safe from the devastating virus. Smallpox visited the palace again, finding new hosts among the family that had not yet been touched by its brutal effects. The first of us to come down with the illness this time was Elisabeth. Beautiful, vain Elisabeth, she told the physicians, "Do what you must to save my face, the rest of my body be damned. If I lose my beauty, let me die, I would rather be dead than to be deformed." She lived, but her face was horribly disfigured.

After Mother contracted smallpox herself, earlier in the year, she had sequestered Josepha, Amalia, Karl, and Maximilian. None of them had had the virus before, and she wanted to make sure they remained safe. Antoinette and I had had the virus when we were young, but we were placed into quarantine right along with the others. The doctors were concerned that we could get it again if we were exposed.

Life sheltered away from the rest of the family was incredibly dull. Brandis lectured Antoinette and me from sunrise until supper. The ogre thought this a great opportunity to train us as proper archduchesses. Antoinette and I, on the other hand, wanted nothing more than to escape the confines of this sorry excuse for palace life. While Brandis droned on and on about long-dead relatives that I could not care less about, I kept my eyes fixed on the perfect spring weather that allured me from outside the window. The palace grounds were filled with lush green lawns and flowers of vibrant blues and pinks.

During the long evenings, we sat in the family parlor, which was called the Yellow Room, but in truth, the only yellow thing about the room was the upholstery on the cushioned chairs. Day after day, we stared at the same white walls with the same loops of ivy painted at the very top. There were no balls or concerts.

No hunts. Our evenings were spent playing chess, reading, or inventing whatever new form of entertainment would keep us from going mad. That is, all of us but Josepha. While Amalia and Karl created elaborate battles with toy soldiers, Antoinette and I made up new card games. We did what we could to make the best of life in isolation, but Josepha was intent on sulking.

"This is no use!" Josepha exclaimed, slamming her book shut. "I can't read another philosophy book or any more history."

"All this studying will make you a better ruler," Amalia said, looking up from the toy soldiers strewn about before her.

"What's the point? I'm going to die anyway."

All of our heads snapped up. "What's that supposed to mean?" I asked.

"I know I am going to die because of Maria Josepha," she said with a sigh, as if we were supposed to know this already. "We share the same name, and that means we are going to have the same fate. I know it. She died of the pox, and so will I."

"That is the most ridiculous thing I have ever heard," I said.

"Oh, please!" Josepha's face reddened. "You went to Mother and had us all call you Charlotte because you didn't want to be connected to our dead sister. And you call me ridiculous?"

"That's different. I didn't want a secondhand name. If I shared the fate of our deceased sister Carolina, I would have died a long time ago." It was a horrid custom, which I despised, that after the death of a child, the next born would be given the same name, as a way to remember the one that had passed. I was the third Maria Carolina. The first had died shortly after her first birthday of severe muscle spasms. The second, born in between Leopold and Johanna, lived barely long enough to be christened.

"You know nothing of these matters. You're just a child," Josepha retorted.

"I know enough not to believe in silly superstitions." Rolling my eyes, I looked at Antoinette. "Come on, let's go to our rooms." She got up and quickly followed me.

The moment we got to our bedroom, Antoinette fell onto her bed. "I swear, if I have to spend one more day with her, I think I will give myself the pox."

"She's like an old lady," I said, coming to join her on the bed. "What if we escaped?"

Antoinette looked at me curiously. "Escape? How?"

"Trust me," I said with a devilish grin.

I learned early that with a well-placed bribe, almost anything could be accomplished. A bit of gold, or even some the jewelry I no longer had use for, when placed in the right maid's palm would allow us the freedom my sister and I so craved. It was with this lesson in mind that we managed to have Brandis occupied while Antoinette and I made our escape.

Our day out in the sunshine was even better than the ones I was forced to watch from a window under the tutelage of Countess von Ogre. Pleasant winds flowed from the east, pushing out all the clouds and revealing a deep-blue sky. Tufts of wild seedlings floated through the air.

"Josepha thinks she is better than the rest of us because she's marrying a king," I lamented as we made our way to a remote part of the grounds. "Just this morning, she called me an ignorant child! How can I be an ignorant child when she is only a year older than me?"

Antoinette spread a blanket out for us to lie on next to a patch of pink peonies. "Ignore her. Soon she'll be married and living in Naples. Then she'll no longer be our concern."

Antoinette picked a nearby flower and began to twirl it between her fingertips, humming as she did, while a feeling of unease grew in my stomach. Mother was already busy making negotiations for my marriage and my sister's. One of us would be married to the Dauphin of France, and the other to nobility with influence that would benefit Austria. "Antoinette, do you think when we get married that we'll ever see each other again?"

Antoinette let out a little laugh that sounded like bells rising into the air. "That may be the silliest thing I have ever heard. If I am queen, I expect you to be one of the members of my court."

I smiled at the thought. She reached over and took my hand in hers. "Oh, yes, I'll need my older sister next to me. If I become queen, you'll provide counsel and, at the very least, beat the heads of state into submission."

We broke into fits of laughter and spent the rest of the afternoon daydreaming about all the ways we would help our future kingdom and how we would be different than our mother. "I will always tell my children that I am a mother first and a queen second," Antoinette said, suddenly growing serious. "That's the way it should be."

I was about to open my mouth to agree, but a dark cloud drifted toward us. Sitting up on my elbows, I eyed the intruder on our perfect day. "Antoinette, I think it's time to head back." Following my gaze, Antoinette agreed.

Only we weren't quick enough. On our way back to the palace, a downpour let loose. We ran through the pouring rain as thunder rippled through the air. We turned a corner, and I slipped, pulling my sister down with me. Mud splashed up, staining both our dresses. I got up and hoisted Antoinette from the muck. "Quick, through the servants' entrance!"

Normally, that was a safe place to enter without notice, but this time as we rushed through the door, I discovered we were in great danger. The fearsome sight of our mother stood before us. Her large form took up most of the doorframe, blocking our escape to the hallway, and she was furious. Both of our heads snapped down in submission, to look at our mud-covered shoes.

"What were you two thinking?" She scowled at us, with her arms crossed in front of her broad bosom. This alone caused

Antoinette and me to tremble with fear. She never needed to yell; she needed only to whisper, and men would cower. "Do you know how worried Countess von Brandis was? How worried I was? Of course you don't, because you are selfish girls who think only of themselves."

I dared to look into my mother's gray-blue eyes, now as stormy as the world outside, but I cast my gaze back down as she glared at us.

"I probably shouldn't even ask whose idea this was," she growled. "Should I, Charlotte?"

"Mother, I—" At that precise moment, a glob of mud fell from my hair. It bounced off my nose and fell with a splat on the brown stone floor.

Her scowl deepened, and her face became crimson. "You are future queens. One of you will be the queen of France. Charlotte, you are always the source of gossip, and your attitude is appalling You are the elder sister. You should be setting a pious example for Antoinette. From this day forward, you will be separated from each other."

We began to protest but she raised her hand.

"Not another word. Antoinette, you will have a private tutor, and Charlotte, you will be placed with Josepha and Amalia. There will be no more secret confidences, no more contact at all whatsoever."

With that, our mother turned on her royal heels and left. Antoinette's grip on my hand tightened. "What are we going to do?"

"We'll pretend to follow her rules, of course," I said. But deep in my heart, I feared that not even my well-placed bribes would get us out of this.

October 15, 1789

Dearest Sister,

Do you remember when we were children and confined to the palace? You were driven mad from the boredom. Even then, you were reluctant to be placed in a cage, and given where I am now, I can understand how you felt.

Those days, though troubling for you, were some of the happiest days of my life. When I close my eyes, I can still see Josepha by the fire, her face bent over her books, and Amalia and Karl, lost to the war games of toy soldiers. Back then, most of the family was too busy for us. What a wonderful childhood. I had you all to myself, from our games with Brandis to our endless adventures. Though the last one ended in disaster. I still laugh at the memory of mud falling from your head as you attempted to plead your case to Mama. These are the memories I return to over and over during these dark times.

We may not be able to visit again for a long time, but know that I cherish these memories when you were my Charlotte, and we were happy.

Your Loving Sister,
Antoinette

ABOUT THE AUTHOR

DIANA GIOVINAZZO is the co-creator of *Wine, Women and Words*, a weekly literary podcast featuring interviews with authors over a glass of wine. Diana is active within her local literary community as the president of the Los Angeles chapter of the Women's National Book Association. *The Woman in Red* is her debut novel. For more information, please visit her website: https://dianagiovinazzo.com/.

YOUR
BOOK
CLUB
RESOURCE

VISIT
GCPClubCar.com

to sign up for the **GCP Club Car** newsletter, featuring exclusive promotions, info on other **Club Car** titles, and more.

@grandcentralpub

@grandcentralpub